THE I LOST-A BRIDE

BY
KATE HARDY

MIRACLE: MARRIAGE REUNITED

BY
ANNE FRASER

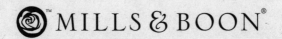

™MILLS & BOON®

Meet two couples who were too busy saving
patients' lives to fight to save their marriages.

But now these doctors
have been given a second chance—and this time
they're determined to get their happy ending!

MARRIAGE REUNITED

It's never too late…

THE DOCTOR'S LOST-AND-FOUND BRIDE
by Kate Hardy

MIRACLE: MARRIAGE REUNITED
by Anne Fraser

THE DOCTOR'S
LOST-AND-FOUND
BRIDE

BY
KATE HARDY

First published in Great Britain 2010
Harlequin Mills & Boon Limited,
Eton House, 18-24 Paradise Road, Richmond, Surrey TW9 1SR

© Pamela Brooks 2010

ISBN: 978 0 263 87682 6

Harlequin Mills & Boon policy is to use papers that are natural, renewable and recyclable products and made from wood grown in sustainable forests. The logging and manufacturing process conform to the legal environmental regulations of the country of origin.

Printed and bound in Spain
by Litografia Rosés, S.A., Barcelona

Kate Hardy lives in Norwich, in the east of England, with her husband, two young children, one bouncy spaniel, and too many books to count! When she's not busy writing romance or researching local history, she helps out at her children's schools. She also loves cooking—spot the recipes sneaked into her books! (They're also on her website, along with extracts and stories behind the books.) Writing for Mills & Boon has been a dream come true for Kate—something she wanted to do ever since she was twelve. She's been writing Medical™ Romances for over five years now, and also writes for Modern Heat™. She says it's the best of both worlds, because she gets to learn lots of new things when she's researching the background to a book: add a touch of passion, drama and danger, a new gorgeous hero every time, and it's the perfect job!

Kate's always delighted to hear from readers, so do drop in to her website at www.katehardy.com

Recent titles by the same author:

Medical™ Romance
FALLING FOR THE PLAYBOY MILLIONAIRE
  Brides of Penhally Bay
THE CHILDREN'S DOCTOR'S SPECIAL
PROPOSAL
  The London Victoria
THE GREEK DOCTOR'S NEW-YEAR BABY
  The London Victoria

MODERN HEAT™
TEMPORARY BOSS, PERMANENT MISTRESS
PLAYBOY BOSS, PREGNANCY OF PASSION
  To Tame a Playboy
SURRENDER TO THE PLAYBOY SHEIKH
  To Tame a Playboy

Praise for
Kate Hardy:

CHAPTER ONE

'EXCUSE me. I couldn't help overhearing the shouting. I'm coming in.'

Marina froze as she heard the voice on the other side of the curtain.

No; of course it wasn't him.

Apart from anything else, Max Fenton didn't work at the London Victoria. So it was completely ridiculous that she'd think he was standing on the other side of the curtain. And she was furious with herself for, yet again, hearing a slightly posh voice and thinking immediately of her ex.

After four years, she should be over him—completely over him. Yet every time she had an oblique view of a man with dark hair that flopped over his forehead, every time she heard someone who sounded faintly like him, she immediately thought of Max. And every time it turned out to be a stranger and she ended up cross with herself for being such a fool.

Of course he wouldn't have followed her to London— not after all this time. He'd signed the divorce papers a year ago, and they'd been separated for three years before that. Sure, Eve had said something about a new senior registrar taking over from Ed, but she hadn't mentioned his name and, as far as Marina knew, the new doctor wasn't starting until next week.

And then the curtain to the cubicle twitched open.

Shock kept her silent.

Since when had Max been working at the London Victoria?

He was definitely staff. Apart from the fact that he was wearing a white coat with a stethoscope flung casually around his neck, his name-badge sported the hospital logo and his name was printed underneath his photograph. But how on earth had she missed the news that he'd joined the team?

She stared at him. There were lines she didn't remember etched on his face, and he was thinner. Too thin. But his hair was just the same, still flopping over his forehead. And she'd forgotten just how blue his eyes were, a smoky, slate-blue that still managed to make her heart miss a beat when she looked at him, even after all the mess and misery that had happened between them.

For one crazy moment, Marina almost reached out to touch him, to press her palm against his cheek and make absolutely sure that he was really here, that this wasn't some weird kind of hallucination.

But she didn't have the right to touch him. Not any more. For all she knew, he could be married.

With a child.

The pain at that thought was so intense that she nearly gasped out loud. Then anger bubbled up to block out the pain. What the hell was he doing here? There were plenty of other hospitals in the world. Why did Max have to muscle into hers, push his way back into her life?

Max's face was completely unreadable. She had no idea

what he was thinking, or whether he was filled with the same confusing mixture of pain, anger and longing that she was.

He glanced at Marina's name-badge before turning to the woman who'd been yelling at her; when he spoke, his voice was clipped, and made it very clear that he was in charge. 'You're disturbing the other patients. I suggest you leave, so Dr Petrelli can concentrate on treating her patient—or do I need to call security to escort you out?'

The woman curled her lip at him and continued to chew gum loudly. 'It's all *wrong*, that lot coming over here and taking jobs off English people.'

'Not that it's any of your business,' Max said, 'but Dr Petrelli is as English as you are. And, even if she wasn't, this department operates a zero-tolerance policy. Our staff have the right to do their job without abuse.'

'I know my rights,' Ms Gum-Chewer said, folding her arms. 'And you're not getting away with bullying me.'

'The way you're bullying my staff, you mean? Three seconds and I'll be calling security to escort you out. Or you can step outside and let Dr Petrelli treat your friend without interruptions. Your choice.' He gave her an implacable stare. 'One…two…'

'I'll be just out here, Ally. And you make sure she treats you properly.' The gum-chewing woman sniffed loudly and stalked out of the cubicle.

Grumbling, and with a last, hostile look at Marina, the woman left the cubicle.

Marina still hadn't got over the fact that Max had called her *his* staff.

Ha; she'd stopped being *his* anything a long time ago.

'May I have a word?' Max looked at Marina and gestured to the cubicle curtain.

'Excuse me, Mrs Marshall,' Marina said to her patient. 'I'll be back in just a moment.'

Max closed the curtain behind them. 'Are you all right?'

His voice was formal and polite. How different it had been when they'd first met. She'd been a fresh-faced graduate in her first job as a pre-registered house officer. Everyone had been rushed off their feet on the first day, and Max had introduced himself swiftly in the five-minute break she'd managed to take, before giving her half a chocolate bar to keep her going, along with a cup of lukewarm coffee that she could gulp straight down. His warm, open smile had turned her weak at the knees, and she'd discovered that love at first sight wasn't a myth at all. She'd fallen dizzily, headlong in love with Max Fenton within seconds of meeting him.

But a lot had happened in those five years. And, given their shared past, and the fact that they were clearly going to have to work together, polite, formal and distant was definitely the best way forward.

She glanced at his name-badge again to check his rank and what she should call him. 'Senior registrar': so he *was* the guy who'd taken over from Ed. Still 'doctor' rather than 'mister', then. Odd, because he'd been so focused on his career that she'd expected him to make consultant at a scarily young age. 'I'm fine, thank you, Dr Fenton.'

That was a complete lie. Seeing him again had made her feel as if she'd just ridden an enormous rollercoaster—at double speed, and sitting backwards. She managed to pull herself together. Just. 'Thank you for coming to my rescue.'

'Not a problem.' He gave her an equally cool nod. 'I'll let you get back to your patient.'

'I'm really sorry,' the woman on the bed said when

Marina returned to the cubicle. She bit her lip. 'Claire's really kind-hearted.'

Maybe, on her own terms; Marina forbore to comment.

'It's just that sometimes she can come on a bit strong.'

That was putting it mildly, but it wasn't Mrs Marshall's fault that her friend was so overbearing. 'I've had worse—you should see the bad-tempered drunks who end up in here on a Friday night,' Marina said with a smile, wanting to put her patient at her ease. 'Don't worry about it.'

'It's because her husband always looks at your bit in the paper on a Wednesday—he fancies you something rotten,' Mrs Marshall confided.

'I'm very flattered,' Marina said, 'But your friend really doesn't have anything to worry about.' Even if she had been in the market for a relationship—and right now life was too complicated for her to cope with dating someone—she only ever went out with single men.

'I've told her how much Stewie loves her, but she's convinced he's going to look elsewhere because of her weight.' Mrs Marshall sighed and shook her head. 'She's trying so hard to make herself look good for him. She put on three stone when she stopped smoking. That's why she chews gum all the time—to stop herself going back on the ciggies.'

Marina knew that people with low self-esteem often lashed out at others as a way of making themselves feel better. Though it still hurt when you were the one they decided to pick on. 'She's done the right thing for her health, giving up the cigarettes. But we really should talk about *you* rather than your friend,' she said gently. 'I think you've broken your wrist, Mrs Marshall. From what you've told me about the way you landed, and the way your wrist looks, I think you have what's called a Colles' fracture. I'm going to give you some pain relief to make you more comfortable, then send you for an X-ray. When I've had a look at your X-ray and I'm happy that everything's straightforward, I'll put a temporary plaster on your wrist to keep it stable until the fracture clinic can see you.'

'You mean I'm going to be in plaster?' Mrs Marshall looked shocked.

'Modern casts are really lightweight,' Marina reassured her. 'But, yes, you'll need a cast for a few weeks, while your wrist heals.'

'Will I be able to go back to work?'

'It depends what you do for a living. If you use that hand a lot, then it's a good idea to have some time off to let your wrist heal properly. And I'd definitely say no lifting or carrying.'

Mrs Marshall looked upset. 'I don't get paid if I don't work.'

'But if you go back too early, and put too much weight on the fracture, there's a strong chance you'll make it worse and you'll be off work for even longer,' Marina said gently. 'I know it's not going to make you feel much better, but you're the fourth patient I've seen today with a Colles' fracture. When it's icy like this, no end of people slip, put their hands out to save themselves and end up breaking their wrists.'

She gave Mrs Marshall some painkillers, then directed her to X-ray. 'Come back when you've had the X-ray and I'll finish treating you,' she said with a smile.

Max grabbed a file and started to read his next patient's notes, needing a couple of minutes to get himself back under control. When he'd heard someone shouting in the cubicles, and realised that someone was haranguing one of his colleagues, he'd instinctively gone to the rescue.

What he hadn't expected was to see his ex-wife standing there.

He'd had no idea that Marina even worked at the London Victoria, so he hadn't been prepared to face her again. It was a double shock to see her again for the first time in four years.

She was still as gorgeous as ever, with that long, silky, dark hair he'd so loved playing with, albeit tied back for work; those expressive, dark eyes, and the perfect rosebud mouth he'd fallen in love with the very first day he'd met her. She was twenty-eight now, but still looked younger than her years, all soft skin and lush curves. Just as she'd done the first time he'd met her, she'd taken his breath away.

He only hoped that it hadn't shown on his face.

Then again, Max had spent months stuck in a hospital bed with nothing to do except brood and teach himself to mask his feelings. Between that, and three years of working for Doctors Without Borders, he was pretty sure he could keep his expression blank and professional in just about any situation.

Including unexpectedly coming face-to-face again with the love of his life.

He'd told himself that he was ready to work in England again, that he was over Marina. But seeing her just now had taught him how wrong he'd been. He wasn't over her at all. He never had been, and if he were honest with himself he probably never would be.

Not that he was going to do anything about it. Marina's expression had been pretty clear—shock, followed by hurt and anger. Given that she'd been the one to start divorce proceedings, it was obvious that she'd keep her distance from him. For all he knew, she could be in a serious relationship—married, even. He hadn't noticed a ring on her left hand; then again, he'd been too busy trying to look professional and detached to think of even looking. The idea of seeing another man's ring there made him feel sick to the stomach, but what right did he have to protest? He'd signed the papers, after all, agreed to end their marriage instead of fighting for it.

He'd been angry when he'd signed them—angry with Marina for walking out on him, and angry with himself for not doing more to keep them together. But he knew now that the anger had been just a mask for the hurt, something to cover the pit of loss so he couldn't see how deep it was.

He swallowed hard. What a mess. Now they were going to have to work together, and there was a fair chance that they'd be rostered onto the same team in Resus. So, for both their sakes, he was going to have to keep a lid on his feelings and pretend they'd never met before.

Thank God he'd chosen to specialise in emergency medicine, where he'd be kept way too busy to think about his ex-wife. He strode out to the reception area and called his next patient.

As always, when the weather was icy, the waiting area in the department was standing-room only. Most of the patients had fallen; some were badly bruised, but there were several with Colles' fractures that needed backslabs to keep the break stable before referral to the fracture clinic. But even though Marina was too busy to have a proper break she made sure she spent enough time with each patient to reassure them—particularly one elderly patient who suffered from osteoporosis and had cracked both arms and a hip. Rather than sending her up to the geriatric ward with a porter, Marina took the old lady herself and spent time settling her in to the ward.

Lunch was a sandwich eaten while sorting paperwork between patients. Halfway through the afternoon, Eve, the charge nurse, caught Marina before she saw her next case. 'You haven't had a break today. Go and grab a coffee.'

'We're busy,' Marina protested. 'And you haven't had a break either, Eve.' Nobody in the department did when it was as busy as this. There just wasn't time.

'Go and grab a coffee,' Eve directed. 'You need a break. And you're off at five today, yes?'

Marina nodded. 'I feel awful, leaving early when we've still got a full waiting-room.'

'You were in at eight, and you haven't stopped since you've been in. So leaving at five isn't exactly leaving *early*, is it? And we all know where you're going to be, anyway, if we need you.'

Yes. Picking up Phoebe, then going upstairs to the maternity department and spending a while at her elder sister's bedside.

Eve smiled at her. 'How's Rosie doing?'

'Getting there. She's feeling well enough to moan about being stuck in here and wanting to be at home with Neil and Phoebe.'

'That's a good sign. And the baby's doing OK?'

'Doing fine.' Marina bit her lip. 'Though I think we'll all be a lot happier when he or she's here safely.'

'Rosie's in good hands. You know as well as I do, Theo Petrakis is the best.' Eve patted her shoulder. 'Now, scoot.'

'Five minutes and I'll be back.'

'Make it fifteen,' Eve said.

Marina had no intention of taking that long, not when they were so busy. But she went through to the staff kitchen, made herself a mug of coffee and added enough cold water so that she could drink it quickly.

'Is the kettle still hot?' a voice behind her asked, and she nearly dropped her mug.

Max.

Longing surged through her, but she stifled it. Fast. 'Yes, Dr Fenton.' She forced herself to sound cool, calm and professional; the last thing she wanted was for him to realise that his voice was enough to turn her to a gibbering mess inside.

If there was an atmosphere between them people would start asking questions. Marina really didn't want to be the hot topic on the hospital grapevine. So, much as she hated it, she forced herself to make small talk. 'I didn't know you were going to be working here,' she said.

'I had an interview two weeks ago,' Max replied, making himself a coffee and topping it up with cold water, the same way Marina had.

Two weeks ago: that explained it. Life had been so crazy since Rosie had been admitted to the maternity ward with pre-eclampsia sixteen days before that Marina really hadn't paid much attention to what was going on at work. She just did her shift, visited her sister before and after every shift and helped her brother-in-law Neil to look after Phoebe, Rosie and his two-year-old daughter.

'I didn't realise you were here, either,' Max added. 'You weren't here when I had a tour of the department.'

'I was probably off duty.' Not that he needed to know what

she'd been doing. He hadn't kept in touch with her family at all; as far as she was concerned, he wasn't part of her family any longer, and she didn't owe him any explanations.

'How long have you been working here?'

'Nearly a year.' She glanced at him, and was gratified to see a slight flicker in his eyes. Good: so he *did* remember what had happened a year ago. He'd taken long enough to sign the divorce papers. Her solicitor had had to send them to him three times because he hadn't bothered replying; the ending of their marriage had clearly been as low a priority in his life as their marriage itself.

But at last she was free. She'd gone back to using her maiden name. At the London Victoria, they'd only ever known her as Marina Petrelli—and that was the way she wanted it to stay.

'It's a good place to work,' she said.

He raised an eyebrow. 'Is it going to be a problem, my working here?'

Trust Max to cut to the chase.

Yes, it was a problem. She'd much rather they didn't have to work together. But she couldn't change the situation, only make the best of it. 'I think,' she said carefully, 'We're both professional enough to put our patients first.'

'Good.'

There was a long, long pause. Marina couldn't think of a single thing to say.

Actually, that wasn't true. There was a lot she wanted to say. Answers she wanted to demand. But the emergency-department kitchen wasn't the right place to say any of it.

If anyone had said to her five years ago that she'd find it difficult to talk to Max, she would've laughed in disbelief. They'd never stopped talking, right from the start. And Max had fitted right in to her noisy, talkative family. The Petrellis had adored him as much as she had.

Until their marriage had gone so badly wrong. Then she and Max had stopped talking completely.

Marry in haste, repent at leisure: how horribly true that saying had turned out to be.

'Well, I'd better get back,' she said, rinsing out her mug and trying to avoid eye contact.

'Me, too.'

Oh, no. Please don't let him suggest walking back to the department together. She wasn't ready for this. But, to her relief, Max was still finishing his coffee, which meant she could escape.

'Bye, then,' she said brightly, and left the room.

How on earth had they come to this point? Max wondered. They were awkward, embarrassed strangers who could barely make small talk in a staff kitchen.

Though he knew exactly how they'd got here: through pain and hurt that they'd both been too young to deal with at the time. Marina had walked out and gone home to her parents for the comfort he hadn't been able to give her. And he'd responded by going off to work for Doctors Without Borders, where he'd known he'd be too busy to think about the wreck of their marriage.

And now they had to work together. He'd seen on her face that, yes, it was a problem for her. It was a problem for him, too. But they'd better deal with it—and fast—because he sure as hell didn't want to be the subject of the hospital grapevine. He'd been there before and he wasn't in any hurry to repeat the experience: people whispering and stopping conversations dead as soon as they saw him walk in, the pitying glances.

If he'd known that she worked here, he wouldn't have taken the job.

Then again, this had been too good an opportunity to turn down: a position as senior registrar in a busy London emergency-department. Added to his experience abroad, it would stand him in good stead for future promotion, for the consultant's post that was the focus of his life right now.

Luckily the rest of his afternoon was too rushed to let Max think about Marina. There were several victims of road-traffic accidents who needed checking over—including one with broken ribs and a pneumothorax that needed very careful attention. Even so, he was aware that Marina left the department a good half-hour before he did.

Then, as he walked out through the double doors, he heard a voice he recognised, saying cheerfully, 'Right, Miss Beautiful. Let's go and meet Daddy.'

Daddy?

Max couldn't help looking, and immediately wished he hadn't. Because at the far end of the corridor Marina was carrying a toddler: a little girl who had the same dark hair, dark eyes and sweet smile as Marina herself.

Marina had a daughter.

For a moment, Max couldn't breathe; it felt as if someone had just sucker-punched him in the stomach and all the air had been driven out of his lungs. The little girl looked as if she was around two years old—which meant that Marina hadn't even waited for their divorce to be finalised before she'd moved on to another relationship and had a baby with her new partner.

Yet she still used her maiden name in the department.

Maybe she hadn't yet remarried. Or maybe she'd decided to keep her maiden name for work.

Whatever.

It was none of his business any more.

All the same, it shook him. Especially when a man came walking down the corridor towards them, kissed Marina lightly on the mouth and scooped the child from her arms.

'Daddy!' the little girl said, beaming as the man kissed her and lifted her onto his shoulders.

Marina tucked her arm through his and they walked off together, chatting easily. Looking exactly like the close, loving family they obviously were.

Exactly like the close, loving family he and Marina had planned to have.

Max swallowed the bile that had risen in his throat. Now he understood why Marina had left her shift dead on time. She'd had to pick up her daughter from the hospital nursery before meeting her partner.

What made the whole thing so much worse was that, if circumstances had been very slightly different, Max would've been the one meeting Marina with a bright, lively pre-school child, and maybe a baby with chubby hands and a wide, wide smile. He would've been the one they smiled at, the one they greeted with a kiss.

He swore under his breath. He'd promised himself that he was over it, that he could cope with working in England again. But seeing that little tableau made it feel as if someone had cracked his heart wide open and stomped on it.

Marina had a child. With someone else.

He'd thought that he'd reached the depths of pain. Now he knew there was more—and it felt as if he were drowning. Someone else had the life he'd planned, the life he'd wanted: Marina, their baby, a fulfilling job.

Why the hell hadn't he tried harder to make it work?

Because he'd been an idiot.

Because he'd been hurting too much at the time to work out what he'd needed to do—what *they* had needed to do—as a couple.

And now it was too late. Way, way too late.

There was only one way of getting this out of his system. So, instead of making himself a sandwich when he got home, Max grabbed his gym gear and headed out again. What he needed was a workout that would leave him too damn tired to think. He'd sleep on it, let his subconscious come up with a way of dealing with the fact that Marina Petrelli was back in his life—and she was very firmly off-limits.

CHAPTER TWO

THE roster fairy definitely wasn't on his side, Max thought the next morning as he walked into Resus and saw his team.

To think he'd been so cool and calm yesterday, asking Marina if it would be a problem for her, working in the same department. He'd been so sure that he could handle the situation.

Though, that had been before he'd seen her with her daughter.

And he was shocked by how much that thought still hurt, like a bruise that went right through his soul.

'Good morning, Dr Fenton,' Marina said.

She sounded bright and breezy, as if nothing was wrong—although he'd noticed that her smile didn't quite reach her eyes, and she was using his formal title rather than his first name. OK; he'd take the lead from her. Bright, breezy and surface-friendly it was—even though he felt like punching something. He forced himself to unclench the fists in his pockets. 'Good morning, Dr Petrelli.'

'We've just had a shout,' she told him. 'RTC, elderly female passenger, ETA six minutes.'

'Any details?'

'Query fracture and internal injuries. They've put a line in and she's on a spinal board.'

Max met the ambulance crew at the door and quickly went through the handover, and the team swung into action to treat Mrs Jennings. Clearly they were used to working together and, whatever the problems between himself and Marina, she obviously took her job seriously, and she hadn't been exaggerating when she'd said that she could push the personal stuff into the background and put her patient first. Max quickly discovered that over the last four years Marina had become a fine doctor, confident and capable, and whenever he was about to give her some instructions he found she was already doing it, having second-guessed him.

As they assessed their patient for hypovolaemic shock—Max wasn't happy with her blood pressure or the capillary refill—they both noted the pattern of bruising across her abdomen, the lap-belt imprint. On examination, Mrs Jennings' abdomen was tender. Not good.

'I'm not happy with this,' Max said quietly to Marina.

'I'd need to see the X-ray to confirm it, but my guess is that the impact fractured her pelvis,' Marina said, equally quietly.

He nodded. 'There may be some splenic involvement as well, or even damage to other organs. We need a CT scan and an X-ray to see what's going on.'

'Agreed. Let's get her stabilised first,' Marina said.

Quietly, Max asked Stella, their senior nurse, to bleep the orthopaedic-surgery team and put Theatre on standby, and then he turned back to the patient. 'Mrs Jennings, I'm going to put a mask over your face,' he said, 'to give you some oxygen, which will help you to breathe more easily.

And I'm going to give you something to help with the pain, so it makes things a bit more comfortable for you while we take a look at your injuries. If you're worried about anything, just lift your hand and we'll take the mask off for a few moments so you can talk to us, OK?'

Mrs Jennings whispered her consent. Max fitted the oxygen mask over her face and gave her analgesia through the IV line that the paramedics had put in, while Marina inserted a second IV line and set up a drip. Marina took blood samples for rapid cross-matching, all the while talking to Mrs Jennings, reassuring her and assessing her. Max was impressed by Marina's calm, kind manner. Although they were faced with a potentially life-threatening emergency—compound pelvic fractures, especially if there were abdominal injuries as well, were associated with a mortality rate of more than fifty per cent—Marina made sure that Mrs Jennings didn't realise how worried they all were. She behaved as if this was a completely everyday occurrence, and nothing more worrying than a dislocated elbow, which meant that their patient relaxed rather than panicking—and in turn that made their investigations just that touch easier.

If it wasn't for the personal stuff between them, working with her would have been a dream.

As it was, it was a living nightmare. Her voice echoed through his head: *Let's go and meet Daddy.*

Daddy. Daddy.

It should've been him.

He shook himself. This wasn't the time or the place. And there was nothing he could do to change the situation, so it was pointless ripping himself apart over it. He forced himself to stay in professional mode, and reviewed the

X-rays with Marina against the lightbox. 'Classic open-book fracture,' he said.

'That's fixable. What worries me more is that her BP is still dropping.'

'Which means she has internal injuries.' He grimaced. 'We don't have time to wait for a CT scan, and even a DPL's going to be risky.' A diagnostic peritoneal lavage or DPL was a quick way of checking for internal haemorrhage when a scan would take too long. 'We need to get her up to Theatre now. Fast-bleep the orthopods, please, Stella,' he said to the nurse. 'I'm sending Mrs Jennings up.'

He turned to Mrs Jennings. 'The X-rays show that the accident broke your pelvis,' Max explained gently, holding her hand and looking into her eyes. 'I'm going to send you up to Theatre so the surgeons can fix it for you. We want to keep you as still as possible on the way, so we're going to put sandbags either side of you to make sure you don't move on the trolley.'

'But don't be afraid,' Marina added. 'It won't be uncomfortable, and it's pretty much routine-procedure for anyone who's got a break right there. I'm going to come up to Theatre with you and introduce you to the surgical team.' She took Mrs Jennings' other hand. 'And I'm not going to leave you until you're happy that you know what's going on. Is there anyone you'd like us to call for you while you're with the surgeons?'

Mrs Jennings reached up with her free hand and lowered the mask. 'My daughter,' she whispered.

Marina made a note of her name and number. 'I'll call her myself as soon as you're in Theatre,' she promised.

'And my friend,' Mrs Jennings whispered. 'The one who was driving me. Was she hurt in the accident?'

'She hasn't been brought in here,' Marina said. 'But I'll talk to the ambulance crew and find out what happened and how she is. Then, when you're out of Theatre, I'll come and see you and let you know what's going on. Now, let me put this mask back on you and make you more comfortable.'

When Marina returned from taking Mrs Jennings up to Theatre and phoning her daughter, Max was about to send her on a break, then the phone in Resus rang.

Stella answered it. 'Marina, it's the nursery,' she said, handing the phone to Marina.

'Marina Petrelli speaking.'

Even though Max tried hard not to listen in, he couldn't help noticing that Marina went white.

'What's happened? Right. I see. Yes, of course.' She replaced the receiver and blew out a breath. 'Phoebe's just thrown up everywhere. The nursery needs me to collect her and take her home, as in *right now*.' She bit her lip. 'Dr Fenton, I know I'm rostered in here with you today, and we're short-staffed, but—'

'Just go,' Max cut in. 'The child obviously needs you.' He couldn't bring himself to say 'your daughter'; the words made his throat feel as if it were closing, and he was angry with himself for not being able to get a grip. He should be happy that Marina's life was on track and that she'd clearly found a partner who loved her the way she deserved to be loved. The fact that he hadn't moved on and found someone else himself was his own stupid fault, and it wasn't fair to blame her for his own shortcomings. 'I'll arrange cover.'

'Thank you.' This time, her smile was genuine, gratitude, clearly mixed with fear for her child; she looked worried sick. And for good reason; he'd been told that the previous month the hospital had had to put a ban on visitors because so many patients and staff had been struck down by the winter vomiting-virus.

He didn't have time to add that he hoped it was nothing serious, because Marina had already left, walking very quickly, the way junior doctors soon learned to do so they could cover the ground between the on-call room and a department at maximum speed and with minimum risk.

To his surprise, Marina was back in the department again within two hours.

What the hell was she doing here? Her daughter was ill and needed her, and yet Marina was at work. Her priorities were *way* out of line. 'Shouldn't you be at home?' he demanded.

Marina shook her head. 'It's OK. Mum's taken over. I rang her on the way to collect Phoebe.'

'Your mother's looking after Phoebe?' He stared at her in disbelief. Just what was going on here? He knew that family was important to Marina, and given the way she'd fallen apart when she'd lost their baby he would've bet good money that she would always put her child before her job—before anything else. How could she just dump her sick daughter on her mother's doorstep?

Then again, the cost of living was high in London. Perhaps she and her partner were struggling financially and needed her salary to survive—what was left of it, after the cost of childcare.

'What about the child's father?' The question was out before he could stop it.

She looked defensive. 'Neil's really busy at work. I can't expect him to drop everything. Not when—'

'Save it. It's none of my business,' he cut in. He knew

he was being rude, but he was angry—with himself, as much as with her. Why couldn't he get his head round the fact that Marina had moved on, that she'd found happiness with someone else? Why was he so selfish that he couldn't be pleased for her, or relieved that she wasn't stuck in the same limbo of misery that he was?

She said nothing, but her face looked pinched, and her dark eyes were wary whenever she spoke to him for the rest of the afternoon.

As Max's anger faded, he realised how just unfair he'd been. Which was why he sent Marina off the ward at five o'clock sharp.

'I can't leave when we still have a patient to treat,' she said in a low voice.

'We'll manage without you.'

'But—'

'Phoebe needs you. Go home.'

'But—'

'Go *home*,' he repeated, trying to make his voice gentle. It was obvious that Marina was torn between her child and her duty; he had no intention of making the choice any more difficult for her.

But he thought about it for the rest of the evening—and wondered. Had their child been ill, how would he have acted? He was pretty sure he knew—and his choice wouldn't have been the same as Neil's.

Then again, he hadn't exactly been a perfect husband to Marina. He hadn't been there when she'd needed him. Yes, work had been busy, but he'd used his career as an excuse to avoid facing the misery at home. He hadn't known how to make things better, for either of them, so he'd put his job first. Her second husband was clearly out of the same mould, so Max knew he was hardly in a position to criticise the guy. It didn't stop him feeling angry about the situation, though, or thinking that Marina deserved better.

Wednesday; thank God it was Wednesday, Marina thought. As part of her training as a specialist registrar in emergency paediatrics, her boss had arranged for her to spend one day a week in the Children's Assessment Unit. She was covering in part for Katrina Morgan, who was on maternity leave. Rhys Morgan—the consultant, who was also Katrina's husband—had taught her a huge amount.

Marina loved every second of the time she spent on the CAU and always looked forward to it, but the fact that she didn't have to face Max today made it even better.

'Are you OK, Marina?' Rhys asked. 'You look a bit pale.'

'I'm fine,' Marina fibbed with a smile. 'Just tired.' She hadn't slept particularly well the previous night, brooding about Max and how hostile he'd been towards her. Yes, she'd been the one to walk out—but they were both equally responsible for the collapse of their marriage. And hadn't they agreed that they were going to put their patients first? If he carried on like that, there was no way they'd be able to work together—and it wouldn't be fair on their patients or the rest of the team.

'Not studying too hard, I hope?' Rhys said.

'No, just worrying about my sister.' It was true: just not the *whole* truth. Not that she was going to burden Rhys with the mess of her personal life. 'And, yes, I know she's in good hands and Theo Petrakis is the best maternity specialist for miles.' Theo's wife Madison and Rhys's wife Katrina were cousins, but were as close as sisters—though

Marina knew that Rhys would have put the family connection aside when he'd assessed his colleague's medical skills, just as she would have.

'But Rosie's still your sister—and where your own family's concerned all your medical knowledge goes out of the window. You end up being like a medical student again, poring through textbooks and convincing yourself that you can see the symptoms of really rare complications,' Rhys said, smiling back. 'Katrina says I'm going to be a nightmare when she goes into labour, just as Theo was with Maddie.'

'Doctors, eh?' Marina said wryly. 'How is Katrina, by the way?'

'Blooming,' Rhys said. 'It's our first anniversary next week. I had planned to take her to Venice for the weekend, but with her being seven-and-a-half months' pregnant I don't want her to fly. So instead we're going to Southwold, on the coast of Suffolk.' He grinned. 'And, yes, I know that this cold snap means that the east coast is going to feel like Siberia. We'll just have to tough it out and snuggle up in front of a proper log-fire in the little thatched cottage I booked.'

'That sounds lovely. Really romantic,' Marina said, trying to keep the wistful note out of her voice. Rhys was deeply in love with his wife and had planned something special to celebrate their first anniversary, whereas she and Max hadn't even made it to their first anniversary.

They hadn't even made it to six months before their marriage had imploded.

And now he was back in her life, and all her feelings were turned upside down again. Anger, hurt, longing, love and hate, all shaken together so thoroughly that she couldn't work out which was which.

She pushed the thought aside. 'Righty. What do you have for me this morning?'

'Severe asthma—cold-induced. Several cases, actually.'

'And if it isn't brought back under control properly they could end up with silent chest—in which case they'll be downstairs with my lot,' Marina said. With asthma, the child's airways were inflamed, and responded rapidly and strongly to stimuli, so the child wheezed and coughed; the airways narrowed so much that the child couldn't breathe out properly. The child might then panic and the situation could spiral. If it got really out of control, the wheezing could stop, which was far more dangerous. 'Silent chest', as it was known, meant that the asthmatic patient wasn't moving enough air through their lungs to even create a wheeze—and that was life-threatening.

'And then, once you've stabilised them, back up with me for admission and overnight observation…' Rhys began.

'Because if there's a history of severe attacks there's a very good chance that a child who's had an attack during the day will have another one at night,' Marina finished.

'Exactly,' Rhys said. 'So part of today is going to be about prevention—talking to the parents about using their inhalers properly, how to use them and when. And it's worth making the point that the steroids we give aren't the same as body-building steroids—these are the ones that are produced naturally in the body.'

Marina nodded. 'And we'll make a note for the GP and health visitor.'

Rhys smiled. 'Working with you is almost like working with Katrina—she's spot on about kids, too. You know, I'm looking for someone to cover her maternity leave properly.

Working up here for a while would be really good for your career development.'

Marina shook her head. 'Ellen agreed to let me work here for a day a week. I'm not sure she'd go for a year's secondment.'

'I can talk to her, if you like? Think about it,' Rhys said. 'The offer's open for a couple of weeks.'

'Thanks.' It was good to know that she had a potential bolthole. Working with Max and dealing with all the memories would've been tough at the best of times but, coming on top of her worries about Rosie and the baby, it just ratcheted up the tension.

At least here in the CAU she could relax.

And she could try not to think of Max.

CHAPTER THREE

ON THURSDAY morning, Max was walking into the department when he heard Kelly on Reception say, 'Hey, Marina! How's Phoebe doing?'

'She's on the mend. It's just a tummy bug.' Marina smiled. 'That's the worst thing about being a medic—you know the worst-case scenarios, and instead of seeing a simple tummy bug you imagine it's the winter vomiting virus and all the complications that go with it.'

Max knew exactly what she meant, though sometimes medics went the other way, going into complete denial when faced with the evidence—just as they had done four years ago. They'd managed to convince themselves that Marina wasn't having a miscarriage, that the baby they hadn't planned but had both wanted so much would be just fine… And when they'd finally had to face the truth it had hurt even more.

'Though Rosie's pretty upset that she's not getting her usual visitor on the ward this morning. I rang her at breakfast, so Phoebe could say hello down the phone, but it's not the same as being able to cuddle her.'

Max knew he really shouldn't be listening in—it was nothing to do with him any more—but he'd always liked

Marina's elder sister. Unless Rosie had changed career and become a medic like Marina, it sounded as if something was wrong. Why would Rosie be in hospital? And why was Marina taking her daughter to visit her sick aunt every single day?

'How's Rosie doing this morning?' Kelly asked.

'She's fine. Missing Phoebe and Neil like crazy, of course, but everyone knows she won't stick to bed rest at home.' Marina spread her hands. 'I mean, you can't if you have a toddler as lively as Phoebe.' She laughed. 'Mum's always telling Phoebe that she's exactly like her Aunty Rina was at the same age—covered in glitter and paint half the time, and pedalling round on her tricycle the other half.'

Everything suddenly fell into place for Max, and for one crazy moment he found himself on the point of whooping with delight and doing a happy dance all round the department.

The toddler Marina had been carrying—the one she'd gone to pick up from the nursery—was her *niece*, not her daughter.

As Rosie had the same colouring as Marina, and similar features, of course there'd be a strong physical resemblance between aunt and niece. And that in turn meant that the man Marina had kissed in the corridor had been her brother-in-law, not her partner. The Petrelli family had always been warm and tactile, and Max had kissed Marina's sister, mother, aunts and grandmother exactly the same way himself before their marriage had fallen apart.

How *stupid* he'd been.

Then again, Max had never been able to think straight around Marina. Not from the moment he'd met her as a wet-behind-the-ears junior doctor who made very sure she pulled her weight on the team and did her best to reassure her patients. They'd gone for a coffee after that first shift, and had dated every night after that. The more time he'd spent with her, the more deeply he'd fallen in love with her.

Small wonder that they'd gone to bed together within a week and had moved in together within a month. They hadn't wanted to spend a single moment apart.

Yet they'd spent the past four years as far apart as they could be: Marina in London, and he moving from disaster zone to disaster zone, pushing himself to the limit so he wouldn't have to think about how much he'd lost.

He closed his eyes briefly. Now wasn't the time or the place. He and Marina were going to have to talk about it, but not now, and definitely not here. Right now, he had a job to do. And so did she.

Marina was rostered on the children's section of the emergency department that morning; that was good, because it meant she didn't have to see Max. Not unless there was a really difficult case where she needed a second opinion. But she was in luck: her first case was a toddler who'd stuffed a plastic bead up his nose, her second was a child with a cough that she suspected was asthmatic, and her third was one who'd fallen in the playground and gashed his arm deeply enough to need stitches and a lot of reassurance. All things that needed a bit of time, reassurance and TLC as well as medical treatment, and she knew she was perfectly capable of dealing with all of them on her own.

Everything was fine until she took her break. The second that she made herself a mug of coffee in the kitchen, Max walked in, as if he had some weird kind of radar that told him exactly when she'd be there.

'How's Phoebe?' he asked.

'Doing OK, thanks. Mum's looking after her today again.'

He made himself a coffee, then took a bar of chocolate from the pocket of his white coat, snapped it in half and handed half to her.

She accepted it without thinking, the way she always had when they'd worked together. 'Thanks.' Then she stared at the chocolate, suddenly realising what they'd both done.

Just like old times.

Except they'd both come a long way in the last four years.

'I didn't have time for breakfast this morning,' he said with the quirky smile that had once made her knees melt.

She remembered those days. Even though their flat had been a ten-minute walk from the hospital, they'd never had time for breakfast. Because they'd been too busy making love.

She took a gulp of coffee and willed the memories to stay back.

'So what's wrong with Rosie?' he asked. 'I overheard Kelly asking you how she was.'

'Pre-eclampsia,' Marina explained. 'They've kept her in so she'll get some rest and they can monitor how the baby's doing.'

'Is it OK if I go and see her?' he asked.

She frowned. 'Why would you want to do that?'

He sighed. 'Look, I know things didn't work out between us, but I liked your family.'

And they'd liked him. A lot.

Pity that the same couldn't be said of the way Max's family had felt about her. Kay Fenton had seen Marina as a rival for her son's affections, and Andrew Fenton had usually been away on business trips. Marina had found them distant and cold, the complete opposite of her own family. And when everything had gone wrong, and Marina had been at her most vulnerable, the Fentons had made it very clear that they weren't going to offer her a shoulder to cry on. Andrew, as usual, had been absent, and Kay had actually said that it was for the best—that it was the wrong time for Max to have a baby when he had his career to think about.

How could anyone possibly say that a miscarriage was 'for the best'? All this time later, it still took her breath away.

'Marina?'

It wasn't Max's fault that his mother was supremely tactless. 'It's not up to me to give you permission. If you want to visit Rosie—' she spread her hands '—then visit her. But bear in mind she has pre-eclampsia. The last thing she needs right now is any kind of worry that'll make her blood pressure rise.'

'As a medic, I'd just about worked that one out for myself,' Max said drily.

'Sorry. I didn't mean to be rude.' She blew out a breath. 'It's just…'

'She's your big sister, you love her and you worry about her,' Max supplied.

'Yes.'

'It's good that she has family who care.'

Marina was careful not to comment, and she took refuge in eating the chocolate he'd given her.

He sighed. 'Look, if you're worrying—nobody here knows about Bristol. And I'm happy for it to stay that way. I don't like being gossiped about, either. If anyone twigs that we know each other, we'll just tell them we worked together years ago and lost touch.'

It was the truth. Just not the whole truth. And it left out a hell of a lot of pain in between. 'Thank you,' she said quietly.

He looked away. 'We have to work together, and there's enough tension in an emergency department as it is without adding to it.'

'Agreed.'

'So can we just drop the formality and treat each other like any other member of staff?'

'Sure.' But he wasn't just 'any other member of staff'. He never could be. But Marina had already been there, done that and had her heart well and truly broken. She wasn't going to take that risk a second time. No matter that she still found Max incredibly attractive physically; she knew that they weren't compatible. And, although part of her would've been more than happy to walk back into his arms, part of her knew that it'd be a huge mistake. She'd simply be setting herself up for more misery. So she was going to have to learn to think of him as just a colleague.

Somehow.

She drained her coffee. 'I'd better get back. Thanks for the chocolate.'

'Pleasure.'

During his lunch break, Max called in at the hospital shop to buy chocolates and a puzzle magazine—he'd already learned that the hospital had a clear-locker-top policy, and flowers were discouraged, to help in the battle with hygiene—and went up to the maternity ward.

'We have protected lunchtimes, I'm afraid,' the senior midwife told him firmly. 'Sorry. You'll have to come back later.'

'Is there any chance you can bend the rules for me, as

staff?' Max asked. 'I promise to be quiet. And I have a feeling that this particular patient hates being on bed rest. So that's fifteen minutes or so when you won't have to keep an eye on her and nag her, because I can do it for you.'

She glanced at his name-tag. 'Ah. You work with Rosie's sister?'

'I do indeed.' Max had no intention of giving the more complicated explanation—that Rosie was his ex-sister-in-law. He held out his free hand. 'Max Fenton, emergency senior registrar.'

She shook his hand and introduced herself. 'Iris Rutherford, senior midwife. No doubt we'll be working together at some point.'

'Good to meet you outside of a crisis.' Max gave her his most charming smile.

'All right. You can have fifteen minutes,' Iris said. 'But you'd better make sure she rests and doesn't move, or I'll be forced to scalp you.'

He laughed, enjoying her direct approach. 'I will. Thank you, Iris.'

Max followed her directions; Rosie was in a room on her own, flicking listlessly through a magazine and looking very fed up.

'Psst. Open for visitors?' he asked from the doorway.

She looked at him, and then gave him a broad smile. 'Max Fenton! What on earth are you doing here?'

'Visiting you,' he said, walking into the room and closing the door behind him.

Her eyes widened. 'We're not allowed visitors at lunchtime.'

'I know.' He laughed. 'I begged.'

'Charmed, more like. You always could melt women's

knees with that gorgeous smile of yours.' She grinned and held her arms open. 'Come and give me a hug, Max. It's good to see you.'

'And it's good to see you, Rosie Petrelli.' And even better to be hugged like that again. He'd missed the warmth of Marina's family, and his own. Well…he'd always found his mother's hugs stifling rather than warm. Though, now that everything was finally out in the open about his father, he could understand the way she behaved. Could sympathise, even.

'I'm Rosie Brown nowadays.' She bit her lip. 'I'm sorry I didn't invite you to the wedding, Max. But, apart from the fact that you'd cut off all contact with us, it would've been a bit—'

'Awkward, given who was probably your chief bridesmaid,' he finished wryly, sitting on the chair next to her bed. 'You did the right thing. I would've brought you some flowers, but I gather they've been banned from the hospital for a while. I hope these will do.' He placed the goodies on her lap.

'My favourites; you remembered I love white chocolate.' She beamed at him. 'And you managed to find the only puzzle magazine I haven't already gone through. Thank you. That's so, so sweet of you, *caro*.'

'My pleasure. So how long have you been in here?'

'Nineteen days, and counting,' Rosie said with a rueful smile, 'thanks to my bossy little sister.'

'Marina picked it up?' Max looked at her, surprised.

'She was on a day off, so she came to have lunch with me. I wasn't feeling brilliant; I thought it was just a bit of indigestion and a headache. But when I told her where the pain was she wasn't happy about it. She said it was rare to get pre-eclampsia with a second baby, but she wanted it checked out. She made me call the midwife and then drink loads of water.'

Ready for a urine test, no doubt. Rosie wasn't in the high-risk group, though: she was under thirty-five, her weight was average and it wasn't her first pregnancy. As far as Max knew, there wasn't a family history of pre-eclampsia, and Rosie wasn't a diabetic. Plus, from what Marina had said, she was only expecting one baby, not twins or triplets. 'So where was the pain? Just under your ribs?'

Rosie rolled her eyes. 'Spoken just like a doctor! Yes. And, yes, before you ask, there turned out to be a little bit of protein in my urine and my blood pressure was a bit on the high side.'

Knowing Rosie, that was a major understatement.

'So they're keeping me in to monitor the baby and keep an eye on me,' she finished.

'How far are you?'

'Thirty-three weeks—and it's driving me insane, being stuck here.' She shook herself. 'And here's me being ungrateful. Marina's been absolutely brilliant. And, yes, I do know she probably saved my life.'

If Rosie's symptoms hadn't been picked up so quickly, she could have been very ill—and there would've been a serious risk both to the baby and to Rosie herself. If Rosie's condition had turned into eclampsia, both of them could have died.

'She's sorted out a place at the hospital crèche for Phoebe while I'm here, and she brings my baby in to see me every morning before her shift. She picks her up, too, if she's on an early. Neil's boss has been really good about him working more flexible hours, but it's smack in the middle of the busy season.'

'Busy season?'

'It's March—coming up to the end of the tax year. He's an accountant,' Rosie explained, 'so normally he'd be working silly hours in the office, but because I'm stuck in here he's having to bring work home and do it when Phoebe's asleep. Mum and Dad have been brilliant, too. Dad's painting the baby's room and Mum's keeping the house ticking over and making sure that there's food in the fridge, so Neil can spend time here with me and Phoebe instead of worrying about housework and shopping and what have you.'

Exactly what Max would expect from the Petrellis, being there to help with practical things in a crisis. Part of him wondered: had he and Marina lived in London instead of Bristol, would her family have rallied round them and kept them together, helped them to work things through?

Too late for that now.

'So when are they going to induce you?' he asked.

'It depends how things go. I know that it's best to deliver the baby as late as possible, but the idea of being stuck here for another seven weeks, having injections and blood taken…' She grimaced. 'I tell you, if I was ever scared of needles, I've learned to overcome my phobia! Anyway, enough about me. We're doing fine—aren't we, Bambino?' She rubbed the bump and smiled. 'So, how are you doing?'

'I'm fine.'

She raised an eyebrow. 'Right. And that's why you've got dark shadows under your eyes and you're too thin. Don't try to bluff me, Max.'

'New city, new job. It takes time to settle in,' he said lightly.

'Maybe.' She gestured to his name-tag. 'But you're also

working in the emergency department with my sister. That can't be easy—for either of you.'

He shrugged. 'We're professionals. Our patients won't suffer.'

'I'm not talking about the *patients*—I know you're both professionals. I was talking about you two.' She reached out and took his hand. 'I was really sorry when you and Marina broke up.'

Tell me about it. He forced himself to keep the words back. 'Things happen,' he said lightly.

'So are you with someone now? What's she like?'

He'd forgotten the other thing about Marina's family: they had no scruples about asking personal questions. For a moment, he considered making up a story, but Rosie would know he was lying. 'There's nobody,' he admitted. And then, to stave off further questioning, he added, 'I spent a few years working for Doctors Without Borders. There wasn't time for anything other than work.'

He wished he hadn't said it when Rosie gave him a very perceptive look. 'So *that's* why we never got a Christmas card from you. Hmm. I happen to know someone else who throws herself into work. Someone who either finds excuses not to date, or makes it friends-only after just a couple of dates.'

Rosie wasn't even trying to be subtle and, although part of him was annoyed, part of him was also amused. The Petrellis were notorious fixers. They were the kind of people who made lemonade out of lemons, who always saw the bright side. It was one of the things he'd adored about Marina; she was unlike anyone else he'd ever met. And the complete opposite of his mother: she saw sunshine where Kay Fenton saw clouds, was light where Kay was intense. Just like the rest of her family. 'Don't get your hopes up, Rosie. Marina and I are colleagues. End of.' He smiled to take the sting from his words.

'It's four years now since you split up. You're both still single. That,' Rosie said, 'is extremely telling.'

'And I think you've been teaching too much *Romeo and Juliet*,' he said, still managing a smile. It was impossible to be offended with someone who so clearly wanted life to be happy. 'A nice story.'

She scoffed. 'Of course it isn't a nice story. It's a tragedy, Max. They both die at the end!'

'And it unites their families.' He flapped a dismissive hand. 'You know what I mean. Marina and I won't be getting back together, Rosie. There's way too much water under the bridge.'

Rosie gave him a telling look, but to his relief she didn't try to labour the point. 'Marina didn't tell me you were working here.'

He shrugged. 'I only started a couple of days ago.'

'Hmm,' Rosie said.

'And neither of us knew the other was working here. It was a bit of a surprise for both of us.'

'I'll say,' Rosie said drily.

He ruffled her hair. 'I have to go. Iris says you have to sit still and be good, or she'll scalp me. Is it OK if I come back tomorrow?'

'Of course it is.' She frowned. 'Why are you even asking me that?'

'I don't want to make things awkward.'

'With Marina, you mean? Or the rest of my family?' She patted his hand. 'Stop worrying. Of course it's not going to be awkward. If anything, they'll be pleased I've got someone else to come in and nag me to rest.'

He couldn't help laughing. 'Good.'

She smiled at him. 'Thanks for coming, Max. It's been really good to see you again.'

'You, too.' He hugged her, and left for the emergency department.

But he couldn't stop thinking about what Rosie had told him.

Marina didn't date.

He hadn't dated much since he'd split up with Marina, either. Most of the time, he'd been too busy at work to bother with a relationship. But when he'd come back to England and had started dating again something had always been missing. He'd always ended up finishing a relationship before it had even got started.

If he was honest with himself, he knew why: because nobody had ever matched up to his ex-wife.

And Rosie had told him that there was nobody serious in Marina's life, either.

Quite what that meant, he didn't know. Did Marina still have feelings for him? But, in that case, surely she would've talked to him and asked him to give their marriage another try, instead of sending divorce papers to him? Or maybe marriage to him had disappointed her so much that she wasn't prepared to try again with anyone else.

The only way to find out was to ask her.

Though, it wasn't the easiest of subjects to broach. Particularly as they had to work together. Right now, they had a guarded working-relationship; not an easy one, but a tolerable one. Asking the wrong questions at the wrong time could tip it over into being intolerable—which wouldn't be fair to their colleagues.

Last time, they'd rushed into things, and it had gone spectacularly wrong. This time, maybe he should try being patient.

And when the time was right, Max decided, then he'd ask those questions.

CHAPTER FOUR

OVER the next week, Marina found herself growing more and more aware of her ex. She knew exactly when Max walked into the department, even if she was busy treating a patient in cubicles and couldn't see him. And, when they were working together in Resus, she was conscious of every single movement he made. Time and again she found herself glancing at him, only to find that he was looking at her too.

This was insane. They'd crashed and burned last time round. So why couldn't they keep their eyes off each other?

Every time his hand brushed hers as she handed him an ampoule, or he passed her a syringe, or they looked at an X-ray together, her pulse started racing—because her body still remembered the way he used to touch her: the feel of his skin sliding against hers, the roughness of the hair on his chest, the softness of his mouth as he'd kissed her awake. The scent of his skin, the way his eyes crinkled at the corners and dimples appeared in his cheeks when he laughed, the way desire flared in his eyes and turned them from slate-blue to hot black whenever he looked at her.

She really had to get a grip. If this carried on for much longer, she'd go crazy.

She and Max were *not* an item. They were never going to be an item again. And it was about time her head got that straight.

Rosemary; Max would've known that scent anywhere. So Marina still used the same shampoo, then.

Her hair was driving him insane. She wore it in a French pleat at work, but he could remember what it looked like when it was down, glossy and spilling over her shoulders. Flowing over his pillow, soft and sensuous. He'd loved brushing her hair, playing with the ends and feeling its silkiness against his skin.

It would have been so much easier if she'd had her hair cropped. At least then he wouldn't have had to keep battling with the memories.

He glanced at her mouth, and wished that he hadn't. Because he could remember that beautiful mouth exploring every inch of his skin, her eyes full of mischief as she'd turned him on so much that he couldn't even see straight. Even the memories made his whole body tingle with desire.

Working with Marina was becoming more and more of a challenge for Max. She was a great doctor, and he'd never been one for throwing his weight around, so teamwork on the ward wasn't a problem.

It was Marina herself, and the way his body seemed to operate completely independently from his head. Every time his hand accidentally brushed hers, or he caught the scent of her hair, he wanted to yank her into his arms, dip his head, brush his mouth against hers, tease her until she slid her hands into his hair, opened her mouth and kissed him back.

For pity's sake. He knew he didn't have the right to do that. But he still wanted to touch her. *Needed* to touch her.

This was crazy, particularly as he didn't have a clue how she felt about the situation. She was perfectly professional with him, and since their brief chat in the staff kitchen she'd stuck to first-name terms and treated him just like she treated everyone else on the ward. But whenever he caught her eye there was something unreadable in her gaze. He couldn't even begin to work out what it was.

Get a grip, he told himself savagely. *Be professional*. Because he knew it was way too late to go back. No way would Marina give him a second chance.

'Max has been to see me,' Rosie said.

Marina frowned. 'He hasn't upset you or anything, has he?'

'No. He's good company. And he's dropped in every day.'

Every day? From what he'd said, she'd expected him to visit Rosie maybe once—not every day. And he hadn't said a word to her about it.

Rosie took her sister's hand and squeezed it. 'I always liked him, Marina. We all did.'

'I know.' Marina sighed heavily, guessing what Rosie was going to say next, and knowing that she had to head her sister off right now. 'But it didn't work out and we've both moved on.'

'Mmm-hmm.' Rosie paused. 'You know, Max isn't seeing anyone.'

'That's none of my business, Rosie.' Trust her sister to have asked the question. Marina deliberately hadn't.

But now she knew.

And it sent a weird mixture of delight and panic through her.

Delight, because it felt as if Max had waited for her. And panic, because it had gone so badly wrong last time; did they really have a chance to get it right, second time round?

If Max had wanted them to try again, he would have followed her to London years ago. He would've refused to sign the divorce papers. He would've *talked* to her.

But, all the same, she couldn't help wondering: why was Max still single? OK, so their marriage had been a disaster, but Max was a nice guy. A good doctor.

A thoughtful lover. Marina suppressed that line of thought immediately. She really didn't need to remember how she'd felt in Max's arms. How his clever hands and mouth had made her blood feel, as if it were singing. How he'd taken her to the edge of pleasure.

'Did you know he spent three years working for Doctors Without Borders?' Rosie asked.

'No.' But it explained why he'd taken a while to respond to her solicitor's letters—and it also explained why he was single. No way would Max have had any spare energy to start a new relationship, working under those kinds of pressures.

'I think,' Rosie said, 'that it's time you two sat down and talked. Properly.'

Ha. That had been one of the biggest blows to their marriage. After she'd lost the baby, they'd stopped talking. 'There isn't anything to say.'

'Isn't there?' Rosie arched one eyebrow.

'No. Now, stop worrying.' Marina patted her hand. 'As I said, we've both moved on.'

Rosie folded her arms. 'Right. Which is why neither of you are dating.'

'If he's been working for Doctors Without Borders, he wouldn't have had time to see anyone,' Marina pointed out. 'And I'm training to be a specialist registrar in paediatric emergency—which means I don't have time to see anyone either.' She gave her sister her brightest smile. 'Right now, my career needs to come first.'

'I worry about you, Marina. I want you to be happy.'

'I *am* happy.' Though, even as she said it, Marina realised it wasn't strictly true. She still missed Max. Or maybe she missed the idea of him: the man she'd thought she'd married, who'd turned out to be not quite the same as the man she'd actually married. 'Stop fussing and let me look at your chart,' she said to put Rosie off the scent.

Rosie groaned. 'They hate you doing that, you know.'

Marina laughed. 'No, they don't. Iris knows that I'm not going to interfere with the way they're looking after you. And this saves her some precious time—she doesn't have to spend ages with me while I grill her about how you *really* are.' She took the clipboard from the holder next to her sister's bed. 'Good. Your temperature's fine, your urine's fine… Hmm; your blood pressure's still not what I'd like it to be, but it's holding. And Bambino here seems to be doing very nicely, thank you. Excellent.'

'I've been here for ever and ever,' Rosie complained. 'I want to go home and play with my little girl.'

'I know you miss her, but she'll be here in a minute.' Marina gave her sister a hug. 'Hang on in there, sis. You're doing brilliantly.'

As if perfectly on cue, their mother walked in, holding Phoebe's hand.

'Mummy!'

Louise Petrelli lifted her granddaughter so Phoebe could

sit next to her mother, and Rosie enfolded her in a hug, holding her tightly and pressing her face to the little girl's hair so she could breathe in her scent.

If things had been different, Marina would've met her baby from school with that same mother-daughter hug. The one that said how much they'd missed each other, even though both had been happily busy all day. The one that said how glad they were to be together again.

She envied Rosie that closeness. Funny; she thought she'd cried herself out over the miscarriage. But even now she was still yearning. Still wishing things had been different. Still not really over it.

Whereas Max… She had no idea how he'd felt about it, back then, and even less idea as to whether he still thought of their baby that might have been. He hadn't broken down the way she had—which didn't mean that he'd felt nothing—but he'd pushed her away, hadn't let her comfort him. Hadn't given her the support she'd needed so desperately.

Pushing the thoughts away, she gave her own mother a hug. 'Hi, Mum. Have you both had a good day?'

'Brilliant. We went to the park this morning and played on the swings, and this afternoon we've been busy making cookies, and pictures with glitter and glue—oh, and singing songs.'

Just the kind of thing that Marina remembered doing in her own childhood. The Petrelli household had been noisy, chaotic and messy, and chock-full of love. There had always been a tin full of fresh-baked cookies or cupcakes in the kitchen, and all the neighbours had seemed to congregate at their house. The mums would be round Louise's kitchen table with mugs full of good coffee, and the children would be playing noisy, messy games in the huge conservatory that opened off the kitchen, far enough away to feel independent, and yet near enough to be scooped up and kissed better within seconds if they fell over.

Completely the opposite of Max's family home, where nothing was ever out of place and the silence was practically deafening. She'd just bet that Max had never been allowed to do anything with glitter, and there wouldn't have been a cork board in his mother's kitchen where his newest paintings from school had been pinned up—because a cork board would have looked so out of place and scruffy in Kay Fenton's immaculate designer-kitchen.

'Sounds like fun,' Rosie said, looking as wistful as Marina felt.

'Hey, Mum, guess who's been visiting me this week?' Rosie asked.

Uh-oh. Marina had hoped that the delight of seeing her daughter would push the subject out of her sister's mind. Now she'd have two of them on her case.

'Who?' Louise asked.

'Max. *Marina's* Max.'

'Oh, really?' Louise looked intrigued.

'He's not *my* anything. We just work together.' Marina rolled her eyes. 'Mum, don't listen to her. She's bored and making up stories to amuse herself.'

'I am not,' Rosie said indignantly.

Phoebe snuggled into her mother. 'Story?' she asked hopefully.

Marina took the chance to escape before her mother could grill her any more, but she knew that the reckoning was only being delayed.

And, just as she'd expected, her mother phoned later that evening. 'So, what's the real story about Max?' Louise asked.

'There isn't one. He joined the team last week, so we're working together. We're both professional enough to put our patients first, so it isn't a problem.'

'Hmm.' Louise sounded as suspicious as Rosie had. 'Are you sure you're OK about this?'

'Really, Mum, there's nothing to worry about. It's fine.'

Louise sighed. 'All right. I won't nag. Your sister can do enough of that for both of us. But if it gets tough you know where I am.'

'I know, and I appreciate it,' Marina said, meaning every word. 'I love you, Mum.'

'Max, we're one short for Friday night,' Eve told him. 'Are you busy?'

'One short for what?' he asked.

'Ten-pin bowling.'

He smiled. 'Thanks for asking, Eve, but I haven't done that for years. I'd just let the side down.'

'Of course you wouldn't. Now's your chance to brush up your skills. And it's a good way of getting to know people outside work.'

Max had already worked out that Eve was the sort of person who took new members of the team under her wing and made sure that they felt welcome. And he knew that Marina was off duty on Friday, so it was highly likely that she wouldn't be there—she was bound to be doing something with her family. So Max judged that it was pretty safe to agree. 'Sure. Just let me know where and what time you want me to turn up.'

'Brilliant.' She gave him a broad smile. 'You won't regret it.'

* * *

Though he did regret it, the moment that he walked into the bowling alley and saw the group of people there.

Seeing Marina in a white coat was one thing. Seeing her in figure-hugging jeans and a loose, long-sleeved T-shirt with her hair down was quite another. At work, she was professional and detached; here, she looked like the girl next door. Just like she'd looked when she'd been his wife.

Five years ago, he would have strode over to her, swept her off her feet, spun her round and kissed her lingeringly, not caring who was watching. Five years ago, she'd have been sitting on his lap, laughing with him and stealing kisses while they were waiting for their respective turns at the bowling alley.

But this was now.

And, with the emotional distance between them, she might just as well have been standing on the moon.

He shoved his hands into the pockets of his jeans, just in case he was tempted to reach out and smooth his palm over the curve of her bottom. For pity's sake. He'd told himself this enough times; he knew he didn't have the right to touch her any more. The fact that he wanted to yank her into his arms and kiss her until they were both breathless and had forgotten the rest of the world...

They really needed to have that talk.

And it looked as if it had better be sooner rather than later.

'Sorry. I didn't realise you'd be here tonight, or I would've made some excuse and not come,' he said quietly as he joined the group.

She lifted one shoulder in a half-shrug. 'Nothing to apologise for—you're part of the team. You have as much right as I do to be here.'

She sounded all cool, calm and neutral—though he

could see the tension in her face, in her mouth, and knew that she too was wishing herself thousands of miles away. This was as much of an ordeal for her as it was for him.

As luck would have it, they ended up on the same team of four. Max's turn to bowl was right after Marina's; short of standing with his back to her when she was bowling—which would've made it look way too obvious that he was trying to avoid her—there was nothing he could do but stand and watch her. The sight of the curve of her bottom, encased in soft, soft denim, sent his blood pressure up a notch, and he had to stuff his hands in his pockets to stop himself reaching out and touching her. Stroking her. She was still the most gorgeous woman he'd ever met, all softness and lush curves. He wanted her so badly, it was a physical pain. Worse, because he could remember how it felt when she touched him, could remember how it felt to lose himself inside her.

When their waiter brought cold drinks and hot, crispy nachos, Max's discomfort was magnified a hundred times, because he reached for the snacks at the same time as Marina and his fingers brushed against hers. It was the lightest, most casual touch, but every nerve-end in his body screamed into life. It felt as if his blood were fizzing through his veins.

He was extremely glad that his jeans were relatively baggy. The last thing he wanted was anyone noticing his arousal, or guessing his reaction to Marina—especially Marina herself.

Cool, calm and casual. That was how Marina had decided to play it tonight, when Max had turned up.

Except he *would* have to wear a T-shirt that brought out the slate-blue of his eyes. She'd fallen in love with his beautiful eyes all those years before, though she'd forgotten how long his lashes were. How he'd looked when he was asleep, like a fallen angel. Sexy as hell.

Yet there were also definite changes in him. She could see dark shadows underneath his eyes, and there was a kind of wariness and a reserve about him that she didn't remember from before, though maybe that was a result of his years working for Doctors Without Borders. She knew from talking to colleagues in her last hospital that the experience changed you.

But the thing that she really noticed was that Max looked...*unloved*.

It made her want to hold him close, tell him that everything would be OK because she was there, and she...

Oh, hell. She really had to stop thinking like this. It hadn't worked out last time; admittedly, they were both four years older and wiser now, but there was too much debris from the past for it to work out this time.

Though she couldn't deny that the attraction was still there between them. When their fingers had accidentally brushed each other's over the nachos, pure desire had rippled down her spine. And when she'd glanced at him he'd masked his expression quickly—but not before she'd noticed how huge his pupils were. Given how bright the lights were in the bowling alley, she had a pretty shrewd idea that Max was remembering the same kind of thing that she was.

Touching.

Tasting.

Losing themselves in each other.

They were really going to have to talk about this. But not at the hospital, and nowhere that they were likely to be spotted together or overheard; the last thing she wanted was for them to become the hottest topic on the hospital grapevine. She'd think about it over the weekend. Plan her strategy. And she'd tackle him on Monday.

CHAPTER FIVE

EXCEPT on Monday there wasn't any time to think. Marina was working with Max in Resus, and there was a constant stream of cases—a woman with chest pain, a man with severe abdominal pain and an elderly man with a transient ischaemic attack. The team was working flat out, and they had just about enough time to grab half a sandwich before the next shout.

Max looked grim. 'We have a teenager on his way in. He was on his bike, not wearing a helmet; a car clipped him and he came off and hit his head. GCS 7.'

A Glasgow Coma Score of 7 meant that the boy was unconscious and unresponsive—and it was harder to judge his injuries. Given that he'd hit his head, his injuries could be severe. Life-threatening, even.

'Stella—can you warn radiology that we'll need an urgent CT scan, please, and get neurology on standby?' Max asked.

Moments after the handover, Marina could see that the neuro obs weren't good. She wasn't happy with the boy's pulse rate or his blood pressure, and even less happy that he still hadn't regained full consciousness twenty minutes after the accident.

'Witnesses say he was playing chicken, crossing the

road on his bike between parked cars,' Max told her drily. 'Apparently the car driver tried to avoid him and did an emergency stop, but he didn't stand a chance.'

'The boy or the driver?'

'Both,' Max said. 'They're bringing the driver separately. He has whiplash—and he's pretty distressed.'

'Anyone would be, in his shoes.' She'd once accidentally backed into a car and broken her rear light, and that had been upsetting enough; when the collision hurt a person rather than a fixable object, even if it wasn't the driver's fault, it must be unbelievably frightening. 'What a mess,' Marina said.

Max swiftly intubated the boy and they set up ventilation. The boy's cervical spine was still protected by the board. 'I've got a bad feeling about this one,' Max said.

'Skull fracture?' Marina said.

Max nodded. 'And maybe a haematoma.' A blood clot that caused the brain to swell and pressure to rise within the cranium was a problem often caused with head injuries, and it could be fatal.

Max grimaced as he reviewed the CT scan. 'Look,' he said, pointing out the fracture at the base of the boy's skull. 'And here.' There were definite signs of a haematoma.

'Hurts,' the boy said, opening his eyes and closing them again almost straight away.

But at least he was talking; that was a good sign.

'Where does it hurt?' Marina asked.

The boy mumbled something neither of them could catch—and then was silent.

Marina and Max shared a glance. 'I hope this isn't a textbook case,' Max said.

She knew what he meant: 'talk and die'. They'd both

seen cases like this before in Bristol, where a patient seemed to start recovering, said a few words—and then died just minutes later.

'His BP's rising,' Marina said.

'And he's bradycardic. Looks like a Cushing response to me.' Max's mouth tightened.

The Cushing response was when blood pressure rose and the heart rate fell; it meant there was increased intracranial pressure. Given the circumstances surrounding the boy's accident and what they'd seen on the CT scan, Marina knew Max thought the problem was caused by the haematoma getting bigger.

'I'll call the neuro team,' she said. A few moments later, she came back over to Max. 'The neurosurgeon says give him a bolus of mannitol—it'll buy time to get him upstairs to Theatre so they can drain the haematoma.'

But they both knew it might not be enough time.

Max administered the mannitol, and the boy was rushed upstairs to Theatre.

Although they were rushed off their feet for the rest of the afternoon, Marina knew that Max was thinking of the boy, just as she was. And the longer it went without any news the more worried she became. Neurosurgery was delicate and draining a haematoma took time, especially when a fracture was involved too, but surely they should have heard by now?

In the one break she managed to snatch between patients, she called her mother to say that it was frantic in the department and asked her to pick up Phoebe. So at the end of her shift, while Max was doing the handover, instead of rushing to the hospital crèche she called the neuro team to see if there was any news on their patient.

'I was on my way down to see you.' Fergus Keating, the neurosurgeon, sighed heavily. 'Sorry, Marina. We did what we could, but right when I thought we were on our way out of the woods we lost him on the table.'

'I'm sorry, too.' Brief, bare words, but she knew that Fergus understood what she meant: sympathy, because he'd tried his hardest, but the boy's injuries had been too severe for him to save the lad. And he also had the task of breaking the bad news to the boy's parents; giving bad news to the next of kin was one of the toughest parts of their job. 'I'll tell the others.'

'Thanks.'

She put the phone down and took a deep breath.

Max, who'd been doing the handover, noticed the pallor in Marina's face as she replaced the receiver.

'Marina?' he asked, going over to her.

She shook her head, as if unable to speak, and just walked out of Resus.

Max recognised the signs. Apart from the fact he'd seen this happen to colleagues a few times in his Doctors Without Borders days, he'd seen Marina crumble like this before. He also knew what it probably meant: that Marina had just been talking to the neurosurgeon and it was bad news.

He remembered that losing a patient had always hit Marina hard, and she'd always taken it personally. Four years' more experience in the emergency department clearly hadn't changed that. Her family was so good at fixing things that she simply couldn't deal with it on the rare occasions when it didn't happen—and it didn't matter that nobody else could've fixed things in the situation, either. In her view, she'd failed.

He followed her into the staff kitchen. She was halfway through filling a glass of water when she doubled over, shaking and not saying a word.

He put his arms round her, spun her round and held her close. 'It's OK,' he said softly. 'Talk to me. Let it out.'

She was still shaking, but clearly she was too upset for tears. 'He—he didn't make it,' she whispered.

Max had guessed as much.

'I hate losing patients, Max. I *hate* it when we can't save them.'

'We do our best, but we're only human. We can't save everyone. You know that.' He stroked her hair; he could smell the familiar scent of rosemary, and it felt so good to have her back in his arms. What kind of selfish pig was he, to be thinking of his own gratification and pleasure when she was upset? 'Marina, we did our best for him. So did the neuro team. Nobody could've done more.'

'I know.' She shuddered. 'But it always feels so much worse when we lose a child. It's bad enough when someone's old, but at least they've had a chance to live— a child has barely started living. And what about his family? There's going to be a huge hole in their lives. I mean, if he was playing chicken he was probably a difficult kid and hell to live with, but even so he was still their child. Losing…' She choked on the word.

'I know, honey.' He kept his arms round her, telling himself it was so she could draw strength and comfort from him, and knowing full well that he was taking just as much strength and comfort back from her.

But he really needed to make her feel better, and there was only one way he knew how.

'I'm pulling rank. Making an executive decision,' he said.

'What?' She looked at him, her dark eyes filled with incomprehension.

'At a time like this, the only thing that works is comfort food. Come on. We're both off duty, and I've done the handover.'

'Max, where are you…?'

'Taking you for some comfort food,' he repeated. 'And, before you ask, I'd do the same for anyone on my team.'

It wasn't a complete fib. He'd take an upset team member for a coffee and a sandwich and let them talk it out; debriefing was important. But he'd probably take them to a quiet corner of the cafeteria, whereas he intended to take Marina somewhere much more private.

He shepherded her to the staff room; they collected their coats and she grabbed her handbag from her locker. Then he took her back to his flat. During the five-minute walk, she didn't say a word and she was still shivering.

'Where…?' she began as he opened his front door for her and stood aside.

'My flat. I'm making you something to eat,' he said.

'Max, I…'

He smiled wryly. 'Don't worry, I'm not going to leap on you.'

'That wasn't what I was worried about.'

'Then what?'

Her eyes were huge, dark and anguished.

He gave a muffled exclamation and hauled her back into his arms. This time, she wrapped her arms round him too. He kissed the top of her head, feeling as if he were drowning in the scent of rosemary from her hair. He really had to stop this, before it was too late.

But then her arms were round his neck, her fingers were

sliding into his hair, and she was pressing tiny kisses into the column of his throat.

It was like lighting touch-paper; the next thing he knew, his mouth was jammed against hers, his arms were wrapped tightly round her and her fingertips were pushing hard against his scalp, urging him on.

Unable to help himself, desperately needing the feel of her bare skin against his fingertips, he untucked her white shirt from the waistband of her tailored, black trousers. He slipped his hands underneath the cotton and splayed his fingers flat against her bare midriff. Her skin felt so soft—and he'd missed this so much.

Then she was doing the same to him, tugging his white shirt out of the waistband of his suit trousers and smoothing her palms along his back.

This was all so familiar, and yet so new at the same time. It was more than four years since Marina had last touched him like this, and they were different people now, yet they were still the same. They still responded to each other in the same way. It almost felt as though they'd never been apart.

Lost in the moment, Max moved his hands higher, his palms stroking against her ribcage. She inhaled sharply and he traced the lacy edge of her bra with one forefinger. One thing that definitely hadn't changed: Marina still wore ultra-feminine underwear. And right now he really, really wanted to see it. Wanted to see her. Wanted to touch and taste, and let her fill the emptiness inside him.

He undid the buttons of her shirt, his hands shaking; to his relief, she didn't stop him. He pushed the soft cotton off her shoulders, revealing pure-white lace against her slightly olive skin, and desire licked down his spine. He could see her nipples through the lace, hardening as he looked at them, and he just couldn't help himself. He dipped his head, closed his mouth over one nipple through the lace, and sucked hard.

Marina moaned aloud and slid her fingers back into his hair, urging him on rather than pulling him away, and he was completely lost. He undid the clasp of her bra and let the lace fall to the floor; he cupped her breasts in his hands, remembering their weight and their warmth.

This felt like coming home.

Where he longed to be.

Where he *needed* to be

He wanted Marina so urgently, so desperately. But, more than that, he needed her to want this as much as he did.

He kissed his way up the column of her throat, then took her mouth again, nibbling tiny kisses along her lower lip until she opened her mouth and let him deepen the kiss. Then she was kissing him all the way back, unbuttoning his shirt and tugging it off his shoulders with the same urgency.

Working purely on instinct, Max lifted her up and carried her through to his bedroom, still kissing her. He set her back on her feet again by the window, drew the curtains and switched on the bedside lamp. Still neither of them had said a word; they were lost in a deep, deep hunger and need.

He kissed her again, and then her fingers were fumbling with the buckle of his belt. Struggling. He gently pushed her hands aside, still kissing her, and dealt with it himself.

He wasn't sure which of them removed which items of clothing, but at last they were how he wanted them to be, skin to skin. And she felt so good: soft and warm, just as he remembered. Just as he dreamed. He drew her closer, and simply fell back on the bed, pulling her with him so she landed on top of him, her glorious hair falling all over his face and her bare skin right next to his.

Heaven.

Marina knew this was all wrong, that she shouldn't be doing this. That Max was off limits. For goodness' sake, he was her ex-husband and her colleague, and when this all blew apart it would be impossible to work together. Not to mention all the mess of their shared past. This was a seriously bad idea.

But she was lying on top of him. Both of them were completely naked, with Max's arms wrapped tightly round her. And, oh, it felt good. Like coming home.

Being in his arms, kissing him, seeing his slate-blue eyes darken almost to black with desire… She'd missed this. Badly. Missed the way Max made her feel as if she were the centre of his universe. Missed the way he made her feel that he were the centre of hers. There was nothing else outside this room, outside this bed. Nothing but the two of them.

The miserable day she'd spent at work, the sense of failure and despair, had all vanished: there was only Max. Max, who was kissing her as if he couldn't get enough of her—just as she couldn't get enough of him.

She shifted slightly, eased a hand between them so she could position the tip of his penis just where she wanted it and gently lowered herself onto him.

Lord, it felt good, the way he filled her, stretched her. The perfect fit. He always had been. Experimentally, she tightened her internal muscles around him.

He sucked in a breath.

And then he began to move. Slowly, at first, then faster,

harder, pushing deep inside her. She matched him thrust for thrust, drive for drive, needing this as much as he did. Needing to feel her body sing at his touch. Needing to reaffirm the fact that she was alive, and life was good.

As her climax slammed into her, rippling through her body, Max sat up straight; he wrapped his arms round her and kissed her hard, and she felt the answering pulse of his body.

She had no idea how long they stayed there, locked together, just holding each other, but at last he gently eased out of her. He moved slightly so he could grab the duvet, then pulled it over them both and drew her back into his arms, keeping her close.

Neither of them had said a word since they'd started kissing in his hallway. And Marina was unwilling to break the silence, to shatter this strange peace between them. She simply wrapped her arm round his waist and rested her head against his shoulder.

'Marina,' he said at last. 'I really didn't intend this to happen.'

Was he saying it was a mistake? That he regretted it?

She couldn't bring herself to ask. Couldn't face him rejecting her again.

'I was going to make you something to eat. That was all. Taking you to bed wasn't something I planned.'

'Uh-huh,' she said, carefully keeping her tone noncommittal.

He played with the ends of her hair, just as he had a hundred times before. 'I'm sorry.'

'It's not your fault. I could have said no.' Except she hadn't wanted to. If anything, she'd been the one to incite it. She'd been the one to start the kiss. And she was still here, still naked, still in his bed, still lying in his arms.

'Neither of us was thinking straight.'

She swallowed hard. He could say that again.

He sighed. 'Marina, we need to talk.'

'Not now.' Not when she hadn't got things straight in her head.

'Yes, now,' he insisted. 'There's one elephant in the room we really can't avoid. We both got carried away just now—and neither of us was in a fit state to think about contraception.'

He thought they might have made a baby, an unplanned child, like they had before? She flinched at the memory. 'There's no need to worry. I'm on the Pill.'

He went very still. 'Are you…seeing someone?'

'It's a bit late to ask now,' she said wryly. 'But I'm not the cheating type; you should know that, Max.'

'I know. Of course you're not.' He grimaced. 'Sorry. I'm not thinking straight.'

Neither was she. 'No, I'm not seeing anyone. As I'm sure Rosie told you.'

'She did,' he admitted. 'So why are you on the Pill? To sort out your periods?'

'Yes. After the…' Her throat closed. Why was it so hard to say that word to him? *Miscarriage.* Ah, hell. He'd know what she meant. One of the biggest elephants in the room. The thing they'd never been able to talk about. The thing that had widened the gap between them day by day, until she hadn't been able to bear it any longer. 'My system went a bit haywire. My GP suggested trying the Pill, and it worked.' She swallowed. 'Though, just in case you were wondering, I don't make a habit of sleeping around. So you won't end up with any—'

He pressed his forefinger lightly against her lips. 'I

already know that, and I wouldn't insult you by thinking otherwise. Just for the record,' he added, 'it's the same for me. You're safe.'

'OK. So we know the score.'

'Do we?' He shifted onto his side, so they were looking each other in the face, and gave her a level stare. 'We've spent the last couple of weeks trying to avoid each other as much as possible—and being ultra-polite and professional when we can't.'

She acknowledged the truth of that with a sardonic smile. 'And just now we ripped each other's clothes off and ended up in bed together.'

He gave her a wry smile.

'It's probably because we both needed comfort after the day we've had.'

'Probably,' he agreed.

Oh, that hurt: the acknowledgement that what they'd just shared had simply been comfort for him. Even though she'd been the one to say it, she wished he hadn't agreed with her so quickly.

And then he gave her the most wicked grin. 'So. Mission accomplished?'

'Max Fenton, you're…'

She really hadn't expected that.

How had she possibly forgotten Max's sense of humour—the way he could say something completely inappropriate or surreal and make her laugh? She couldn't help smiling back. 'Yes. Mission accomplished.' She paused. 'You?'

He nodded. 'I think we both needed that.' He stroked her face. 'We always were good together, Marina.'

True. Until it had gone spectacularly wrong.

And then he said something that really shocked her. 'I've missed you.'

She stared at him, not quite believing what she'd just heard. 'What did you say?'

'I've missed you.' His face was utterly open and candid. 'Having you back in my arms just now made me realise how much.'

He'd missed her.

And what he'd just said... He could have been speaking for her, too. Given how long they'd been apart, it must have cost him a lot to make that admission. The least she could do was match his honesty. 'I missed you, too,' she said. Making love with him just now—for a while, the empty spaces in her soul had been filled again. Max had made her feel complete, the first time she'd felt that way since they'd separated.

'So where do we go from here?' he asked.

She shook her head. 'I have no idea.'

'Maybe we could start seeing each other?' he suggested.

Was he serious? He really thought that they could pick up where they left off?

'Though we should probably take it slowly,' he added.

She raised an eyebrow. 'Slowly? Considering your bed's all rumpled and I have no idea where my clothes are—or yours...'

He gave her a lopsided grin. 'OK, so we're not very good at doing "slowly".'

She returned the smile. 'We never were. A week, wasn't it?'

'Five and a half days.'

He remembered that precisely—from all those years ago? Marina looked at him, stunned. So was he thinking about the very first time they'd made love? She remembered that night, too. How right it had felt. Even that very first time had been like a kind of homecoming, as if she'd found a place she wanted to be for the rest of her life.

In his arms.

And for four empty years they'd been apart.

'Max, I'm not so sure this is a good idea. I mean, we know that it works between us in bed. But…' She shook her head. 'We crashed and burned last time.'

'I know. But we're both older and wiser now,' Max said, his gaze steady. 'And I think there's still unfinished business between us. Otherwise we wouldn't be right here, right now.'

She swallowed hard. 'We can't change the past.'

'But we can learn from it.'

'And if it all goes wrong again? I don't think I could face picking up the pieces a second time.'

'I don't think either of us is in a fit state to make any sort of decision right now,' he said softly. 'But we do need to talk.'

She blew out a breath. 'About the other elephants in the room? There are quite a few of them.'

'Too many to deal with all at once. But if we tackle them one by one we might stand a chance of sorting it all out.'

'One by one,' she repeated.

'When we're ready. But right now I think you need comfort—because you're one of life's fixers, and you take it personally when you can't make something right. Even if nobody else could've made it right, either.'

Since when had he figured her out that well?

'I need comfort, too,' he said softly. 'Stay with me tonight, Marina.'

'That's your idea of slowly? Asking me to spend the night with you?'

'No. I'm trying to be honest. Right now, I think we both need this.'

'All cats being grey in the dark.' So this was just comfort. Sex. A way of celebrating life when you'd just had to face death.

'Absolutely *not*.' His voice was very clear. 'I wouldn't have done this with anyone else in the department, Marina, and neither would you.'

She couldn't deny the truth of that. She hadn't slept with anyone since Max, even though she'd had offers.

Had he?

It was none of her business what he'd done since she'd walked out. But the idea of Max making love with another woman cut her to the quick. 'I can't stay. I can't go to work tomorrow in these clothes.'

'I have a washer-dryer. I can put your stuff through the machine overnight, and your clothes will be clean for the morning. And I have a spare toothbrush.'

It was an easy solution. And she was oh, so tempted. She normally wore dark trousers and a white or cream shirt at work, so it wasn't as if it would be obvious that she was wearing the same clothes. She could stay, spend the rest of the evening in bed with Max, exorcising some of their demons. Comforting each other.

Making love. Because it wouldn't be just sex—not for her.

'The sensible thing,' she said, while she still had a few vestiges of self-control, 'Would be for me to go home.'

He cupped her face with one hand, tracing her lower lip with the pad of his thumb. 'We've had a rough day; it's not the time for being sensible. You need to be held and so do I.'

'But you've seen worse than today if you've been working for Doctors Without Borders.'

He frowned. 'How do you know about that?'

'Rosie told me.' She paused. 'Why did you go?'

'I thought we weren't talking about any of the elephants. Besides, I promised to feed you.'

'Why did you go?' she repeated.

He shrugged and sat up, drawing his knees up to his chest and wrapping his arms round them. 'If you really want to know, it felt like the right thing to do. You'd gone to London, and I didn't want to stay in Bristol without you. There were too many memories and I was miserable. I hated going home to that empty flat. To me it showed I was a failure, that I couldn't make my marriage work.'

She couldn't let him take complete responsibility for the break-up. That wasn't fair. 'It wasn't just your fault, Max. There were two of us in that marriage, and I was the one who left.'

He reached out to touch her cheek for a moment. 'Thank you for that. But I still felt a failure, and facing it every day was too much for me. I couldn't fix my own problems, but working for Doctors Without Borders meant I could make a difference to other people's lives. And I really needed to feel that I could do that. That I could fix *something*.'

She could understand that. Wasn't that part of the reason why she worked in emergency medicine, so she could make a difference?

He looked down at her, unsmiling. 'As we're tackling elephants, why did you—' He stopped abruptly. 'Why did you leave Bristol?'

She knew exactly what he'd been going to ask: why had she walked out on him? Because he'd shut her out and she'd felt that she was the only one making an effort in their marriage. 'Same reason as you,' she said. 'I was miserable in Bristol. Every time I walked through the city centre I saw pregnant women, and I couldn't handle it.' Maybe this was going too far, but she was going to be honest with him. She dragged in a breath. 'I needed support, Max.' Support that Max and his family wouldn't—or couldn't?—give her. 'You shut me out. And what happened to us… It was more than I could deal with on my own. I needed you and you just weren't there. So I came home, because I knew my family would help me get through it. I knew at least here that I'd be loved.'

He still wasn't smiling, and his expression was unreadable. 'Enough elephants for now, I think. Though I do owe you an apology.' He swallowed hard. 'For not giving you what you needed.'

And in that moment Marina realised. The way he'd acted back then wasn't because he hadn't cared. It was because he hadn't known how to deal with the situation, either. 'I was the one who walked out.' She hadn't stayed to fight for him. 'So I guess we're even. I owe you an apology, too.'

He spread his hands, the gesture telling her he didn't know what to say.

That made two of them.

And the breakup of their marriage was too complicated for them to work out in a single conversation.

'I'll make us something to eat.' He paused. 'So, do you want me to put your stuff in the washing machine?'

Working for Doctors Without Borders had clearly made him more practical. The old Max wouldn't even have thought about it until the next morning—when it would've been much too late to do anything about it.

Stay or go?

If she stayed, she knew she'd end up making love with him again. Clouding the issues between them.

But, if she left, he'd take it as a rejection and he'd clam up on her. Which meant they would never get the closure they both needed. They'd still be stuck in limbo, unable to move on.

Sleeping with Max didn't mean that she was still in love with him, or that he was in love with her. They'd already agreed that for tonight this was just comfort—comfort of a kind that only they could give each other. No strings.

Should she stay or should she go?

CHAPTER SIX

'ONE thing: this is just tonight? No strings?' Marina asked.

Max's expression was completely unreadable. 'No strings.'

'Then, yes. I'll stay.'

'OK.' He climbed out of bed, grabbed a pair of jeans from his wardrobe, pulled them on, then took a navy bathrobe from the back of the door and handed it to her. 'If you want a shower before you come downstairs, the bathroom's first on the left—and the towels are clean.'

'Thanks.'

Considering how well they knew each other's bodies, and what they'd just done, Marina knew it was ridiculous to wait until he'd left the room before climbing out of bed. But she did so anyway, feeling shy—as well as enormously grateful that Max had clearly picked up on it and wasn't putting any pressure on her.

Max's bathroom turned out to be very plain and functional, just like his bedroom. Then again, he hadn't been in London for long. Less than a month. Given that Max had been working abroad, his things were probably still in storage. Certainly she'd seen nothing she remembered from their old flat in Bristol. When she'd left Max, she'd taken only her clothes, a few books, precious photographs and her omelette pan, not wanting anything around to remind her of the disaster of their marriage.

Another off-limits topic, unless they wanted to tackle another elephant. Though right at that moment Marina thought it would be better to keep things light. Extremely light. Especially as they'd agreed that tonight meant no strings.

She stepped out of the shower, dried herself then pulled his bathrobe on and drew the belt tight. The robe was soft to the touch and smelled of him; it felt like being wrapped in his arms.

She padded through to the kitchen. Max had obviously collected her clothes on the way; she could hear the gentle whirring of the washing machine, and he'd put the kettle on to make coffee.

Though she couldn't see any sign of the food he'd promised.

'OK?' he asked.

She nodded. 'And hungry. Do you want a hand?'

'Thanks.' He smiled wryly. 'You know, I really was going to be nice and make you dinner.'

'But?' Something in his expression made her brave. Cheeky. She opened the first cupboard, peered inside and raised an eyebrow when she saw it was completely empty. And so was the next one. 'I see. You did some training at Old Mother Hubbard's school of cookery.'

He rolled his eyes. 'Very funny. Not everyone likes cooking, you know.'

Didn't they? 'You used to enjoy it.'

'No, I used to like being in a kitchen with you,' he corrected. 'You used to do the actual cooking. I just fetched things and washed up and talked to you.'

She hadn't thought of it that way. She just remembered doing what she always did with her family, everyone joining in and doing a bit, talking, laughing and singing as they washed up, mixed, tasted and cooked—the normal things that families did together. She remembered preparing meals with Max, sharing a single glass of wine with him, and half the time having a long break between preparing the meal and actually cooking it, because they'd ended up in bed together, needing to sate desire more than they'd needed to sate hunger.

She looked in his fridge. There was a lump of cheese he hadn't wrapped up properly that was going hard round the edges, a carton of orange juice and a carton of milk. So he didn't even have the makings of an omelette or a basic dish of pasta with tomato sauce. And he didn't have a fruit bowl of any description. 'Max, this is atrocious. No wonder you're so thin. Do you eat at all?'

'Of course I do.'

'Like what? Do you live on takeaway food or something?'

'Anyone would think you were the food police,' he grumbled. 'There's nothing wrong with takeaways.'

'In moderation. But it's not the same as eating a properly balanced meal.'

'All right, if you must know, I normally eat at the hospital canteen at lunchtime so I don't need to do more than make myself a sandwich when I get in.'

She couldn't help laughing. 'A fresh-air sandwich, would that be? And an invisible piece of fruit?'

He sighed. 'I admit, I'm out of bread right now. And fruit. I forgot to buy some today.'

'Uh-huh.' That wasn't all he'd forgotten to buy, from the look of it.

He rolled his eyes. 'Don't rub it in. So I'm out of sandwich fillings as well.'

'I noticed.'

'And I'm *not* too thin.'

'No?' She raised an eyebrow. 'My mother would take one look at you, make you sit down at the kitchen table and start cooking for you. I bet Rosie said something to you too, didn't she?'

'Well—yes,' he admitted. 'But your family doesn't do subtle.'

'No.' Though he'd never seemed to mind. She was used to people being open and honest rather than reserved and masking their true feelings with a polite smile. It was so much easier to sort out any problems if you talked about them, instead of expecting the other person to guess what was going on inside your head, the way Max's family seemed to do.

'That wasn't a criticism, by the way,' Max added.

'Wasn't it?'

'No. I've always liked your family. Even when they're being really full on.'

Because her family always acted out of love, Marina thought. There were no hidden agendas. You always knew exactly where they were coming from, and they said exactly what they meant.

He pulled open a kitchen drawer and extracted a handful of leaflets. 'Since we've established that neither of us is going to be cooking tonight, and I promised to feed you, I'll order a takeaway. What would you like?'

'I don't mind, as long as there isn't a really long wait.' Her stomach rumbled, as if to make the point, and she grimaced. 'Sorry.'

'It's OK. Neither of us had time for lunch today. I'm hungry too,' he said.

'If you have a corner shop nearby that sells eggs, I could make us an omelette,' she offered. 'That'd be quicker than a takeaway.'

'Technical hitch,' Max said. 'I don't actually have an omelette pan.'

Because she'd taken it with her when she'd left. Somehow it didn't surprise her that he hadn't replaced it. 'Do you have any saucepans of any description?'

'My kitchen isn't that bad.'

By her standards, it was. 'Yes or no, Max?'

He opened a cupboard door to show her. 'Satisfied?'

'I can work with them, sure. If you can go and buy some eggs, bacon, cream, dried pasta and salad,' she said, 'I'll make us pasta carbonara. It'll take ten minutes.'

'So much for me looking after you,' Max said wryly.

'As you just said, not everyone likes cooking. You don't—but I do. It soothes me,' she said. 'And, if I'd been thinking straight, I would've suggested going back to mine.'

'Would you?' Max asked, giving her a searching look.

She wrinkled her nose. 'Truthfully? No. I wouldn't have asked you into my space. But there's no way I'm going back to my flat right now wearing nothing but your bathrobe. So if you want feeding you'll have to go to the shop. What did I do with my handbag?'

'Uh—I put it over here.' Clearly he'd retrieved it, along with her clothes, from wherever she'd dropped it. 'But this was my suggestion, so I'm paying. I'll be back in a tick.' He pulled on a sweater and a pair of battered running shoes and left.

While Max was gone, Marina laid the table in the

kitchen, rummaged in his almost-bare cupboards to find the equipment she needed then wandered into his living room. It was as spartan as his kitchen and bedroom; there were no pictures on the walls, no photographs anywhere, and nothing personal to give a single clue about the person who lived in the flat. There were a few medical textbooks on the bookshelves, but that was all. The décor and furnishings were completely neutral, and his sofa didn't have so much as a cushion to soften its stark lines.

Max's flat wasn't a home, it was just a place to sleep. He might just as well be living out of a suitcase, and it made her heart ache for him. How different it was from her own flat, filled with colour, photographs and memories.

She shook herself. It was none of her business any more. He'd signed the papers. They were officially divorced.

Yet here she was, cutting the hard edges off the lonely lump of cheese in his fridge and grating the rest of it into a small bowl.

She must be mad.

She'd been here before, had her heart broken into tiny pieces that had taken years to glue back together. Yet Max's words kept echoing in her head.

We're both older and wiser now.

And I think there's still unfinished business between us.

Was he right? Could they learn from the past, try again and avoid the mistakes?

Somewhere deep inside, she felt a flicker of something that might just have been hope.

When Max came back from the corner shop and walked into the kitchen, it didn't feel anything like the room he was used to in his rented flat. He couldn't quite put his finger on what the shift was: simply that Marina had laid the table for two and was sitting there, mug of coffee in hand, flicking through a medical journal.

'Sorry—I took liberties with your kettle and your magazine,' she said. 'Hope you don't mind.'

'Of course not.' He handed her the carrier bag. 'Is this lot all OK?' He'd remembered the brief shopping list she'd given him—eggs, bacon, cream, salad and dried pasta— and added a loaf of bread, plus a decent bottle of Pinot Grigio he'd found in the chiller cabinet.

She looked through them, then glanced up at him and smiled. 'Fabulous. Do you want to sort the salad while I do this?'

'Sure.'

'Did you want a coffee? The kettle's still hot.'

'No, I'm fine. But thanks for asking.'

It felt oddly domestic, washing the salad and placing it in a bowl; Max was surprised to discover how much he'd missed being in a kitchen with her. He enjoyed watching Marina cook, the deft way she beat the eggs with the cream, then kept an eye on the pasta at the same time as she was dry-frying the bacon. For the very first time since he'd moved into the flat, the kitchen smelled fantastic. It reminded him of the way it had been when they'd first moved in together, how he'd teased her that she could go on one of those TV shows where people were given random ingredients, and however strange they were that she would manage to come up with something edible—a feast, even.

Although he remembered Marina avidly flicking through foodie magazines, she hardly ever stuck to a recipe; she used them as springboards for her own imagi- nation. And most of the time she cooked without weighing things, either—a practice he guessed was born from cooking with her mother and her sister from an early age.

As he opened the wine and poured two glasses, she dished up—Max noticed that she'd warmed the plates, too, which he would never have bothered doing—and they sat opposite each other at his kitchen table. Familiar, comfortable, just like he'd done so many times before. He was glad then that he'd agreed to her request of no strings; it avoided any awkwardness between them. Because he wouldn't have missed sharing this with her, not for the world.

If somehow they could pick their way through the mess of the past, work out how to make a new start…

Too far, too fast. There was a long way to go before they could start to do that.

But it was years since he'd felt that weird lightness inside, a feeling that took him a while to pin down and categorise as hope.

He took a mouthful of the pasta. 'This is fantastic.'

'It's the best comfort food I know,' she said. Then she gave him a speaking look. 'It's not exactly *difficult* to make, Max. And it's practically as quick as making a sandwich.'

He forbore to comment, knowing that he'd never bother to cook for himself; it didn't seem worth it, cooking for one. But he loved the fact that she'd made it for him and didn't fish for extravagant compliments on her skills. She was secure in who she was, and didn't need anyone to pump her ego for her. He'd always liked that about Marina, her self-sufficiency.

And then, when she'd crumbled, he hadn't known what to do. What to say. How to make things right. He'd panicked and buried himself in work to block out the feeling of failure. Except the sense of failure had only deepened when he realised that he'd pushed her away, that she'd walked out on him.

'The wine's lovely,' she said.

'I'm glad you like it. You always used to prefer white wine to red, as long as it wasn't oaky.'

She blinked. 'You remembered that?'

'Yes.' There were a lot of other things he remembered about her: the shape of her body fitting against his as he fell asleep; the scent of her hair—and the shadows in her eyes. The shadows they weren't going to talk about tonight, but that he knew were still there—just masked for a little while until they worked out how to deal with them.

After dinner, they washed up together. Although they didn't say much, it was a companionable silence rather than the loaded silence that had haunted the end of their marriage. Max switched the washing machine over to the tumble-drying cycle, then ushered her through into the living room. 'Sorry, I haven't got round to sorting out a television. Though, if you really want to, we could maybe watch a film on my laptop.'

She smiled. 'You're trying too hard, Max. I'm fine. Though, if you want to put some music on, that'd be nice.'

'Music I can do.' He connected his MP3 player to the small speakers, selected a playlist of the mellow kind of music he remembered she used to like, and topped up their glasses before joining her on the sofa. He rested the arm nearest to her along the back of the sofa, and was relieved when she curled into him, letting him curve his arm along her shoulders.

'When did you move in here?' she asked.

'The day before I started working at the hospital.'

'So most of your stuff is still in storage?'

He shrugged. 'I travel light nowadays. I guess it's a

hangover from working with Doctors Without Borders; I got used to living out of a suitcase.'

'What made you come back to England?'

'Do you really want to talk about another elephant?' he asked softly.

She was silent, but he waited, guessing that she was thinking about it.

'No,' she said finally. 'We said no strings tonight. That means no elephants.'

'Well, that's your answer.' He didn't want to tell her about the accident, because he didn't want her to pity him. And he didn't want to tell her about his father, because it would be all too easy to tell her the whole story—and he still hadn't quite come to terms with it himself. 'We're going to have to talk about it properly at some point. But you're right: not now.'

'We've made a start,' Marina said. 'That's enough for tonight.'

They lapsed back into silence, but it was still a comfortable silence, and she was still cuddling into him. Right at that moment he was happy just to be there with her in his arms, chilling out and forgetting about their lousy day.

When the music finally ended, he said, 'I think we could both do with some sleep. Come to bed.' He stood up and held his hand out; when she took it, he pulled her to her feet, twined his fingers through hers and led her back to his bedroom.

She bit her lip, looking faintly embarrassed.

'What?'

'Max, I'm not wearing anything under this robe.'

Guessing what was making her uncomfortable, he lifted her hand to his mouth, kissed her palm and curled her fingers round where he'd kissed. 'I know that. OK. Turn your back.'

'Why?'

'So I can get undressed too.' He gave her a wicked grin. 'Unless you'd rather watch me take all my clothes off? I can strip for you, if you like.'

Colour shot into her face. 'Max!'

'Just a thought,' he said mildly. But at least he'd made her smile.

He pulled off his sweater, and stifled a chuckle when she hastily turned her back to him. He stripped swiftly, climbed into the bed and pulled the duvet over him. 'OK, I'm in bed—and my back's turned, so it's safe for you to take off my robe and get into bed.'

He felt the mattress dip slightly with her weight, then she curled into him. 'Thank you.' She pressed a kiss against his spine.

'What for?'

'Being nice. When I'm behaving ridiculously, in the circumstances.'

He shifted so that he was facing her. 'It's not a problem.' He kissed the tip of her nose. 'Good night, Marina.'

'Good night.'

He turned the light off. It was a while before he slept, though he was aware when she fell asleep, as her breathing became regular and deep. With Marina lying in his arms, he felt oddly at peace. Funny, in his brief relationships over the last couple of years, he'd never once stayed the night with anyone. He realised now how much he'd missed that closeness.

Ha. Who was he trying to kid? More like, how much he'd missed Marina. And that was why he'd never spent the night with anyone else. Because they hadn't been her.

Finally, Max slid into sleep.

* * *

'No!'

The agonised yell woke Marina instantly. She sat bolt upright, slightly disoriented and wondering where she was.

Then it all snapped back. She was in Max's flat. Max's bed. And Max was thrashing about next to her, clearly in the middle of a nightmare. His breathing was fast and shallow; he was almost at the point of hyperventilating.

She laid a hand on his shoulder and shook him. 'Max. *Max*. It's OK. You're here. In London. With me.'

He groaned and shuddered; she continued talking to him, reassuring him quietly, until at last he was still.

'Max?' she asked softly. 'Are you OK?'

'Uh, fine.'

She didn't believe him. 'You were having a nightmare.'

'I'm fine. Sorry for waking you.' He sounded embarrassed.

'It's not a problem.' She sighed. 'If I knew where your bedside light was, I'd turn it on.'

Without comment, he switched on the lamp.

His face looked absolutely ghastly, very pale, and he was in a cold sweat. Whatever he'd been dreaming about, it had clearly been distressing in the extreme. 'Stay put,' she said. 'I'll get you some water.' She retrieved the bathrobe, belted it tightly round herself, then fetched him a glass of water and sat on the bed next to him.

He took a sip of water and placed the glass on his bedside table.

'So what was that about?' she asked.

'Nothing.'

She laced her fingers through his and simply waited.

Eventually, he sighed. 'I get bad dreams from time to time.'

'About something that happened while you were working abroad?' she asked.

'Yes.'

'Tell me.'

He shook his head. 'It's old stuff.'

She had no idea where he'd been working—whether it had been a war zone, or whether he'd been helping out after some kind of natural disaster—so she couldn't even begin to imagine what he'd seen to affect him so badly. 'Did you have any counselling about it?'

'I didn't need it.'

'Tell me,' she said neutrally. 'If a colleague had been through whatever it was you went through, would you advise them to have counselling?'

'I'm fine. Don't fuss.'

She'd seen that look on his face before—when he'd shut himself away from her, after she'd miscarried their baby. Clearly this was one respect in which he hadn't changed. Even now, Max was pushing her away, refusing to talk.

Maybe she should take the hint.

'I think,' she said quietly, releasing his hand, 'maybe I should go home.'

He glanced at the clock. 'It's three in the morning. The Tube won't be open.'

'I'll call a taxi, then.'

'Marina.' He sat upright and wrapped his arms round her. 'I'm sorry. Don't go. It's…not that easy for me to talk about things.'

She wasn't going to throw his apology back in his face; four years ago she might've done that, but as he'd said himself she was older and wiser now. Instead, she slid her arms round him, and he rested his forehead on her shoulder.

'I was working as part of the rescue team after an earth-

quake. While I was stabilising a little girl so we'd be able
to move her, there was a second tremor—and the building
came down on us. It took them a while to dig us out.'

'How long?'

'I was unconscious for some of it.'

'How long?' she repeated.

'I don't know. Five or six hours, maybe. It was pretty
unpleasant. Hot as hell; my mouth and eyes and nose were
full of dust, and I couldn't even move to clean it out.'

She tightened her arms round him. She'd just bet that it
had been far worse than his economical description. And
he'd been unconscious. 'Did you have concussion?'

'Yes.'

'And?'

He sighed. 'A broken arm and leg. Which meant I
wasn't much use out there, so they shipped me home.'

And no doubt he'd been stuck in bed for a while. No
wonder he understood exactly what Rosie was going through.

Though Marina was very, very aware of what he *hadn't*
said. And she knew he wasn't going to volunteer the information himself. 'What about the little girl?' she asked quietly.

'She didn't make it.'

Four little words that told her volumes. 'And losing
that patient today must've brought some of the memories
back,' she said.

'Yes.' He closed his eyes. 'I suppose I really should've
warned you that I might dream about it tonight. But we—
uh—I thought I'd be OK.'

Except he wasn't. 'Then I'm glad I stayed,' she said,
stroking his face. 'That I could be here for you.'

'I'm glad you stayed, too,' he admitted.

Then somehow his mouth was on hers, warm and sweet,

asking rather than demanding, yet giving and promising at the same time.

This time, their love-making was slow and gentle, soothing each other rather than filling them with the frantic and desperate need from before. Every touch, every kiss, was like balm being poured over old hurts. This time, Marina's climax was soft, sweet and fulfilling, like summer rain rather than a winter cloudburst. And when Max turned out the light she curled back into his arms and drifted into sleep, feeling warm, safe and secure—and happier than she'd felt in a long, long time.

CHAPTER SEVEN

THE alarm shrilled; Marina rolled over and groped for the bedside table, intending to hit the snooze button, then suddenly realised why the bedside table wasn't there: because she wasn't in her own bed. And Max's alarm clock was over on his side.

She heard a soft click, and the shrilling stopped.

'Good morning,' Max said, his tone completely neutral.

She followed his lead. 'Good morning.'

And now what? She'd never experienced morning-after awkwardness before—not even the first time she'd spent the night with Max. They'd gone to bed laughing, and they'd woken up tangled together and smiling.

Now they were tangled together and…awkward.

'What's the time?' she asked.

'Half-past six.'

An hour and a half until her shift started. And she had things to do. She really, really shouldn't be here. 'Then I have to go. I need to collect Phoebe from Neil, and I need to take her to see Rosie before she goes to the hospital nursery.'

'I'll sort your clothes out while you have a shower, if you like?' Max offered.

'Thanks. That'd be good.'

By the time she'd finished, Max had laid her clothes on the bed—he'd clearly taken them straight out of the dryer rather than ironing them, as they were a little crumpled, but nobody would notice beneath her coat—and she could smell coffee and toast. She went into the kitchen, and Max handed her a mug. 'I've added a bit of cold water so you can drink it straight down.' He also handed her a plate of buttered toast. 'Sorry, I don't have any jam or honey.'

That wry, slightly shy smile, made her decide: Max, too, clearly felt awkward and mixed up about the whole situation, not sure whether he was more relieved or disappointed that she was leaving.

'No jam or honey. Now, why doesn't that surprise me, Dr Hubbard?' she teased.

'Yeah, yeah.' But his face cleared.

She walked over to him and kissed him lightly. 'Thanks, Max. I appreciate this.'

'Is there anything else you need?'

'I'm fine—but thank you for asking.' She finished her toast and drank her coffee quickly. 'In case you were wondering, I really do have to go. It's not just an excuse to avoid you.' Well, not completely. Though she had to admit that it was pretty convenient.

'Uh-huh. I'll see you at work.'

She bit her lip. 'Max, before I go…'

He looked at her. 'What?'

'About last night… I don't want anyone talking about us at work. Can we keep this to ourselves?'

'Sure.' His face was expressionless. 'As you said, no strings.'

She saw the flicker of hurt in his eyes before he managed to mask it. And, even though she knew this was going to lead to complications and was completely dangerous where her peace of mind was concerned, she said, 'I'm not on call tonight, so you could come over for supper, if you like?'

He looked at her for a moment, as if judging whether her offer was genuine or guilt-driven.

It was a bit of both, if she were honest about it.

'I'd like that,' he said finally. 'What time?'

'Seven? That gives me time to take Phoebe to Rosie after my shift and stay with them for a bit.'

'Are you sure that's long enough? I can make it half-past seven, if that's easier.'

'Half-past seven it is. Got a piece of paper and a pen?'

'Sure.' He grabbed a pad and pen from the drawer where he kept the takeaway leaflets and handed it to her.

She scribbled down her address, added a mobile-phone number, then kissed him briefly. 'See you later. I have to run.'

The world seemed a different place this morning, Max thought as he showered. He hadn't felt this relaxed and carefree for years—now he thought about it, not since he and Marina had first been together. There wasn't the worry that had come with her pregnancy and the hurried arrangements for their wedding, or the desolation that had surrounded her miscarriage, or the misery as their marriage had splintered, or the days afterwards when he'd worked to the point of near-exhaustion so that he'd be able to fall into a dreamless sleep and shut out the past.

Then he realised why he felt so relaxed.

Because, for the first time in a long, long while, there was hope in his life.

He knew that he and Marina still had a long way to go; for a start, they had to tackle the things that had gone so badly wrong before, and work through them together instead of running away from the issues. But he was beginning to think that maybe now there was a chance that they could come out the other side. That he could make it with her.

He smiled at everyone on his way in to work that morning, but, even though his heart gave a funny little jolt when he saw Marina, he was careful to treat her the way he usually did, as if she were just another member of the team.

And everything, Max thought, was definitely all right with his world today.

'Someone, please, help my baby!'

The woman staggering into reception was carrying a child Marina judged to be around five years old; her face was white with fear, and the child was wheezing. An asthma attack? Marina wondered.

'Can you tell Max I need him in Resus, please?' she said to Dawn, the staff nurse who was doing triage.

Dawn nodded and went to find Max as Marina walked over to the woman. 'I'm a doctor. Let me help you,' she said, taking the child. 'We'll go into a room over here. Can you tell me what happened?'

'Jessie's had an ear infection; the doctor gave her anti-biotics and she was perking up. I took her to the park because I thought some fresh air might make her feel better, but then she started wheezing. She can't breathe!'

A first glance also told Marina that the child was covered in a rash, tiny red spots that she could practically see appearing on the little girl's skin.

'I know I should've called an ambulance, but the park's opposite the hospital and I thought it would be quicker to bring her over.'

'You did the right thing,' Marina reassured her. 'What were the antibiotics?'

'Amoxicillin.'

'Has your daughter ever had amoxicillin before?'

'No.'

'When did you start giving it to her?'

'Last week. She had the last dose last night. The doctor said it was important to finish them, even if she seemed a lot better.'

To help avoid antibiotic resistance—funnily enough, the topic that Marina had planned to cover in her next batch of articles. 'How long has she had the rash?'

'She had a couple of spots this morning, but…' The woman gasped as she saw the redness over the little girl's face. 'It wasn't anywhere near that bad. I would never have taken her out with that!'

They could practically see the spots appearing and spreading. 'I think,' Marina said carefully, 'Your daughter's reacting to the antibiotics.'

'But—I thought if they were allergic to antibiotics it happened straight away?'

'Sometimes it does, but it often happens a day or so after the last dose,' Marina explained. 'You did the right thing bringing her here, because we can help her. Is she on any other medication?'

'No.'

'Does she have any other medical conditions or allergies?'

The woman shook her head. 'Just the normal coughs and colds kids get, and she was definitely over the ear infection, because she'd stopped saying how much it hurts.'

Marina established the rest of Jessie's patient history on the way to Resus. As they reached the double doors, Max came up. 'This is Max Fenton, our senior registrar,' Marina said. 'Max, this is Jessie, and I think she's having a reaction to amoxicillin.'

'OK.' Max smiled at Jessie's mother. 'I know you're worried, but your daughter's in the best place now. Dawn here will take you through to the relatives' room, and we'll come and get you when Jessie's feeling a bit better.'

The woman shook her head wildly. 'I can't leave my baby. I *can't*.'

'The thing is,' Marina said, 'the medical procedures we need to use can look a bit scary, and we might not have time to explain them to you properly as we're working. I know waiting's going to be hard, but trust me on this. It'll be a lot easier on your nerves than watching us.'

Jessie's mother looked at her. 'You're the doctor in the paper, aren't you?'

'Yes.' Marina gave her a self-conscious smile.

'I read your column every week. It's really good.' She nodded. 'All right.'

While Dawn took the woman through to the relatives' room, Marina filled Max in on Jessie's medical history.

Gently, they removed Jessie's coat and sweater; the rash had spread, and the little girl was fighting for air.

'We'll defer intubation until the epinephrine kicks in,' Max said.

'I'll give her high-flow oxygen and salbutamol on mask,' Marina said.

'Good.' Max deftly put a line into Jessie's vein as Marina hooked her up to the monitoring equipment.

'BP's low,' Marina said. With severe allergic reactions, blood could leak from the veins, causing low blood pressure and hypovolaemic shock.

'Give her a bolus of Ringer's,' Max said. 'How old is she?'
'Five.'

'Normal weight—I'd say about eighteen kilos.'

'Agreed.' Marina mentally calculated the amount of solution she needed to give, based on the child's weight, and sorted it out while Max put in a second line and administered epinephrine.

It took three doses before Jessie finally stopped fighting for air; Max added antihistamines to the mix, and Marina kept a close eye on the monitoring equipment, knowing that the drugs they were using to stabilise the little girl's condition and stop the swelling of her throat could also cause heart arrhythmias.

'I'll call the paediatric ward and tell them we want to admit Jessie,' Marina said. 'We need her under obs for the next twenty-four hours.' With severe drug reactions, there was a risk of a second, delayed reaction, so it was best to be prepared. 'And that rash is going to be incredibly itchy—she'll need some cream as well as the antihistamines.'

By the time Marina had called up to the children's ward and spoken to Lynne, the senior sister on the ward, Jessie had revived sufficiently to want her mother. Max was holding the little girl's hand and telling her a story to distract her, and he was making a great job of it; anyone would think he had children of his own and was used to telling stories at the drop of a hat to ward off tears.

Marina pushed away the thought of what might have been and said, 'I'll go and get her mum.'

The little girl brightened as soon as she saw her mother, and the woman almost collapsed in relief when she saw that her child was safe, and hugged her tightly.

'She's very much on the mend now,' Marina said. 'But we're going to keep her in overnight. When a child reacts to medication as severely as Jessie did, sometimes there's a second reaction a few hours later, so we want to make sure she's OK before she goes home.'

'The rash will take a bit longer to go. It'll probably last for about a week,' Max said. 'And it'll look worse before it gets better—it often seems to work its way downwards. We can give Jessie some antihistamines to make sure she doesn't swell up and to help with the rash.'

'But it'll be terribly itchy, worse even than chicken-pox,' Marina added. 'So we'll give you some lotion to help with that. Lynne on the children's ward is brilliant with kids, and she'll show you ways of helping Jessie to press or pinch her skin rather than scratch. I'll take you up and introduce you to the team—Rhys Morgan, the consultant there, is just *lovely*.'

There was a particular softness to Marina's smile as she said the other man's name, and Max had to suppress a sudden flare of jealousy. How ridiculous. Despite what had happened last night, he had no claims on Marina— though she'd told him that she wasn't seeing anyone. He didn't have the right to be jealous.

Or maybe last night really had been all about comfort, and although she wasn't actually seeing the paediatric spe-cialist she was attracted to him. In love with him, even.

He pushed the thought away. 'We'll tell your GP what's happened and make sure that Jessie's hospital records are labelled, so the medical teams all know to give her a dif-ferent sort of antibiotic rather than penicillin if she needs treatment in the future,' he said to Jessie's mother. 'Though it's worth getting one of those Medic-Alert bracelets in

case you're elsewhere in the country or if you go abroad—
it'll warn the medics that she's allergic to penicillin-type
antibiotics.'

'I will. Thank you both so much. You've been brilliant.'

'It's what we're here for.' Marina smiled at her. 'Come on,
I'll take you both up so Jessie can get settled in to the ward.'

Max watched her leave before he started on the paperwork. They were definitely good together at work—and he
hoped they could sort things out so they were good together
outside work, too. The way it used to be, before everything
had gone wrong.

CHAPTER EIGHT

AT EXACTLY half-past seven that evening, Max rang Marina's doorbell. Her flat was a twenty-minute walk in the opposite direction to his from the hospital, though it was a pleasant walk, past two parks and in a road lined with trees.

A few moments later, she answered the door. Tonight she was dressed in a black, crinkle-pleated, silky skirt that fell almost to her ankles, a matching vest-top and a bright-pink georgette shirt which she'd used as an unstructured jacket; her hair was down, and her feet were bare apart from the nail polish on her toes that matched her shirt. She looked incredibly feminine and Max found it difficult to resist the urge to yank her into his arms and kiss her until both their heads were spinning—but the sensible side of him reminded him that it was a bad idea to push her too hard or too fast. He wanted her to relax with him. So he simply smiled and handed her a bunch of deep-blue irises. 'For you.'

'Thank you, Max.' She looked stunned, then pleased.

Did she really think he'd forget her favourite flowers that quickly?

'I wasn't sure what you were cooking, so I thought I'd play it safe.' He gave her the bottle of chilled Sauvignon Blanc.

'That's lovely. Though you really didn't need to bring anything—it's only supper.'

'I wanted to,' he said simply. 'And I didn't want you to think that I'm taking you for granted.'

'Come in. I'll put these in some water.'

He followed her into the flat.

There were photographs hanging in the narrow hallway, and he'd just bet the mantelpiece in her living room was crammed with more framed photographs. There was a cork board in her kitchen with photographs and postcards pinned to it; some of the photos were clearly of work nights out, as he recognised several of their colleagues, and others were of Marina's family. Several sheets of artwork were fastened to the fridge with magnets—abstract patterns of thick paint, liberally sprinkled with glitter, which he guessed were Phoebe's. Pots of herbs grew on the windowsill, and there was a spice rack on the worktop that Max knew from experience was well used rather than just sitting there for decorative effect.

Marina's kitchen was obviously the heart of her flat, just as it had been in their home together; and suddenly he felt wistful. He could remember how it had felt to come home on days when their duties hadn't matched; walking into a room had been like walking into her arms for a hug, even when she wasn't there, because everywhere had felt so welcoming.

So different from his almost-empty flat.

And so very different from his parents' ultra-formal house, where he felt guilty about putting a dent into a pristine cushion and wouldn't dream of putting his feet up on the sofa.

In Marina's flat, he instantly felt at home. It made him realise again how much he'd missed her. How empty his life had been since he'd lost her.

Could they give each other a second chance?

'Sorry, I'm running a teensy bit behind, so dinner's going to be another twenty minutes. Do you want a coffee, or do you want to start on the wine?' she asked.

'Coffee would be lovely,' he said politely.

She put the wine in the fridge and switched on the kettle. 'Make yourself comfortable. You can go through into the living room, if you like, and I'll bring our coffee through.'

'Do you mind if I sit here?' He indicated one of the chairs at her kitchen table.

'Sure. Help yourself.' She smiled at him and started arranging the irises in a clear-glass vase.

'Anything I can do to help?'

'You can get the milk out of the fridge, if you like.' She busied herself shaking coffee grounds into a cafetière.

He opened the fridge and blinked. 'Your fridge is full,' he said as he retrieved the milk and set it on the worktop.

'That's what a normal person's fridge looks like.' She laughed. 'Yours *isn't* normal, Dr Hubbard.'

The only answer he could give to that was a wry smile, and a change of subject. 'Something smells wonderful.'

'Supper,' she said, frothing the milk in a jug with a tiny whisk before adding it to the coffee and handing him a mug.

It was typical of Marina to make proper coffee rather than instant, he thought, and to add those extra touches without making a big deal out of it.

'Sorry, I haven't had time to lay the table yet.'

'I'll do it, if you tell me where everything is,' Max offered.

'Sure. Cutlery's in the second drawer along, place-mats are in the drawer next to them, and the glasses are on the middle shelf of the cupboard above the kettle.'

So she still kept everything in the same places as she'd

kept things in their kitchen. No wonder he felt as if he knew his way around already.

'I didn't get a chance to see Rosie today,' he said. 'How's she doing?'

'OK, but horribly bored,' Marina replied. 'Mind you, I don't think I'd cope too well with being confined to a hospital bed.'

Max certainly hadn't. He'd brooded and brooded and brooded. Then again, he'd had a lot to brood about. Finding a new job, dealing with his father's death—and then coming to terms with the bombshell his father had left. Not to mention the sea-change in his own feelings afterwards, losing his respect for his father and discovering a new sympathy towards his mother, even at the same time as he loathed the way she fussed over him and smothered him. 'Spending a day in bed with a book is a treat. But if you're forced to do it for a month it'll drive you crazy.'

She raised an eyebrow. 'That sounded personal, Max. Is that what happened to you after the earthquake?'

He backtracked swiftly. Marina didn't know any of the stuff about his family, and he wasn't going to burden her with it, despite the fact that she'd asked. 'Yes. And I know other people who've been stuck on bed rest. Not for pre-eclampsia, admittedly, but the principle's the same.'

'So that's why you visit her almost every day?'

He shrugged. 'I hope you don't mind.'

'No, it's kind of you. And it really does help take her mind off how bored she is.' She looked over at him, seeing that he'd retrieved the cutlery and the place-mats. 'Just stick the books on one of the spare chairs, or on top of the fridge.'

He glanced at the textbooks as he moved them, noting

that the subject was paediatric emergencies. 'Is this what you're doing your special-reg training in?'

'Yes. It's why I spend Wednesdays in the children's assessment unit with Rhys Morgan. He's offered me a temporary post in the paediatric department.'

'Oh, has he?' Again, Max felt that twist of jealousy in his stomach and was cross with himself for being ridiculous. Maybe the consultant recognised Marina's abilities as a doctor. Just because Max himself found her incredibly attractive, it didn't necessarily mean that every other man would. For all he knew, Rhys Morgan could be gay and completely uninterested in Marina as a woman.

And he was even crosser with himself when Marina said, 'It'd be as maternity cover for Katrina, his wife—she's expecting their first baby in just over a month. They're a great team, and I've learned a lot from them both over the last few months.'

How wrong could he get? Not only was the other man completely straight, he was married. Preparing to become a father.

As Max himself had been four years ago. The news of Marina's pregnancy had been unexpected, shocking—and yet when he'd got used to the idea he'd loved it. It wasn't until the miscarriage that he'd realised how much he'd been looking forward to becoming a father, to having a family with Marina. To coming home and being kissed hello by a little girl who was the image of his wife, and who had the same love in her eyes when she looked at him. To coming home and teaching his son how to ride a bike and how to bowl a cricket ball. To telling bedtime stories and going to school nativity plays and sports days.

He pushed the thoughts away. 'Are you tempted to take the job?'

'A bit,' she admitted. 'But I know I'd miss the buzz of the emergency department.' She gave him a rueful smile. 'Maybe I'm just an adrenaline junkie.'

He smiled back. 'No, you're just used to being too busy. You were very good with young Jessie today.'

'Thank you.'

'And I was thinking, if you want anyone to do spot questions with you for the exams, give me a yell.' As soon as the words were out of his mouth, though, he regretted them. He could remember studying-sessions with Marina from her days as a junior doctor. And how he would reward her with kisses for giving him the right answers—but only at the end of the session, so he didn't distract her from learning... 'Am I keeping you from your books tonight?'

'No, it's fine—I've already done some studying. That's why I was running a bit late.' She grimaced. 'Sorry. It's a really interesting subject, and the time ran away with me.'

'No need for apologies.'

Supper turned out to be sweet potato wedges, chicken fillets stuffed with blue cheese and wrapped in parma ham, and steamed green vegetables, followed by bananas that had been studded with chocolate and baked in the oven, served with low-fat Greek yoghurt.

Max ate every scrap. 'That was wonderful.'

'It was just supper.' She flapped a dismissive hand and topped up their glasses.

Then he remembered something else that had been bothering him. 'What was Jessie's mum saying about seeing you in the paper?'

'I do a column in the local paper once a week. Milly in

the press office talked to Ellen about it—' Ellen was the Director of Emergency Medicine and head of their department '—and she suggested I should do it as part of my training. The idea is to give people more of an idea of what we do in the emergency department and what they can do to help themselves.'

'Sounds good.'

'I'm trying to cover the most common cases and keep them as seasonal as I can—so I did Colles' fractures a couple of months back, and I'll do stings in the summer. It's a bit of a mix of first-aid advice and raising awareness of where else people can go for help—their friendly, local pharmacist for minor things, their GP or nurse practitioner for more serious things and us for accidents and emergencies.'

'Do you enjoy it?'

'It's fun,' she said. 'The only downside is that the paper insists on using my photograph. So when people do come in sometimes they're a bit wary of me because they're not a hundred per cent sure that I'm a real doctor.'

'Like that woman who was shouting at you the other week.'

'From what her friend said,' Marina said, 'she was deeply unhappy with her life and I was a convenient target for her to let off some steam.'

'She still shouldn't have taken it out on you.'

'It doesn't matter. You came to my rescue,' she said lightly.

Marina made more coffee, and shepherded him into the living room. As he'd suspected, the mantelpiece was crowded with photographs of her family, and the comfortable sofa was covered with cushions.

What he hadn't expected was the up-to-the-minute television and games console. He didn't remember her being into video games.

Clearly she followed his line of thought, because she laughed. 'I'm still not into "shoot 'em up" or car-racing games. But this is a lot of fun.' She gave him a sidelong look. 'Challenge you?'

'To what?'

'Up to you—there's a ten-pin bowling one, or there are some word games—or there's one that's full of mini-games, where you do all sorts of things, from hula-hooping to pretending to be an elephant. Which sounds completely ridiculous, but it's hilarious.'

'I'll follow your lead,' Max said.

It turned out to be enormous fun. Marina showed him how the controls worked; she beat him at the first couple of games, but as he grew more used to the controls he overtook her.

Finally, she flopped on the sofa. 'Enough! Do you want another coffee?'

'No, I'm fine, thanks.' He sat down beside her. 'I enjoyed that.'

'Me, too.'

He found himself staring at her mouth; when he glanced up, he noticed that she was looking at his mouth too. He leaned forward very slightly, intending to do no more than just touch his mouth to hers in a brief and sweet kiss. But somehow they ended up lying flat on the sofa, with Marina underneath him. Her legs were wrapped round his waist as he traced a line of kisses along her collarbone. How he loved her scent, the softness of her skin beneath his mouth. The tiny little noises of pleasure she made when he rediscovered a place she liked being kissed. The feel of her pulse beating strong and hard beneath his mouth, growing more rapid as she became more aroused.

Then he came to his senses.

He was practically making love to her on her sofa, when she'd invited him over simply for supper. This really wasn't supposed to be happening, and he was acting way out of line.

He pulled back slightly; he could see that her eyes were huge and dark, her mouth reddened from his kisses, and she was clearly as turned on as he was. Yet there was an undercurrent of worry beneath it all.

Was she scared that if she let him close again they'd end up making the same mistakes they'd made last time?

'Sorry. I didn't intend this to happen.'

She gave him a dry smile. 'Neither did I. This was really just an invitation to dinner.'

'And I've really overstepped the boundaries. Overstayed my welcome. I'd better go.'

But her legs were still wrapped round his waist and she hadn't moved. She reached up to stroke his face. 'Max, you don't have to go.'

'If I don't, I'll end up carrying you to bed and making love with you,' he warned. 'Because I still can't keep my hands off you.'

'Funny, that. I'm having the same problem. And, right now, you feel so good.' She slid her hands round his neck and drew his face down to hers, then touched her mouth to his.

As the kiss deepened, Max was completely lost. It was only when they rolled off the sofa together, she landed on top of him and all the breath hissed out of his lungs that he stopped kissing her.

'Uh. Remind me that I'm thirty, not eighteen,' he said.

She stroked his face. 'I'm not that far behind you. Only two years. Hey, do you realise that we're practically halfway to being pensioners?'

It was so crazy that he couldn't help laughing. 'I think we might have a way to go yet.'

She smiled at him, climbed off him and lithely got to her feet; then she held out a hand to help haul him up.

Except, once he was standing next to her, he couldn't stop himself pulling her back into his arms and kissing her.

'Enough of the teenage stuff,' she said with a grin when he broke the kiss. 'Let's finish this somewhere more comfortable.' She laced her fingers through his and led him through to her bedroom.

The room was painted soft duck-egg blue and cream; her double bed had a silver-painted wrought-iron frame, and there was a huge pile of pillows. Max could hardly wait to see her hair spread across them.

Except he still had the guilty feeling that he was taking this all too quickly. 'Are you sure about this, Marina?' he asked softly.

Her eyes were clear as she looked at him. 'I'm sure. Are you?'

He nodded. 'We're both crazy, you know that?'

She kissed him lightly. 'Stop thinking, Max. Let's just *be*.'

Telling him, in typical Marina style, that he was being too intense. That he should just relax and enjoy what was happening—because she intended to enjoy every second of it.

She untucked his shirt from his trousers and began to unbutton it.

Slowly they undressed each other, item by item. It took a long, long time, because they both had to kiss every centimetre of skin they uncovered. How much Max loved exploring her like this.

'I didn't tell you,' Max said 'You look lovely tonight— and I love your hair down like this.'

She smiled at him. 'Thank you. I can't wear it like this for work because it isn't hygienic.'

He couldn't resist playing with the ends of her hair, all soft, silky and curling round his fingers. 'It's still beautiful. Like you.'

'Flatterer.' But there were dimples in her cheeks, and he knew she'd appreciated the compliment.

She drew the pad of her thumb along his lower lip. 'You're still beautiful, too.'

He raised an eyebrow. 'Yesterday you said I was too thin.'

'You are. But you've also got the longest lashes of anyone I've ever met, and your mouth is irresistible. Sexy as hell.'

'So,' he said, stealing a kiss, 'is yours.'

Kissing turned to touching. And then they were in her bed, with her hair spread over the pillow, just the way he'd wanted it, and her head tipped back in offering, and he was kneeling between her thighs.

As he eased inside her, again he had that odd sensation that he was coming home. It was more than just familiarity: this was where he wanted to be. And they were definitely making love—because this wasn't just sex. It was a lot, lot more than that.

He still loved Marina from the depths of his soul. Always had, always would.

And he wanted her back in his life. For good.

Now wasn't the time to tell her—at least, not in words, but he could let his body do the talking. Rediscover where she liked being touched, what pleased her, what thrilled her. What made her make little breathy noises of surprised delight, what made her quiver and what made her grab onto him and practically hyperventilate.

As he felt her body tighten round his, the initial shimmer of her climax, he looked into her face and whispered, 'Open your eyes, Marina.'

She did. He saw the exact moment that she reached the peak—and it pushed him into his own climax.

I love you, Marina Petrelli, he said inside his head. *I love you.*

Afterwards, he lay on his back with Marina curled into him. 'So, what are we going to do?' he asked.

'About what?'

'The elephant in the corner.'

She pressed a kiss against his shoulder. 'If we're honest about it, Max, there is more than one.'

'Let's tackle the smallest first, then—this thing between us.'

She sighed. 'I don't know, Max. Maybe it's just a physical thing.'

It was more than that for him—and, from what Rosie had said, Marina had kept other men pretty much at arm's length, rarely going on more than a second date. So it gave him hope that this was more than just sex for her, too. Marina Petrelli was warm, sweet and giving, but she didn't give her whole self lightly.

He smiled. 'I never could keep my hands off you.'

'Me, too.' She paused. 'I know this is going to sound mad, but maybe we should have a fling and get it out of our systems.'

That was the thing: he didn't think it would get her out of his system. 'We've already been there, done that and made a mess of it. And we made a complete mess of our marriage as well,' he reminded her.

'I'm not blaming you for that,' she said softly. 'There were faults on both sides.'

He hadn't talked to her, and she'd walked out. Neither of them had really given the other a chance to work it out. 'So what are we going to do about this?'

'Can't we keep it just between us for now?'

'Which makes me your dirty little secret.'

'Not *dirty*.' She shook her head in frustration, trying to work out the right way to say it. 'Just… I don't know where this is going, neither do you, and until we get things sorted out in our heads it's better not to raise anyone's expectations.'

'So you're saying this is just sex?'

'Yes. *No*.' She frowned. 'Max, please don't push me. There's a lot going on in my life right now, what with Rosie being in hospital and my studies. I really don't need the extra pressure.' She sighed. 'Look, what I'm trying to say is, I know we have issues and I know we need to talk about things. But I don't think tackling everything head-on is going to be the best way to deal with it.'

'So what do you suggest?'

'That we get to know each other again. Understand where each other's coming from. Learn to trust each other a bit before we tackle the tough stuff.'

'You mean, dating each other?'

'But *not* under a spotlight. Max, everyone in the department's lovely, but they're all incurable matchmakers.' As was her sister. 'If they have even a hint that there's anything between us, they'll have us married off faster…'

'Than we were last time?' he finished.

She nodded. 'Marry in haste, repent at leisure: there's

a lot of truth in that. We didn't really get to know each other properly last time. We just leapt into—' She stopped as he burst out laughing, and frowned. 'What?'

'Did you hear what you just said, Marina? Considering where we are…'

Reluctantly, she laughed. 'All right, you have a point.'

He stroked her face. 'We managed to hold out for a week longer this time before we ended up in bed together. But we're not very good at keeping our hands off each other, Marina.'

'Maybe we should try a bit harder.'

'So there's going to be a rule about no kissing and no touching? I'm not sure how long that's going to last, but we can give it a try.' He paused. 'Are you off at the weekend?'

'Yes.'

'Got any plans?'

'Visiting Rosie and spending time with Phoebe.'

'Can you spare Saturday afternoon? If, say, I help you study in the evening?'

The offer was tempting. Incredibly tempting. She'd always loved studying with Max. 'What did you have in mind?'

'You suggested it,' he said. 'A date. You don't have to dress up, just wear something you can walk in.'

'We're going for a walk?'

'We're going to play tourist,' he said. 'Spend some time together. Get to know each other again.'

'But no touching and no kissing,' she reminded him.

'Not on Saturday,' he agreed. 'But right now I'm in your bed. And we're both naked. And what I really want to do is…' He leaned forward and kissed her, a slow, hot kiss that made his blood fizz. 'That's on account,' he said. 'Until we're ready to take it further.' He slid out of bed and retrieved his clothes. When she made a move to get up, he shook his head. 'Stay put. I can see myself out—and I think you need to get some sleep.'

She glanced at her bedroom clock. 'I didn't realise it was this late! Um, Max, if you want to stay…'

He finished dressing and sat next to her on the bed. 'I'm tempted. Very tempted. But then I'll break this new no-touching rule within seconds. So I'm going home. I'll see you tomorrow.'

'I'm not working in the department tomorrow. I'm in the children's assessment unit,' she reminded him.

'Then I'll see you on Thursday.' He couldn't resist stealing one last kiss. 'Good night. Sweet dreams.'

Marina smiled as he closed her bedroom door. Yes, her dreams would be sweet tonight. Because they'd be dreams of him.

CHAPTER NINE

MARINA was kept busy in the Children's Unit on the Wednesday, and after visiting Rosie she went home with her parents and helped out with Phoebe, but she still found enough time to miss Max. She didn't do anywhere near as much studying as she'd intended, either, because she kept thinking of him instead of keeping her mind on her textbooks.

On Thursday she and Max were rostered on different parts of the ward, and on Friday they were too busy to say more than a brief hello, but on Saturday morning he sent her a text.

Your place at 1?

C u then, she texted back.

It gave her half an hour to change her outfit three times and redo her make-up twice.

Don't dress up, he'd said. *Wear something you can walk in.*

In the end she opted for jeans, flat ankle-boots, a long-sleeved T-shirt and a light jacket in case it rained.

At precisely one o'clock, her doorbell rang, just as she'd expected; Max always had been the punctual sort. He, too, was wearing jeans, though his were black rather than faded blue, and his sweater was the same slate-blue as his eyes.

He looked utterly edible, and she seriously considered grabbing him and breaking all the new rules.

'Ready?' he asked.

'Sure. Where are we going?'

'The weather's on our side.' He indicated the bright-blue spring sky. 'So I thought we'd get some fresh air, if that's OK with you?'

'Sure.' It was ridiculous to feel this shy with him. She'd been *married* to the man, for pity's sake. She'd ended up in bed with him this week—on two separate occasions, so she couldn't even say it was a one-off mistake.

But this felt exactly like a first date. A step into the unknown. Would they have anything in common any more, apart from that intense physical attraction? Over the years they'd both changed; would they actually like each other now?

She mentally shook herself, grabbed her handbag, locked the front door behind them and walked with Max to the Tube station.

'We're going to Kew Gardens?' she asked when they changed onto the District line. She'd never been to see the display of spring bulbs; it was one of the things she and Rosie had always planned to do, but they'd never quite got round to going.

'It's meant to be lovely at this time of year,' Max said.

It was breathtaking, with the fading drifts of daffodils and crocuses being replaced by tulips, blossom starting to come out on the cherry trees and the tiny flowers of the 'glory of the snow' turning the lawns near the Orangery into a carpet of blue even brighter than the spring sky.

She ended up hand in hand with Max as they walked through the grounds.

'I thought we had a no-touching rule?' she asked with a smile.

'This is our "first date", so I think holding hands is just about permissible,' he said, laughing back.

And, as long as they avoided the subject of the past, the old easiness between them came back. Just like on their real first date, where they'd talked and talked and talked. They wandered through the gardens and the galleries, stopped for tea in the Orangery, and Marina was shocked by just how quickly the time went.

'I know I said just an afternoon,' Max said. 'But can I persuade you to have dinner with me tonight? I'll spot-test you on paediatric complications, if you like.'

She laughed. 'I don't think it'll hurt if I play hooky from my studies occasionally.'

'So that's a yes for dinner?'

'I'd love to,' she said.

They ended up in a Chinese restaurant, sharing a mixture of dishes. And at the end, when they were thoroughly stuffed, they drank jasmine tea and broke open their fortune cookies.

'"Being happy is not always being perfect",' Max read.

That was true. They'd tried to be the perfect couple, and everything had gone downhill after that.

'"He who climbs a ladder must begin at the first step",' she said, reading hers aloud.

'Well, that tells us,' he said with a smile.

He was teasing, she knew, but it was definite food for thought. If they were ever to salvage anything from the past, they'd have to start right back at the beginning—and learn that they didn't have to be perfect. That it was enough just to be themselves.

After Max had walked her home from the Tube station, Marina stood on tiptoe on her front doorstep and kissed him on the cheek. 'Thank you for today.'

He coughed. 'What about the no-kissing rule?'

She gave him a cheeky grin. 'As you said, it's our first date. I'm allowed to kiss your cheek right at the end.'

'Hmm,' he said.

'Seriously, Max, it's been a fabulous day. I really enjoyed myself.'

'Me, too.' He drew her hand up to his mouth and kissed the back of her fingers.

'What was that you were saying about the no-kissing rule?' she teased.

'You just said it was a first date and it's allowed,' he countered. Then his smile faded and his eyes grew serious. 'I hope that today's maybe a new beginning, Marina.'

'Me, too.'

'I know we've still got a way to go,' he said softly. 'And there are a lot of things we're going to have to talk about. But this is a start.'

'Like my fortune-cookie message said.'

'Exactly.' He stroked her face. 'Don't ask me in for coffee. We both know where that will lead. And, much as I want to kiss you right now, and carry you to your bed and make love with you for the rest of the night, I'm going to be sensible about this. I'm going home.'

She understood. Like her, he wanted to give them a proper chance. To go beyond their physical attraction and deal with the demons in their joint past. 'Thank you for today.'

'And thank *you*.' He waited until she'd unlocked her door, sketched a brief salute and was gone.

* * *

Sunday heralded a perfect spring morning, and Max called Marina to suggest a trip on the river down to Greenwich.

'I'd love to, but I'm meant to be helping Mum and Dad with Phoebe.'

'No worries. Some other time,' Max said. 'See you tomorrow.'

But the disappointment must have shown on her face when she ended the call, because her mother immediately asked what was wrong.

'Go,' Louise said when Marina explained. 'Phoebe has a nap in the afternoons anyway—and you have a full-time job in the busiest department in the hospital, not to mention the fact that you're studying for exams. You need a break. Call him back and say you've changed your mind.'

She did. 'Is that offer still open?' she asked.

'Sure.' Max sounded surprised—and pleased. Marina's heart gave a little leap at the realisation that he was looking forward to spending time with her. Just as she was looking forward to spending time with him.

'Meet you at Westminster at one?' she suggested.

'Great. I'll see you on the pier.'

When she arrived, Max was leaning against one of the lamp-posts, wearing black jeans, a grey sweater and a pair of dark glasses. He looked utterly gorgeous, and she wondered if he was aware of just how many appreciative female glances he was attracting.

Then he saw her and smiled, and her heart gave a kick—because that smile was only for her.

'Hi.' He walked over to her, kissed her briefly on the mouth and grinned at her shocked stare. 'Second date.

We've moved from a peck on the cheek to a peck on the lips. That's the rules.'

'Oh, really?'

'Really.' He stole a second kiss, just to prove it.

He helped her on to the boat and held her hand when he sat down next to her.

It turned out the boat he'd booked was one of the fast boats, and they sped along the Thames. Max gave her a sidelong look. 'Feeling brave?'

'Why?'

'I have an idea.' He drew her to her feet and guided her over to the back of the boat. 'I know we're at the stern of the boat rather than the bow, but we have to do the *Titanic* thing, don't you think?'

'You're completely crazy.' But she loved his spontaneity; this was the Max she remembered from years ago. The man she'd fallen headlong in love with.

He stood behind her. 'Step up. I won't let you fall.'

She knew he wouldn't. And a few moments later she was standing there with her arms outstretched, her hands entwined with his, leaning out into the wind. 'Max, I'm flying!' she said with a grin.

'Are you, now?' He drew her hands down, wrapped his arms round her waist and kissed the curve of her neck. 'Better not do the rest of the scene, as we're only on our second date—and we're in a public place,' he murmured into her ear. 'But I'm thinking it. Imagining it. Remembering what it's like to kiss you properly. Feeling your mouth open against mine. And then knowing that I'm going to carry you to our bed and make love with you until neither of us can see straight.'

Desire shivered through her and she brought one hand up to touch his face. '*Max.*'

'I know. Me, too. But waiting's going to make it all the sweeter.' He kissed the curve of her neck again, then stepped down, his hands still entwined with hers to keep her safe; they walked hand in hand back to their seat.

At Greenwich, they disembarked and walked through the streets to the Naval Museum, then through the park behind the huge, sprawling building and up the hill to the Royal Observatory. It was studded with the last of the daffodils, and families were out in force: parents strolling along with pushchairs and children running round. A perfect Sunday afternoon.

Max's hand tightened around hers. 'I thought that would be us by now.'

She stilled. 'Elephant alert.'

'*Enormous* elephant alert,' he corrected, his voice gentle. 'You're not over it, are you?'

The miscarriage. Losing their baby. Losing their marriage. The words felt too big to come out of her mouth. In the end, she said simply, 'No.'

'Me, neither.'

Marina was shocked into silence. She'd always thought that it hadn't affected him as badly as it had affected her. And, even though she knew that his mother's comments had been fuelled by jealousy and resentment, part of her had wondered if there was some truth in them: that deep down Max really was relieved that she'd lost the baby because they had both still been so young and right at the start of their careers. After all, he hadn't tried to get her back after she'd left. He hadn't followed her to London, hadn't called her… He'd just shut off.

'I know we didn't plan to have children quite so soon, but I always thought we'd have them,' Max said. 'More than one, because I didn't want ours to be an only child.'

'Like you were, you mean?'

He shrugged. 'I have no idea if my parents wanted more children. It's not exactly something I could ask my mother, but I sometimes wonder if they might not have been able to.'

That would certainly explain why Kay had clung so desperately to Max, Marina thought. If only she'd realised that she was gaining a daughter rather than losing a son.

Max had had all the pressure of his mother's love and expectations on him. And he'd missed out, too. 'Our house was always full of children,' Marina said. 'But when they'd gone I still had Rosie to play with. Sure, we squabbled—all kids do—but she was always there for me, to cheer with me in the good times and give me a hug in the bad times. She's always given me the space to work things out for myself and listened without judging.' She looked away. 'Rosie was the one who stopped me going under after I…after I lost our baby.'

He sucked in a breath. 'I'm glad you had her support. Though I know it should've been me. And I'm sorry. I just couldn't deal with it back then.'

Her throat felt too tight for her to speak. She made a noncommittal noise and rummaged in her handbag for her sunglasses, jamming them on to her face to hide her eyes.

He stopped dead and pulled her close, wrapping his arms round her, heedless of the people walking by them. 'Are you crying?' His voice was so soft that she could barely hear him.

She still couldn't speak, so she shook her head. She wasn't crying…just. Though her eyes were stinging with unshed tears, and the pressure round her head was almost unbearable.

'I didn't mean to upset you, Marina. I just wanted you

to know that I'm sorry. And I wish I'd been mature enough to support you myself instead of running away and hiding in work. I don't have any excuses. I let you down, and I'm sorry.'

'We were both young. What happened to us was a really big deal. Neither of us knew how to deal with it. And I should've supported you, too. I just didn't think it…' She couldn't finish the sentence.

'You didn't think it bothered me, because I wasn't the one who physically had to go through it?'

Hearing her thoughts spoken aloud was shocking. Particularly as she hadn't expected Max to read her so easily. There was an edge to his voice: anger, hurt, pain? She couldn't tell.

But if they were ever going to stand a chance she owed him honesty. 'Yes.'

He was silent for a long, long time. Then he whispered, 'The day you lost the baby was one of the worst days of my life.'

She could feel him shaking with the pain of the memories and the strain of actually letting the words out.

'I'd been worrying myself sick for weeks, thinking of all the things that could go wrong with your pregnancy, and part of me felt as if it were my fault, for reading up on everything and talking it up.'

She'd never even dreamed he'd felt like that. 'It wasn't your fault. Of course it wasn't. You know as well as I do that one in five pregnancies never comes to term. We were unlucky.' She choked back a sob. 'And it happened after we thought we were safe.' So unfairly. When they should've had the chance to relax and enjoy her pregnancy, to plan the nursery, talk about names and dream about the future.

'It wasn't your fault, either,' Max said softly. 'So I hope you're not blaming yourself.'

She shook her head. 'I'm not. I just wish it had been different. That we'd had our chance to be a family.'

'Me, too. I wanted a family with you, Marina. I know our baby wasn't planned, but I wanted a little girl who looked like you. And a little boy. I wanted to take our kids to the park with you, play on the swings, teach them to swim, read them stories. I wanted all of it.'

'So did I.' A single tear slid under her sunglasses and soaked into his sweater.

They'd wanted exactly the same things. And they'd wanted them with each other. So how the hell had they ended up like this?

'I should've told you,' Max said. 'I know now I should've told you how I felt. But you were in pieces, and I didn't think it was fair to lean on you and make you deal with my misery as well as your own. I couldn't make it right for you and I hated myself for being such a failure—at work I could fix things, but at home I was just useless.'

But if he had leaned on her she would've coped better—because she would've known that they were in the same place. *Together*.

'So working crazy hours was your way of coping?' she asked.

'Yes. And it was the wrong thing to do,' Max said. 'I know that now.'

'I had no idea you felt that way. I thought…I thought that you were sick of me moping about, that you'd lost patience with me and I was being such a pain that you'd rather be at work than with me.'

'No. I'd lost patience with myself.'

She blew out a breath. 'I feel as if an elephant just sat on me.'

'Me, too.' He pressed a kiss against her hair. 'But we're still standing. And we're going to keep standing, Marina.'

It sounded as if he believed they could do this. Together. That they could lay the past to rest and start again.

Was he right? Or was this going to be her biggest mistake yet?

She wrapped her arms round him. 'No more elephants today, OK?' she asked shakily. 'I think that's as much as I can deal with right now.'

'Sure. We'll play tourist. Have some fun. The way it was supposed to be today.' He pulled back slightly, and brushed his mouth against hers. 'And I'm sorry I made you cry just now.'

He was wearing dark glasses, but Marina had a feeling that if he took them off his eyes would be a little too bright— with unshed tears of his own.

'We always knew it was going to hurt when we started dealing with the past,' she said.

'Like lancing an infected wound,' Max agreed. 'But, if we don't do it, we'll never get proper closure. Never really heal.'

'My mum used to soak sticking plasters off in the bath,' Marina said. 'I was never brave enough to let her pull them off quickly.' She raised an eyebrow. 'Did you tough it out?'

'Boys do,' Max said. 'And it's a point of honour not to say a word about how you feel. But I'm trying to un-learn that.' He raised her hand to his mouth and kissed it. 'Just not all at once, hmm? Let's live in the now.'

She walked up the hill with him to the Observatory, hand in hand; she stood on the Meridian Line and Max took a photograph of her on his mobile phone. She did the same for him, then he got her to stand in front of him, wrapped his arm round her waist, pulled her back against him and took a photo of them together, his cheek pressed next to hers, both of them smiling.

It felt as if they were courting again—just as it had years ago, before everything had started getting complicated. And Marina loved every second of it: wandering round Flamsteed's original observatory and marvelling at the Wren-designed interior; looking at the clocks, then wandering round the Planetarium and touching the four-and-a-half-billion-year-old meteorite in the entrance.

Max found them a little bistro for dinner, where they held hands under the table and fed each other morsels of their puddings. Then he saw her back home and kissed her briefly goodbye on the doorstep. 'Sweet dreams. See you tomorrow.'

'See you tomorrow,' she echoed.

'Tell me to go. Before I start breaking rules.'

'Supposing I'd like you to break them?'

He groaned. 'Don't do this to me, Marina. I don't want to rush into this. I want to give us a chance.' But he drew her back into his arms and kissed her until her head was spinning.

'Enough,' he said, pulling away. 'We have more elephants to tackle first.'

She laid her palm against his cheek. 'I know.'

He turned his face and pressed a kiss into her palm. 'Go indoors, Marina. Or I'm going to start behaving like Tarzan.'

She grinned. 'Me Jane.'

He laughed, then his face became serious. 'You're right about one thing, though: in the early films, Tarzan really, really loved his wife. And no other woman ever matched up to her.'

Was he saying…?

As if she'd asked aloud, he said softly, 'Me Tarzan.' He kissed her palm again and curled her fingers over the place he'd kissed. 'I'm going to fight for you, Marina. We're going to fight those demons together. And we're going to win.'

Life somehow had its sparkle back. All was more than fine in Marina's world—until Tuesday, when Max came looking for her in the cubicles, looking serious. 'Would you excuse us for a minute, please?' he asked her patient. 'Dr Petrelli, I need a word.'

She stepped outside with him. 'What's happened?'

'Rosie,' he said. 'Don't panic—she's OK—but Theo Petrakis just called down. He spoke to me, as you were with a patient; he's not happy with Rosie's blood pressure and he wants to take her in to Theatre and deliver the baby.'

Marina's teeth started to chatter. 'Oh, no. Please tell me she hasn't had an eclamptic fit?'

'No, she hasn't,' he reassured her. 'As I said, don't panic—but she's a bit scared and she needs someone with her before she has the anaesthetic. Iris is calling Neil and your parents, but they're at least half an hour away, and Theo wants her in Theatre now.'

'Max, I need to go to her. But my patient!'

'Don't worry, I'll finish seeing your patient and give your apologies.' He took her hands and squeezed them briefly. 'I'll sort cover for you so you don't have to worry about a thing—just go to Rosie, give her my love and come and tell me how things are when you get the chance, OK?'

She nodded, unable to speak; she knew she should thank him, but fear seemed to have paralysed her vocal cords. She squeezed his hand, hoping he'd realise what she wasn't capable of saying, and headed straight for the maternity unit.

'She's OK, Marina, just scared,' Iris said, letting her onto the ward.

Rosie was shivering and tears were running unchecked down her cheeks when Marina reached her bedside. Marina wrapped her arms round her sister. '*Cara*, everything's going to be absolutely fine. I'm here and Neil's on his way, and so are Mum and Dad.'

'If I lose the baby…'

'You're *not* going to lose the baby. He's thirty-five weeks, and loads of babies are born at that age and are absolutely fine. And Theo's the best; he won't let anything happen to Bambino. They're getting you to deliver him a little bit early because you're not very well and Theo believes this is the best thing for both of you. He knows exactly what he's doing.' She stroked Rosie's hair. 'Take a deep breath for me. And another. That's great. And another. Attagirl. Keep breathing like this, nice and slowly.'

Finally Rosie calmed down enough to take her pre-med. Marina stayed with her sister until the moment when she was wheeled into Theatre for the anaesthetic, then she headed back to the maternity unit for a quick word with Iris, to find out the full situation.

A few minutes later, Neil walked in, looking distraught.

Marina met him with a hug. 'She's going to be fine. Stop worrying. It's just that her blood pressure went up overnight and they couldn't get it to settle. They've given her some steroids to mature the baby's lungs, so this is the best thing for both of them. She's having the section under a general anaesthetic, so we can't go in, but I was with her for the pre-med. Oh, and she gave me a message for you—she says she loves you.'

She'd hoped that it would reassure her brother-in-law, but instead he was shaking.

'Marina, she's the love of my life. I can't imagine being without her. If she doesn't make—' He choked off the last word.

'Of *course* she'll make it. We Petrellis are made of tough stuff, you know,' Marina told him lightly. But inwardly she was terrified; she'd read up on Rosie's condition and she knew all the potential complications—including the fact that Rosie could still go into an eclamptic fit even after the baby had been delivered. Not that she was going to tell Neil any of that; she could see that he was worried enough without knowing the worst-case scenario.

And she really, really wished Max was here.

'Let's go and wait outside Theatre. Then we'll get the news as quickly as possible.'

Waiting was awful. Although Marina started chatting, trying to take Neil's mind off the wait and the reason why they were there, he was monosyllabic and distracted. In the end, she resorted to going to the vending machine and getting them both a paper cup of coffee neither of them particularly wanted, just so they'd have something to do with their hands and something to concentrate on.

Time seemed to be moving through treacle. But then at last Theo emerged from Theatre. He was smiling broadly. 'I'm delighted to tell you that Rosie's doing fine and you both have a beautiful baby boy,' he told Neil.

A single tear leaked down Neil's face; he wiped it away with the back of his hand. 'I'm sorry. I'm being so wet.'

Theo clapped his shoulder. 'It's OK. I know how you

feel—I cried like a baby myself when my little girl was born last year. It's the fear and the relief.' He smiled at Marina. 'I know women go through the physical pain of childbirth but, believe you me, men suffer right along with you. We worry all the time about what can go wrong. It's terrifying.'

'Tell me about it,' Neil said drily.

Had Max been this terrified when she was pregnant? Marina wondered. Being an emergency doctor, he'd know all about the potential complications. And he'd admitted on Sunday that he'd read up on things and worried. Had he worried about Marina developing a pregnancy-related condition, something life-threatening like Rosie's?

And then, when she'd miscarried… She knew now that Max had shut himself away in work because he hadn't been able to deal with the pain, the fear and the sheer helplessness.

She was aware that Theo was still talking. 'And if it makes you feel any better, Neil, my Helen was three weeks early and she's doing absolutely fine.'

'Can I see them?' Neil asked.

'You can see Rosie when she's completely round from the anaesthetic in a few minutes. We're taking your little boy to the special-care baby unit now, but that's simply because he's early, so he needs to be kept very warm and have a little bit of oxygen to help him breathe. It's really common with babies born this early, so try not to worry,' Theo reassured him. 'What I suggest is that one of you goes along with him, gets one of the nurses to take a Polaroid and then brings it back so Rosie can see him. It'll make her feel better, too.'

He smiled at Marina and rested a hand on her shoulder. 'And *you* can stop worrying as well. I'm not keeping anything back from you. I've given Rosie mag sulph, so

I'm pretty sure she's not going to develop full-blown eclampsia. She'll be in for the next four days anyway, to give her a chance to recover from the section, and I'm keeping her under obs, but as soon as she's feeling up to it you can take her down to SCBU in a wheelchair.'

'Let's go to see Bambino,' Marina said. 'And I'll text your mum and mine to let them know what's going on.' She swiftly texted both sets of parents to tell them that Rosie and the baby were both doing well, then took Neil down to SCBU. 'It looks much scarier than it really is,' she warned Neil as they rubbed their hands with the hand-sanitising gel outside the main doors. 'There will be machines and tubes and monitors and alarms going off everywhere, but it's nothing to panic about, OK?'

'I'm just glad you're here,' Neil said.

'Hey, it's what families are for.' She squeezed his hand.

Seeing the tiny baby in an incubator was clearly an ordeal for Neil; gently, she talked him through every single one of the machines and what they were for, to reassure him. Meeting the neonatal nurse who was looking after the baby clearly made him feel a bit better, but the clincher was being able to put his finger into the baby's tiny palm for the baby to grip hard.

'Do you see this, Marina?' he asked, awed.

'I do.' She was close to tears herself.

The nurse took a Polaroid photo of the baby for them, and Marina took Neil back to the recovery room where he was able to see Rosie.

'Aren't you coming in?' he asked.

'No. You need some time together,' she said. 'Give Rosie my love—and I'm going up to the ward to meet our parents and fill them in. Take your time, and don't rush.'

Neil hugged her. 'You know, you're the kid sister I always wanted.'

'Stop it. You'll make me start to cry,' she told him. 'And, for the record, you're the big brother I'm so glad I've got. Now, go and see Rosie.'

Back on the maternity ward, both sets of parents had already arrived and were waiting in Rosie's room. Marina filled them in on what had happened, and made sure that all four of them had hot drinks while they were waiting for Rosie to come back to the ward, then headed back down to the emergency department to find Max.

'How are things?' Max asked.

'Rosie's in the recovery room but Theo says she's doing fine. She had a little boy.' She bit her lip. 'He's going to be in SCBU for a few days.'

'Which is pretty normal, given that he's thirty-five weeks,' Max reminded her.

'Mmm.'

'But you're still worried.' He stroked her hair. 'Honey, he's in the right place. Hold on to that thought, OK?'

She nodded. 'My parents are here, and so are Neil's, but everyone's on edge. Neil's mum has a cold, so she can't go to SCBU, and nobody remembered a camera. I know it's a cheek of me to ask, but I said I'd get mine so the parents can at least have a photo of the baby. Would you be able to sort out cover for me for just a couple more hours?'

'Of course I can. But you've got some annual leave owing, haven't you?'

'A couple of weeks,' she said.

'Then why don't you take a couple of days of it now? I have a feeling Rosie and Neil are going to need a bit of extra support. You're not letting anyone in the department down—everyone will understand.'

'Max, I can't.' She looked at him, stricken. 'I want to be with Rosie and Neil and the baby—of *course* I do—but it's my day in the children's assessment unit tomorrow.'

'Don't worry. I'll have a word with Rhys in a minute and let him know the situation so he can get cover. You said he and his wife are expecting a baby, so I'm sure he'll understand. These are exceptional circumstances.' He squeezed her hand. 'It'll be fine. Try not to worry. Give Rosie and Neil my love, and I'll call you later, OK?'

CHAPTER TEN

EVERYTHING was a blur after that. Marina rushed home, found her camera and came straight back to hug Rosie and take photographs of the baby. Neil's parents clearly felt as if they could do nothing to help; Marina suggested that the grandmothers could go and get the photos printed and find some extra-small baby clothes, while the grandfathers went to the park with Phoebe, so Rosie and Neil could spend time with the baby.

'You're a genius,' Rosie said to Marina when their parents had left. 'Now nobody feels left out, and I don't feel that Neil and I have to stay up here and be sociable when I really just want to be with Nathan.'

'Nathan? That's a lovely name,' Marina said with a smile. 'And it suits him.'

She and Max had never got round to discussing names, thinking it unlucky until after the twenty-week scan. Except they hadn't made it that far. She'd lost the baby at thirteen weeks, the week after she'd been so sure it was safe to tell the world that they were expecting.

She pushed the thought away. Now really wasn't the time to brood. She couldn't change what had happened, so it was completely pointless dwelling on it; better to spend her energy supporting Rosie, Neil and the children.

'His middle name's Murray, by the way,' Neil added.

'Seeing as I was stuck in here,' Rosie said, 'it gave me plenty of time to look through all the baby-name books and find a boy's name meaning "from the sea". It's Gaelic.'

Marina suddenly twigged what her sister was telling her: her own name meant 'from the sea'. 'You named him after *me*?' Her eyes filled with tears.

Neil slipped his arm round her shoulders and hugged her. 'I don't know anyone else called Marina, so I guess we must have done.'

'That's…that's…' She was lost for words.

'Don't cry, *cara*,' Rosie said. 'Or you'll set me off and I'll start leaking everywhere.'

'I'll go and get us some drinks and meet you in SCBU,' Marina said, and fled into the corridor so she could give in to the overwhelming rush of tears. Her sister had given her precious baby the masculine version of Marina's name, showing just how much she loved her.

How she wished she'd been able to pay Rosie that same compliment three and a half years ago.

Later that evening, Max phoned Marina. 'How are things?' he asked.

'Fine.'

But he could hear the wobble in Marina's voice. Something definitely wasn't fine. Was the baby ill?

'Rhys sends his best and says not to worry—and he'll pop in and see the baby too.'

'Thank you.'

He heard an audible gulp, and it worried him even more.

'How was your day?' she asked.

'Fine. And don't worry about work. I've sorted cover for you.'

'Thank you.'

There was another wobble in her voice, and Max needed to know just what she wasn't telling him. The only way to satisfy himself about what was really going on was to see her face to face. But he also knew that if he suggested dropping by she'd say that there was no need and everything was fine. Marina always had been self-contained—too self-contained, really. If she'd cried her heart out on his shoulder instead of her sister's when they'd lost the baby, he would've felt that she needed him, that he'd actually been able to do something to help. But after that first horrible day she'd just withdrawn from him, and he hadn't known how to get her sparkle back. He hadn't really explained that to her properly at Greenwich: how helpless he'd felt, facing her pain and knowing he couldn't do a single thing to make things better.

'I'll talk to you later,' he said. 'Call me if you need anything.'

'Thanks. I will.'

Though he knew full well that she wouldn't. She'd try to fix things herself, the way she always did.

This time, things weren't so bleak, but he still needed to show her that she could rely on him. That he'd be there for her, support her the way she deserved. He went to the corner shop for supplies, then drove over to her street and leaned on her doorbell.

Her eyes widened as she opened the door. 'Max! I wasn't expecting to see you.'

'I think,' he said softly, 'you need a hug. Come here,

honey.' He stepped into the hallway, closed the door behind him and held her tightly. She was trembling, teetering on the edge of leaning on him. And he really, really wanted her to lean on him.

'How are things *really*?' he asked, resting his cheek against her hair.

She shivered. 'Max, you know as well as I do, preemies can have real problems. I can't possibly tell Rosie any of this—she's scared enough as it is, without me dumping this on her.'

Marina was using up all her reserves to support her sister; she needed someone to shore her up, too, whether she admitted it or not. 'Talk to me,' Max said. 'Tell me what you're worried about.'

'For a start, the baby's more susceptible to picking up an infection.'

'Which is exactly why they're so hot on hygiene in SCBU. He's in the right place,' Max reassured her.

'And preemies don't have the shiver reflex that full-term babies do. He doesn't have as much subcutaneous fat, he's at risk of hypothermia—and that can lead to other conditions.'

Such as low blood sugar, Max knew. 'Which is why he'll be wearing a hat, why he'll be in an incubator and why it's so horrendously warm in SCBU.'

'And he's at risk of developing RDS.'

Respiratory distress syndrome was one of the biggest risks to premature babies. 'OK, he doesn't have as much surfactant in his lungs as a full-term baby,' Max said. Surfactant stopped the small air sacs in the lungs from collapsing, so the lack of it caused problems for premature babies, making it harder for them to breathe properly. And the sheer effort they had to expend in breathing exhausted them, so they didn't have the energy to feed. 'He might need some extra oxygen to help him for a while, or if he's really struggling they might intubate him and treat him with surfactant—and yes, before you say it, they'll monitor the oxygen carefully. He's in the right place to get the help he needs.'

'And he's a high risk of developing apnea.' The condition made babies stop breathing for twenty seconds or more, and their heart rate slowed down below eighty beats per minute; it was most likely to occur when the baby was asleep.

'Not all preemies do. If he does, the nurses will stimulate him to breathe by touching his feet—and they'll put him on a monitor that will tell them if he stops breathing.'

'And he's more likely to have a haem—'

Max cut off the rest of the word by kissing her, nibbling at her lower lip until she opened her mouth and kissed him back. He walked her backwards into her living room, still kissing her, then sat down in a chair and pulled her onto his lap.

She stared at him. 'Why did you do that?'

'Because you're working yourself up into a real panic here, and that was the only way I could think of to stop you. Yes, there are risks, but your nephew's in the right place, and you know that—they'll be monitoring him really closely and they'll pick everything up.'

She dragged in a breath. 'He's so tiny, Max. He only weighs two and a quarter kilos.'

'That's pretty good, for his dates.'

'And his skin's thin and wrinkled, and his head looks too large.' She grimaced. 'I did a placement in SBCU, so I knew what to expect if he did arrive early—but it's so different when the baby's part of your own family, not just a patient.'

'Of course it is. You're emotionally involved—which is just how it should be.' He kept his arms round her. 'How's he feeding?'

'Through a naso-gastric tube. Rosie's expressing milk and cuddling him during feeds.'

'That's great. It'll help them bond. How's she doing?'

'Frantic with worry—it's not at all like last time, when she had Phoebe naturally and could hold her straight after the birth. She's able to hold him for a little bit, but clearly it's not that comfortable for him right now, and she feels as if she's a bad mother because she can't give him what he needs.' Marina sighed. 'Obviously, she's staying in hospital for observation anyway because she had a section, and they probably won't discharge her until the weekend. I'm going to keep her company and support her with the baby during the day for the rest of the week, and Neil's going to try and delegate as much of his work as he can so he'll be able to spend more time with her and the baby in the evenings.'

'Is Phoebe going to keep going to the hospital nursery?'

'For the next couple of weeks, yes. She's going to stay with my parents, and I'm going to do the nursery run both ends of the day, to take the pressure off Neil, and also give Phoebe the chance to see a bit of her mum.'

'It sounds as if you've got it all sorted out between you,' Max said. Marina's family always had been good at organising things. Louise had been brilliant with the wedding plans, especially as everything had been such a rush, and Marina had been suffering too much with morning sickness to do as much as she wanted to.

They'd married in Kings Weston House, a beautiful Georgian mansion on the outskirts of Bristol that had been designed by Sir John Vanbrugh. His bride had walked down the amazing suspended staircase to meet him for their marriage. His parents hadn't quite forgiven him for not getting married in church—his mother had even mentioned Bristol Cathedral, at one point—but Marina had asked him for something simpler. And he'd wanted to give his bride the kind of day she'd dreamed about. The kind of day he wanted himself.

'Mum's been brilliant,' Marina said, and there was a hint of wistfulness in her eyes; was she, too, thinking of their wedding? he wondered. 'Neil's parents have been good too, but Neil's mum doesn't want to risk Phoebe or Neil picking up her cold, because then they won't be able to see the baby, either—and she's so upset, Max. She hasn't been able to see the baby yet, and photographs really aren't the same at all. She's trying to be brave for Neil and Rosie, but I can see it in her face. She feels useless and miserable because she can't do anything practical to help.'

'Maybe she can help with things like sending birth announcements and pictures of the baby to people,' Max suggested.

'That's a good idea. I'll talk to Neil and Rosie and see what they say.' She bit her lip. 'I just wish I could do more. I wish I could wave a magic wand so Nathan'll be well and ready to go home right now.'

'Of course you do.' He drew her closer. 'But you're already being a brilliant support.'

She swallowed hard. 'They're calling him after me.'

He didn't follow that at all. 'Didn't you just say they were calling him Nathan? Forgive me for bursting your bubble, honey, but Nathan doesn't sound anything like Marina.'

'Not his first name—his middle name. Murray. It's the Gaelic masculine equivalent of Marina.'

'That's lovely.' He stroked her hair. 'And I'm not surprised. Rosie thinks an awful lot of you.'

'I think a lot of her.'

He stole a kiss. 'Look, I live nearer to the hospital than you do. Why don't you come and stay with me for a while? It would save you a bit of time.'

She shook her head. 'That's really sweet of you to offer, but I'd rather stay here. If there's a problem, this is the first place anyone will ring.'

'You'd have your mobile phone on you.'

'Even so. I'd rather be here.'

With all her things round her—at *home*—rather than in his anonymous and impersonal flat. He could understand that. 'In that case, give me your spare key.'

She frowned. 'Why?'

'So I can help you with practical stuff. For a start, I can stop your fridge becoming like mine.' He kissed the tip of her nose. 'And I can work a washing machine nowadays. It'll take some of the pressure off you—and if you call me when you're on your way home, I'll have dinner ready when you get in.'

She shook her head. 'Max, you really don't have to cook for me.'

'I know I don't, but I want to help.' He drew her closer. 'I want to be here for you. You're supporting Rosie and Neil. Let me support you.'

It was such a tempting offer. Someone to lean on. Someone to talk to about her worries—someone who'd understand the things she couldn't say to her family.

But, the last time she'd needed his support, he hadn't been there. She'd had to put a brave face on it and go it alone. Until she'd fled back to her family.

Would Max let her down again? Or could she take the risk and trust him?

'By the way, I brought supplies.'

She hadn't even noticed the paper bag he'd brought with him. But, when he gave it to her and she opened it, she discovered chocolate. Lots of chocolate. And a box of tissues.

'That's so…' She was overwhelmed by his thoughtfulness. 'Thank you, Max.'

'Just in case,' he said. 'I had this feeling there was something you weren't telling me.'

'Not about Nathan. But you know how it is—when you're a medic, you know too much. You know what the worst-case scenario is. I couldn't talk to Rosie or Mum about it without worrying them sick.'

'I'm glad you told me,' he said softly. 'And what you said isn't going anywhere. *I'm* not going anywhere, either.'

'Thank you.' Making the decision, she wriggled off his lap. When he looked wary, she took his hand and tugged him to his feet, then led him into the kitchen. She took her spare keys from the drawer where she kept them. 'You'll need the code for the alarm,' she said, scribbling it on a piece of paper and giving it to him along with her keys.

Max was as good as his word. Marina called him the next evening on her way home from the hospital, and by the time she got in he had a meal ready for her: baked salmon, new potatoes and salad.

'It's all pre-packaged stuff. All I did was follow the instructions and shove it in the oven,' he warned.

'It means I don't have to worry about cooking. Thank you, Max.'

'No problem. As I said, I just want to support you.'

If he'd supported me like that four years ago, Marina thought, if he'd let me support him, we'd still be together now.

The food was good, but Marina found herself picking at it. And she really wasn't in the mood for conversation; in her mind's eye, she could see her nephew in the special-care unit, vulnerable, fragile and struggling to breathe. As if Max guessed, he didn't push her to talk; he simply cleared away their plates and tidied her kitchen.

'Stay put. Visiting someone in hospital is tiring—not so much physically, but it drains you.' He handed her a mug of camomile tea. 'Caffeine's going to make you twitchy and disturb your rest. This might help.'

He'd sweetened it with a spoonful of honey to make it palatable, and Marina's eyelids prickled with tears. This was a whole new side to Max: caring, reliable, thoughtful. Just as he was with his patients and his staff. A grown-up version of the man she'd fallen in love with—a man who could still be spontaneous, but had a serious and responsible side.

The man she was still in love with, if she were honest with herself. She'd been angry with him, hurt and furious, but underneath it all she'd never really stopped loving him.

And she was beginning to think that he felt the same way.

On Thursday, Nathan's condition deteriorated, and when Marina met her sister on the unit Rosie was in tears.

'He didn't need those tubes yesterday.'

Marina knew that the nursing team would have explained everything to Rosie, but she guessed that her sister had been so shocked by the sight of the baby and the extra tubes that she was panicking. Gently, she talked her through the equipment. 'It's not hurting him; it's there to help the nurses look after him. He's probably a bit tired; this is helping him rest, so he gets stronger.'

'But it's all my fault.' Tears ran unchecked down Rosie's face. 'If I'd rested properly, this wouldn't have happened and he would've been fine.'

Marina put her arms round her sister. 'This is your hormones kicking in, *cara*—it's the baby blues talking. You've had a rough time, what with being on bed rest and away from Neil and Phoebe for weeks, having an emergency section under a general anaesthetic, and now Nathan being in here. And *none* of this is your fault. It's just one of these things that nobody could predict—and Nathan's going to be fine. He might get a bit worse before he gets better, but all the nurses here are really experienced and they'll know exactly what to do.'

Marina spent the rest of the day with Rosie, reassuring her, and was grateful to go home to Max's support.

'You know as well as I do that all conditions like this get worse before they get better, whether it's a premmie with RDS, a baby with bronchiolitis or a toddler with pneumonia,' Max said.

She nodded. 'That's what I told Rosie. But it's so hard to see him like that, Max. It makes me feel so helpless— I'm a doctor and I can't do a thing to make things better.'

'You're an emergency doctor, not a neonatal specialist,' he said. 'And you're the one who picked up Rosie's pre-eclampsia in the first place. If it wasn't for you, there might be a much darker scenario.'

She couldn't even bear to think about that.

'It's going to be fine.' He wrapped his arms round her. 'I'm here, and I'm not going away. But I do think you need something to take your mind off things.'

She tensed for a moment, wondering just what he had in mind.

But then he released her, walked over to her games console and slid a disk in. 'Prepare,' he said, 'to be thoroughly beaten and forced to admit that I'm better at ski-jumping than you are…'

He did manage to take her mind off her worries. He even made her smile. But as he prepared to go her smile faded.

'Try not to worry,' he said gently. 'I know it's hard, but Nathan's in the best place, and so is Rosie.'

'I know. I just can't…' She dragged in a breath. 'Max, can I ask you something?'

'Sure.'

'Would you…would you stay with me tonight? I'm not trying to make a move on you or anything. I just don't want to be on my own right now.'

She'd actually asked him for something—which meant she was letting him close. He'd give her the moon and stars if it were in his power, if she only knew it. Staying with her, holding her while she slept, was easy to promise and easy to do. Max wrapped his arms around her. 'Of course I'll stay.'

'I can't even offer you a T-shirt or anything.'

Because his frame—even though he was thinner than he'd been four years ago, as she'd pointed out—was so much larger than hers.

He rested his cheek against her hair and smiled. 'I think I can just about cope. Pink doesn't really suit me, anyway.'

To his relief, it made her laugh. Only a tiny laugh, but it was a start. Being with her was helping push her fears away—and it made him feel ten feet tall. Because he was making a difference. To the woman he loved.

'Come on, honey. Let's go and get some sleep. Do you have a spare toothbrush?'

'No, but you're welcome to borrow mine.'

She suggested that he should have the bathroom first. She was wearing a nightshirt when she climbed into bed beside him. She could've been skin to skin with him, Max thought, and he would have resisted temptation. Because he knew that right now she needed cuddles rather than sex. And he was going to give her exactly what she asked for. Exactly what she needed.

'Roll over,' he said softly, and curled his body spoon-style round hers. He drew her back against him, holding her close. She'd trusted him enough to show him her vulnerable side, and it aroused every single protective fibre in his being. 'Sleep, now,' he said. 'I'm here. And everything's going to be just fine.'

CHAPTER ELEVEN

THE next morning, Max woke with Marina in his arms. Although he knew he really ought to get up, he couldn't resist staying where he was a little longer. Waking up with her like this, on just an ordinary day... Even though the quality of the light filtering through the curtains told him that it was raining, it felt as if the day was full of sunshine simply because he was with her.

The woman he loved more than words could say.

Not that now was the right time to tell her.

Eventually, she stirred in his arms and her eyelids fluttered.

'Morning, sleepyhead,' he said softly.

She opened her eyes, instantly awake. She'd always been a morning person, he remembered. 'How long have you been awake?' she asked.

'Long enough.' He stroked her face. 'I have to go, honey. I need to drive home before the rush hour starts and get changed for work.'

'And I need to pick up Phoebe.' She brushed a kiss across his mouth. 'Thanks, Max. For staying with me, last night—I really appreciate it. And I'm sorry I was so needy.'

If he wasn't careful, she'd pull away from him again, turn all self-contained: and he wanted to avoid that. 'Hey.

I was the one who drove over here, all panicky and convinced something was wrong.'

'You didn't panic at all.' She smiled wryly. 'Nothing fazes you, Max.'

Oh, yes, it did. Losing their baby and then losing Marina had thrown him completely. And he'd tried to outpace the pain by burying himself in work. The second he'd stopped running—when he'd been immobilised in a hospital bed—he'd discovered that his demons had grown to twice the size. And he still hadn't quite conquered them.

'You'd be surprised,' he said. 'But we both have to get going. I'll see you tonight, honey.' He kissed her lightly and climbed out of bed.

'Can I make you breakfast?'

He shook his head. 'No time.' But maybe tomorrow. *If* she asked him to stay tonight…

Max was grabbing a sandwich at his desk during his lunch break, catching up on paperwork, when his mobile phone rang. He glanced at the screen, half-intending to ignore it, until he saw Marina's name on the caller display.

'Marina? Is everything all right?' he asked.

'It's fine,' she reassured him.

It was only then that he realised that he'd been holding his breath, fearing the worst.

'Sorry, I didn't mean to scare you. Nathan's doing a bit better today, so I wondered if you'd like to come and see him this evening.'

'Are you sure Rosie won't mind?' Since Nathan had been in SCBU, Max had stayed out of the way and concentrated on supporting Marina, not wanting to push in, and feeling that he didn't have the right to be part of her family any more.

'Actually, Rosie suggested it.'

'I'd love to.'

Did this mean that she didn't want to see him tonight, though? That she didn't want him to cook for her, the way he had been doing—that she'd ask him to return her keys?

He made an effort to concentrate on his patients rather than his fears, and after his shift he made his way down to SCBU. He identified himself over the intercom, and Marina came to the door to let him in.

'I haven't brought anything for the baby or Rosie,' he said, giving her a worried look. 'I know soft toys aren't suitable for here, and—'

She pressed the tip of her forefinger against his lips. 'Don't worry about it. A visit's enough.'

It had been a while since he'd last been in a special-care unit, and he'd forgotten quite how high the temperature was set. And how noisy the unit was, with monitors going off every few minutes.

He hugged Rosie. 'Congratulations. Sorry I haven't brought you anything.'

She smiled at him. 'Don't be daft! I didn't expect anything—I'm happy just to have you here. You spent so much time with me before he was born, I wanted to introduce you to my son.'

'He's beautiful.' Max stood awkwardly by the incubator, not sure what to do. Funny; in a life or death situation, he knew exactly what to do, knew what to look out for, knew how to direct others. But here he was completely out of his depth. 'I didn't realise how small he'd be.' He grimaced as soon as the words came out. 'Sorry. What a stupid thing to say.'

'He is small.' Rosie patted his shoulder. 'Though he's

not the smallest baby in here. He's feeding well and he's put on a couple of ounces.'

'That's great.'

As if sensing that he didn't have a clue what to do next, Marina said softly, 'Try putting your finger against his palm.'

'Is that…?'

'It's *fine*,' Rosie reassured him. 'Try it.'

He did so. And he wasn't prepared for the emotion that welled up as the baby's tiny fist closed around his index finger: the longing. The way his heart seemed to turn inside out. The way all his protective instincts reared up and made him want to fight dragons to protect this little boy.

This was what it could've been like for Marina and him: the first precious moments of seeing their baby, touching the soft, soft skin, seeing those blue eyes open in wonder…

Of course, he'd seen babies before. He had treated them, sometimes in the most appalling conditions. But it wasn't the same as seeing a baby who was close to you. The baby who, if he'd still been married to Marina, would've been his nephew: a blood relative of the love of his life.

He really hadn't been prepared for this surge of emotion.

Just for a moment, Max was completely unguarded. And Marina could see how overwhelmed he was; she was shocked that someone so tiny and helpless could reduce him to utter mush. She could see the emotion flickering across his face: wonder, awe—and was that wistfulness?

Would he have looked like that the first time he'd laid eyes on their baby?

'He's beautiful,' Max said again, his voice slightly cracked.

'I can't wait to take him home.' Rosie bit her lip. 'I'm

allowed to go home tomorrow, but Nathan needs to be here for at least another couple of weeks.'

'At least you can spend time here with him, and you're not going to be stuck on bed rest,' Max reminded her.

'That's true. And I can't wait to be home with Neil and Phoebe—even though I want to be here, too.'

Almost as if on cue, Neil walked in, carrying Phoebe.

'We'll go and wait outside—give you some room,' Marina said. 'Phoebe, when you've had a cuddle with Mummy, would you like to come and have supper with me before you go back to Grandma and Granddad's?'

Phoebe looked at Max, then at Marina; she nodded shyly and buried her head in her father's chest.

Max hugged Rosie goodbye and shook Neil's hand.

'Come and get me when you're ready,' Marina said. 'I'll be in the café.'

As she left the unit with Max, she asked, 'Would you like to have supper with us tonight? I'm going to make Phoebe's favourite—spaghetti Bolognese and garlic bread.' When he didn't reply immediately, she said, 'Don't feel you have to— we've taken up too much of your time already this week.'

'No, I'd like to—as long as you think Phoebe won't mind being around a stranger.'

'She might be shy with you at first, but if you're any good at building towers out of bricks that she can knock down she'll be fine.'

'I take it you have bricks?'

'I have a *great* toy box. Bricks, those little tray-type jigsaws, dinosaurs and a train set.'

He blinked. 'Phoebe's a girl.'

'She likes dinosaurs and trains as well as princessy stuff,' Marina explained with a grin. 'Let me get you a coffee.'

They'd just finished their drinks when Neil brought Phoebe in to the café. 'I've got her pushchair so she can have a nap on the way back to yours,' he said.

'And I've got a seat in the back of my car, so I'll drop her off at Mum and Dad's,' Marina said.

'You,' Neil said, 'are just brilliant. Thanks so much. Without you, these last few weeks…'

'And Max,' Marina said. 'He's been brilliant, too.'

'I know. Thanks for helping.' He shook Max's hand, then hugged Marina. 'See you later.' He strapped Phoebe into the pushchair and kissed her goodbye. 'Daddy'll be home ready for bath time, poppet.'

Back at her house, Marina dug out the toy box. 'Phoebe, Max will make you a tower while I cook the spaghetti, OK?'

Phoebe looked slightly wary and clutched at Marina's knee.

'What's her favourite colour?' Max mouthed.

'Red,' she mouthed back.

He smiled. 'Shall we start with a red brick, Phoebe? Except, I need you to show me the right one.'

'Red bick,' Phoebe said. She rummaged for a red brick and handed it to him.

'Brilliant. What colour shall we have next?' Max asked.

'Lellow.' She found a yellow brick and produced it triumphantly, balancing it on top of the brick Max had laid.

'Shall we count them as we put them up?' Max asked. 'One, two…'

Marina smiled, half-wishing she could stay to watch them, but then Max might feel uncomfortable and stop. 'I'll give you a yell when everything's ready.'

Cooking pasta while Max was playing with her niece felt odd, almost as if she had the chance to see what might have been. How their life should have been: simple domestic comforts wrapped in deep, deep love. She could hear squeaks of delight from the living room, the sound of tumbling bricks, and then suddenly Max's baritone rendition of a nursery song, punctuated with claps and giggles from Phoebe.

They'd both missed out, she thought. Phoebe on an uncle, and Max… Max on an awful lot more.

Phoebe insisted on sitting next to Max at the table. It meant that he ended up being splashed with spaghetti sauce, but he didn't seem to mind at all. And at the end of the meal he was the one who washed Phoebe's face and hands.

He was a natural.

What an amazing father he would have made.

'Do you want to come with me to drop Phoebe off?' she asked after they'd eaten.

'Better not. Things to do,' he said.

In other words, she thought, he was avoiding her parents. And she could guess why, too: in case they held the divorce against him, which of course they didn't. The Petrellis were nothing like the Fentons.

'But I'm off duty tomorrow. We could take Phoebe out, if you like—maybe to the Aquarium?' he suggested. 'Then Neil and Rosie don't have to worry while they sort out the paperwork before Rosie leaves the hospital.'

'But she's only two—how can we take her on the Tube?'

'I'll carry her. That pushchair's lightweight and easy to put up and take down, isn't it?'

'Yes.'

'Then, you handle that and I'll carry Phoebe.' He smiled. 'It'll be fun.'

A whole day with Max, doing parent-type things. In

some ways, it would hurt; in others, maybe it would help to heal. To heal him as well as her, she thought. 'I'll call Rosie from Mum's and check it's OK with her.'

'Great. Unless I hear otherwise, I'll meet you here at ten.'

At precisely ten the next morning, Marina answered her front door, with Phoebe settled on one hip. The little girl stretched out her arms and gave a beaming smile. 'Max!'

'Hello, princess,' he said easily, and took her from Marina. 'We're going to see the fish. Do you like fish?'

'P'etty fish,' Phoebe said, still beaming.

'I think that's a yes,' Marina said. 'I've got her bag and her pushchair.'

Dealing with the Tube was as easy as Max had suggested, and Phoebe loved the Aquarium. She was entranced by the seahorses, and was wide-eyed in the tunnel where she could see the sharks. Max carried her on his shoulders all the way round the exhibition, pointing things out to her and getting her to count the fish and name the colours.

Again, Marina thought what a fabulous father he would've made.

If only.

Eventually, Phoebe's eyelids started to close; Max gently strapped her back into the pushchair, and found them a space in a café on the South Bank.

'What should I get for Phoebe?' he asked. 'Juice and a sandwich?'

'No need. I've got a packed lunch in my bag for her,' Marina said.

'But it's a warm day. Won't it all be a bit icky?'

'Ice packs,' Marina explained with a grin.

He grinned back. 'Duh. I forget how efficient you Petrelli women are. OK. Cappuccino and a panini?'

He'd remembered her favourite snack. 'Yes, please.'

He made sure that Phoebe's pushchair was parked safely in the shade, then went to fetch coffee and toasted sandwiches for himself and Marina. He greeted her with a kiss when he returned with a tray, and touched Phoebe's cheek gently with the back of his fingers. 'Bless her. I think the sharks really tired her out.'

'She usually has a short nap about now. I'd say we've got about another half-hour before she wakes up,' Marina said.

'Half an hour for just you and me.' He smiled, easing himself onto the bench next to her. 'She looks so cute when she's asleep, doesn't she? Mind you, I know someone else who looks cute.' He moved closer and whispered in her ear, 'Especially when she's asleep.'

Marina couldn't help laughing. 'Max, that's so cheesy!'

'Hey. I didn't claim to be perfect. But I still think you're cute.' He kissed her again. 'And, because you're the sexiest woman I've ever met, you can have first pick of the paninis. Brie and bacon, or chicken.'

'As they've been cut in half, how about a piece of each?' she suggested.

He stole a kiss. 'That's one of the things I love about you—you're so practical.'

A woman carrying a tray and clearly looking for a spare table smiled at them. 'Your little girl's gorgeous,' she said, indicating the sleeping toddler. 'Such beautiful hair. She looks just like her mum.'

'Yes, she does,' Max said without missing a beat. 'Thank you.'

His gaze met Marina's, and she knew they were both thinking of what might have been.

'Easier not to explain,' he said when the woman had moved away.

True. And she and Max were acting like parents—as if Phoebe were their own child rather than her niece—so it was an easy mistake for a stranger to make.

'When I first saw you with Phoebe,' he said, as he if he were reading her thoughts, 'I thought she was your daughter, because she looks so much like you. I saw the way you greeted Neil. And I thought you were a family.'

'We *are* family.'

'That's not quite what I meant.' He paused. 'It hurt like hell to think of you with a child.'

A child that wasn't his. It would've been the same for her. She couldn't have faced seeing him with someone else, either. 'It hurt,' she said, 'the first time I held Phoebe.'

'Because you were thinking of our baby?'

She nodded. 'I wish I'd known whether we were going to have a girl or a boy.'

'You were thirteen weeks. It was too early to tell.'

'But it made it so much harder, Max. It meant I couldn't give our baby a name and grieve properly. All I have are dates.'

'Valentine's Day,' Max said. 'And the twenty-first of August.'

The day she'd lost the baby, and their due date.

She really hadn't expected him to remember that.

Her surprise must have shown on his face, because he said softly, 'I hate those days too. And the only way I get through them is to go to church and light a candle for our baby. When I was in the middle of a disaster zone, and there wasn't a church or a candle anywhere for miles, I looked up at the stars and I thought about our baby.'

'I had no idea.'

He shrugged. 'You never asked.'

'Because you weren't there to ask.' She closed her eyes. 'Oh, hell. This wasn't meant to be a fight. I'm not blaming you for our marriage breaking up, Max. It was just as much my fault as yours.' She dragged in a breath. 'Why didn't you follow me to London?'

'I didn't realise you wanted me to come after you. I thought you wanted some space—and preferably away from me.'

She shook her head. 'I wanted *you*, Max. I wanted to know that you cared.'

He looked shocked. 'Of *course* I cared, Marina. I married you, didn't I?'

'Because of the baby?'

'No. I admit, I probably wouldn't have asked you to marry me that soon had you not been pregnant, but I knew from the first moment I met you that you were the one I wanted to spend the rest of my life with.'

Tears stung her eyelids. 'It was the same for me. But I thought you'd changed your mind about me. That when I lost the baby you realised you'd made a mistake, and that's why you didn't come after me. Because you were secretly relieved.'

He shook his head vehemently. 'I wasn't relieved at all. It broke something inside me, something that still isn't fixed.'

So he'd really meant it when he'd told her at Greenwich that he wasn't over it either.

'That's why you divorced me—because you thought I didn't want you?' he asked.

'I thought you wanted your freedom.'

He took her hand. 'No. I wanted *you*. But you walked out on me, and I thought you'd stopped loving me because I'd let you down. You stopped talking to me, Marina.'

'Because you shut me out, Max, and I couldn't get through to you. I didn't know how.'

'You were devastated about losing the baby, and there wasn't anything I could say or do to make things better. I couldn't cope with that.' He sighed. 'And I hadn't grown up enough to realise that if I'd admitted that, and told you I was as lost as you were but I loved you, then maybe we could've helped each other through it.' The lines on his face seemed deeper, etched in pain.

'You volunteered for extra shifts at work. It felt as if you'd do anything rather than face me.'

'At work, I felt I was making a difference to somebody's life. Getting *something* right. At home, I felt helpless.' He grimaced. 'Useless. I hated that, Marina. I hated not being able to help you when you needed me, and it was a kind of vicious circle. The more you backed off, the more I backed off, and the worse it got.'

'If you'd told me that was how you felt, I would've stayed. We could've got through it together.'

He laced his fingers through hers. 'Just for the record, you were the love of my life.'

Past tense, she noticed. Did he still feel the same about her? Or was he, too, scared of being burned again—scared to believe that this time they could make it?

'And I wanted our baby as much as you did—it didn't matter that it was an unplanned pregnancy.' He blew out a breath. 'You're right. If we'd talked, really talked, we could've worked it out.'

'We can't change the past,' she said, looking away.

'No.' He didn't say anything more, but he tightened his fingers round hers. Almost as if he were trying to tell her that they could change the future.

Could they?

Max came with her to the hospital to meet Rosie and Neil and hand over Phoebe. Marina wasn't sure whether she was more relieved or disappointed when he turned down her offer of dinner.

'We could maybe go to the park tomorrow with Phoebe while Neil and Rosie are visiting Nathan,' he suggested. 'There's a playground in the park opposite the hospital. Meet you at the park at ten?'

'If it's not raining.'

'If it is raining, we'll think of something else,' Max said.

But it turned out to be another perfect spring day. Max got Phoebe to count the boats on the boating lake and tell him which one was her favourite, and then they hit the play area. He checked that she was strapped safely into the swing before pushing her high enough to make her shriek with delight, and then, when she'd had enough, he grinned at her. 'Want to go on the slide?'

It was enormous. Marina eyed it nervously. 'Max, are you sure it's safe?'

'Of course it's safe. Look.'

There were other men taking toddlers onto the slide, walking up the snake-like ramp with them and then sitting the toddlers on their lap and launching themselves off.

'It's safe,' Max repeated softly. 'I won't let anything happen to her. Come on, Princess.'

He already had a pet name for her.

And Phoebe clearly adored him. She toddled happily

alongside him and Marina watched, her heart in her mouth, as Max launched them off the slide.

'Again, again!' Phoebe said, tugging at Max's hand. 'Pease.'

'You heard the lady,' Max said with a grin, and did as the little girl had asked.

This was another side of him Marina hadn't seen. And, once her fear of Phoebe being hurt receded, she found herself enjoying watching them.

This was just how Max could have been with their children. And it put a lump in her throat; how much they'd both missed.

But she didn't want him to see her brooding. She forced a smile to her face and met him at the bottom of the slide. 'You're just a kid at heart, aren't you?' she teased.

He laughed. 'Yes. This is where I miss having brothers and sisters—I don't have a niece or nephew to borrow and do things like this. It's fun, isn't it, Princess?'

'Fun,' Phoebe said, with a smile a mile wide.

If Max had stayed with her, Marina thought, he would've known Phoebe from a babe in arms. They'd probably have a child of their own, too, a cousin for Phoebe to play with.

As if Max realised the direction her thoughts were taking, the next time he reached the bottom of the slide he lifted Phoebe to chest height. 'I think Aunty Marina needs a kiss to make her smile, don't you?'

Phoebe clapped her hands, leaned forward and kissed Marina. Then she looked at Max. 'Max kiss Rina.'

'Your wish, Princess, is my command,' Max said with a grin, then yanked Marina to him and kissed her.

After that, he kissed her every time they slid down the slide.

He kissed her at every curve of the path through the park.

And he slid one arm round her shoulders as they walked along, with Marina steering the pushchair and him holding Phoebe's hand.

It was a declaration, of sorts. And Marina wasn't sure whether she was more thrilled or scared. *Please just don't let it go wrong this time.*

CHAPTER TWELVE

ON MONDAY, Marina was back at work. The triage nurse came in with her first case. 'Brianna's twenty; she's got a headache, feels sick, tired and dizzy, and her tummy hurts. I'd say she had the flu, but she doesn't have a temperature, and she says it's been going on for a while but she feels worse today.'

'I'll come and see her,' Marina said. She introduced herself to the patient in cubicles. 'Sorry to ask you this— and I'm not judging, I'm trying to narrow down the causes of why you're feeling ill so I can help you—have you been drinking or taking anything?'

Brianna grimaced. 'I don't feel well enough to drink, and I'm not stupid enough to do drugs.'

'Could you have eaten anything that might have disagreed with you?'

'I wondered if it was food poisoning but I haven't eaten anything dodgy.'

'You're a student, aren't you?' At the girl's nod, she asked, 'Has anyone else in your house had the same symptoms?'

'My flatmate's away on a field trip, but she's been getting headaches too. I'm sorry, I'm wasting your time. I've been to the doctor at the university health-centre twice, and they say it's probably post-viral syndrome, and that I've been studying too hard or something because I've got finals this year. They say third-years always overdo it and they have loads in with the same symptoms at this time of year.'

Studying too hard might make someone feel tired and give them a headache, but stomach pains suggested something else. 'How long have you been feeling like this?'

'Since before Christmas. I felt so rough this morning, my mum nagged me to go and see someone else.'

'Did the doctor say the same thing to your flatmate?'

'Yes.' Brianna smiled weakly. 'I'm really sorry. I'm beginning to feel a bit better now; my headache isn't as bad as it was.'

'Do you find this normally—your headache's bad first thing in the morning, and then better when you've been outside for a bit?'

'Yes.'

Marina had a feeling she knew what the problem was. 'Do you have any pets?'

'No, and I'm allergic to animals anyway.'

'I want to check something with a colleague first, but I'd like to give you a breath test and a blood test.'

'For drugs?' The girl looked shocked. 'But I just told you, I don't do drugs.'

'Not for drugs,' Marina said gently, 'for carbon monoxide. What you've described are classic symptoms, but I need to test your breath now and measure it again in a couple of hours to see if the measurement changes, and if I'm right I'll need to give you oxygen therapy. Do you have gas heating in your flat?'

'Yes, but the landlord's got a safety certificate. Everything's legit.'

'Do you have carbon-monoxide testers installed?'

'No, but we've got smoke alarms.'

'I have a hunch on this, and if I'm right I'll be talking to the council so they send someone out to do a carbon-monoxide test on your flat.'

'So I don't have post-viral syndrome?'

'No, and I'm glad you listened to your mum instead of dismissing it as nagging. I'll be back in a minute, OK?' She emerged from the cubicle and went to find Max. 'Can I run something by you?'

'Sure.'

'I've got a patient presenting with flu-like symptoms but no temperature, and she's been to the health centre a couple of times and they say it's a mix of overwork and post-viral syndrome.'

'But you don't think so?'

'I researched an article last year on carbon-monoxide poisoning, and I think she's a classic case, especially as she feels better outside and her flatmate has the same kind of symptoms. What are the chances of them both having post-viral syndrome?'

'Carbon-monoxide poisoning isn't exactly something you come across in a disaster zone,' Max said thoughtfully. 'But I do remember a couple of cases at Bristol. Can you see the natural colour of her lips?'

'Yes, and she looks normal. I know it's when they're critically ill that the lips go cherry-red.'

'Check out the carbon-monoxide levels in her breath and a pulse oxymeter,' Max said. 'But you also need to check how long she's been away from her flat, because carbon monoxide has a half-life of about four hours in clean air. And if she's having arrhythmias or neurological symptoms it's better to opt for hyperbaric treatment rather than an oxygen mask.'

The test showed Marina that Brianna had higher levels of carbon monoxide in her breath than she should have, even though she'd been out of the flat for two hours.

'Carbon monoxide can have other effects,' Marina said. 'So I want to check how your heart's beating. I'm going to wire you up to a monitor, but it won't hurt. Have you had any fits or blackouts, or felt a bit disoriented?'

'No.'

'That's good.' As she set up the ECG, she explained what she was doing and why. 'Your red blood cells contain something called haemoglobin—it's what gives your blood its red colour. As it goes through your lungs, it takes up oxygen to carry it round your body, and you breathe out carbon dioxide. But, if you're exposed to carbon monoxide, the carbon monoxide bonds to the haemoglobin and stops it taking up the oxygen, so your body doesn't get enough. That's why you're not feeling very well. It also tends to make your blood vessels a bit leaky, and that's giving you a headache. So how we fix it is by giving you oxygen— basically it'll turn the carbon monoxide into carbon dioxide and you'll breathe it out.'

She checked the ECG monitor. 'The good news is that your heart's beating absolutely normally, so I can give you oxygen right here through a mask. The important thing is that you don't go back to your room until it's been checked over properly and the source of poisoning's been removed. Is there anywhere you can stay tonight, a friend's place where they haven't been suffering the same kind of thing you've been?'

Brianna nodded.

'Good. And I'm going to call the environmental health people myself, to make sure they do a test on your flat. I'll also be sending the results of your test to the health centre, and I'm going to suggest to the head of the centre that the team gets some training on carbon-monoxide poisoning.'

Over the next few days, Nathan became stronger; he was gradually spending more time without supplementary oxygen, taking larger quantities of milk and putting on weight. Max came with Marina in the evenings to visit him, and made a huge fuss of Phoebe. And, ever since Marina's hesitant suggestion, Max had started staying over, picking up a change of clothes from his flat before going over to hers, and keeping his razor and toothbrush in her bathroom.

It was almost like the early days of their relationship, when they'd first moved in together. And even though Marina was still worried about Nathan she also felt strangely at peace. As if everything was finally starting to become all right in her world.

'You look happy,' Rosie commented on the Friday.

'It's been a good day—I had a visitor today.' She smiled. 'And we have a big box of chocolates in the staff room.'

'Who's been buying you chocolates?' Rosie asked.

'One of my patients.' She looked at Max. 'Remember the girl I thought had carbon-monoxide poisoning?'

He nodded.

'The environmental health people sent someone round with a carbon-monoxide tester and it turned black overnight. It turns out the gas cooker wasn't installed properly and there was carbon-monoxide pollution in the kitchen—and her bedroom, which was next door to the kitchen.'

'So, if it wasn't for you asking the right questions, she might have been seriously ill. Died, even,' Max said.

'Yes. It's good when things turn out right and there's a happy ending,' Marina said.

Rosie gave them both a thoughtful look. 'Indeed.'

The following Wednesday, Max was sitting with Phoebe on his lap, reading her a story while Rosie fed the baby and chatted to Marina, when Louise arrived.

Max stilled. 'Sorry. I'm intruding. I'll be out of your way.'

'You're not intruding at all. Finish Phoebe's story,' Louise said with a smile. 'It'll be more than my life's worth to take her home with an unfinished book.'

He finished the story, but Marina could see the wariness on his face.

At the end, he transferred the little girl to Marina's lap. 'I'll see you later,' he said.

'Max.' Louise put her arms round him and hugged him. 'It's good to see you.'

He looked utterly taken aback; had he really thought that her mother would push him away?

'Thank you for all the support you've been giving my girls. Rosie told me. And Phoebe's been telling us about the fish and the slide.'

'She's a sweetheart,' Max said.

'And she adores you all the way back.' Louise paused. 'Please don't feel I'm pushing you out, Max. Stay as long as you like.'

'I ought to be going, anyway. Paperwork,' Max said.

Louise raised an eyebrow. 'You sound just like Marina.'

'Funny you should say that. Actually, I need to leave, too, as I have some studying to do,' Marina said.

'Oh, *you*!' Louise rolled her eyes. 'Don't be a stranger, Max,' she said gently, laying a hand on his arm. 'See you soon.'

When Marina had settled Phoebe with Louise and said her goodbyes, Max walked out of the unit with her.

'Are you really studying tonight?' he asked.

'Yes, but that doesn't mean you have to go back to yours. I can work in the kitchen, if you want to watch a film or listen to some music in the living room. And I'll make supper for us.'

'Thanks. That'd be good.'

He didn't say much until they were back at her flat. And then he sighed. 'Your mother knows about us, doesn't she?'

'Guessed,' Marina corrected.

'I didn't expect her to greet me like that. I didn't think she'd forgive me for what went wrong between us.'

'It takes two to break a marriage,' Marina said drily.

'And it takes two to make one.' His eyes were intense. 'Marina, we're good together. These last couple of weeks...'

They'd been full of worry. But they'd also been full of joy, and a burgeoning understanding between them. After that first chaste night, when she'd simply slept in his arms for comfort, they'd given in to the overwhelming attraction between them. Right now they were so in tune, both at work and at home.

'Let's give it another go.'

The words that part of her wanted so very much to hear: Max wanted them to try again. To get back together properly.

Yet fear held her back, like icy water slowly seeping through her, and she didn't know how to stop it. How to make the chill go away.

'Marina?'

She couldn't bluff this. Couldn't fudge the issue. If they were ever to have a chance, she had to be honest with him and admit her doubts. 'I'm not sure,' she hedged.

He frowned. 'Why not?'

'It didn't work last time. If it goes wrong this time, I'm not sure I'd be able to pick up the pieces.'

'Back then, we were both completely unprepared to deal with what life threw at us. It's different now. We've both grown up. Changed.' He paused. 'Marina, I want you back in my life. Permanently. And I want to make a family with you. The time we've spent with Phoebe has shown me how it could be for us.'

'So you're saying you want children?'

He nodded. 'With you.'

'What if—' she dragged in a breath, remembering how desolate she'd felt when she'd lost their baby, how empty and lonely '—what if we can't?'

He took her hand. 'Marina, lots of women have a miscarriage, sometimes even more than one, and then go on to have a baby. Just because we lost one baby, it doesn't automatically mean we'll lose another.'

She knew that—intellectually. But emotionally was another matter. Inside she was panicking, her stomach churning, still wondering: *what if?*

'And, if it does turn out we can't have children of our own, there are other ways to make a family. IVF, fostering, adoption—there are lots of options. It isn't just biology that makes a child ours.' His fingers tightened round hers. 'Let's cross that bridge when we come to it. But be very clear on this: if we *are* unlucky, if we do end up losing another baby, I won't shut you out. I won't use work as an excuse not to talk to you.'

Wouldn't he? She really wasn't so sure. 'You're going to have to put the hours in if you want to make consultant.'

He shrugged. 'I know. And senior consultant after that, and maybe even director of emergency medicine—but you and our children will come first. *Always*.'

She wanted to believe him. So badly.

But how could he be so sure it would work out? How could he be sure that panic wouldn't set in, making him react the same way he had last time?

Her doubts must have shown on her face, because he sighed. 'Life doesn't come with guarantees, Marina. Tomorrow, you or I could be knocked over crossing the road. So I can't promise you eternal happiness, and I'm not going to patronise you by saying that we're going to have a perfect life. All I can promise is that I'll try my hardest to make you happy—and I'll be right by your side in the good times as well as the bad.'

Yes.

She willed the word to come out of her mouth.

And yet she couldn't utter a single sound.

'I guess this is a case where silence *doesn't* mean consent.' He looked grim. 'So that answers my question.' He took her spare keys from his pocket. 'I think I'd better give these back to you. And, in the circumstances, supper's not a good idea.'

She stared at him in shock. He was walking out on her?

'Goodbye, Marina,' he said. 'I don't think there's anything left to say.'

The fact that he closed the front door quietly, rather than slamming it, made things worse. He wasn't stomping out in anger: he was saying goodbye with a cool head.

It was over.

* * *

Marina had no idea how she got through the next week. The roster fairy at least was on her side, as she wasn't working in the same area as Max; when he was in Resus, she was in cubicles, and when he was in cubicles, she was in the children's section. The one time when she did need help from him—with a lumbar puncture on a toddler with suspected meningitis—he was perfectly professional, but he was utterly cold to her. No eye contact, no smile, and not a single word more to her than was absolutely necessary. And it broke her heart.

The only good thing to happen was that Nathan was discharged, and Rosie was ecstatic to have him home. Although Marina was genuinely happy for her sister, she wasn't completely successful in hiding her own misery, and Rosie picked up on it the second that both Phoebe and Nathan were asleep.

'You look awful. Is something wrong between you and Max?'

'There is no me and Max. We're just colleagues.'

The deadness in her voice must have been obvious, because Rosie simply put her arms round her. 'I'm so sorry. I thought you two were working out your differences. Phoebe said you kissed when you took her out.'

'We did,' Marina admitted.

'Then what's the problem?'

'He wanted us to get back together properly.'

'But that's good, isn't it?'

When Marina didn't reply, Rosie sighed. 'Why not?'

'Because.' Marina wrinkled her nose and flapped a dismissive hand. 'It doesn't matter, Rosie, you've got enough on your plate.'

'Listen, *cara*, you were there for me when I needed

you, and I'm here for you now. And I'm going to worry an awful lot more if you don't tell me,' Rosie warned.

Marina swallowed hard. 'It didn't work out last time. How can we be sure it'll work out this time?'

'Well, there aren't any guarantees.'

'That's what he said.'

'Look at the last few weeks,' Rosie said gently. 'It's been a pretty tough time for our family, and he's been there to support you. He's even cooked you a meal every night, even though he hates being in the kitchen. Why would he do that, if he didn't love you? Cut him a bit of slack.'

'It sounds,' Marina said miserably, 'as if you're on his side.'

'I'm not taking anybody's side. I just want to see my little sister as happy as I am,' Rosie said. 'You never got over Max, and he never got over you. I know it was a mess last time—but you've talked through what went wrong, haven't you?'

Marina nodded.

'You've both changed over the last four years. If you'd lost the baby now, it would've been completely different—you both would've coped a lot better.' Rosie's eyes widened. 'You're not pregnant again, are you? Is that what you're not telling me?'

'No. Of course not.'

'So it's not hormones making you look like that.' She sighed. 'It's because you're missing him. And I bet he's just as miserable as you are. Marina, when are you going to stop punishing yourself—and him?'

'I'm not punishing myself. Or him.'

'No?' Rosie raised an eyebrow. 'What are you holding back?'

Marina sighed. 'I'm just scared that it'll all go wrong again, and I don't know how to get past the fear.'

'Then talk to Max, *cara*. Tell him how you feel. Because the only way you're going to work this out is together.' Rosie patted her shoulder. 'Remember that Tennyson poem I studied for my finals? He had a point: "Tis better to have loved and lost Than never to have loved at all",' she quoted. 'Do you really want to give up on everything you could have with Max just because you're scared of losing it?' She spread her hands. 'From where I'm standing, you're losing it right now. Talk to him, Marina—before it's too late.'

Marina slept badly that night, brooding over what her sister had said. And at stupid o'clock she finally came to a decision: the only way to get past the fear was to face it head on. To talk to Max. Work it out with him.

Though she knew she'd hurt him. Badly. She owed him an apology before she could ask him to help her sort things out in her head.

But she didn't have the chance to talk to him at work, to ask him to meet her for lunch or after their shift. He was already in Resus when she arrived, and she was with a patient just before lunch when Ellen, the head of the department, put the department on alert for a major incident.

'There's a huge fire at a hotel just down the road—a boiler exploded and the whole place went up. So we're expecting an influx of patients with burns, scalds, smoke inhalation and possibly crush injuries; right now, we don't know what to expect,' Ellen said. 'I've sent Max out to head up the rapid-response team.'

It made sense, given Max's experience in disaster zones, but it also meant that he was walking straight into danger.

Ice trickled down Marina's spine. Fires were notoriously unpredictable. All it would take was a change in the direction of the wind, and he could end up surrounded by the inferno. And he might not make it back.

Please let him come back safely. Let her have another chance to apologise and explain, and tell him how she really felt about him.

She listened to Ellen's instructions about the procedures; she'd be working with the Resus team on the priority one patients, Eve was heading Triage at the main ambulance entrance, and they'd use the pre-prepared major-incident folders for all patients because there wouldn't be time to use the computerised system.

They'd just about cleared the reception area of patients when the first casualties came in. She assessed each patient as quickly and as carefully as she could, taking blood samples and giving fluids. Patients with burns needed plenty of fluids to support their circulation and avoid the risk of ending up with pulmonary oedema; during the first four hours, the extra fluid needed was calculated by the percentage of burns multiplied by their weight in kilograms, divided by two, so she double-checked the calculations to make sure.

Patients came in, already on oxygen and with IV lines in, their burns covered with sterile sheets. One particular patient had severe burns to his chest, which restricted his chest movement and in turn his ability to breathe. Marina had seen an escharotomy done before but had never done one herself; however, with the rest of the senior doctors busy with cardiac arrests and patients with severe inhalation injuries, she had no option. Her patient couldn't afford to wait. Although the experience was one of the grimmest she'd ever had in her years in the emergency department,

Marina reassured her patient, cut the burnt areas of his skin down to the viable tissue along the line of his ribcage, across his sternum, and then made eight parallel-downward cuts. Just as she'd finished and her patient was able to breathe again, Ellen came across. 'Good job, Marina,' she said approvingly.

They were so busy that Marina completely lost track of time. She forced herself not to think of Max and worry about whether he was safe—with his experience in disaster zones, she just knew that he'd ignore any risks. Wasn't that how he'd ended up with a house collapsing on him in an earthquake zone? Something that still gave him nightmares.

Eventually, the flood of patients steadied to a trickle, but Max still wasn't back.

She was walking through the reception area on the way back from the loo when she heard the news reporter saying that one of the rescue team was hurt.

No names, no details: but her first thought was Max.

And if he was hurt badly there was a possibility that she would lose him before she could tell him how she felt about him. Before she could tell him that she loved him. Before she could tell him that she was scared stupid about things going wrong again, but she was willing to take that risk—if he was still willing to give her the chance.

She headed for the triage area to talk to Roland, the ambulance controller.

'Roly, I just heard the news. One of the rescue team's been hurt. Do you know who it is?' Not caring any more whether the hospital grapevine would start to talk about her, she asked urgently, 'Please tell me it isn't Max. Please. I need to talk to someone on site to be sure it's not him.'

* * *

Max—tired and dirty after a very long day—walked from the ambulance bay to the triage area. He recognised Marina instantly and he could hear the panic in her voice as she asked Roland about him—panic, desperation and fear.

So did that mean she cared after all?

'Marina,' he said.

She whipped round and burst into tears as she saw him.

'It's all right, mate—no need to ring in to the RRT,' he said to Roland. 'We're all back now.'

Marina was shaking. 'Max, I thought you were…'

He wrapped his arms round her and drew her over to a quiet corner. 'In need of a shower and a cold drink, and some sleep, but I'm OK. It was one of the firefighters who was hurt, but he's going to be fine. What about you? It must've been pretty bad here, too.'

'Not like being in the front line.' She was holding him just as tightly. 'Max, if you'd been hurt and I hadn't had a chance to tell you—'

'I know,' he cut in softly. 'Me, too. I was just glad you weren't out there. I'd have gone crazy with worry about you. At least I knew you were safe here. Rushed off your feet and under a huge amount of stress, but *safe*.'

They were both shaking now.

'I stink of smoke and sweat,' he said.

'I don't care.' She refused to let him go, holding him more tightly.

'I need a shower and a change of clothes.' He rested his cheek against her hair. 'Come home with me?'

The word she'd wanted to say a week ago—the word she should've said a week ago—finally she was able to say it.

'Yes,' she whispered.

CHAPTER THIRTEEN

THEY went back to Max's flat, their arms wrapped tightly round each other all the way.

'Have you had a chance to eat today?' Max asked as they walked into his kitchen.

'I had a sandwich earlier.' She had no idea how long ago it had been. 'But I'm not hungry.'

'Too tired?'

She nodded.

'Me, too,' he admitted. 'Which is probably just as well, because my kitchen's in Dr Hubbard mode. But I do need a cold drink.' He filled two glasses of water and handed one to her. He downed his in two swallows and refilled it, this time drinking it more slowly. Then he sniffed his armpit again and grimaced. 'I *really* need that shower. Come and wash my back?'

It was a ridiculously tight squeeze in the cubicle, but she didn't care, and she could see on his face that he didn't care either. Right then they needed to have each other in their sight, just to be sure each other was safe. Tenderly, she washed him clean, washed all the smoke, dirt and grit out of his hair, and he did the same for her.

Usually, when they were naked and in a shower, passion

would flare between them: but tonight it went deeper than that, emotion so raw that only gentleness would do.

Finally, they dried each other. Max pulled on a pair of clean jeans and wrapped Marina in his bathrobe. She held him tightly, resting her cheek against his chest. 'I'm sorry, Max. Sorry for pushing you away and hurting you.'

'So why did you do it?'

'Because I was scared. Scared that it might all go wrong again.'

'Scared that I'd let you down, the way I did last time?'

She dragged in a breath. 'I know I was wrong.'

'Marina, honey, what do you think I've spent the last few weeks doing?' he asked.

'Being there for me. Helping to take the worry away.'

'With actions, not words. Doesn't that prove to you that it'll be different in the future—that I've changed? That we've *both* changed?'

'I know.' She closed her eyes. 'But I couldn't get past the fear. Not until today, when I thought you were hurt— when I thought I might have lost you and I wouldn't be able to tell you how I feel about you.'

'Now might be quite a good time to tell me,' he said softly.

So she was going to be the one to say it first. To take the risk.

Though when she looked at him his expression told her the same as the words stuck in her throat. And she could see that he needed to hear it as badly as she did.

Given that she'd been the one to push him away, she was the one who needed to make it better between them. To say it.

'I love you,' she said. 'I thought I hated you at one point. But underneath it all I always loved you. A bit of me hoped that when you got the divorce papers it'd be like chucking cold water over you: you'd wake up, realise what we had and come and get me back.' She swallowed hard. 'But you just ignored them. My solicitor had to send them three times.'

'I didn't get them until I came back to England. And even then I wasn't in a position to sign because I'd broken my right arm and couldn't hold a pen.'

'But you signed them eventually.'

He nodded. 'I thought that was what you wanted.'

'I told myself it was what I wanted.' She sighed. 'I tried to move on. But nobody ever quite matched up to you. I always ended things after the second date.'

'Same here. I dated, and there was always something missing. It was because she wasn't you.'

She stroked his face. 'Max, we've wasted so much time.'

'In one sense, yes. But it's given us both time to grow up and learn what's important.' He dipped his head and brushed a kiss across her mouth. 'Do you know now that I love you and that's not going to change?'

'Yes. And I love you.'

'But?'

He'd picked up on her last doubts. 'There is one thing.' She bit her lip. 'Your parents never liked me, Max. I know you're close to them, and I don't want to make you feel torn between us. It isn't fair to them or to you.'

'You're not marrying them, you're marrying me—at least, I hope you are,' he said. 'Besides, it might not be the issue you think it is. None of my girlfriends before you were ever good enough for me either, in my mother's eyes. But this time I think she'll accept that I'm an adult and I've found the woman I wanted to share the rest of my life with.'

'Will she?' The words came out before Marina could stop them.

His gaze held hers. 'She's changed. A lot of things have changed. Even if the accident hadn't happened when it did, I would still have had to come home.' He paused. 'Dad had a heart attack.'

'Is he all right now?'

'He died. About two hours before I could get to the hospital.'

Marina stared at him in shock. She'd had no idea that Andrew Fenton had even been ill, much less that he was dead. Max hadn't said a word.

Then again, maybe he'd been too busy supporting her and hadn't wanted to burden her with his grief.

He hadn't had the chance to say goodbye to his father. Hadn't had the chance to hold his hand while he lay dying and say 'I love you'.

'Max, I'm so sorry. I know you thought a lot of him.'

'Past tense,' he said drily. 'It wasn't just that he had a heart attack, Marina. I found out after the funeral that it happened while he was in bed with his mistress.'

'Oh, Max. That's… I don't know what to say.' Not only had he lost his father, then, he'd also lost his ideals and had his family blown apart. She tightened her arms round him. 'That must've been so hard for your mother. And for you.'

'It turned out,' Max said, 'that he'd been having affairs for years. All those business trips… Half the time, he had another woman accompanying him. My mother turned a blind eye because— Well, I suppose because she loved him, and she hoped that if she put up with it he wouldn't leave her.'

'And it's why she clung to you so much,' Marina said

softly, enlightenment dawning. 'Why she couldn't bear the idea of losing you to another woman, the way she was losing her husband.' She kissed him lightly. 'Yet she did lose you, because you went abroad. It must have been hell for her, watching the disaster zones on the news and worrying herself sick because you were out there. It was bad enough for me today, and I only had one day of it. She had three years of worry.' She blew out a breath. 'Maybe we can find some common ground this time round—because we both love you. And love stretches, Max; it isn't like a cake that you have to cut into smaller and smaller pieces.'

'I think my mother's beginning to see that that now,' Max said. 'Because she's found someone else. It's still early days, but Rupert treats her better than my father ever did. I think she's beginning to realise that if you love someone it's safe to let them go, because they'll want to come back, whereas if you smother them they'll pull away and not want to be near you.' He frowned. 'Maybe it's why Dad had all those affairs—because she was so anxious to be the most important person in his life that it made him feel trapped, and it was his way of escaping.'

'And it was a vicious circle—the more he did it, the more scared she became, the more she tried to bind him to her, and the more he tried to escape. Poor Kay.' She stroked his hair back from his forehead. 'And poor you. I know you looked up to your dad.'

'He wasn't who I thought he was.' Max lifted a shoulder in a half-shrug. 'I had plenty of time to think about it.'

'While you were stuck in a hospital bed.'

'I wasn't the best of patients,' Max admitted.

'Medics never are—and you'd already had enough dumped on you. Being hurt so you couldn't work, your father dying and then having to deal with all the emotional fallout of what you'd learned.'

'I stopped believing in love and marriage for a while.' He stroked her face. 'Though your family's restored my faith there.'

'I'm glad.' She bit her lip. 'Though it couldn't have helped, having divorce papers waiting for you when you got back to England.'

'When I finally opened them, I was livid. I had a fit and threw them over the other side of the room,' Max said ruefully. 'Except then, because of my leg, I couldn't get down to pick them up again. Luckily a friend came in to visit me before my mother did, and she got rid of the evidence for me.'

'She?'

'It's possible for a man to have female friends,' Max said. 'And, believe me, I was in no fit state to think about anything more than friendship. I was either stuck in traction or stuck in a wheelchair.'

Max wasn't the still, quiet sort. He was happiest in the thick of action. 'It must have driven you crazy.'

'It did. I had hours and hours and hours with nothing to do except brood. I thought of you—a lot. And ranted a bit. Your ears must've been burning.'

'I ranted about you, too,' Marina admitted.

'I was so sure I hated you,' Max said. 'And then I came to London and opened that curtain and saw you.'

'In all the emergency departments in all the world, you had to walk into mine,' she quipped.

'Yup. And then I discovered that, actually, I didn't hate you. That was just a mask, a way of coping with what I'd lost. I couldn't keep my eyes off you. And when I thought that Neil was your husband... Well, put it this way, my physio would've taken me to task for overdoing it at the gym that evening.'

'Oh, Max.'

'And you wore those jeans to taunt me at the bowling alley.'

'My jeans are perfectly respectable,' Marina said. 'Besides, I didn't know you were going to be there that night. Might I point out that *you* were wearing soft, very touchable denims yourself?'

A teasing glint lit his eyes. 'You wanted to touch me, then?'

'I wanted to take you home, rip your clothes off and have my wicked way with you,' Marina said.

The glint intensified. 'I seem to remember you did that a few days later. In my flat. Come to think of it, not very far from where we are right now.'

'This isn't home,' Marina said.

'Actually, it is.' He leaned forward and stole a kiss. 'Home's wherever *you* are. Everything else is just trappings.' He stroked her face. 'I think we've been given a second chance. Are you brave enough to take it?'

This time, she didn't hesitate. Didn't need to. 'Yes,' she said. 'Because I know you'll be there right beside me.'

His kiss was warm and sweet and full of promise.

'So, are we going to take it steady this time? Court each other all over again?' she asked.

'Not on your life,' Max said. 'I've spent four years missing you, and the last week in the uttermost reaches of hell. I want you back in my life permanently, starting right now.'

'Marry in haste...' she warned him. 'Didn't you learn that last time round?'

'We don't have to set a date right now. Actually, you don't even have to marry me, if you don't want to.' His eyes were very, very blue, full of sincerity and love. 'Just be with me, Marina. You're the love of my life; I've missed you so much that it hurt even to breathe, and I don't want to spend any more time without you. I don't care where we live, or whether you call yourself Fenton or Petrelli. I just want you back with me. For good. And starting right now.' He paused. 'One more thing: we talk. Even if we think what we say might be upsetting, if we're unhappy about something, we talk about it. No hiding in work. Deal?'

'Deal.' And she sealed it with a kiss.

EPILOGUE

Fourteen months later

'How did we get to be so lucky?' Max asked, coming to stand behind Marina and wrapping his arms round her waist. He rested his chin on her shoulder and looked through the kitchen window to the garden. His mother and Marina's were sitting next to each other in the shade, chatting away and cooing over Carly Rosamond Fenton, the youngest member of the family. Rupert, his mother's partner, was manning the barbecue with Marina's father. Rosie was taking dishes of salad through to the huge table set ready for lunch under the gazebo, and Neil and various Petrelli aunts, uncles and cousins were chatting in groups and playing with the children.

Max had grown up with a small, intense family. Now he was part of a huge, noisy one that believed in fun and love and laughter—and his mother and Rupert had been accepted right along with him. Over the last year his mother had relaxed, discovering that she wasn't losing a son but gaining a daughter, and a whole new family to boot. Marina had made a point of sitting down and talking with her, and making her realise that she was always going to be part of their lives—that there would be room for her.

'I think,' Marina said, turning round in his arms and kissing him, 'That we make our own luck.'

'Tut tut. Put each other down, you two,' Rosie teased from the doorway to the garden. 'You're supposed to be getting drinks, Max. And you're supposed to be sorting out the buns for the burgers and the rolls for the hotdogs,' she told her sister. 'Dad and Rupert sent me in to find out where you'd got to because everything's almost ready.'

Marina laughed. 'Is it my fault that I have the sexiest husband in the world? He distracted me.'

'On the contrary, *you* distracted *me*,' Max countered. 'So I think that deserves a forfeit.' He stole another kiss.

Rosie spread her hands. 'Honestly, you two. Anyone would think that you were newlyweds!'

'We are. We only got married a year ago today,' Marina said.

'And what a year it's been,' Max said softly. Marrying the love of his life; being promoted to consultant in a unit where he was most definitely part of the team. And becoming a father to a baby girl who'd taught him that the Petrellis knew exactly what they were talking about: love stretched and grew along with the family. 'Life doesn't get any better than this.'

'Tell me that in twenty-five years,' Rosie said. 'When we're celebrating your silver wedding and you've got grandchildren in your arms.'

Max looked at his wife and smiled. 'You know, I think you might just be right…'

MIRACLE: MARRIAGE REUNITED

BY
ANNE FRASER

MILLS & BOON

First published in Great Britain 2010
Harlequin Mills & Boon Limited,
Eton House, 18-24 Paradise Road, Richmond, Surrey TW9 1SR

© Anne Fraser 2010

ISBN: 978 0 263 87682 6

Harlequin Mills & Boon policy is to use papers that are natural, renewable and recyclable products and made from wood grown in sustainable forests. The logging and manufacturing process conform to the legal environmental regulations of the country of origin.

Printed and bound in Spain
by Litografia Rosés, S.A., Barcelona

Anne Fraser was born in Scotland, but brought up in South Africa. After she left school she returned to the birthplace of her parents, the remote Western Islands of Scotland. She left there to train as a nurse, before going on to university to study English Literature. After the birth of her first child she and her doctor husband travelled the world, working in rural Africa, Australia and Northern Canada. Anne still works in the health sector. To relax, she enjoys spending time with her family, reading, walking and travelling.

Recent titles by the same author:

SPANISH DOCTOR, PREGNANT MIDWIFE*
THE PLAYOY DOCTOR'S SURPRISE PROPOSAL
FALLING FOR HER MEDITERRANEAN BOSS
POSH DOC CLAIMS HIS BRIDE

Brides of Penhally Bay

CHAPTER ONE

DR ROBINA ZONDI studied the austere man addressing the conference delegates and sucked in her breath. Dr Niall Ferguson, the keynote speaker and the man on whom the success of her book depended, was disturbingly good looking and surprisingly sexy. Somehow she had expected someone middle-aged, not this Adonis with a beak of a nose that prevented fine features from being too beautiful. He couldn't be more than thirty—thirty-five tops. Young surely to exude such easy confidence. As he spoke, he pushed a lock of dark hair which kept flopping across his brow aside with impatient fingers.

She had looked him up on the internet, but there had been no photographs accompanying the rather dry but impressively long list of credentials. She certainly hadn't expected to be enthralled—as everyone else in the conference appeared to be—by his presentation. No polite, bored coughing had interrupted the smooth flow of words, as he emphasised key points in his lilting Scottish accent. It was a flawless and professional performance and as soon as the question-and-answer session was over, he was surrounded by journalists and attendees all vying for his attention.

This was going to be harder than she'd anticipated.

The butterflies that had been setting up home in her stomach were creating havoc. It was very likely that he would send her away with a flea in her ear, but Robina had never been one to give up without trying. If her easy-to-read guide on infertility were to be taken seriously, she needed someone of his stature to give it his seal of approval. Her publishing company had sent him a copy, but he hadn't even had the decency to acknowledge its receipt. To be fair, he probably had loads of people wanting his views or his endorsement. When she had read on the internet that he was to attend a conference in Cape Town, the opportunity to ask him face to face had seemed too good to miss.

Robina waited until he was finally alone before approaching him.

'Dr Ferguson, may I have a word?' Blue eyes, the colour of the rarest of Kimberley diamonds, looked up. He frowned as if trying to place who she was.

'You don't know me,' she said quickly. 'I'm Dr Robina Zondi. I know you're a busy man, but could I have a minute?'

He stood and Robina was disconcerted to find that he towered over her. Taller than he had appeared at the podium, he had to be at least six feet three. It was all she could do not to take a step back.

'Of course,' he said politely. 'Please have a seat.'

Robina dipped into her briefcase and pulled out a copy of her book.

'I hope you don't mind, Dr Ferguson,' she said quickly before her courage failed her, 'but I have a favour to ask you.' She handed him the book.

'*A Guide to Infertility,*' he said quietly, glancing at the cover. 'How can I help?' He smiled encouragingly and his face relaxed, making him seem more human and even more devastatingly handsome.

But before she could launch into her carefully prepared speech, a short, dark-skinned man appeared and elbowed his way past Robina. 'Dr Ferguson, I'm Professor Lessing, based at Groote Schuur Hospital. I've been trying to get a hold of you for weeks now, and I wondered if I could have a moment?' He glanced at his watch, making it clear that he was a busy man.

'I'm sorry, Professor,' Dr Ferguson said in his deep lilting voice that made Robina think of water rushing over rocks, 'but I'm afraid this lady got here first. Perhaps we could schedule a time later on?'

'Please, go ahead,' Robina interrupted. 'I can wait. Actually, I'm dying for something to drink, so can I get you something while you speak to this gentleman?'

'You wouldn't mind? In that case a glass of iced water would be great.' He grinned and a dimple appeared at the side of his mouth. Robina's heart skipped a beat. She tried to tell herself it was just nervousness about her book that was turning her legs to jelly and her mouth to dust. February in Cape Town was hot enough without being in a crowded room where the air-conditioning had broken down. If Dr Ferguson was feeling the heat, he gave no sign of it.

By the time she fought her way back through the crowds with three glasses of iced water on a tray, it looked as if whatever the professor had been discussing with their guest speaker hadn't made him very happy. Just as Robina approached, the older man leapt to his feet, knocking the tray of drinks from her hands. Robina watched in horror as three glasses spun in the air, spilling ice cubes and water over Dr Ferguson and his companion.

'For God's sake, woman,' Professor Lessing growled, dabbing at his suit. 'How can you be so careless?'

Robina glared back. It hadn't been her fault. If he hadn't jumped to his feet without looking, the drinks would have stayed on the tray. She bit back the words and glanced at Niall. A small smile tugged at the corner of his mouth.

'I don't know about anyone else,' he said slowly, 'but a cool shower was just what I needed.' He looked at Robina and grinned.

'Stupid girl,' the professor muttered irritably, still dabbing at his suit.

All of a sudden the smile left Dr Ferguson's face. 'What did you say?' he asked quietly.

'She should have looked where she was going.'

Dr Ferguson's eyes glittered. 'I think we all know whose fault it was. Now, Professor, if you would excuse us?'

The older man looked as if he were about to protest, but something in Niall's expression stopped him in his tracks. 'I don't see any further need to meet again,' he said tightly. 'You've made your position quite clear.' And with that he turned on his heel and left.

'I'm so sorry,' Robina said.

'Don't be. The man has an over-inflated opinion of himself. And he's a bore—even more unforgivable. You did me a favour, actually. He wants me to put my name to some paper he's presenting, but I told him I'm not interested. I'm afraid he wasn't too happy.' He sat back down in his chair, indicating to Robina that she sit too. 'Now, where were we?'

Robina wiped droplets of water off the front of her book and pushed it across the table. 'I know I have a cheek asking, but I wondered…' She paused. Now it came to actually asking the question it seemed ridiculously forward. But she was here now and she could hardly just get up and leave. 'I wondered if you would read my book and consider writing the foreword?' There, it was out. He could laugh in her face, or send her packing, but at least she had asked.

He turned the book over in his hands. 'As a matter of fact, I have already read it. It was sent to me by your publisher. I've been kind of busy, otherwise I would have replied by now.' He leaned back in his chair and scrutinised her face. Robina felt her pulse kick up a gear. What if he'd hated it?

'I thought it was well written,' he said, to her relief, 'and very accurate. I particularly liked the style—informal without being patronising. I can see the need for a book like this. We specialists aren't always the best people to explain complicated medical issues to the general public.' He grinned and Robina's heart somersaulted.

'But what makes you qualified to write it? I haven't heard your name associated with the sub-specialty, and I know most people,' he continued, his eyes never straying from hers. The way he was looking at her made her feel they were the only two people in the room. Her heart thudded against her ribs.

'I'm a doctor—a GP—but before that I was a journalist.'

'And being a GP makes you qualified to write such a book?' he queried, his eyes drilling into hers, but then his gaze softened. 'Or is there a more personal reason?'

She shook her head. 'Purely professional. I saw loads of women at my surgery who wanted to know about infertility, but didn't know where to go. Often they didn't know if they even needed treatment. Their questions were what gave me the idea for the book.' She stumbled slightly over the words. When she said it like that, it did sound a little simplistic. He wasn't to know about the hours she had spent researching the area and more particularly, talking to women, finding out what they wanted to know rather than what the experts thought they *should* know.

His eyes dropped to the bare fingers of her left hand and then he looked up at her and grinned again. Robina caught her breath. Never in her twenty-eight years had a man had such an effect on her and suddenly, crazy though it was, Robina knew that she was smitten.

Niall looked over her shoulder and Robina turned to see a group of people bearing purposefully down on them. Niall stood suddenly and whispered in her ear.

'Let's get out of here,' he said, 'before I get trapped.'

Robina could no more have refused him than she could have walked across the Atlantic. She tried to pretend to herself that the opportunity to have access to one of the leading lights in infertility was the reason, but gave up that notion the second he gripped her elbow and steered her outside. Suddenly the last thing she wanted to talk about was work. Instead she wanted to know every personal detail about this man, down to the name of his first pet.

He led her to an open-top sports car and helped her into the front seat.

'Where are we going?' she asked, not really caring.

'I thought you could show me a bit of your country. In return for me endorsing your book?'

'So you'll do it, then, Dr Ferguson?' Her heart was still doing its ridiculous pitter-patter and it had nothing to do with the relief she felt at his words. What was the matter with her? She was reacting like some star-struck groupie.

'Yes, but only if we have a deal. And by the way, it's Niall.'

Robina forced herself to breathe normally before she replied. 'Have you been to Cape Town before?'

'Once, but I never got out of the hotel.'

'You are kidding, right?' she said incredulously. 'You came all the way here and didn't see anything? Not Table Mountain, Chapman's Peak, the vineyards? Nothing?'

All of a sudden his smile vanished and his expression turned bleak. 'There wasn't time,' he said shortly. 'I had…' he paused '…only a couple of days. I didn't want to leave my daughter for too long.'

So he was married, Robina thought, aware of a crashing sense of disappointment. He hadn't been wearing a ring, but many men didn't.

'And your wife?' she said lightly. 'Did she come with you?'

'My wife's dead,' he said quietly. 'She died two years ago.'

This time there was no mistaking the raw pain that shadowed his face.

Before she could help herself, she reached across and squeezed his hand. 'I'm so sorry. She must have been very young.'

'Thirty.' He sucked in a breath as if it hurt him to say the words. 'Mairead died just six months before that last conference. Unfortunately, these things are arranged months—even years—in advance. I couldn't get out of it, but I didn't want to leave my daughter for a second longer than I had to. I flew back as soon as the conference finished. I don't think I saw anything apart from the inside of my hotel.'

'But you've got more time this trip?' Robina thought it wise to get the subject onto safer ground.

'I have the rest of the weekend,' he said. 'The first flight back I could get is on Monday. So until then, I'm all yours.' He looked at her and Robina felt the world spin. Never before had she experienced such an instant, overwhelming reaction to a man. 'So where are we going first? What do you recommend?'

'What do you want to see? The tourist Africa or the real Africa?'

'The real Africa, of course, that's why I've kidnapped you.' Her heart lurched. If only that were true! The thought of being kidnapped by this enigmatic man sent all sorts of fantasies spinning around her brain. Stop being ridiculous, she told herself. He wanted a guide in exchange for his help, nothing more. From the expression on his face when he'd mentioned his wife, he must have loved her very much. And he had a daughter. All very good reasons for Robina to run a mile.

'So, where to?' he asked a little later as he put the car into gear and exited the conference car park. They came to a T-junction. 'Left or right?'

'Right.' She paused as a thought struck her. 'You're not afraid of heights, are you?'

'I'm probably going to regret this but, no, I'm not. Why, are you?'

'Terrified!' Robina admitted with a smile. 'But I would never forgive myself if I didn't take you up Table Mountain—especially on a beautifully clear day like today. I know it's a bit touristy, but everyone has to go up at least once in their lifetime. So why don't we start there? And then…'

'Then we'll see,' he finished the sentence for her. There was something in the tone of his voice that sent a shiver up Robina's spine. It was a promise and a warning. She knew that if she wasn't to get in too deep, now was the time to call a halt. But even as the thought formed in her mind, she knew it was too late. She could do nothing except allow this man to pull her along in his wake and enjoy the ride. For once she was going to throw caution to the wind and let life take her where it would.

As they waited in the queue for the cable car, they chatted easily about work. When their turn came to board, Robina's heart began to race. Although she had made the trip many times before, each time she was swamped by a rush of anxiety. The doors opened and Robina immediately clutched the handrail that encircled the oval cable car. But she knew it would be worth it once they got to the top— the views over Cape Town and the South Atlantic Ocean were breathtaking. Niall would be impressed.

'Are you all right?' he asked quietly, and she could feel his breath on her neck.

'I'm fine, really. Like I told you, I'm just not very good with heights.' She looked up at him and smiled with as much reassurance as she could muster.

'For some reason, I didn't think of you as someone who could be afraid of anything.' He placed a comforting arm on her shoulder and she felt the heat of his fingers burning her bare skin.

And suddenly she wasn't frightened any more. Before she knew it, they had reached the top and were spilling out onto the flat top of Table Mountain.

Two hours stretched into three then four as they explored the trails along the top of the mountain, eventually retreating to the outside restaurant for a late lunch. A cool breeze tickled their skin and Robina thought she had never felt as happy as she did at that moment.

Niall topped up their water glasses. 'So is this where you take all your guests?' he asked.

Robina took a sip of her drink and pointed to an island in the distance. 'Do you see that strip of land over there?'

He nodded.

'That's Robben Island. Where Nelson Mandela was incarcerated.' She felt the tears prickle behind her eyes and she blinked furiously.

But she was too late. Niall touched her hand. 'Hey, are you all right?' he said gently.

'I come here at least once a year,' Robina said.

Niall raised an eyebrow in a silent question. 'On the anniversary of my father's death,' she continued.

'Was he there too?' Niall probed gently.

'For six months. When he was a young man.' She turned to face him. 'It's open to the public now, but I somehow can't bring myself to go there. It would be too painful. So I come up here and pay my respects instead.' Robina took a deep breath.

'You know the prisoners spent their free time teaching each other whatever they knew, so that by the time they were released, they would have the skills and knowledge to lead a government. My parents had to leave South Africa when they got married. At that time it was still illegal for a white woman and a black man to marry. They continued their work in the UK, before returning here in the early eighties. My father said not living in Africa was like not being able to breathe.'

'He sounds like a remarkable man.'

'He was. I've spent my whole life trying to be someone he could be proud of.'

Niall grinned and, taking her hand in his, rubbed her fingers. 'It looks like you succeeded.'

'I don't know. Maybe. Perhaps if he were here to tell me himself...' She shook her head. 'Anyway, enough about me.' Suddenly she was appalled. How had she let herself go on like that? She never discussed her private thoughts with anyone, yet here she was spilling her heart out to a relative stranger. 'I just wanted you to experience Table Mountain—even if you see nothing else,' she added lamely.

'Thank you for showing me. And sharing with me.' Gesturing the waiter over, Niall peeled off a pile of rand notes.

'Where to next?' he asked as they stood up. When he took her hand, it felt like the most natural thing in the world.

'I want you to meet my grandmother,' Robina said impulsively. 'She lives about an hour's drive from Cape Town.'

'I'd like that,' Niall said simply.

As they drove into the township, leaving a flurry of dust in their wake, Niall kept glancing at the woman sitting beside him. It wasn't just that she was the most beautiful creature he had ever seen, with her exotic almond eyes, smooth dark skin and elegant long limbs, but her strange mix of nervousness and passion enchanted him. Every minute he spent with her, he felt himself falling more and more under her spell. Never in a million years had he ever thought he would meet anyone again who made his pulse race the way this woman did.

Now that the heat of the day had passed, people were beginning to emerge from the cool shelter of their houses. Women were returning from the well, balancing enormous pots on their heads, while still others carried long sheaves of firewood in the same way. A number of schoolgirls mimicked the older women, balancing their school books in neat piles on top of their heads. It could have been a different world.

Robina pointed to a mud house with a neat fence and a small verandah where an old woman was rocking gently as she worked with her hands.

As Robina got out of the car, the old woman stood unsteadily, leaning heavily on a stick. When she saw Robina, a smile spread across her broad face. 'Mzukulwana!'

Niall waited as Robina hugged her grandmother. There followed a long stream of words incomprehensible to Niall. Finally Robina stood back and beckoned him forward.

'Niall, I'd like you to meet my grandmother. Makhulu, this is Dr Niall Ferguson.' She repeated her words in the same language she had used to greet her grandmother and listened carefully to the reply.

'My grandmother says you are welcome to her home and asks if you would sit. I'm afraid she only has a little English—she speaks mainly Xhosa.'

'Could you tell her that I'm honoured to meet her?' Niall said, taking the older woman's hand. The old lady shook his hand warmly.

They sat on the verandah drinking tea as the shadows began to lengthen. Before long there was a group of curious women gathered in front of the house.

'Sisi,' they called. 'Who is this good looking man you have brought to meet your grandmother?' And then they added something in Xhosa that made Robina blush. She replied in the same language and it seemed from the appreciative laughter that she was giving as good as she got.

Niall could have sat there all afternoon just listening to the babble of voices and looking at Robina. He had never met anyone like her before—she was a strange mix of the modern and the traditional. One moment shy, the next joking with her grandmother's neighbours and friends. He was happy, he thought, surprised. He hadn't felt like this since Mairead had died.

Eventually Robina stood. 'I have one more place to show you,' she said as she kissed her grandmother goodbye. 'Unless you want to get back to the hotel?' she added anxiously. 'Perhaps you've had enough for one day?'

Niall shook his head. 'No,' he said quietly. 'Right now there is nowhere I'd rather be than with you.' Robina blushed again at his words and Niall knew she wasn't immune to him either.

By the time they arrived at their next destination, the sun was beginning to set, casting a rosy hue over the mountains and turning the sea red-gold.

They pulled up outside a house set on its own, almost overhanging a cliff. Niall got out of the car and drank in the views. The front of the house seemed to be almost suspended over the waves that crashed against the rocks, spraying a fine mist. Below was a stretch of beach as far as the eye could see. There were no other houses in sight. They could have been the only people left on the planet. Perfect.

A notice-board outside the house proclaimed that the house was for sale and gave a number for enquiries.

Curious, Niall raised a questioning eyebrow.

'This was my mother's parents' house,' Robina said. 'They lived here up until they retired to Gauteng a couple of years ago. They passed it on to my parents after that to use as a holiday cottage. It's where I spent all my school holidays. Mum and Dad planned to move here when he retired, but then he died. Mum only recently got around to putting it up for sale—she can't bear the thought of living in it without him. I'll miss it when it sells.'

Niall followed her down a steep path by the side of the house onto the beach. Robina looked out at the ocean. 'In spring and summer the whales come in here. When I was a little girl I would sit out here for hours watching them.'

Niall studied her. All of a sudden he had an image of the girl she must have been, sitting on the rocks, her knees pulled to her chest as she dreamed her childhood dreams. He smiled. The image was so different from this cool, elegant woman standing beside him.

'What are you smiling about?' Robina asked.

'I don't know. This, you, everything. It's the first time I've felt…' he struggled to find the right words '…at peace since Mairead died.'

Niall sat on a rock and threw a stone into the sea, where it skidded across the water.

'Tell me about her,' Robina said, finding her own rock close to him to perch on. They sat in silence for a few moments. Then Niall started to speak.

'I'd known her since I was a child. I can't remember a time when she wasn't around. We both grew up in a place called Applecross in the far north-west of Scotland. Our parents were good friends. She was younger than me, and at first she used to irritate me the way she kept hanging around. But eventually, as boys do, I started to notice that she wasn't a pesky kid any more but a pretty teenager with a mind of her own. I went away to university and when I came back after qualifying I discovered that the once irritating tomboy had turned into a beautiful, funny and amazing woman. We fell in love, married and moved to Edinburgh. We tried for kids for years—I guess that's what sparked my interest in fertility—and finally we were blessed with Ella. It seemed as if life couldn't get any better. My career was going well, Mairead loved being a stay-at-home mum, and she seemed content to have only one child. I have never known a woman so satisfied with her lot.'

The familiar ache seeped into his chest. This was the first time he had talked about his wife. He had never been a man to talk about himself and was surprised he could now. Robina, listening in silence, made it easy.

'That's more or less it. Two years ago she started getting bruises. She told me it was nothing, just her being clumsy, and I guess I chose to believe her. But one day the bruising was so bad, I forced her to see a colleague of mine. He diagnosed aplastic anaemia. Three weeks later she was dead. Ella was only two years old.'

He felt a cool hand slip into his. 'I'm so sorry, Niall. It must have been hard.'

But Niall felt he had said more than enough—too much, in fact. Whatever he wanted from this woman, it wasn't pity. Something stirred inside as he looked at her. For the first time since Mairead had died, he wanted another woman. This woman. Before he could stop himself he leaned towards her and found her lips. They were cool under his own and as they parted he groaned and kissed her with a hungry need he'd thought he'd never feel again.

His heart was pounding as she returned his kisses with a passion that matched his own. Eventually they broke apart, both breathing heavily. As Robina looked at him shyly, he stood and pulled her to her feet.

'Come back with me,' he said, knowing that he couldn't bear to leave her.

'What? To your hotel room?' She blushed, the redness darkening her honey skin.

'Yes. There first.'

Robina shook her head, her blush deepening. 'I'm sorry…I can't.'

He froze. It hadn't crossed his mind that she wouldn't be free. But why not? A woman like her was bound to be involved. 'Why?' He forced the words past a throat gone dry. 'Are you in love with someone else?'

'No, it's nothing like that.' Squaring her shoulders, she tilted her chin proudly. 'I know it may be old-fashioned, but I don't believe in sex before marriage,' she said primly.

Niall threw back his head and laughed, pulling her back into his arms at the same time. He kissed the tip of her nose. 'Then we are going to have to spend a lot more time together.' He cupped her face and traced her high cheekbones with the pad of his thumb. 'I'm going to enjoy getting to know everything about you.' Then he remembered they had hardly any time. 'Will you come and see me in Scotland?' he asked urgently.

Robina's lips parted as she turned her face to his. 'Just try and stop me,' she said before he brought his mouth back down on hers.

CHAPTER TWO

'NO WAY! It's out of the question!' Niall slammed his mug down on the desk, noticing but not giving a damn as the coffee splashed across his desk.

'Really?' Robina raised perfectly groomed eyebrows. 'Why not?' she asked, her calm, cool tones underpinning the determination in her dark eyes. Niall leaned back in his chair. The woman he had met a year ago was almost unrecognisable behind the practised, almost cold, façade.

'Why not?' he echoed incredulously before lowering his voice. 'Surely you can see why it's impossible?'

'Let's keep this professional,' she responded calmly, but he flinched inwardly from the reproach in her eyes. How could brown eyes, the colour of acacia honey, which had once sparkled up at him with suppressed laughter, now look so distant? 'Why don't you give me your reasons and I'll respond to each one in turn?'

'For a start, there's patient confidentiality. Then there is the fact that these are a particularly vulnerable group of women, and then finally, if all that weren't enough, how do you expect us to work with cameras in our faces? We'd be tripping over wires, sound recordists and God knows who all else. That's why it's impossible.'

'Quite the opposite.' Robina crossed one slim leg over the other, only the tightening of her lips giving away her determination to have her own way. 'But let's take each of your objections in turn, shall we?' She tapped her pen against her lips. 'Patient confidentiality; we will, naturally, check with the patients whether they are prepared to appear on camera. Only those who are one hundred per cent happy and who our company psychologist thinks can handle it will be asked to participate, and they will be allowed to withdraw their permission at any time. Secondly, yes, they are a particularly vulnerable group of women, I agree. Anyone going through or considering IVF has usually been on a very emotional journey before seeking treatment. However, that is the very reason why making a documentary of this kind is important. It will provide an insight into the process that cannot be gleaned from books on the subject, no matter how detailed or how professional.' She arched an eyebrow at him. 'Even my book on infertility, popular though it is, cannot truly prepare women for what it is really like to undergo treatment. Following the actual experiences of other women, on the other hand, will. That's why this documentary should be made.' She tilted her head, and raised a questioning eyebrow at him, daring him to find a fault in her argument.

Niall started to interrupt, but she held up a manicured hand, stopping him. 'And papers published in medical journals, no matter how worthy or how accurate, simply do not deal properly with the emotional aspect of infertility. And that is the angle we wish to focus on. Women considering IVF will be able to see first hand what a roller-coaster ride it can be, and the effect failed treatment can have on couples, before they decide whether or not to proceed with treatment. Of course we will portray the other side too. The fact that IVF has given so many women—and their partners—the opportunity to have the children they so desperately want.'

He had to admire the way she demolished his arguments. But he had seen her in action before. In front of the camera, faced with an expert from a medical field, she never let them bamboozle her or the audience with science. No, he had to admit, although it pained him, she had a knack of making even the most complicated medical condition understandable to the layperson.

'And as for staff getting in the way, you'll hardly know we're there, I promise you.'

'The answer is still no,' he said. 'This is my unit and as long as I'm in charge, I will decide what is and what isn't allowed.'

Once again the eyebrow was raised. 'I have to say that view sounds a little dictatorial. Is that really how you like to run things?' Her lips twitched. 'And I thought you took pride in being up to date, cutting edge in fact.'

Niall gritted his teeth. It was a sly dig and they both knew it. Just as he opened his mouth to retaliate there was a brief knock on the door and Lucinda Mayfair walked into the room. The unit's general manager was in her early fifties with short grey hair and a wide, determined mouth. Niall had worked with her for a number of years and although they had had their differences of opinion, he had enormous respect for her skills. Without her fighting their corner it was unlikely that the unit would have gained the recognition it had as the foremost centre in the UK, even given his international reputation.

'I'm sorry I had to leave you to get started without me.' Lucinda's smile relaxed the severe contours of her face.

Despite her fearsome reputation, and her forbidding exterior, she had a soft heart. More than once he had seen her eyes suspiciously moist when a patient had been given the news they so desperately wanted or sometimes, sadly, dreaded.

Lucinda had shared his dream of making the unit the best in the UK, and so far, working together, with the support of their hand-picked team, they had succeeded. Which, he thought grumpily, they couldn't have done, if it had been anything except cutting edge.

'Don't you think Robina's idea is great, Niall?' Lucinda continued.

Niall frowned. It seemed that they were on opposite sides in this argument. Still, they had been before and he had always managed to talk Lucinda round. He didn't foresee any difficulties this time either.

'I have just been telling Robina that it's impossible. We're a working unit. We certainly don't have time to appear on a TV show. God, is there no aspect of life that reality TV doesn't want to ferret around in?'

'Niall,' Lucinda said warningly, 'you and I need to talk about this. And as for people *ferreting around*, as you so elegantly put it, Robina's a doctor and completely professional. She's not going to go about this in an insensitive manner. You know that.'

Robina stood, flicking an imaginary speck of dust from her beautifully cut Chanel suit. Every inch the professional media woman, Niall thought. Looking as if butter wouldn't melt in her mouth. But there had been times lately when he'd thought he'd seen naked pain in the depths of her deep brown eyes.

'Why don't I leave you two to discuss it? I need to get back to the office. We can speak later.'

As she bent to drop a kiss on Lucinda's cheek, Niall studied Robina surreptitiously. Her closely cropped dark hair, long neck and high cheekbones, along with her chocolate skin, all added to the exotic look known to thousands, if not millions, of viewers. She wasn't just beautiful, she was stunning. At least five-ten, she was slim, recently almost painfully so. If she had chosen a life as a model, Niall had no doubt she would have been equally successful.

Robina walked around to Niall's side of the desk and bending, kissed him on the cheek.

'I'll see you at home, darling. Try not to be too late. You know Ella won't go to sleep unless she can kiss you goodnight. Make sure he leaves on time, won't you, Lucinda?'

And with that, Niall watched his wife sweep out the door.

'Robina gets more beautiful every day,' Lucinda said wistfully. 'How she manages it, looking after a young child with a full-time job *and* her writing, is beyond me. She must be some kind of superwoman! I hear she has a new book coming out in the spring.'

The last thing Niall wanted to talk about was his wife and her career, particularly since she hadn't even mentioned until now that her company was thinking of doing a documentary in his unit. There was no doubt in his mind that the two women had been planning the project long before he had been told about it, and he was furious. How had Robina managed to get to Lucinda without him knowing? Robina must have known damn well he would oppose the project, and not just for the reasons he'd outlined earlier. For her even to be thinking about doing the documentary was crazy. It was far too soon and far too close to home. But that was probably why she had gone directly to

Lucinda. The unit's general manager didn't know about the baby and even if she did, it wouldn't have crossed her mind that he and Robina hadn't discussed the documentary beforehand. Neither could Lucinda even guess that he and his wife were barely on speaking terms these days, and that the kiss Robina had deposited on his cheek had all been part of the façade they kept up in front of others.

'What in God's name made you think I would agree to this?' he said, trying to keep the anger from his voice. 'We should have discussed it before you set up the meeting with Robina.'

Lucinda looked at him warily. 'Money,' she said flatly. 'Real Life Productions will be paying a lot for this. Money that we could use either for research or to help sponsor more women into the programme.'

Niall hated the funding aspect of the unit, hated anything that took him away from his patients or his research, and was only too happy to leave the finances of the unit in her capable hands.

'I was sure you and Robina had talked about this.' Lucinda's grey eyes were puzzled. 'Otherwise, I wouldn't have gone ahead with the meeting. I assumed when Robina came to me that you must have agreed in principle.'

Niall returned her gaze steadily. The last thing he was prepared to discuss was his personal life.

'Money isn't the only issue here,' he said evasively. 'I see no reason why we should be selling our soul to the devil, and believe me that's exactly what we'd be doing. We'd be exploiting the very women who come to us for help.'

'I'm afraid I don't see it that way. Not at all.' Lucinda regarded him severely and Niall groaned when he saw the determination in her eyes. 'We do need the money, Niall.

You are always waiving fees.' She threw up her hands anticipating his protest. 'And I support you. But we can't keep doing it. If we don't generate some extra funding, and soon, we'll have to start turning away all non-paying patients, and neither you nor I want to do that.'

Niall was stunned. He'd had no idea that the unit was in financial difficulty.

'Why didn't you tell me this before?' he demanded. 'You and I are supposed to be partners.'

'I tried to tell you.' Lucinda drew a weary hand across her brow. 'But it is so hard to pin you down these days. You are always so damned preoccupied with one thing or another.'

Niall looked at her sharply. Her eyes looked hollow; her mouth pinched with fatigue. He felt a pang of guilt. Why hadn't he noticed? But even as he thought the question he knew the answer—because he had been too busy trying to block out everything except his work.

'The trouble is, Niall, between your patients and your research, it's almost impossible these days to catch you so we can have a discussion about the business side of things.'

Niall knew she was right. He had little patience for the business side of things, as she put it, at the best of times. And lately, well, he'd had other stuff on his mind. But nevertheless he should have noticed that something was wrong. He shouldn't have let Lucinda carry the burden on her own. The trouble was that he had become used to her taking care of the financial aspects of running the unit and had been only too happy to let her get on with it. He felt a fresh spasm of guilt.

'We can find the extra funding from elsewhere, from my own pocket if necessary.'

Lucinda half smiled. 'I appreciate the sentiment, but

your pocket—generous as it's been—isn't enough any more. The kind of money we need has to come from ongoing investment. The kind of investment that would come from a documentary such as the one your wife, or at least the company she represents, is proposing. But,' she continued, 'that aside, I would never even consider it, not even for millions of pounds, if I didn't think it was a good idea. But I have to agree with Robina. Infertility is something so many women suffer from, and I think it is in the public interest to inform a wider audience of the reality. As for your concerns, I'm sure Robina has told you that only patients who are willing to share their experiences on TV will appear and we will, of course, ask them to sign the appropriate waivers. It will be an inconvenience to us, I admit that, but there must be ways we can minimise the disruption. At least say you'll think about it.'

Niall stood and crossed over to the older woman. He placed a hand on her shoulder and squeezed. 'I've been selfish,' he said. 'And I'm sorry. You shouldn't have to worry about funding on your own. Why don't you give me a copy of the latest financial forecast and I'll look at it over the weekend? Then we will talk again,' he promised. 'But in the meantime I have a clinic about to start. Could we discuss this again on Monday?'

Lucinda nodded and then smiled up at him. 'Hey,' she said, 'don't beat yourself up. If you weren't so obsessed with work, the clinic wouldn't have such a fine reputation.'

'You've made your point,' Niall said, smiling. 'The last thing I want to do is turn patients away, knowing that we are their last hope.'

'Like the Dougans?' Lucinda said, referring to a couple Niall had talked to her about the day before. Ineligible for treatment on the NHS, they had paid for one cycle of treatment, which hadn't worked. Mr Dougan had recently lost his job, and there was no way the couple could afford to pay for another cycle of IVF.

'I did tell them we'd only be able to offer them one cycle free—we still have enough in our endowment pot for that, surely?'

Lucinda smiled ruefully. 'Yes, but barely. Without raising more funds, the Dougans might be the last couple we'll be able to subsidise. I know you mean well, Niall, but we have salaries to pay as well as our not inconsiderable overheads. We are a business after all.' She got to her feet. 'You'd better get to your clinic. We'll discuss it again after the weekend. I'm a great believer that, one way or another, things have a habit of working out.'

When she'd left the room Niall closed his eyes for a moment, trying to banish the image of his wife from his mind. If only Lucinda knew the truth she wouldn't be so quick to tell him things had a habit of working out. It was ironic, really. He and his wife spent so much time trying to help others with their lives, yet they couldn't seem to do a thing about the almighty mess they had made of their own.

Robina rushed into the house, glancing at her watch. It was almost seven! She had planned to be home earlier so she could sit with Ella while she had her supper and then read her a story before bed. It was the one time in the day that was precious to her. When she was in the middle of filming, she'd often have to spend the night in London, returning late the following evening. So while her show was off the air, and when she was based at home in Edinburgh, she tried to be home at a decent hour whenever she could—especially when it was unlikely that Niall would be home before her. He often worked late particularly when he knew she was around, so that he could have most of the weekends free to spend with his daughter.

But to her surprise, as she flew into the kitchen discarding her bag and coat in the hall, she saw his dark head bent over Ella as he helped her cut up her fish fingers. Robina's heart squeezed as she paused in the doorway. They were so alike, from the determined mouth to the clear blue eyes. Similar too in temperament. Both equally stubborn. Both so dear to her.

Niall looked up. For a second she thought she saw a flicker of warmth in his blue eyes, but she knew she was mistaken when the familiar coolness cloaked his expression. Despite herself, her spirits drooped with disappointment. When would she ever truly accept that it was over between them? They were married, but for the last few months in name only. God, they could barely be civil to each other these days.

Niall looked at his watch. 'We expected you home earlier,' he said.

'Sorry, I got caught up at the office.' Robina bent to kiss her stepdaughter, who flung her arms around her neck. She savoured the feel of the little girl's marshmallow-soft skin under her lips and the dear, familiar smell of her. Whatever differences she and Niall had, she couldn't love Ella more had she given birth to her, even if she were a constant reminder of Niall's first wife—and an even more painful reminder of the baby she had lost too early, five short months after their marriage. But all that would have been bearable if only she could be coming home to a husband who loved her. Someone who would want to know about the trivia of her day and would rub the tension from her shoulders, making everything seem all right.

But shoulder rubs and evenings by the fire, sharing the day's stresses, was never going to happen. Had rarely happened even when they had first married, and certainly not these days. The breakdown of her marriage had happened in such little steps she had hardly noticed until—well, until the miscarriage when it had all fallen completely apart.

'Would you like me to read to Ella while you have dinner?' Niall asked formally, as if they were complete strangers, which in a sense she supposed they were. Falling in love, her coming to Scotland for a visit, Niall proposing to her, their marriage, it had all happened so fast they hadn't really had time to get to know each other. They had both thought—*if* they had thought about it at all—that there would be plenty of time later to get to know each other properly. But to her delight and amazement, the book for which Niall had written the foreword had been an immediate run-away success and she'd been asked to appear on a show to talk about it. The producer had been so impressed with the way she had been able to translate medical jargon into simple language he'd asked her to stand in for the presenter of the show, *Life In Focus*, who had to unexpectedly withdraw. The timing hadn't been great, coming right on the heels of their wedding, but she and Niall had both agreed it was too good an opportunity to miss. And that was when it had all started to go wrong.

'No, I'd like to read Ella her story, if that's okay,' she said, realising Niall was waiting for a response. She hated the way her tone was equally formal.

'I told Mrs Tobin that it was okay for her to leave. She's

left a casserole in the oven,' Niall continued, referring to their housekeeper, who had stayed on after they had married and also doubled as a childminder for Ella.

'Oh, Daddy.' Ella looked up at him imploringly. 'Can't I stay up later tonight, with you and Robina? I never get to be with both of you at once any more.'

A flash of regret darkened Niall's eyes.

'Not tonight,' he said firmly. 'It's a school night. But why don't I get you ready for bed and then Robina will read to you before lights out? How does that sound?'

Ella pouted, but the little girl knew her father well enough to know he wouldn't budge. She scrambled to her feet. 'Come on, Daddy. Let's hurry up, then.' Taking her father by the hand, she led him upstairs.

Robina sat at the table and picked at the beef casserole. Most evenings, Niall arrived home after she and Ella had had supper, then one or the other of them would organise Ella for bed. When Niall's daughter was asleep, they would retreat to separate rooms, Niall to his study and Robina to the small sitting room that had, over the last few months, become hers. When the interminable and lonely evening had dragged to an end and they were ready for bed, she would go to the room they had once shared, while Niall slept in the spare room. It was a cold, unhappy home these days and if it hadn't been for Ella, perhaps she would have found the strength to leave—even if it would have shattered her already fractured heart.

Scooping the remains of her half-eaten meal into the dustpan, Robina took her coffee into her sitting room. Before she had left for the night, Mrs Tobin had lit a fire against the cool of the late February evening and Robina warmed her chilled hands. If only she could so easily chase away the chill in her heart, she thought as she picked up the proofs of her latest book. She sighed when she saw the title. *How to keep your relationship happy—in bed and out of it.* If her readers knew the truth, they'd be astonished. She flung the book aside, in no mood to concentrate.

She looked around the room with its tasteful carpets and elegant furnishings. It was beautiful, she admitted, but not really her taste. Perhaps if she hadn't moved into the home Niall had shared with his first wife, things might have been different. But Niall hadn't wanted to unsettle Ella so soon after their marriage, and Robina had wholeheartedly agreed it was the right thing to do. She had been so in love, she would have lived in a cave if Niall had asked her to. What did it matter as long as she and Niall were together? But it had come to matter—a lot. Everywhere she looked she was reminded of the woman who had been the perfect wife and mother. A woman who was as unlike her as it was possible to be.

She became aware of a presence in the doorway and, looking up, found Niall standing there, watching her intently. He hesitated as if unsure he was welcome in her domain.

'Are you okay?' he asked softly, and for a moment Robina could almost make herself believe he still cared. Almost, but not quite.

'Just tired,' she said. 'It's been a long and…' she slid him a look '…difficult day. And I still have the proofs of my book to finish. My editor expects them early next week and…' She bit off the rest of her sentence. Why was she even bothering to tell him? He wasn't remotely interested in her work.

He looked as if he was about to say something, then changed his mind.

'Ella's waiting for you,' was all he said.

Robina's heart felt as heavy as her legs as she slowly mounted the stairs. This wasn't the life her parents—particularly her father—had envisaged for her, surely? Away from her country, her people, her family. Unable to carry a child—and perhaps never able to conceive again. Robina sighed. Perhaps she should end her marriage, even though it went against every grain of what she believed. She could return to Africa and give Niall a chance of one day finding happiness with someone else, even if the thought of leaving him almost tore her in two. Robina blinked hot tears away. They couldn't go on this way, she decided. She had to do the right thing. And ask him for a divorce.

She paused for a moment outside Ella's bedroom and composed herself, wiping away any evidence of her unshed tears. Pushing the door open, she saw that Ella was snuggled under her duvet, her favourite soft toy cuddled in her arms.

'Can we have *Mr Tickle*?' her stepdaughter asked, holding out the well-thumbed book.

Robina smiled as she inwardly suppressed a groan. They had already read *Mr Tickle* three times that week. Surely Ella was tired of it? But it seemed not. Robina climbed onto the bed and waited until Ella made herself comfortable in the crook of her arm.

She read the story as Ella's eyes drooped. When she had finished, she gently eased Ella out of her arms. But as two bright blue eyes fluttered open, it seemed the little girl wasn't quite ready for sleep.

'Robina,' Ella whispered. 'I've been thinking. Would it be okay if I called you Mummy?'

Robina's breath stopped in her throat. 'Of course,

darling. If you would like to.' Her heart twisted. Why now? When she had been gathering the strength to leave?

'It's not as if I will ever forget I had another mummy. But I can hardly remember her. I used to ask Daddy about her, but it made him sad to talk about her, so I don't ask any more.'

'I think,' Robina said carefully, 'that you could talk to him now. At first, when somebody dies, it hurts so much that it's difficult to talk about it. But in time it becomes easier. So maybe you should try talking to him again. I'm sure he doesn't want you to forget.' As she said the words her heart ached. She should try taking her own advice! She and Niall had never talked about the loss of their baby either.

'You won't leave me too?' Ella asked. 'I couldn't bear to lose another mummy.' She looked at Ella, her eyes—so like her father's—round with anxiety. Robina squeezed her eyes shut, forcing away the wave of sadness that washed over her as she pulled the little girl into her arms and kissed the top of her head. She chose her words carefully. 'I'll always be here for you, *mntwana*—little one,' she promised. 'For as long as you need me. So whether you like it or not, you're stuck with me. Just like a piece of chewing gum on your shoe. Only much nicer, I hope.'

Ella giggled and snuggled down in bed. 'Okay, Mummy. Night-night.'

Robina stayed on the bed until she was sure Ella had fallen asleep. How could she ask Niall for a divorce now, when she had just promised Ella that she would never leave her? Whatever mess she and Niall had made of things, the little girl had been through enough heartbreak in her short life.

Her head throbbing with unanswered questions, Robina returned downstairs to her sitting room. To her surprise

Niall was still there, gazing into the fire, apparently deep in thought.

He flung another couple of logs on the fire. The flames lit the room, chasing the shadows away.

'I told Lucinda I would think about your proposal,' he said. 'We should have an answer for you by Monday.' He stretched. He had changed out of his suit into more casual gear and his T-shirt lifted slightly with the movement, revealing a glimpse of his muscular six-pack. A memory of the sensation of his muscles tightening under her fingertips as she trailed a hand across the dark hairs of his abdomen flashed across Robina's mind. Whatever their difficulties, she knew she still wanted him. Up until the miscarriage, sex had been what had kept them together even as emotionally they had drifted apart. Was it possible, she thought, to still fancy someone like mad even when you weren't sure that you still loved them? Or them you?

Niall crossed the room, placed his hands on her shoulders and looked directly into her eyes. 'Are you sure that doing this documentary is the right thing for you? Isn't it too soon? Too close to home?'

Robina flinched and backed away from him. She could just about cope with anything these days—except his kindness.

She turned her back to him and watched the flames flicker in the fireplace. 'Perhaps my…' she took a breath to steady her voice '…experience makes me the best person to be doing this.'

'Maybe it does,' he said gently. 'I wouldn't know. I don't know how you feel. You've never told me.'

Robina shied away from his words. She had never talked to him about the loss of their baby, because she had refused to let herself think about it. It was still too raw. Every time she thought about the baby that almost was, the pain threatened to crush her. So it was easier, and better, not to think about it at all. But was he right? Should she be doing the documentary when she still felt so wretched? But all she had left right now was her career and she would do nothing to jeopardise it. And she needed to keep busy. It was the only thing that stopped her from going crazy.

'I'm a professional,' she countered. 'I'm still a doctor. My personal feelings don't come into it.'

He made no attempt to hide his disbelief.

'I just wish you had discussed it with me first,' he said tersely.

Robina swung round to face him.

'I would have,' she retorted. 'If we ever spoke these days. I know you don't want to hear about my work. You've made it clear enough that you don't approve of what I do,' she added bitterly.

'That's where you're wrong,' Niall protested. 'I only ever worried that you were doing too much, especially when…' He stopped.

'Especially when I was pregnant and should have known better,' Robina flashed back at him. 'Anyway, I don't want to talk about it right now.'

'When are we going to talk about it? You're never here to talk about anything.' Niall's voice was cold. 'Maybe if you were…'

That was rich, coming from him. Why did he think it was okay for him to work most evenings just because he was a man? It was an old argument. She knew he held her responsible for the miscarriage—and she could hardly blame him. God knew, she blamed herself. He had asked her enough times to slow down. But she'd refused to listen.

Her fledgling career had just been taking off and she hadn't wanted to take time off. She had argued that millions of women worked until just before their babies were born. She had thought there would be plenty of time to take it easy after the baby was born. How terribly wrong she had been, and if she could have the time over, she would do it all differently. But thinking like that was pointless. What was done was done.

'It's no use, Niall. Perhaps it's time we both accepted our marriage is over.'

The shock on Niall's face was unmistakeable.

'Divorce—is that what you want? Is life with me so unbearable?'

Yes, she wanted to shout. Living with you, living like this, knowing you don't love me any more—if you ever did—is tearing me apart. But she just looked at him in silence. Perhaps if they had shouted, argued when things had started to go wrong, they might have been able to fashion some sort of life together. As it was, they had barely been speaking when she had miscarried.

'No, I don't want a divorce. Upstairs, just now, I promised Ella I'd never leave her. But we have to find a way of living together—for Ella's sake. You can't be happy either.'

'Why did you marry me, Robina?' Niall ground out. 'I thought you wanted the same things I did. A home and a family.'

'Instead you got landed with a woman who can't have children and whose career *is* important.' Despite her best intentions, Robina felt her voice rise. They stood glaring at each other.

'Daddy, Robina.' A small voice broke into the room.

'Why are you shouting? Why are you angry? Did I do something wrong?'

'No, oh no, Ella,' Robina said, turning to the forlorn figure in the doorway. Niall held out his arms and Ella flew into them, burying her head in his shoulder.

'You could never make me angry, pumpkin,' he said. 'Never, ever. Not in a hundred years. Not unless you don't go to bed when I say so, or hide my newspaper or…' He pretended to look cross.

Unconvinced, Ella lifted her head from his shoulder and looked him straight in the eyes. 'Then you must be angry with Robina. What has she done?' Her face crumpled. 'You're not going to divorce, are you? My friend Tommy's parents are getting a divorce and he has to stay with his mummy during the week and go and live with his daddy at the weekends and he doesn't have any friends where his daddy lives and his mummy is always crying and his daddy is always angry. That's not going to happen to us, is it?' She placed her small hands on either side of her father's face. 'Robina isn't going to go away and leave us, is she, Daddy? Not like Mummy did. Robina *promised* me she would always be here for me.'

Niall looked at Robina across the top of his daughter's head, the anguish in his eyes like a kick to her solar plexus. He was a proud man, and Robina knew he would never beg, but he was pleading with his eyes. Not because he wanted her to stay for himself but because he knew it would break his daughter's heart if she left, and one thing Niall loved more than anything else in the world was Ella. She had thought that she had managed to reassure Ella, but she obviously hadn't. Ella had taken her words literally. *She'd always be here for her.* And she wouldn't break that promise, no matter how much living with a man who no longer loved her was eating her up inside.

'We are not going to divorce, silly,' Robina said firmly, aware of the relief in Niall's eyes as she said the words. 'Grown-ups argue sometimes, but then they make up and everything's all right again.' She flicked a glance in Niall's direction, knowing he wouldn't fail to notice the irony of her words. 'We are a family and families stay together, just like I told you. Your mummy wouldn't have left you if she'd had any choice and now I am here to look after you and love you for ever. Or at least until you are a big girl and have a family of your own.'

'I'm glad,' Ella said with a tentative smile. 'Cos I'm never going to get married. I'm going to stay with you and Daddy for ever. Because I love Robina very much, Daddy. Not as much as my real mummy, but almost.'

The flash of anguish in Niall's eyes made Robina's heart twist.

'And you love Robina too, don't you, Daddy?' Ella persisted. Robina realised she wasn't going to give up until she had the reassurance she craved.

'I married her, didn't I?' Niall said evasively. He tossed his daughter into the air. 'Remember? You were there.'

Robina's heart cracked a little more as she remembered their wedding day, only three months after they had met. The spring day brilliantly bright, not a cloud in the sky. The pipers, wearing full highland dress, playing them in and out of the small seventeenth-century church; dancing with Niall, who had held her close in his arms as if he couldn't bear to let her go; everyone so happy for them, her silent toast to her absent family, and her dead father the only shadow on an otherwise perfect day. With her new family around her, and her new, exciting career ahead of her, she hadn't thought it was possible to be so happy.

Oh, yes, he had married her. But how quickly it had all gone wrong. Niall had spent so much time at work and her career had taken up so much time that they had barely seen each other after the wedding. Slowly the doubts had started to creep in. Then in one awful series of events, it had all come crashing down. She closed her eyes against the familiar sweep of pain. Would she ever get used to the gut-wrenching sense of loss?

'So why don't we do anything together any more?' It seemed Ella still wasn't convinced. They had completely underestimated how much the sensitive child was picking up of the strain between them.

'Robina and Daddy are busy,' Niall replied. 'But we still have the weekends. Last weekend we went to the zoo. Or have you forgotten?' He wriggled his eyebrows at her in an attempt to make her laugh. But Ella was having none of it.

'No, we don't. Sometimes I have you, like at the zoo, and sometimes I have Robina—I mean Mummy—but I don't have you together. And you just said we were a family.'

Niall's eyes darkened when he heard Ella call Robina Mummy for the first time in his hearing. How did he feel about his daughter's explicit acceptance of Robina? Did it make it that much harder for him to acknowledge their marriage had broken down? Possibly irretrievably? There was no way of knowing. The little girl had picked up on the tension between her parents and it had obviously been worrying her for a while. It shamed Robina that they had been too busy, too wrapped up in their own problems, to notice.

'Then we will have to do something about that,' Niall said firmly. 'But right now it's bedtime, pumpkin. Come on, let's get you tucked in.' And before Ella could protest further, he carried her out of the room and up the stairs.

Robina sank into her favourite chair and stared into the fire. Whatever she and Niall felt about each other, however angry they were, they needed to make sure Ella was happy. It wasn't fair to let the child sense that they were having problems. And for the little girl to worry it was her fault! That was unforgivable.

In keeping with her mood, the wind hurled rain against the window and Robina wrapped her arms around her body in a bid to draw some warmth into her chilled soul.

'She wants you to go up and say goodnight again.' Niall's voice came from the doorway. Despite his size he moved quietly.

Robina eased herself out of her chair. 'Of course,' she said.

But as she passed him he grabbed her wrist, forcing her to stop. The touch of his hand sent shock waves through her body. How long had it been since he had touched her?

'If you want a divorce, I won't stand in your way.'

'Is that what *you* want?' Robina said tiredly, not knowing if she had the strength to fight him any longer.

'No, you know it isn't.' It sounded as if the words were being dragged from his lips. Her heart lifted. Did he still care? Enough not to want to let her go?

'I don't want my daughter to lose another mother—and you are her mother now. God knows, she's known enough sadness in her short life already. I'd do anything to protect her.'

Robina's heart plummeted. Was that the only reason he wanted her to stay? For his daughter's sake? Not for the first time, she wondered sadly if that was the real reason he had married her. Wasn't that what he had just said? He wanted a home, and by that she assumed he meant someone to run it, and a family. Things hadn't exactly turned out the way he had expected.

'Neither do I want to cause Ella any more pain,' she said sadly. 'As she said, I promised her I would never leave her. You know I love her. So no, we're married and we'll stay married. I made my vows and I'll stick by them. For better or for worse. We've had the better, let's deal with the worse.' She pulled her hand away. 'Goodnight, Niall, I'll see you at breakfast.' Knowing that she was moments away from breaking down and that all she had left was her pride, she hurried away to the sanctuary of her room.

CHAPTER THREE

'MOST of you have met my wife.' Niall indicated Robina with a nod of his head. 'And you all know why she is here.'

There were a number of smiles and nods of recognition from around the room. It was the first day of filming and Robina and her cameraman, John, who would be doubling up as sound recordist, were sitting in on the clinic's regular update meeting. Niall had told her that he was reluctantly—and he had emphasised the word reluctantly—agreeing to let filming go ahead, but he would stop it if he thought it was no longer in his patients' best interests.

'We meet once a week to discuss cases,' Niall explained. 'This gives everyone an opportunity to share any concerns they may have about patients' treatment. It is also where we discuss the more complex cases and agree on a way forward.' Niall folded his hands on the table and leaned forward.

He looks so distant, Robina thought, at least when he looks at me. Dressed in his dark suit, his shirt blindingly white and with a dark blue tie, he was the epitome of the successful doctor and Robina was reminded of the first time she had seen him. He had seemed intimidating then too, at least until she had spent time with him and realised that under that formal, serious demeanour was a man who had a dry sense of humour, who was kind and thoughtful and who could make her pulse race like no other. Where had that man gone?

She glanced around the room. There was an embryologist, whose name she hadn't quite caught, Niall and one of the other doctors, a part-timer called Elaine, two specialist nurses, Sally and Mairi, as well as the nurse manager, Catriona. All the other staff were busy in the lab or seeing patients.

'I would guess that not everyone is happy that we are being filmed, but now that we have agreed to go ahead, I know you will all do your best to make it as smooth as possible,' Niall continued easily.

He knows his staff will do whatever he asks, Robina thought as everyone nodded. They trusted him completely.

'I've contacted all our patients who are either on treatment or scheduled for an appointment, asking whether they wish to take part,' Catriona said. 'And have passed the names of about ten patients to Robina.' The older woman smiled at her. 'For what it's worth, I think it's an excellent idea—as long as the patients are happy and as long as I don't have to appear on camera.'

'I don't mind being filmed,' Sally, the dark haired nurse with an impish grin, said, smoothing her hair, 'I just worry I might say something daft.'

'Don't worry,' Robina reassured her, 'you'll soon forget about the camera, believe me. And if you say something daft, we'll edit it.'

'I'm not appearing, if that's okay,' Mairi chipped in. 'They say the camera puts on ten pounds, and with the extra weight I'm carrying already, I don't think I could face it.'

Everyone laughed and a spate of good-natured teasing broke out.

'Can we move on?' Niall said when everyone had settled again. 'We have a number of cases to discuss before I have to check on my patients in the labour ward.'

On top of his patients at the clinic, Niall still carried a full workload of obstetric cases. No wonder we hardly see each other, Robina thought sadly. Either she was working, or he was, and that included most evenings and weekends.

'Annette is coming in for her seven-week scan this morning,' Sally announced. 'Keep your fingers crossed, everyone.' The mood in the room turned sombre.

'This is Annette's third attempt,' Catriona explained to Robina. 'The first time the embryos didn't implant, the second time, she had a positive pregnancy test, but her seven-week scan, the one we do to determine whether the pregnancy is ongoing, showed no evidence of a heartbeat. As you can imagine, she was distraught. She and her husband have agreed that this will be their last attempt—she was thrilled when this most recent pregnancy test was positive—but they are naturally extremely anxious. I think she might be one of the women who said they'd be happy to talk to you.'

'Who's doing the scan?' Niall asked.

'I am,' replied Sally. 'I looked after her through her other treatments.' She chewed on her lower lip. 'I don't know how she'll cope if we don't find a heartbeat. And I will hate being the one that has to tell her.'

'Let's just wait and see,' Catriona said soothingly. 'There's no point in getting ahead of ourselves.'

'I have a patient I'd like to discuss,' Niall said. 'It is a difficult case and I'd like to know how everybody feels—particularly the embryologists—before I see this lady.'

Everyone turned curious eyes on Niall.

'I have been approached by a woman who wants us to carry out PGD—pre-implantation genetic diagnosis,' he said to Robina, for the benefit of the camera. 'She has a family history of breast cancer in the family and all the female relatives in her family have either died or have had the disease. As a precaution, she decided to have a prophylactic double mastectomy when she was eighteen, after genetic testing showed that she carried the variant BRCA1 gene.'

There was a sharp intake of breath followed by a murmur of sympathy from around the room.

'Now that Isabel has joined us…' he smiled at the curly-haired embryologist sitting on his right '…we are in a position to offer this service. But I want to know how everyone feels about it.'

'Could you explain what it involves, Niall?' Robina asked, knowing that this was exactly the kind of thing her viewers would be interested in. She only had a vague memory from researching her book of what the procedure involved and progress in this area was rapid.

'I'll let Isabel explain, as she's the one who'd be doing the procedure.'

'I'll try and make it as simple as possible.' Isabel took a sip of water. 'We stimulate the ovaries, in the same way we do for our infertile ladies, and then fertilise the eggs in the lab. Once the eggs are fertilised they start dividing—one cell becomes two, two become four and so on. We wait until we have eight cells, then we remove one and test for the BRCA1 gene. If it's positive, we move on to the next embryo and so on until we find one that doesn't carry the gene. When we do, that is the embryo we replace.'

'Don't some people think this is too close to eugenics?' Robina asked. 'As in designer babies?'

'Not at all,' Niall interrupted quietly. 'This isn't select-
ing embryos based on hair colour or intelligence or
anything like that. This is selection that will prevent
someone almost certainly suffering from breast cancer
later on in life.'

'I know some people find it distasteful,' Isabel continued, 'but the truth of the matter is that we select embryos
anyway to put back.'

Robina was puzzled. 'What do you mean?'

'We add sperm to all the eggs we retrieve. Say we have
fourteen. Out of those, sometimes only a proportion will
fertilise. We study the ones that are under the microscope
and grade them according to specific, recognised criteria.
We select the ones with the best grades, and choose one
from these to replace. So in a way we are already select-
ing. PGD only takes it a step further.'

Robina was fascinated and knew viewers would be too.
Some might find it controversial, but she had never shied
away from controversy. She would present both sides of
the argument and leave people to make up their own minds.

'Isn't destroying perfectly healthy embryos wrong?'

'Sometimes we freeze the leftover embryos—the ones
that are of good quality, that is—in case the women want
further treatment. If they don't, then yes, we dispose of the
remainder,' Isabel continued, her face animated. It was
clearly a subject that was close to her heart. 'In many ways
it's no different to what happens in normal pregnancies.
The ovary starts to produce several eggs, but there is always
one dominant egg which then releases a hormone that stops
the other competing eggs from developing further. In a
way we are simply replicating nature.'

'The issue I have is more of a scientific rather than a

moral one,' Niall said. 'Not for this gene, which would be present in every cell of the embryo, but when we are testing for other genetic conditions, for example Down's syndrome, there is the risk that out of the eight cells, we test the one cell that doesn't carry the genetic abnormality and are led to falsely believe that the embryo is free of the condition. It is important that anyone considering PGD understands this.'

'She wouldn't be considering it if she weren't desperate,' Mairi interjected. 'And she's already shown how serious she is by having a double mastectomy. I'm not surprised she doesn't want her daughter to go through the same thing.'

Robina leaned back as lively discussion broke out around the table. She wondered how it felt to have to make these kinds of decisions on a daily basis, knowing you held people's dreams in the palm of your hand. Her heart went out to all the couples. The people in this room had such power over their lives. How could so many women bear to put themselves through so much potential disappointment and heartache? She knew she couldn't put herself through it again. Never, ever. She had thought she would never get over the pain of losing one baby. How could she possibly risk doing it all over again?

'Let's take a vote,' Niall said. 'Everyone in favour of my seeing this lady, remembering I intend to make sure she understands the pros and cons before we proceed, raise their hands.'

It seemed that everyone was in agreement.

'Let's move on then,' Niall said, but before he could continue, the receptionist popped her head around the door.

'Annette has arrived for her scan, Sally. I've made her

a coffee, but I don't want to keep her waiting—she looks terrified.'

Sally stood. 'Are you coming?' she asked Robina, who immediately got to her feet. 'Keep your fingers crossed, everyone,' she added over her shoulder as Robina and her cameraman, John, followed her out of the room.

Sally showed Annette and her husband into one of the consulting rooms and then left them with Robina and John while she went to set up the scan.

Annette was pale and held on to her husband Mike's hand as if for dear life.

Robina asked the nervous couple if they were sure they were happy to be filmed. 'You can still change your mind,' she told them gently.

'No, we said we'd do it and we will.' Annette raised her chin. 'We want people to know what it's like to go through IVF.'

Robina nodded to John, who focussed the camera on Annette.

'Only people who have been through this know what it's like.' Annette's voice was so soft, Robina had to strain to catch her words.

'At first, every month you hope that this will be the month, but you tell yourself not to get too excited, but you can't help yourself. You just want it so much. And then, when it doesn't happen, it's like a dark cloud descending on top of you. So you ask yourself, why me? What is wrong with me? And then eventually you realise that you have to seek help, because it's not going to happen on its own—no matter how much you want it to. Suddenly, you can't bear seeing babies. Sometimes you'll cross the street so you don't have to look at them, and you even avoid friends and relatives who are pregnant or have young children—even though you know it's wrong and selfish.'

She took a shaky breath. Robina wanted to reach out and put her arm around Annette's shoulders and tell her she knew how she felt, but she forced herself to stay still and let her have her say.

'People tell you to relax, that it will be all right, that there is always adoption, and yes, for some people adoption is the right thing. But although they mean well they just don't know how much it hurts not being able to have children of your own.'

She paused for a moment, her eyes welling up with tears. 'And then, when you decide to go for IVF, you think that this is it. That soon you'll be pregnant. Oh, you know the treatment might be unpleasant, but you don't care. And they tell you it might not work, but you're not really listening, cos you have hope again. So you do everything you are told, and loads of other stuff that you read about on the internet and in magazines—just in case. You go through the injections, do the diets, try the alternative treatments—put up with the hormones making you a little crazy, because you just know that soon you'll be holding a baby in your arms, and you'll do anything to have that feeling. Then when the drugs work, and they take you to Theatre, the hope is almost painful. So you have your eggs collected, but you have to wait again to see if they fertilise, and if they do, and one or two are replaced, you have to wait again to see if they implant. And even if you know there is still a chance you won't fall pregnant, you go out and buy the cot, and start to think of names. And it's the longest two weeks of your life as you wait. You are almost too scared to do anything, even though you know it won't make a difference, and every twinge and niggly pain terrifies you. Then, at last, it's pregnancy test day. And you tell yourself you must be pregnant because you couldn't bear it if you are not.'

Annette took another deep breath. 'But if you are like me, then the first time the test was negative, and I couldn't believe it. I was devastated. But Mike wouldn't let me give up, so we tried again. And this time the test was positive. We were so excited, even though Sally warned us it was only the beginning.'

She paused as Sally re-entered the room. 'We didn't listen, did we? We told everyone and they were so happy for us. But something didn't feel right. I tried to tell myself I was imagining things, but I wasn't. This time we got as far as the seven-week scan—like the one we are having today. But there was no heartbeat. We had lost our baby.'

Robina swallowed the lump in her throat. She also recognised the terrible feeling of loss; even though her baby had been no more than a few centimetres in length. A baby was no less mourned because it was only a tiny embryo.

'C'mon,' Sally said gently. 'Let's get you scanned. I think you've waited long enough for this moment.'

A few minutes later, Annette lay on the bed looking even paler and on the verge of tears. She's expecting bad news, Robina thought. It's written all over her face. Or at least she's preparing herself for the worst.

The room was deathly silent as Sally ran her probe over Annette's abdomen. Annette clutched Mike's hand as if he were a life-raft and if she let go, she would drown.

But a few minutes later a huge smile spread across Sally's face. 'A clear, strong heartbeat.' She swivelled the monitor so the couple could see. 'See just there.'

Robina craned her neck to see where she was pointing

and, sure enough, the steady movement of a heartbeat flickered on the screen.

'Are you sure?' Annette whispered.

'One hundred per cent. You can relax, we've got an ongoing pregnancy.'

Annette burst into gut-wrenching sobs and her husband gathered her into his arms. 'I can't believe it,' Annette hiccupped once she had regained her composure. 'We're going to have a baby. Thank you, oh, thank you.'

'Congratulations,' Robina said. 'I'm so happy for you both.' With a bit of luck, in a few months' time this couple would be holding a much longed-for baby in their arms. Robina's throat tightened and she knew that tears weren't far away. Annette's story had brought too many painful memories flooding back.

Leaving the ecstatic couple with Sally, Robina found the staff in Reception gathered around a woman who was proudly showing off a baby, who, judging by its size, was somewhere around two to three months old.

'Isn't he just gorgeous?' Linda was saying. She noticed Robina. 'Dr Zondi, come meet our latest arrival, little Matthew.'

She held out the baby and, before Robina could protest, handed her the tiny bundle as everyone looked on. For a second Robina's heart froze. She hadn't seen, much less held, a baby since her miscarriage. Now she had no choice but to accept the infant.

John was filming, his camera trained on her face. He was one of the few people who knew about the miscarriage, but the thought probably hadn't entered his male head that she would find cuddling a baby difficult. She forced herself to look down at the tiny bundle she held in her arms. His eyes were closed, and impossibly long lashes fanned plump cheeks. She inhaled the baby smell of him and the numbness in her throat spread into her chest, making her feel as if she could hardly breathe. If her baby had lived, she would be due about now. Don't let me cry, she thought. Don't let anyone speak to me, cos there is no way I could force any words past my throat.

She glanced up and over the heads of the nursing staff and saw Niall watching her intently. Without a word, he crossed the room and gently took the baby from her arms.

'Ah, let me see,' he said, holding the baby as if he'd had years of practice, which, of course, he had. 'What a fine-looking lad. You must be very proud of him.'

Robina backed away as Niall diverted attention away from her. She was shaking and desperately needed some time on her own to compose herself. Mumbling something about the Ladies' to no one in particular, she walked as steadily as she could, on legs that had turned to mush, towards the bathroom.

Inside, she slumped to the floor and laid her head on her knees, taking deep, gulping breaths. Her hands were still shaking and she could feel the pressure of tears behind her eyes. It should be *her*, holding *her* baby. She caught her breath as a fresh wave of grief washed over her. She couldn't break down, not here. She needed to regain her composure before she went back out. Maybe Niall was right and she should never have agreed to this programme. She was still too raw, too vulnerable. Thank God, he had seen how close she had been back there to losing it, and had rescued her. How on earth was she going to manage weeks of this? Especially if every time she saw a baby, she thought she would disappear inside herself from the pain of it?

But it was too late for second thoughts. She had made a commitment and she never backed out of anything, regardless of the personal cost. Somehow, although she didn't know how, she would have to lock her feelings back down, deep inside. It was the only way she could continue. She had done it before, and she could do it again. Couldn't she?

CHAPTER FOUR

NIALL sat across the desk from Mr and Mrs Thomas trying, but not quite succeeding, to ignore the cameras. After studying the financial projections, he had been forced to agree with Lucinda. The clinic needed to attract extra funding. So he had agreed to the documentary, but it didn't mean he had to like it. And to add to his discomfort, Real Life Productions had insisted that Niall, given his international reputation, be the one to appear on camera. Mark, the third doctor, and Elaine had made no secret of their relief that they wouldn't have to.

'You're used to appearing in public,' they had teased. 'God knows, your picture has appeared in the press often enough recently.'

They were right, but only because the press wanted pictures of Dr Zondi and her husband, out together and still very much in love. The press hadn't a clue, Niall thought bitterly, and it was just as well. The thought of having his personal life discussed in the papers made him squirm.

Robina had chosen an unobtrusive spot, just to the left of his patients. She was looking drawn, Niall thought with a stab of anxiety. Holding that baby had hurt—she had put her professional face back on, but the way she was nibbling her lip told him she was struggling to hold it together. Damn it! He should never have agreed to this project. Never mind about the finances of the unit, they would manage somehow—but would Robina? He didn't care what she had said about being able to cope—she was more affected than she'd imagined she'd be. But the woman was stubborn. He knew *that* to his cost. He dragged his thoughts away from his wife, concentrating on the anxious man and woman in front of him.

Mrs Thomas, Eilidh, was 38, and her husband already had a child by a previous marriage. Either of these reasons on their own made them ineligible for NHS treatment.

'We only met a year ago,' Eilidh was saying with a fond look at her husband Jim. 'I had more or less given up on meeting the man of my dreams. Then he walked into the room and, bam—just like that. We fell in love.'

Niall couldn't stop himself from sliding another glance at his wife. He knew exactly what Eilidh was talking about.

But if the same thought occurred to Robina there was no sign of it. In the last few moments she seemed to have managed to get her emotions under control. Cool, calm Dr Zondi was back, and she was concentrating intently on what Eilidh was saying.

'We started trying for a family…when was it, love?' Eilidh turned to Jim for confirmation. 'About six months ago. I know it isn't long, but my GP thought that, given my age, we shouldn't wait before we sought expert advice. So here we are.'

She's anxious, Niall thought as Eilidh chewed on her thumbnail. But then again, almost everyone who ever sat in that chair was nervous. They came to him filled with their hopes and dreams, hoping that he'd be able to work some magic that would give them the child they so desperately longed for. And most of the time he did. But not always. However, he knew there was a good chance he could help the hopeful couple in front of him.

'I have the results of your tests here,' he said.

Eilidh gripped Jim's hands and chewed more fiercely on the thumbnail of her free hand.

'Bill's sperm test is perfectly normal—that's the good news. But the test we did for your ovarian reserve, Eilidh, shows that, as we'd expect from someone your age, your fertility is declining.' Niall kept his voice matter-of-fact.

'What does that mean?' Eilidh asked. Her pale face lightened another shade.

'It means that you are unlikely to conceive naturally, but are a good candidate for IVF,' Niall explained.

Eilidh sank back in her chair and smiled with relief. 'Thank God,' she murmured. 'I was terrified you were going to tell us it was hopeless. That getting pregnant was impossible for me.'

'It doesn't mean I can promise you a pregnancy,' Niall continued. 'Sometimes, no matter what we do, women still fail to conceive. And sometimes they conceive but are unable to carry the pregnancy to term. I don't want to paint a negative picture, but you should be prepared.'

But Niall suspected even as he said the words that Eilidh and Jim weren't really listening. Like so many couples, they couldn't bring themselves to think about the possibility of failure. 'That's why,' he added, 'we suggest you make an appointment with our counsellor. You don't have to see her but I would recommend it. She's excellent and is there should you need to talk to someone neutral at any time through this process.'

Niall couldn't prevent another glance at Robina. Sure enough, her eyes had widened in surprise. When they had first started experiencing problems in their marriage, she had suggested a counsellor. But he had refused. The thought of airing their dirty linen to a stranger was just too much. If she had truly loved him, they should have been able to sort things out themselves. Now he wondered if he should have agreed.

He took the couple through the process; how the clinic would take control of Eilidh's cycle and give her drugs which she would need to inject every day for roughly ten days. In addition, Eilidh would have to come in for regular scans of her ovaries as well as blood tests.

He went on to describe the side effects of the drugs and didn't mince his words when he explained the more unpleasant aspects of the treatment.

'Are you sure you want to put yourself through this, love?' Jim asked his wife. 'I didn't think it would be so…awful for you.'

Eilidh looked her husband straight in the eye. 'What does it matter if we get a baby at the end? I'll be all right. I can do anything as long as I have you!'

They smiled at each other and Niall felt a flash of envy. If only he and Robina could share their troubles in the same way.

'Once your ovaries are producing enough follicles and are at the right stage,' he continued, 'we take you to Theatre and you'll be given a sedative. We remove as many eggs as we can from your follicles and then we will use Jim's sperm to fertilise them in the lab. At that point the fertilised eggs become embryos. Depending on how many fertilise, we will make a decision on when to put one, or two, back. Either day two, three or day five. Are you following me so far?'

Eilidh and Jim nodded mutely.

'How do you decide whether to replace one or two embryos?' Jim asked.

'Essentially it's up to you. The HFEA, the UK regulatory body for fertility clinics, recommends that only one embryo is replaced at a time. That's because twin pregnancies carry a greater risk of complications. However, the chances are smaller of one embryo implanting successfully. We'll go over it again when we get closer to that time but, as I said, the final decision will be yours.'

Jim and Eilidh nodded sombrely. 'I think we'd like to know more before we decide how many embryos to have put back,' Jim answered for them both.

'Good decision. It's a lot to absorb in one go,' Niall said gently, 'but you'll be seeing one of our specialist nurses on a regular basis. They will be only too happy to answer any questions you may have as we go along, and they have stacks of literature that you can take away with you. Does that sound okay?'

'Does it hurt—I mean the bit where you take the eggs?' Eilidh asked.

'It can be uncomfortable,' Niall admitted. 'That's why we sedate you. But, I can promise you, you won't remember a thing about it afterwards. You might be a little sore for a couple of hours, but we'll give you something for the pain.'

He spent a few more minutes going over the same ground with the excited couple before he called in Mairi, who would be co-ordinating their treatment.

'Mairi will answer any other questions you might have,' Niall assured the couple, 'but if you ever want to speak to me, you have my number.'

'Thank you, Dr Ferguson.' Eilidh was beaming and two bright spots of colour stained her cheeks. 'I know there's a chance treatment won't work, but you have given us hope. That's all we can ask for.'

When the couple had accompanied Mairi from the room, John made to follow, but Robina stopped him. 'We'll pick them up later through their treatment,' she said, 'but in the meantime, let's give them some privacy.'

When John left the room in search of some coffee, Robina turned to Niall. 'Thank you,' she said quietly, 'you kept everything very simple. I'm sure our viewers will appreciate that.'

Niall smiled wryly. 'It's the way I speak to all my patients,' he said slowly. 'My God, woman, don't you know me at all?'

And there was the rub. She didn't really know him or, for that matter, he her. Niall had always thought they would have the rest of their lives and had looked forward to years and years of learning about the complicated, complex woman who had agreed to become his wife. Instead, he thought bitterly, it had all started to go wrong almost as soon as they'd married. Truth was, things hadn't being going well even before the miscarriage. He had been so busy at work, and Robina's new career in the media had taken off like a bullet. At first he had shared her excitement about the job, even though it had meant postponing the honeymoon, which had somehow become permanently postponed.

He hadn't realised how little he would see of her. How much her new job would take her away. Then when, to the delight of both of them, she had fallen pregnant, it had seemed that everything was going to work out fine. After the series finished she would take time off to prepare for their child. At last they could begin to be a family. But, boy, had he got that wrong! Whilst he'd assumed she'd spend less time at work, she had worked even harder, determined to establish her career before the baby arrived.

Two days before she had miscarried they had argued bitterly. Robina had returned home from London looking exhausted. She had barely managed to find the energy to eat and Niall was worried that she was losing weight.

'You need to slow down, Robina. You can't keep working at this pace.' He tossed the words down like a gauntlet.

'I will, soon. C'mon, Niall, you and I both know that pregnancy isn't an illness. In Africa, women often keep working until days before the baby is born.' She touched him gently on the cheek, but he grasped her hand and held it in his. He knew if he allowed her to touch him, he'd end up wanting to take her to bed. God knew, that was the one thing that was still okay, more than okay, between them.

'You can't keep burning the candles at both ends. You're working on the show then on your book and they still want you to do public appearances. It's too much.'

'Are you trying to tell me you don't think I should do the show?' she retorted, a dangerous glint in her deep brown eyes.

'Yes, that's what I'm saying. It's all too much. And what about after the baby is born? I thought we agreed you'd be staying at home to look after it and Ella.'

'Did we?' Her eyes deepened and her full, generous mouth tightened. 'Is that why you married me, Niall? To provide a full-time mother for your child and any other children you might want? Because, and let me make this clear, I am not Mairead. I'm not the kind of woman to give up her career just to submit myself to my husband's wishes.'

'Leave Mairead out of this,' he responded furiously.

'But I can't, can I? Not when she's everywhere. I'm living in her house, married to her husband, looking after her child. How can I possibly leave her out of this?' Suddenly a shadow crossed her eyes. 'I know she was a wonderful woman. God knows, everyone tells me, and I can see it for myself.'

'Don't tell me you're jealous of her. She's dead, for God's sake.'

'I'm not jealous of her, Niall,' Robina responded quietly, 'I just can't live up to her any longer. I will never be good at what she was. I can't cook, I can't sew, I'm not good at sports, all I am good at is my job. Please don't take that away from me.'

But he refused to see what she was so desperately trying to tell him. That night they went to bed, but instead of reaching for each other, they lay stiffly side by side, neither prepared to give an inch. Two days later, she went into labour, losing their baby, a little boy, at 12 weeks. The memory of Robina's face, tight with fear and pain, still tormented him. She had looked at him, needing him to do something, anything, to stop her losing the baby—but for the second time in his life, he had been powerless to help. The sadness in his wife's eyes when she had known that there was nothing anyone could do had almost torn him apart. When he had tried to comfort her, she had turned away. Then, a few days later, she had been in ITU with an infection, fighting for her life, and he had been terrified he was about to lose her. Robina's illness had brought back memories of Mairead and the gut-wrenching weeks and days leading up to his first wife's death. He hadn't been able to save Mairead and the thought he was going to lose Robina too had almost driven him mad with fear.

Not once had they spoken about their child or the fact that Robina was probably infertile. They had never shared their grief, or given or taken the slightest amount of comfort from one another, and one way or another their marriage had never recovered. When Robina had come home from hospital she had asked him to move into the spare room, saying that she wanted time and space on her own for a while. After a couple of weeks he had suggested he move back into their bed, but she had shaken her head and asked for more time. He didn't ask her again and that was the way it had been ever since.

Niall dragged a hand through his hair. It was a mess. And for once in his life, he didn't have a clue what to do.

Robina had been watching him in silence. He wondered what she was thinking.

'Our baby would be due in a couple of weeks.' Robina spoke softly, almost to herself. 'Just about the anniversary of the day we met. Seeing baby Matthew just now…' Her voice shook '…was so hard.'

The familiar mask he had become too used to seeing slipped for a moment. Right now she looked so vulnerable, so sad, so different from the public persona which was all he ever saw these days. For the first time in months he glimpsed the Robina he had met and fallen in love with. He wanted to gather her into his arms but he was afraid to break the spell. It was the first time she had mentioned the baby and Niall felt a surge of hope. Perhaps this documentary wasn't such a bad thing after all. Not if it meant they would start talking. He sat in silence, waiting for her to continue, but just then there was a knock and Sally burst into the room.

'Dr Ferguson, I need you to come and see one of our ladies. I think she might have OHSS.'

Niall was torn. He wanted to comfort his wife, seize the moment when she had opened up to him, but if Sally was right and the patient did have ovarian hyper stimulation syndrome, he needed to see her straight away. Although in the early stages the condition was fairly benign, it was still a potentially life-threatening illness.

Robina also jumped to her feet, the professional mask back on her face.

'I think you should stay here,' Niall said firmly. 'I'll let you know what's happening as soon as I can.'

When Sally and Niall left the room, Robina slumped back down in her chair. Just for a moment there she had been ready to talk to Niall, and it looked as if he had been ready to listen. But the moment had passed, and Robina wondered whether she would find the strength to raise the subject again.

After a working lunch, where Robina and John had a look over the clips they had filmed, Robina went in search of Niall.

'I have decided to admit our lady with the suspected OHSS,' Niall told her.

'Would you mind explaining the condition for our viewers?' Robina asked. When Niall nodded, Robina signalled to John to start filming.

'Infertility treatment, although fairly benign,' Niall said thoughtfully, 'is not without its risks. We do our best to minimise these, which is why we take blood and scan our patients every couple of days and readjust their treatment protocol as appropriate.' Although his expression was serious, he looked calm and relaxed. This was his field and he knew it well. 'Sometimes the hormones we prescribe over-stimulate the ovaries and it can lead to very real complications, which if not treated can lead to the kidneys failing, and even death. It is rare, but something we take very seriously. Thankfully, we have never had a full-blown case, but on average one woman dies every year in the UK from this condition.'

'I wonder how many women know and understand the risk,' Robina said quietly.

'We do tell them—we make a point of it. If we didn't we'd be negligent,' Niall replied.

'Does it ever put anyone off?'

Niall smiled wryly. 'I think you know the answer to that. And anyway, as long as patients are monitored closely, as most are, the chance of it happening is greatly reduced.'

'But you had a potential case today,' Robina persisted. 'So it does happen.'

Niall narrowed his eyes at her. 'As I said, it is a risk and one that we manage. I admitted the patient who presented with symptoms of OHSS to the ward this morning, but more because she was anxious. I fully expect her to be discharged tomorrow.'

Robina opened her mouth to speak, but before she could say anything, Niall held up a hand.

'Whatever anyone might think, we always have the health of the mother foremost in our minds. But any pregnancy, whether through IVF or through normal intercourse, carries a risk, however careful the expectant mother or however vigilant those looking after her are. We can't always guarantee a positive outcome.'

This time he looked directly into her eyes and she knew that he meant his words for her. He lowered his voice. 'No matter how much we wish we could.' He leaned forward, his eyes locking with hers, and Robina caught her breath at the intensity in his eyes. For a few moments there was silence, then Niall stood.

'I will be doing the Strains' embryo transfer this afternoon,' he said, changing the subject. 'I understand they are one of the couples who wish to appear on your documentary.'

Hiding the fact that her emotions were all over the place, Robina rifled through her papers and found their name. In total ten couples had agreed to be part of her programme. Most of them already knew her work from television and were keen to do anything to help other couples. One or two of them had even read her *Guide to Infertility*, the book that had started her new career.

'Trevor and Christine. They are a lovely couple, I interviewed them yesterday to get their back story. I understand this is their first attempt?'

'Yes, and I'm optimistic. This time the problem, if you can call it that, lies with Christine's partner. He has a very low sperm count, so we did a procedure called ICSI. It is where we searched for and selected motile—that is swimming—sperm from Trevor's semen sample and injected one directly into each of the eggs we retrieved from Christine. She responded well to the drug protocol we prescribed for her, and we managed to remove a good number of eggs. And because we injected the sperm directly into the egg, we managed to fertilise several embryos. You can go into the lab some time if you like to see how it's done. It involves a high level of expertise and a very steady hand—so no drinking for our embryologists the night before.' He grinned. 'Anyway, they'll be here about three for the transfer of their embryo back into the uterus. But I want to make it clear that if they change their mind about you being there, you must respect that. Even if they have given permission before.'

'Of course!' Robina replied, stung. 'Niall, you need to remember that I was a GP—I still am. I have taken the Hippocratic Oath to do no harm. And that means psychological as well as physical.'

'I'm sorry.' Niall looked contrite. 'That was uncalled for. I know you could never be accused of being unprofessional. Forgive me?' He smiled at her, and her heart flipped.

'Anyway,' Niall said, looking serious again, 'please remember if you are planning to come into Theatre you can't wear perfume or make-up. Not even deodorant. Is that clear? We don't want to risk affecting the embryos in any way.'

'Clear as crystal,' Robina replied, before turning on her heel and going in search of her team.

Later, in Theatre, Robina watched from a safe distance while the staff prepared Christine for the transfer.

The clinic hadn't stinted on equipment, Robina thought approvingly, taking in the latest high-tech anaesthetic monitor and ultrasound scanner. Niall, dressed as all the staff were, including Robina and John as well as Mr Strain, in blue scrubs, slowly and carefully replaced the embryo into Mrs Strain's uterus. The procedure didn't take long, but although Christine joked with Sally, there was an undercurrent of tension in the room. All anyone could do now was wait.

'Patients tell us the next couple of weeks are the worst time of the whole process.' Sally addressed Robina while looking at Mrs Strain. 'Up until this point it's all still possible. They see us regularly, but when they go away from here after the ET—the embryo transfer—there is nothing more they, or we, can do. Whether the embryo implants or not is in the lap of the gods. Patients tell us it's the longest wait of their lives.'

Niall half smiled at Christine. 'I wish we could make this part easier, but we can't. If you do want to speak to us—if you have any worries at all—you get on the phone. Don't worry that we'll think your question is trivial, we'd rather you asked. Okay?'

Christine nodded.

'We'll let you rest for half an hour or so, then you're free to go,' Sally said. 'We'll see you when you come back for your urine test. In the meantime, we'll all be thinking of you.'

Once again, Robina marvelled at the way that the staff genuinely seemed to care about every one of their patients. It was as if every pregnancy mattered personally to every member of staff. Niall had managed to gather the best possible team around him. No wonder he was so wrapped up in his work.

Later that evening, Robina was getting Ella ready for bed. Niall had telephoned to say he would be late as he had a paper to finish but he wanted to say goodnight to Ella. Robina couldn't help a pang of disappointment. Despite everything that had happened, she still missed him when he wasn't there and she had been looking forward to discussing the day's events with him.

They had come close to talking back in the clinic. Maybe there was still a chance they could start talking again—maybe even find a way back to each other.

She handed the phone to Ella. 'It's Daddy, he wants to speak to you.'

Robina busied herself setting the table, smiling to herself as she caught Ella's side of the conversation. 'I love you too, Daddy, and I'm sending you a big kiss down the phone.' She puckered her lips and blew down the mouthpiece. She giggled at something Niall said. 'I got your kiss, Daddy, but what about one for Mummy? She needs one too. Hold on a minute, I'll get her for you.' Ella turned to Robina. 'Here, Mummy, Daddy wants to send you a kiss goodnight.'

Robina stared at the receiver, horrified. What could she do? She couldn't very well refuse—what would Ella think? With a thudding heart, she held the phone to her ear.

'Well,' Niall said dryly, 'are you going to blow me a kiss?'

'You first, darling,' Robina replied, forcing her tone to remain light, painfully aware of Ella watching her with delight.

'This is ridiculous,' Niall replied, his voice echoing his embarrassment down the wire. 'That daughter of mine is too smart for her own good. Okay—here goes.' He made a smacking noise. 'Now your turn—and remember you've got an audience.'

Robina couldn't help smiling. Niall was right, it was ridiculous, but there was something bitter-sweet about it too. She pursed her lips, emphasising the required smacking sound, playing up to the watching Ella. 'Mmmmmwhah!'

They both laughed and for the first time in months Robina felt her sadness ease.

When she put the phone down, Ella asked, 'When will Daddy be home?'

'After you're asleep, darling,' Robina answered. 'But he'll be here when you get up in the morning. We both will, so we can have breakfast together.'

'Then after that can we go ice-skating? Please, Mummy. Sophie went with her mummy and daddy and they had so much fun.'

Robina kissed the top of her stepdaughter's curly blonde head. She was so like her father it made her heart ache. But her blonde hair must have come from her mother. The sloe-eyed Mairead. Beautiful, maternal Mairead who had been everything she wasn't.

'Sure we can, as long as Daddy doesn't have to work. I know tomorrow is Saturday, but sometimes his patients need him.'

'*I* need him,' Ella persisted. 'He's my daddy, not theirs.'

Robina hid a smile. 'But he's helping lots of people become mummies and daddies—you understand that, don't you? People who without his help would never know how wonderful it is to have a lovely little girl like you.'

'I s'pose,' Ella said, settling herself in the crook of Robina's arm. 'But I need *some* time with my daddy. They can't have him all the time. Just some of the time.'

Robina's heart ached for the little girl. Although their work made enormous demands on both of them, they had to find time to spend with Ella. They had promised her and it was about time they made good on their word. Although Mrs Tobin was great and Ella loved her to bits, it wasn't the same as having her parents around.

Robina made up her mind. The documentary would take three months, including the follow-up of patients in nine months' time. The new season of her show wasn't due to start for a couple of months. Her last book was selling well, and she had almost finished the proofs of her latest. She would put off starting a new one until after the summer. That way she'd have more time to spend with Ella. Robina sucked in her breath. She couldn't blame Niall for everything that had gone wrong with their marriage. She had, as he had pointed out, been so immersed in her new career she hadn't given her new marriage, or Niall, the time and attention it had needed. When things had started to go wrong, had she been too quick to lay the blame at Niall's feet? One thing was for sure, she couldn't keep going the way she was with a show and book tours and still have enough time for Ella, let alone her marriage. The more she thought about it, the more she wondered why she hadn't seen it before.

'Why don't we ask Daddy whether we can do something next weekend? Just the three of us? We can do anything you like,' she suggested to Ella.

'Could we really?' Ella said, looking up at her with achingly familiar blue eyes. 'Daddy too?'

'Yes, darling,' Robina promised. 'Daddy too.'

But Robina didn't get the chance to discuss it with Niall that night. She waited up, reading a book on the sofa of her small sitting room. The room was still exactly the way Mairead had left it, all pale walls and deep rugs. Even the overfilled sofas were pale and there was a wood-burning stove for the cool evenings. The only item Robina had brought with her from her old life was an African stool. She stretched out a finger and felt the deep grooves of the intricate carving. Her father had given her the stool when she had graduated. It had belonged to his father, who had been a master wood cutter, and Robina cherished it. Every time she touched it, she thought of the village where her father had been raised in the old African traditions and could almost feel the heat of the sun and hear the undulating voices of the women as they called to each other. How she missed Africa and especially her mother and grandmother.

Sighing, she glanced around the room that had belonged

to her predecessor. The walls were lined with floor-to-ceiling bookshelves. It seemed that along with a similar taste in men, she and Mairead shared the same literary taste. All her favourites were on the bookshelf, from the classics to the contemporary romances she liked to read before bed. Unfortunately, reading them only made her acutely aware of the lack of romance in her own life.

Despite her best intentions, she was unable to stop herself falling asleep and woke to find Niall covering her gently with a blanket. Still half dreaming, she smiled up at him and went straight back to sleep but not before she thought she felt his fingertips like a caress against her skin.

CHAPTER FIVE

'YOU'RE cutting it a little fine, aren't you?' Niall said the next evening, glancing at his watch.

Robina had almost forgotten about the charity dinner she had promised to attend. Although it was the last thing she felt like doing, she knew they were expected. She had been called in to work for an unexpected meeting and still hadn't managed to speak to Niall about the promise she had made to Ella.

'I can get ready in half an hour if need be. Ella will be in bed before then. Won't you, darling?'

Niall scooped his daughter into his arms and tickled her until Ella was shrieking with laughter.

Robina watched them for a few moments with an ache in her heart. 'I'll start running the bath, shall I?'

As she switched on the taps in the bathroom that had once been Mairead's, her thoughts turned, as they inevitably did, to her loveless marriage. At least loveless as far as Niall was concerned, she mused, but how did she feel? She had loved him once, loved him so much that she'd thought she'd burst with it. She'd been so happy, never suspecting for one minute how easily it would all come crashing down about her.

Hearing footsteps behind her and the deep growl of Niall's voice as he teased his daughter, Robina blinked furiously lest he see the moisture in her eyes. She couldn't bear him to know that she still cared. All she had left was her pride and she was damned if she would let him take that too.

Niall strode into the bathroom and deposited his giggling daughter gently on the bathroom floor.

'I'll leave you to it while I get changed,' he said. Robina ached, knowing that he couldn't bear to be in close proximity to her. 'I suppose I have to come?' he added. 'Couldn't you ask someone else to accompany you? I have something I'd really prefer to be doing this evening.'

'Of course I can't force you to come,' Robina said between stiff lips. 'But you know the press will have a field day if you don't. They'd like nothing better than to sense trouble between the author of *How to keep your man happy— in bed and out of it* and her husband.' How bloody ironic it all was.

It seemed as if the irony wasn't lost on Niall either. His lips twitched in a half-smile as he looked at Robina, his eyes glinting. To her mortification, she felt her face burn. Was he remembering how good it had been? Her book had been written from memory, it was true, but only because every moment of their love-making was burnt into her brain. She could remember every touch of his lips, the feel of his hands on her skin, the way they couldn't get enough of each other, and the memories tortured her. Her heart thumped as he held her gaze and something flickered in his eyes. If only he would tell her he still loved her, then sweep her into his arms and take her to his bed, perhaps they could find a way back to each other again. She knew he still wanted her as much as she wanted him. But what good was sexual attraction, however intense, without love? She shook her head slightly.

Niall gave her one last lingering look before he turned and walked away.

'Dr Zondi and Dr Ferguson, could you look this way, please?'

Cameras flashed in a maelstrom of light and noise. Robina supposed she should be used to it by now. But the speed with which her career had taken off and the media interest had taken her by surprise. She had gone from being a GP to a best-selling author and presenter of *Life In Focus* all within a few months, and her head still reeled. Never in a million years would she have imagined the life she found herself living. But for all its glamour and wealth and adulation, Robina knew she would have traded it all in a heartbeat for the life she had envisaged when she had fallen in love with Niall.

She sneaked a sideways glance at her husband. Although he hated these functions, no one except her would be able to tell. He cut a devastatingly handsome figure in his tux. Tall, dark-haired and incredibly good-looking, the media loved him. As a couple they were portrayed as Mr and Mrs Perfect. If only people knew the truth, Robina thought bitterly. They were as far away from perfect as was possible.

Niall took her elbow and steered her through the photographers and into the hall. As Robina had expected, it was filled with a veritable who's who from the TV world. Instantly they were surrounded, and Robina felt a pang as Niall moved away, leaving her to talk with the presenter of one of TV's most popular chat shows.

'Ah, Dr Zondi,' the presenter, a grey-haired

distinguished-looking man in his early fifties, was saying. 'I was hoping we'd get a chance to talk. I would love it if you would do a slot on my show as one of the celebrities.'

Robina nodded distractedly, watching Niall from the corner of her eye as he was cornered by a journalist from one of the national newspapers. Niall had recently published a paper on a new treatment for infertility, which was causing quite a stir. She watched him bend his head to listen to what the journalist was saying, before he threw his head back and laughed. Whatever his feelings about events like this, he would play his part. Robina knew he would never do anything to embarrass her publicly. She felt the familiar stab of regret. Once she had made him laugh like that. Robina swallowed a sigh, before turning her attention back to the presenter, who was still speaking. She was on duty, and for the time being, at least, would forget about the mockery that was her private life.

'You want me to talk about the documentary I'm doing?' she asked.

The presenter frowned. 'Documentary? No, not really. People are interested in Dr Zondi the woman. Especially your new book. They know about the doctor, now they want to know what makes the woman tick.'

Robina shook her head. 'I don't do chat shows,' she said dismissively.

'Of course you do.' Richard Christchurch laughed. 'You have your own show every week.'

'That's different,' Robina insisted. 'That's not about me.'

'Isn't it?' Richard raised an eyebrow.

'It's not a chat show,' Robina persisted. 'It's a chance for patients to talk about their medical problems and get some answers. And for viewers to get information. They come on and talk about how illness affects their lives and what help they have found. It's not entertainment!'

'Isn't everything on TV entertainment?' Richard continued. 'But if, as you say, your programme is more of a public service, then you appearing on my show can only help get information to the public.'

Robina still wasn't sure. She didn't altogether trust Richard Christchurch as he had a reputation for taking cheap swipes at his guests. On the other hand, he was right. If she appeared on his show, it would help raise public awareness about her own show. And that was good. Wasn't it?'

'I'll need to speak to my agent,' she hedged. 'But I don't know if I'll have the time. I'm in the middle of this documentary, and my own programme returns in a couple of months. And somewhere in between I have to find time to promote my latest book—at least my agent tells me I have to.'

Richard smiled. 'Of course. It was only a thought, but I'll get my agent to speak to yours, shall I? In the meantime, perhaps you want to discuss it with your husband?'

Discuss it with Niall? Who was he kidding? Niall was the last person she'd be discussing it with. She glanced across the room to find her husband's eyes on her. He was too far away for her to read his expression, but as their eyes held, she felt her heart thump against her ribs. There had been a time when their eyes would have met across the room and she would have known exactly what he was thinking. That he wanted to leave, so he could make love to her. At one time, they couldn't get enough of each other. At one time no words had been necessary.

At dinner, she and Niall were placed at different sides of the table and she was thankful that they wouldn't have to pretend to everyone to be wrapped up in each other.

Throughout the seemingly endless meal she would look up from conversations she was having with the guests on either side to find Niall's unfathomable eyes on her. Whenever he caught her eye he would smile dutifully and she would grin back as if her heart wasn't breaking.

After the main course, the band struck up and Niall got to his feet, came over to her side, and held out a hand to her.

'Shall we, darling?' he drawled. As usual he was playing the attentive husband role and if he had a sardonic look in his cool blue eyes, only Robina saw it.

Conscious of several pairs of eyes on them, she let him whirl her around the dance floor. His hand was low on her back as he guided her and she could feel his fingers on her bare skin, burning into her. The movement of the dance brought her body tight against his and she let her body melt into him, taking the opportunity to let herself believe, even for a few minutes, that they were a normal couple, still in love.

Her head only reached as far as his shoulder, and she rested her head against the rough material of his suit, breathing in the scent of soap and the faint smell of his aftershave.

'What did Richard Christchurch want?' he murmured into her ear, his breath like a caress.

'He wants me to appear on his show.' She smiled up at him, conscious that people would be watching.

'And will you?' He frowned. 'Be careful, Robina. He's a snake.'

The concern in his voice was unexpected. 'I can look after myself,' she responded lightly.

Niall's answer was to pull her closer and Robina let herself relax into his arms, enjoying the feeling of his arms around her, even if it was all for show. All too soon the music ended and they returned to their seats.

The evening was almost over when Robina heard a commotion coming from the rear of the room. Looking across, she noticed several people had jumped out of their seats and were standing about in confusion.

She glanced across at Niall. The noise had attracted his attention too.

'Someone call an ambulance.' The voice cutting across the room was shrill, panic not far away.

Wordlessly, she and Niall were on their feet moving swiftly across the room. As the crowd parted, Robina's heart missed a beat. On the floor lay a middle-aged man, his face grey and his lips tinged with blue. He didn't appear to be breathing. Immediately Niall took command of the situation. Squatting beside the stricken man, he loosened his tie and felt for a pulse.

'What happened?' he asked the woman who had cried out.

'Bill…my husband…he said he had indigestion earlier. He took something for it, but then all of a sudden he said the pain was getting worse and he would go to the bathroom. But when he stood he clutched his chest and just dropped to the floor.' The woman's teeth were chattering with shock. Niall looked at Robina.

'No pulse. We need to start CPR.'

'Call an ambulance,' Robina told one of the bystanders. 'Tell them we have a cardiac arrest.' In the same breath she dropped to Niall's side. Aware of the eyes of the room on her and the flash of cameras, she shut them out of her mind. First and foremost she was a doctor and this man needed their help. It had been some time since she had done any clinical practice and she was hugely relieved that Niall was with her. She knew that, as a practising clinician, he was required to keep his resus skills up to date.

He was pressing on the stricken man's chest, counting off the beats under his breath. She waited for him to count to thirty before she bent over the stricken man and, taking a deep breath, tipped his head back and blew twice into his mouth.

The room was deathly quiet as she and Niall worked together, completely in synch as they once had been in everything. As long as they could keep blood circulating in his system until the ambulance arrived, the man had a chance. They worked silently, until after a couple of minutes the man coughed.

'I've got a pulse,' Niall said. He looked at her and grinned. Robina's heart rate escalated further. With his help she turned Bill onto his side, into the recovery position. There was little they could do now until the ambulance arrived, but it looked as if Bill would make it.

'Is he all right?' his wife was asking frantically. 'Please tell me he's going to be okay.'

Robina stood, easing the stiffness from her legs. 'It's early days yet, but he's breathing on his own now. And that's good. The paramedics will be able to give him something when they arrive, and the sooner he gets to the hospital the better.'

'Oh, thank God. Thank you. Thank you.' The woman dropped to her knees and cradled her husband's head in her lap. She looked up at Robina, her eyes wet. 'Thank you, Dr Zondi. You've saved his life.'

Robina was embarrassed. 'It's Dr Ferguson you have to thank,' she said. But as she smiled into Niall's eyes she was dismayed to find the shutters had come back down and he looked as distant as he always did these days.

The doors swung open as the paramedics rushed into the room, carrying a portable defibrillator and medical supplies.

Robina stepped back, knowing that Bill was in safe hands.
She turned to look at Niall, but he had already turned away
and was striding away from her. She bit down on her disappointment as the cameras continued to flash.

'Please,' she said, suddenly furious. 'Give this man and
his wife some privacy, can't you? This isn't a live TV
show, for goodness' sake.'

Chastised, the photographers lowered their cameras and
stood about looking shamefaced.

The paramedics lifted Bill onto the stretcher and moved
briskly towards the exit, Bill's wife following closely
behind. As they left, the photographers picked up their
cameras again and focussed on Robina, the flashes
blinding her.

She had to get out of there. She whirled around, trying
to remember what she had done with her coat, and then Niall
was by her side, holding it out for her to slip her arms into.

'I think my wife has earned the right to some privacy,
don't you?' he told the reporters. His tone was even, but
Robina could hear the suppressed fury behind the words.
He would hate the way the man's heart attack had turned
into a circus. All because she was there, and everything she
did was newsworthy. Robina had no doubt that her picture
would be splashed all over the morning's newspaper. It was
one thing not to have any privacy, it came with the terri-
tory after all, but quite another for photos of the unconscious man to make the news. She felt Niall's hand on her
elbow and then she was being steered out of the room and
into their waiting car.

Inside the safety of their limousine, Robina felt the
adrenaline seep out of her body. Uncomfortably aware of
the length of the hard muscles of his thigh against her leg,

she shifted slightly in her seat, wanting to put some distance between them. Despite the tumult of different emotions she felt towards him, he still had the power to send her senses into overdrive. Tonight, working with him over that poor man, she had remembered why she had fallen in love with him in the first place. He was a good man, a kind man. Couldn't they try to put the past behind them and move on? Try to be friends at least? It had taken little steps to destroy their marriage—could little steps take them back?

She reached for his hand as she prepared the words in her head.

Niall brought her fingers to his lips and kissed the back of her hand, the feel of his lips sending shock waves through her body. But then, his eyes glinting in the semi-darkness, he took her hand and replaced it in her lap with a little pat, as if she were a child.

'Well done, darling,' he drawled. 'Another opportunity to get your name in the press. You must be delighted.'

She glared at him. Every time she thought she was softening towards him, he would do, or say, something that would cause her to clench her fists in fury. How was it possible to lust after your husband, even though you weren't even sure you liked him? And what kind of woman did that make her? In that respect she was just like him.

'Yes,' she hissed through clenched teeth. 'How very clever of me to arrange for that man to have a cardiac arrest. Just for another photo opportunity. God, Niall, what kind of person do you take me for?'

'A woman who would do anything to promote her career.' His voice was gentle, almost caressing. 'As we both know very well.'

Stunned, she edged even further away from him. 'At least you know now who you married—just as I know the kind of man I married.' Why had she thought even for a minute they could be friends when clearly he despised everything about her? It seemed the only way she could save her marriage was by giving up work and becoming some sort of earth mother. And there was no chance of that.

Niall closed his eyes as they sped towards home.

Why had he said that? It was grossly unfair and he knew it. But she got under his skin. When he had seen her dressed in a gown of simmering bronze that fell to her feet, her short black hair highlighting that impossibly beautiful face, the diamonds he had given her as a wedding present sparkling at the base of her long neck, she had taken his breath away.

He had needed every ounce of self-control he could muster to stop himself from picking her up and carrying her off to…to where? His bedroom? Hers? And there it was. She hadn't spent a night in his bed since the night they'd argued before the miscarriage. She had made it perfectly clear that she couldn't bear him to touch her. He had tried to be patient, hoping she just needed time. He smothered a groan, thinking back to the night he had gone into the room they had once shared, thinking—hoping—they could comfort each other. But when he had reached out for her, she had recoiled and the look of fear in her eyes had shocked him. He clenched his teeth, pushing away the bewilderment and pain of her rejection. Although he had known it would take time for her to recover from the miscarriage, that had gone deeper. He was sure of it. It was almost as if she hated him. Every day she had drawn further and further away from him, throwing herself back into her work. If he'd hoped that with time she would come round, he had been badly mistaken. All that time had done was to drive a wedge between them. A wedge the size of the Grand Canyon. And as far as he could see, there was no way across.

CHAPTER SIX

IT WAS the second week of filming and, once again, Robina was sitting in with Niall as he consulted with couples. At home, everything had carried on the same as it had before, with the two of them spending as little time together as possible, meeting only over breakfast or when Ella's school functions demanded their presence. She had spoken to him about her promise to Ella and Niall had wholeheartedly agreed that they needed to make some time for the three of them to spend together. Despite this, they still hadn't managed an outing as a family. Niall had been on call the day after the charity dinner and had spent the whole day seeing emergencies at the hospital.

The patients they were seeing today, the Davidsons, were an ordinary couple with an ordinary life. Patricia, an anxious looking woman with short brown hair, was a primary school teacher and her husband, Luke, was a farmer.

Niall introduced her as usual, although she had met the couple before, and reminded them that they could withdraw from the filming at any time. Then he leaned forward and asked them to explain why they had come to see him. Once again Robina was struck by his warm, encouraging manner with his patients. How could she have forgotten the way his eyes crinkled at the corners, the way his mouth lifted when he smiled, how sympathetic he could be?

'We've been trying for ages to have a baby,' Patricia was saying. 'We wanted to wait until my career was established first. Then one thing after another happened. My mother became very ill and I had to look after her as well as work full time, so we kept putting it off. Sadly she passed away just over a year ago, but as soon as everything settled down we started trying. But months have passed and nothing.' She glanced over at Robina. 'I saw you on the telly, talking about your book on infertility, and I went out and bought it. It made me realise we had to do something, and quickly. So that's why we're here. To see why it isn't happening.'

'I see from your notes that you are forty-three,' Niall said gently.

'That's not too old, is it?' replied Patricia anxiously. 'I mean, I don't feel old. I'm fit, I exercise regularly. I feel as good as I did in my twenties. Anyway, don't they say your forties are the new thirties?'

'Yeah, she even drags me to the gym,' Luke added. 'I don't know where she gets her energy from.' He smiled fondly at his wife. 'She'll be a great mother. We're even looking forward to the sleepless nights.'

Robina felt a pang of envy. Whatever difficulties these couples were experiencing, it was obvious they loved and supported one another.

'Unfortunately, people don't realise that a woman's fertility begins to tail off once they are thirty-five,' Niall said quietly. He passed the couple a chart illustrating his point. 'And once they get to forty, their fertility is dramatically reduced. It doesn't really matter how fit and healthy they are, although for younger women, being a reasonable weight does help.'

'What are you saying?' Luke was frowning. 'Are you telling us you can't do anything for us, that you won't treat us?'

'Not at all,' Niall said. 'But I do have the results of your fertility tests here; the semen analysis from you, Luke, and the blood test we did on you, Patricia, at your first visit.'

Patricia grabbed Luke's hand. It was clear to Robina that she was beginning to realise that she wasn't going to like whatever it was that Niall had to tell her.

'Go on,' Patricia said quietly. Robina could hear the tremor in her voice.

'Luke's tests came back normal, but I'm afraid, Patricia, that your ovarian reserve is so low as to make the possibility of you falling pregnant, even with IVF, just about zero.'

Robina could tell he was choosing his words carefully, and that he knew he was giving the couple the worst possible news.

'Just about zero?' Patricia echoed, clearly shocked. 'Are you sure?' Her voice cracked. 'No chance at all?' Her eyes shimmered.

'I'm sorry,' Niall said. 'There really is no point in going down the IVF route. It's not just the number of eggs you have left, it's the quality. In my opinion, even if we did manage to collect some eggs from you, and I think that is extremely unlikely, there is every chance that they won't fertilise. And even if they do, the chance of you miscarrying is about sixty per cent. And lastly, even if a pregnancy were to continue, there is the much increased risk of foetal abnormality. I'm sorry if all this sounds harsh, but you need to know the truth.'

Patricia started crying in earnest, deep, racking sobs as

if her heart was being shattered, which it very probably was, Robina thought sadly. Luke placed an arm around his wife's shoulders. 'Is that it then?' he said. 'We have to give up? Never have a family?'

Robina ached for them. She felt a lump the size of a pebble form in her throat. She knew only too well how the couple would be feeling, especially Patricia. It was a devastating blow to their hopes and dreams. She gripped her hands together tightly, not wanting to let Niall see how much she was affected.

'I think it's only fair to be brutally honest with you, no matter how difficult it is for you to hear. But there are other options.'

Patricia looked up and Robina shied away from the naked hope in her eyes. 'But I'm warning you—what I am about to suggest is not for everyone. You would need to think about it very carefully, and before we went ahead, you would have to talk it through with a counsellor.'

'Please, tell us.' Luke spoke for his wife.

'The only way your wife could get pregnant is by using donor eggs. That's where we use the healthy eggs of another woman, fertilise them with your sperm, Luke, and then place one of the embryos back in you, Patricia.'

Patricia glanced at her husband and then back at Niall. 'But it wouldn't be my baby.'

'Not genetically, no. It would, of course, have half of Luke's genes, but, no, none of yours. The positive thing about using donor eggs is that the chances of achieving and maintaining a pregnancy are the same as if you were the donor's age. And since we don't accept donors over thirty-five, there is a greater than fifty per cent chance of you falling pregnant on your first cycle.'

'I don't know,' Patricia said slowly. 'It's all so much to take in. I never imagined for one moment that I wasn't going to be able to have children of my own. I guess I knew it wouldn't happen naturally, but I wasn't prepared to find out that it wouldn't happen at all except with another woman's eggs.'

'I don't expect you to make a decision right away,' Niall said. 'In fact, I would actively encourage you to have a long hard think about it. As I said, it's not for everyone. But if you think it is something you might consider, I suggest you put your name on our waiting list. I'm afraid it's about a year's wait at the moment.'

'A year! As long as that?' Patricia's face fell. Then she looked curious. 'Do these women sell their eggs? Is that how it works? Maybe if we paid someone more…'

Niall shook his head. 'I'm afraid that's illegal. There is no money involved. The women either donate their eggs because they have had their families and want to help someone else achieve their dream, or they are women who donate a proportion of their eggs in order to help fund their treatment. There are very strict regulations around all of this. No clinic in the country can try and get around them without running the risk of losing its licence. The regulations are there to prevent women, who are often pretty desperate, from exploiting or being exploited.'

Robina was conscious of leaning forward in her chair. Of course she knew that couples could use donated eggs or donated sperm, she had written about it in her book after all, but that had been before…before she had known that there was every possibility she had joined their ranks. Listening to Niall talk to the couple was almost as if he was talking to her.

'There is one other option, and I am not necessarily recommending it either, but I think you have the right to know. There are other clinics, overseas, that have more donated eggs than we do in this country. Not all of these clinics are above board, but there is one which I'd be happy to refer you to, if you want. You need to think about it. Speak to the nursing staff who will be able to put you in touch with others who are going through the same thing. Most people find that it helps. Then, if you think you may want to go forward, make an appointment to chat things over with the counsellor. She'll help you decide whether it's the right thing for you.'

After answering several other questions from the shaken couple, Niall showed them out to where one of the nurses was waiting to talk to them.

By the time he returned, Robina had managed to get her trembling hands under control. How on earth was she going to manage another couple of months of this? When every patient's story left her feeling like a wrung-out rag. But over the last couple of weeks Robina had known that something was shifting inside her. Seeing the way couples were able to deal with their grief and move on with their lives— together—was planting the tiniest seed of optimism inside her. Maybe, in time, she too could come to terms with *her* loss. And if she was too scared to risk another pregnancy, or if her tubes had been damaged by the infection, there were other options. None of which she'd even considered. But then, unlike her, all these women had loving, supportive marriages. And that made all the difference.

'So you are saying that women are encouraged to donate a proportion of their eggs in order to fund their treatment?' she said, signalling to John to keep filming.

Niall sat down in his chair and stretched his long legs in front of him before regarding her steadily over steepled fingers.

'You'd prefer women not to have the opportunity?' he said quietly. 'Do you have any idea how short the supply of donor eggs is? There are so many women, like Patricia, whose only hope of having a child is through the generosity of those women who are prepared to donate their eggs.'

'I can see the point when it comes to altruistic donors...' Robina replied. 'Those women who have nothing to gain except the satisfaction of helping someone else, but these other women, the egg sharers—aren't they under impossible pressure to donate in order to fund their own treatment? Is that morally correct?'

Niall brought his brows together. 'Don't you think we've considered all that?' Underlying his calm tone was a thread of steel. 'Do you think for one moment that any of us here would force women, or even steer them, towards a decision that wasn't right for them? And as I explained to Patricia, it's not only the recipients who have to undergo counselling. The donors aren't permitted to donate unless we are absolutely convinced that they know exactly what they are letting themselves in for.'

'But,' Robina persisted, 'I can see how desperate these women are to have children. Surely you are taking advantage of that?'

Niall stood. He towered over her, his eyes glinting. He signalled to the cameraman to stop filming. 'Could you leave us for a moment, John?' He waited until John, after a nod from Robina, left the room.

'Don't make this about us, Robina,' he said. When she opened her mouth to protest he held up his hand. 'I told you that I thought this was too close to home for you, but you wouldn't listen.'

'It isn't about us,' Robina retorted. 'There *is* no us. Oh, we may be married but we both know it's in name only. We haven't been married, not truly, since…' She broke off, unable to bring herself to say the words. 'Actually, I can't even remember if I ever felt married.' Furious with herself, she tried to blink away the tears before Niall could see, but it was too late.

He crouched down by her side and touched her arm. She looked into his diamond eyes. 'Are you sure?' he said quietly. 'We were happy once. We can be happy again. If we are both prepared to try.'

Robina's skin burnt at his touch and she desperately wanted to say, Yes, let's start again, go back to where we were, before it all went so badly wrong. But she couldn't. She was no longer the woman he'd married.

She shook her head. 'I don't know, Niall. So much has happened. You know you want more children, but I don't. I won't risk it.'

'We could adopt.'

'We could. But do you think having children would sort what's wrong with our marriage? Because I don't.'

He dropped his arm and turned away, but not before she saw the flash of disappointment in his eyes. Despite herself she felt a flicker of hope. Was there a chance? Did he still care? Even after everything?

'But maybe,' she said tentatively, 'maybe we can be friends. Not just pretend like we do around Ella but really try. Maybe make a start this weekend. Like we promised Ella. Do you know how long it's been since we did something all together?'

Niall's expression was hooded. 'You know I'd do anything to make my child happy. And if having you and me spend time with her together makes her happy then naturally I'll do whatever she wants. You know that.'

And just like that the flicker of hope was snuffed out. Whatever Niall said, the reason he wanted her in his life was to be a mother to his child. And she'd do well not to forget that, even for a moment.

'Come on, Daddy,' Ella demanded. 'Robina's programme is about to start.'

Niall switched on the TV and sank into the leather sofa. Richard Christchurch had phoned Robina the Monday after the charity dinner, explaining that a scheduled guest had been unable to appear on the show later that week due to a family crisis. The presenter had wheedled and begged a resisting Robina to step in at the last minute. When her agent had added her entreaties, Robina had eventually agreed.

Ella cuddled in beside Niall, popping her thumb into her mouth. He resisted the temptation to pull it out again. She'd get over the habit in her own good time.

They were just in time to watch Robina's entrance into the studio. She paused and smiled as the camera focussed in on her. She looks every bit the TV star, Niall thought proudly. She looked elegant in a floor-length gown that clung to her curves, a simple gold necklace highlighting the length of her neck, her height putting her at least a couple of inches above her host. For the programme she had chosen to dress in traditional African style and Niall thought she looked stunning.

As she settled into the chair the host Richard Christchurch held out for her, she appeared cool and at ease. They shared a couple of words off camera as they waited until the applause died down.

'Robina. May I call you Robina?' Richard asked. When she nodded he continued. 'For those few viewers who don't know you, could you tell us a little bit about your work?'

'I present a weekly show called *Life In Focus*,' Robina answered. 'It's a programme that covers a different medical topic every week.'

'Could you tell us how you came to present the show?'

'I am a qualified GP,' Robina answered. 'About a year ago, I had a book published—an-easy-to-read guide on infertility. When it came out, it was very well received and I was asked onto the show to talk about it. Shortly afterwards, the producer offered me the opportunity to present *Life In Focus*.'

'Aren't you a bit young to be offering medical advice on a range of topics?'

Robina smiled, her perfect teeth a flash of white against her deep copper skin. Niall felt something shift low in his belly. God, he loved her smile. It was one of the first things he had noticed about her. It lit up the room.

'I have a team of experts who work with me. They provide most of the answers because you're quite right—there is no way I could be an expert on all the different conditions we cover. All I do is translate the medical jargon into simple language the patients and viewers can understand. All of us have been in situations where we didn't grasp everything the doctor was telling us, partly because we didn't know the right questions to ask.'

'I have a clip from one of your programmes to show the audience.'

The snide smile on Richard's face made Niall uneasy, and he wondered if his wife knew what she could be letting

herself in for. A couple of minutes of a show Robina had
presented on autism came up on the screen. She was
sharing a sofa with parents who had children with the
illness. Opposite them on a separate sofa were the experts
who were there to answer questions. It was evident as the
couples spoke that Robina's empathy was genuine. As the
screen faded Richard turned to her again.

'Before we talk about your future projects and your
books, tell us a little about yourself. What about the woman
behind the medical degree?'

'I was born in South Africa,' Robina answered with a
smile. 'My mother is a journalist, and my father was
Xhosa. He used to be a lawyer and a political activist. He
died just over five years ago.'

'Isn't that how you started? As a journalist? What made
you decide to take up medicine?'

'I was sent to Sudan to cover a refugee camp there,' she
said. Niall saw something shift in his wife's eyes. 'The conditions were awful, completely unbearable. There was so
little anyone could do. But there was a team of doctors and
nurses and other outreach workers who were there, doing
a tremendous job. I watched them work for three weeks and
realised that medicine was the career for me. I wanted to
do something—not just report it.'

'But yet here you are, working as a high-profile TV per-
sonality. Not exactly front line medicine, is it?'

Ouch, Niall thought. He'd suspected all along that
Richard hadn't brought Robina onto the show for a cosy
chat. He felt his fingers curl into fists.

'No.'

Niall sighed with relief when Robina refused to let the
presenter rattle her.

'But one thing I did realise, after working as a doctor in a similar scenario when I finished my training, was that what really makes a difference is education and information. Doctors do what they can in these situations, but really it's just like sticking plaster on a wound. Without going to the source of the problem, we will never reach a long-lasting solution.'

'So tell me how all this relates to your work here in the UK.'

Richard's smile made him look like a shark. Niall would have given anything to wipe the supercilious grin off his face.

'It doesn't,' Robina admitted. 'But what I do is provide information to as many people as I can. Take my book on infertility, for example. If it helps even one person understand what the process involves, or points them in the right direction to find help, it can only be good. And as for the clip we have just seen, autistic spectrum disorder affects far more of the general population than most people realise. There was so much incorrect information given out about the MMR vaccine and its association with ASD that people stopped immunising their children, with a resultant increase in measles. The clip you have just seen is an attempt to share the challenges of living with an autistic child as well as debunking some of the myths that have sprung up around this condition.'

'Apart from making you a substantial amount of money,' Richard said snidely.

'Most of which I put into programmes that provide immunisations and clean water to the people in war-torn countries such as Sudan,' Robina replied without missing a beat.

Niall was taken aback. She had never told him that. It was hardly surprising since they barely spoke let alone

discussed their individual bank accounts. He was beginning to realise that there was a lot more to his wife than he
had suspected.

Her answer obviously took Richard by surprise too. For
a moment the smile faltered, but then it was back. 'That's
not public knowledge,' Richard said.

'No reason it should be.' Robina smiled sweetly, but
Niall could see a hint of iron in her eyes. 'What I choose
to do with my money is private.'

Niall was beginning to enjoy himself. 'Way to go, Robina!'
he called out, only to find Ella looking at him with bafflement.

'Way to go, Mummy,' she chimed in anyway, making
Niall laugh. God, he loved his daughter.

'Let's discuss your latest project,' Richard continued. 'I
understand you are doing a documentary following women
undergoing IVF treatment?'

'That's right. It will be airing in the autumn.'

'Don't you think it's a little invasive? After all, these
women are going through a particularly difficult time in
their lives.'

'I couldn't agree more. That's why only those women
who wish to take part are filmed. We make it clear they can
withdraw their consent at any time. But most of them want
others to know what it's like to undergo treatment. A book
can't really show the reality. It can be a terribly difficult and
unpleasant experience for women and as my documentary
will show, women are only prepared to put themselves
through it because their need for a child is so overwhelming.'

'Do you think IVF is good use of scarce resources?'
Once again the shark-like glint was back in Richard's eyes.
'After all, as you have so eloquently pointed out, there are
so many other places where funding is needed.'

'Do you have children of your own, Richard?' There was a dangerous sparkle in Robina's eyes.

He nodded.

'When you watch my documentary, one of the things that will become clear is how much these women want children. If they can be helped, why deny them?'

'Especially when it helps make your husband richer. I understand he works in the private sector as well as the NHS. I'm sure the publicity of your film will do his business no harm. Quite the contrary, it's bound to generate quite a bit of income for him, wouldn't you say?' This time there was no mistaking the look in Richard's eyes—he had pinned his prey, now he was going to finish her off. Niall groaned aloud. He'd had a bad feeling about this appearance all along. He should have listened to his gut and tried to talk her out of it.

But it seemed once more he had underestimated his wife. She smiled. 'Yes, I can see why you might think there is a conflict of interests. But I can assure you, my husband makes no personal profit from his private work. He uses any income from fee-paying patients to subsidise those who can't afford it and who aren't eligible for treatment on the NHS. Any funding left over goes to research. I'm sure you know that he is a world leader in this area? His research has involved looking at taking ovarian tissue from teenage girls with cancer prior to treatment. This may be the only way these young women will be able to have children. Before, it was an impossibility, now there is hope. His research also involves polycystic ovary syndrome, one of the main causes of infertility but also a factor in significantly increasing morbidity in this group of women.'

Niall sat bolt upright. How did she know all this? Not about his reputation, that was why she had sought him out back when they had met, but about him not taking any profit from the business? Just as she hadn't shared her finances with him, neither had he felt the need to share his with her. She must have winkled the information out of Lucinda, he guessed. Part of her journalistic training. That would teach him to underestimate his wife.

'I should also tell you that my husband takes none of the profit from any new treatments his research generates. He believes that new discoveries in science shouldn't belong to an individual but to society as a whole.'

Could he be hearing right? Niall thought, growing more surprised by the minute. But was that pride he heard in her voice?

Applause broke out from the audience. Robina had clearly disconcerted Richard. Her response not what the presenter had expected.

'Oh? But you live an affluent lifestyle, don't you? A large house in one of the more expensive parts of Edinburgh, a couple of flash cars, holidays abroad.'

'I have explained my finances as far as I'm prepared to,' Robina replied coolly. 'I'm sure you wouldn't want me to ask you publicly about yours.' She arched an eyebrow at Richard. Once more Niall felt like cheering. Obviously she knew something about Richard that wasn't in the public domain. Once again, it seemed that she had put her investigative skills to good use.

'Returning to your documentary for a moment,' Richard continued. Although the famous smile was still fixed to his face, the strain was beginning to show. 'Do you really think that you can empathise with the women appearing in your documentary? What would you know about the pain they are going through?'

Niall caught his breath. This was different, much more dangerous. Ella who, since his outburst, had been watching quietly, eyes fixed to the screen, looked up at her father.

'What is it, Daddy? What did that man say to make you angry?'

Niall put his finger to her lips. 'Not now, darling.' He could hardly bear to watch as he saw the emotions flit across his wife's face. He saw shock, pain and confusion. It seemed, like Niall, she had realised that Richard knew about the miscarriage. The presenter was too clever to ask her outright, knowing that she would wonder how he had found out. Apart from the hospital staff involved in her care, only Robina, her mother and he knew. But clearly there had been a breach of confidentiality somewhere.

For a long moment Robina sat in silence and Niall wanted to put his hand through the TV screen and strangle Richard Christchurch. But then she sat up straight and slowly crossed one leg over another, only the tell-tale nibbling of her lower lip indicating to Niall how anxious she was.

'I can empathise,' she said slowly, 'because following a miscarriage a few months ago, which resulted in an infection, the likelihood is that I too am infertile.' Her eyes shimmered and she blinked furiously.

Niall could only guess at the strength it had taken her to say the words live on TV. Especially when she had been unable to even talk to him about it. Hadn't talked to anyone as far as he knew, except perhaps for her mother, but he didn't even know that for certain.

Richard's jaw dropped, her response apparently not what he was expecting, or hoping for.

'I am sorry,' he said insincerely. 'I had no idea.'

'It's not really something that has come up,' Robina

said quietly. 'Obviously it is not a secret, but neither is it something I have spoken about in public before. But I think you would agree that I am well placed to be doing the documentary.'

She turned and looked directly into the camera, raising her chin. 'When my show returns, we will be covering mis- carriage. I ask anyone who has gone through this and wishes to share their experiences on TV to get in touch with the producers of my show. But for you out there, for whom it is all still too raw, you are in my thoughts and my prayers.' She blinked rapidly once or twice. Niall knew that anyone else would have let the tears fall, letting their public know that they too were human. But not his Robina. She could never pretend in public what she could barely allow herself to feel in private, and he admired her for it. But at the same time he wondered what keeping it all inside was costing her.

After Ella was in bed, Niall poured himself a whisky, stoked the fire and waited for his wife to come home.

He looked around the small sitting room she had made her own and felt a wave of sadness wash over him.

The cosy room was still exactly how it had been when Mairead had been alive except for one item; a small, intri- cately carved African stool Robina had brought with her.

It hit him like a sledgehammer. He'd never really thought about it before, but what had it been like for her to live here surrounded by his first wife's belongings and her taste in furnishings? Although he liked the little room with its plain white sofas, elegant furnishings and pale walls, it wasn't Robina's taste. He knew enough about his wife to know she preferred richer, more vibrant colours, abstract paintings instead of landscapes. In fact, her taste couldn't be further from his first wife's.

Picking up his whisky, he started pacing. What a blind, stubborn fool he had been. Why hadn't he realised what it must have been like for Robina? To come to a strange country, to live in the house he had once shared with his wife, to look after her child? He had been only too glad to know that Ella had someone who loved her, but if he were honest with himself he had been resentful of the way Robina's career had got in the way of the life he had thought they had mapped out. He had treated her as if she were some kind of replacement for his first wife. Not a woman in her own right with her own needs and desires. Stupidly he had thought that their love for one another was enough. Seeing her on TV just now had removed the last vestige of self-delusion from his eyes. She was lonely and lost and he had failed her when she had needed him the most. He had refused to see how much living Mairead's life had eaten away at her confidence. They had married without really knowing each other, and again that had been his fault. Having fallen deeply in love with her, he hadn't been able to bear her living several thousands of miles away, and had persuaded her to marry him, although they had barely known each other. And she had unquestioningly uprooted herself from everything she had known and loved to live with him and his daughter in Scotland.

And she had mentioned the miscarriage. Publicly. What strength that must have taken when she couldn't even talk to him about it. Did that mean she was beginning to come to terms with it at last?

He drained his whisky. Somehow he needed to win his wife back, make her believe he loved her and only her.

Make her understand that he could no more live without her than cut off his right arm. It was probably too late, he thought miserably, but he was going to try. Damn it! He was going to do more than try. Suddenly inspiration hit him. He had a plan. All it would take would be patience.

CHAPTER SEVEN

'DADDY says we're going out all together today. And I can choose.' Ella was practically hopping from foot to foot in her excitement. It was Saturday and for once neither Robina nor Niall planned to go into work.

Niall lowered his paper and looked at Robina. 'If that's all right? We did promise her.'

'I think it's a great idea,' Robina said, ruffling Ella's hair. 'We're all yours, sweetheart. Where do you fancy going?'

'I can't make up my mind. Swimming or ice-skating or the beach.'

Robina shuddered. 'I think it's a little cold for the beach. And I'm a hopeless ice-skater and not much cop in the water either.'

'How do you know you can't ice-skate?' Niall asked, cocking his eyebrow at her. 'Have you ever tried?'

'Not exactly,' Robina admitted. 'But I have two left feet, so I'm bound to be hopeless.'

'You can't be hopeless. You are good at everything,' Ella replied. 'Anyway, Daddy can't skate either. Can you, Daddy?'

'That's what you think, pumpkin.' Niall chucked his daughter under the chin. 'Just wait until you see my moves.'

'He can't even dance,' Ella said scornfully. 'My first

mummy said he always stood on her feet.' She looked glum for a moment. 'At least I think she said that. I can't really remember her any more.'

'Tell you what,' Robina interrupted hastily, hoping to distract Ella. 'There's a place I know, not too far from here, that I hear has a swimming pool with lots of slides, and an ice rink. What if I go swimming with you and Daddy takes you ice-skating, then we can all have dinner together? How does that sound?'

But to her dismay, Ella shook her head. 'You said I would have both of you—together.'

Niall rose from the table. 'So we did. And so you shall. If we have to pull Robina around the rink, so be it. Off you go then, and get your costume.'

Ella shot upstairs as if she were scared Niall would change his mind.

Niall grinned at Robina and her heart flipped. Damn the man, why did he still have the power to make her pulse race? It would be so much easier if she didn't still fancy him rotten. It had been so long since they had spent any time together and, despite the horrors of the ice-rink in store, Robina couldn't help but look forward to spending time with Niall and Ella. Perhaps this could be the start of them being a proper family?

'I'll just go and get my costume as well then,' Robina said, feeling suddenly shy under Niall's amused stare. 'I may not be able to ice skate, and not be much of a swimmer, but I can paddle with the best of them.'

The pool was busy with schoolchildren and the noise was deafening when Robina and Ella emerged from the changing rooms. Ella was wearing water-wings, but Robina warned her to stay close in case she got into difficulty. As soon as they spotted Niall, looking lean and sexy as hell in his Bermudas, Ella ran up to him, dragging Robina by the hand.

Robina was acutely aware of Niall's eyes raking her body. She felt the heat rise in her cheeks as his eyes travelled from her face down to her toes and back up to her face. He could only have looked at her for a couple of seconds, but to Robina, her body tingling under his gaze, it felt like for ever. She resisted the impulse to shield her body from his gaze. Once he had known every inch of her, and she of him. She recalled the scar he had below his left shoulder, where he had fallen from his bike as a child. She remembered tracing the grooves with her tongue, after tracing the contours of the raised skin with her fingertips. And how Niall had whipped over and grabbed her hands, pulling her down on top of him, kissing her until she was breathless. And then slowly, ever so slowly he had… She shook her head, horrified to feel languorous warmth spreading across her body. She had to stop thinking like that. She had to stop thinking of how it used to be, or she would go mad. But from the way his eyes darkened she guessed he was remembering too. Whatever their differences now, there had been a time when they hadn't been able to keep their hands off each other.

Thankfully, Ella was oblivious to the tension between her parents and was soon dragging them up several flights of steps to the slide. Robina tried to protest, the thought of being even the height of the slide frightening her, but one look at Ella's face and she knew she had to put her fears aside. This was Ella's day and Robina wanted it to be perfect.

Ella insisted that Niall go down the slide first, and then she followed, leaving Robina to go last. Telling herself she was being ridiculous to be scared and holding her nose, Robina flung herself down the slide and was soon caught up in a circular basin which spun her around in ever-decreasing circles. Taken by surprise, she let go of her nose and by the time she plunged into the bottom pool, she was gasping and spluttering. Her head popped up and then Niall was by her side, grabbing her under her arms. Instinctively, she wrapped her legs around his waist to keep her head out of the water. Niall's hands tightened around her waist and she felt her body being pressed into his. Despite her panic, she could feel the heat of his muscles through the cool water and the solid strength of his hips supporting her. Again there was that dizzying sense of the world spinning. She looked down to find Niall looking up at her, his expression unreadable. All of a sudden he released her and in her surprise she sank beneath the water again. This time he grabbed her arms and dragged her unceremoniously to the edge of the pool where Ella was waiting in fits of giggles.

'I thought you said you could swim,' Ella accused Robina, still laughing.

'I can swim,' Robina said, trying to hang onto her dignity. 'But no one told me about that bowl thing. It took me by surprise.' She was damned if she was going to admit there was *another* thing she couldn't do. Mairead probably swam in the Olympics, she thought bitterly. And then as Ella and Niall shared a grin, she had to laugh. She wagged her finger at the pair of them. 'Just you wait, you two, I'll get my own back.'

But her fear had left her, and for the next hour they swam and slid down slides and splashed each other in the wave machine. Robina couldn't remember the last time she'd had so much fun. It was the first time since she had lost the baby that she hadn't felt an overwhelming sense of loss and sadness. It was almost as if they had put the last few terrible months behind them and were the family they had been in those early, blissful weeks following their marriage. Seeing Niall laugh, Robina realised that it had been a long time, far too long, since she had seen him so relaxed and carefree. Why hadn't they tried to do something like this before? How could they both have been so stubborn? Even if their marriage was dead, was there a chance that they could be friends at least?

Ice-skating turned out to be just as embarrassing as Robina had expected. She just couldn't get the hang of gliding forward on her skates; instead she pushed herself around like a baby giraffe finding its legs for the first time, while holding onto the side. Niall and Ella, on the other hand, soon had the hang of it, and while not contestants for the next celebrity ice-skating TV programme, were making valiant attempts at getting around the rink.

Eventually they skated up to her.

'If we hold your hand, can you let go of the side?' Ella asked.

Robina could see that Niall was having difficulty controlling his amusement.

'I don't think so, darling.' Robina said. 'I will definitely fall on my bottom if I do.'

'No, you won't. Not if we hold onto you.'

Reluctantly Robina gave in and with Niall holding one hand and Ella on the other they skated off, with Robina doing her best not to wobble. Soon they had completed a circuit, but just when she thought she might be getting the hang of it, she tripped, pulling Niall and Ella down in an untidy heap beside her.

Robina hoped that with her woolly hat pulled low on her ears, no one would recognise her. The last thing she wanted was to spoil the day, or to have pictures in the press of her collapsed on the ice. Somehow she doubted her viewers would be impressed to see the normally cool and collected Dr Robina Zondi making an enormous idiot of herself.

Still grinning, Niall got to his feet and helped Robina to stand. But as he pulled her up, she lost her footing again and fell against him, knocking him to the ice with her on top of him. Ella stood by, watching, in a fit of giggles.

The world stopped as Robina felt the length of Niall's body underneath hers. Once again, the feel of him brought vivid memories back of their love-making. She looked into his eyes to find him regarding her with what? Pain? Hurt? Desire? She couldn't tell. Hastily, she scrambled to her feet.

'I think I've had enough,' she said, hoping that Niall would put her breathlessness down to her exertion. 'You two carry on for a bit while I grab us some burgers and drinks.'

Ella protested half-heartedly, but Robina could tell she was happy to have her father to herself for a little bit. They accompanied her back to the side, and she left them to it.

As she waited for them to join her, Robina thought back to her earlier resolve. She was the one who had pushed Niall away after the miscarriage and it was up to her to make the first move. On the other hand, Niall wanted more children, children she couldn't give him... She shook her head. What was the point? She kept going round in circles. She needed to speak to someone. Maybe her mother? Although she hated the thought of revealing the pathetic state of her marriage to Grace, she had to talk to someone.

* * *

Later that evening, once a happy but tired out Ella was in bed, Niall joined Robina in her sitting room. She had showered and was wrapped in her silky dressing gown, toasting her feet in front of the fire.

'It was a good day,' he said softly, coming to stand beside her. 'We should do it more often.'

'I know,' Robina said equally softly. 'Ella had so much fun.'

'Why don't we rent a cottage near Ella's grandparents for the weekend?' Niall suggested. 'Ella hasn't seen Mairead's parents since we got married and they are desperate to see her and her them.'

Robina's heart skipped a beat. Did he want to spend time with her or with Ella? And did it matter? She had promised Ella a trip, but the thought of being away with Niall was unsettling.

His eyes were on hers, and if she hadn't known better, she would think that her reply really mattered.

'There are some great easy walks, and some of the most beautiful hills in Scotland to climb. I haven't really had a chance to show you my country,' he coaxed.

'Okay,' she said finally. 'Why not? I'll ask my PA to try and find something in the area, shall I?'

'No,' he said firmly. 'I'll arrange it. I have the perfect place in mind.'

'Oh?' Robina felt a chill run down her spine. 'Somewhere you and Mairead stayed?'

'For God's sake, Robina. Of course not. I'm not that insensitive.' He pulled a hand through his thick dark hair then smiled sheepishly. 'Sorry. I know I deserved that. No, it's nowhere Mairead and I have ever been and you don't have to do anything except pack a bag. I'll see to everything else. In fact, I've already booked it for this weekend.'

Monday was spent watching Niall in Theatre as he collected eggs from three patients. He looked more relaxed than Robina had seen him for a long time. Gone was the distant, polite man she shared her home with. Instead, here was the man she had met twelve months before—the man she had fallen in love with.

As he worked he seemed oblivious to the camera, explaining to each of the patients exactly what he was doing and why. Every now and again he would catch Robina's eye as if he wanted to be reassured that she was okay.

The last patient of the day was a young, single woman. Maisie had been an unexpected appointment so Robina hadn't had the opportunity to meet her in advance. However, as soon as the woman, a pretty redhead in her mid twenties, had heard about the filming she had been adamant she wanted to be part of it.

'I want other people in my situation to know if there is anything that can be done,' she said firmly.

Maisie was attending with her mother. At twenty-four, Maisie wasn't married, not even in a relationship, but earlier in the week she had received the devastating news that she had cervical cancer. Luckily the doctors had caught it in time, so while Maisie would need to undergo chemotherapy, as well as radiotherapy, the prognosis was very good. However, the treatment that would save her life would destroy her ovaries and any chance of her having children. Maisie was still reeling from the news that she had cancer, but she was friendly with one of the specialist nurses at the clinic who had suggested she see Niall.

'They've told me that it's likely I'll go through the menopause as a result of the treatment,' she said quietly, but Robina could see from the whiteness of her knuckles as she gripped her hands together that she was struggling to maintain her composure. 'And that it means that it is unlikely I'll be able to have children. Hearing that was almost the worst thing about finding out about the illness. The doctors reckon that with treatment I should make a full recovery, but that I should accept that children aren't for me.' Her voice cracked a little. But she took a deep breath and continued. 'I have always wanted children. Ever since I can remember. I can't bear it if I can't. Mairi said you might be able to help me.'

Niall leaned forward in his chair. His voice was gentle. 'The most important thing is to ensure that your illness is treated successfully. You do realise that?'

'Of course. I know that they wouldn't recommend I have chemo and radiotherapy unless it was necessary, but they say they won't be starting until next month.'

'When I read the referral letter from your GP, I phoned your oncologist,' Niall continued. 'I wanted to be clear what the treatment plan was before we spoke. I didn't want to get your hopes up.'

The spark of hope in Maisie's eyes cut Robina to the core. Why was life so unfair? Just when the woman in front of her thought she had everything to look forward to, her dreams were snatched away.

'When did you last have a period?' Niall asked.

When Maisie told him, Niall looked satisfied. 'The timing is good, then,' he said. 'What we can do is to stimulate your ovaries to produce eggs, then freeze them using a process called vitrification. Then later, when you are ready, we could thaw them and fertilise them with your partner's sperm. It would give you a chance at a pregnancy. Your oncologist would be happy for us to treat you as long as we act quickly. I'm afraid it doesn't give you much time to think, but it is an option.'

Tears were rolling down Maisie's cheeks and Robina felt tears prick her own eyes. She blinked rapidly. Despite the tears, hope had brightened Maisie's eyes. Robina just hoped Niall knew what he was doing. Surely he wouldn't take chances with this young woman? What use would she be to a child if she were no longer alive to care for it?

'But won't the hormones you need to give her speed up the spread of her cancer?' Maisie's mother asked anxiously. 'Because, darling, if they do, can't you see it's not worth taking the chance?'

'I wouldn't recommend this course of action if I wasn't absolutely certain that it won't affect the outcome of Maisie's treatment,' Niall said. 'The level of hormones we use in order to stimulate your own hormones is tiny compared to that which floods a pregnant woman's body. The latest research shows that the amount we would be giving you, along with the very short time span you'd be receiving the hormones, has no material effect on your cancer, but of course it's entirely up to Maisie. All I can do is tell you what is possible, along with the pros and cons— but the decision is entirely up to you.'

'Mairi said if anyone could help, it would be you.' Maisie smiled before turning to her mother and taking her hand in hers. 'Mum, I need to do this, do you understand? Can you support me? I don't want to live if it means not ever being able to have children. And my treatment won't be starting for a few weeks anyway.'

'You can always adopt, darling. Have you thought about that?'

'I could, Mum. Possibly. But who knows if it would ever happen? There's such a shortage of babies. Besides, I know this is really selfish of me, but I want a child that is mine genetically. If it is at all possible.'

'Well then, my love, it's up to you.' Maisie's mother tried a smile, but it didn't quite work. 'I'll go along with whatever you want.'

Maisie hugged her mother. 'Thanks, Mum. I don't want to go through this alone. I need you with me every step of the way.' Then the two women were in each other's arms, crying as if their hearts would break. Niall indicated with a nod of his head that they should be left in privacy.

Robina mumbled an excuse and fled for the privacy of the ladies' toilet. How could Niall do this every day and not be affected? she wondered. And what about the nursing staff? They saw the patients on a regular basis throughout their treatment, became involved, she knew they did, because they had told her it was impossible not to. But they had all said that for each sad and disappointing outcome, there would be successes, some against all odds. And they had hundreds of photographs of happy families to prove it.

She had to keep believing that. Just because life had been unbearably cruel to her, it didn't mean that these women didn't have every chance. The irony was that it was Niall who was helping them when he was patently unable to help her.

CHAPTER EIGHT

By the time Robina finished for the day, she was emotionally exhausted and looking forward to spending some time with Ella. After she had read her a story, she would work on her book before collapsing into bed. Sometimes she wondered if it *was* all too much, the filming and the writing. Most people would be happy with just one career and she had two. Perhaps she was tearing herself into pieces just trying to prove she could do it all? But prove it to whom? Niall, herself—or her dead father? The time off she had promised Ella was her first break from work since her marriage. Robina felt a shiver of guilt, remembering that she and Niall hadn't even taken a honeymoon because of her work schedule.

The thought of the weekend away was becoming more appealing by the minute. Even if it did mean Niall and her circling each other like two wary tigers. But since their day out with Ella the tension between them had eased. So perhaps it was what she and Niall both needed. But how would they cope? Thrust into one another's company for two whole days? Her heart rate upped a notch. Maybe they could build on the fragile truce of the day out.

Her thoughts turned to her mother. She missed her

terribly. Something was worrying her—that much was obvious to Robina from their last phone call, no matter how much her mother tried to pretend nothing was wrong. Perhaps she should go and see her? They were due to have a break from filming in a couple of weeks. She could take Ella with her—show her Africa, and introduce her to her family. Her spirits lifted. It was an appealing thought—a couple of weeks back in the country she yearned for, with her mother, would give her time to think at least.

Once Ella was tucked up in bed, Robina popped a lamb joint into the oven and left it cooking while she ran herself a bath. Perhaps Niall would be home in time to join her for dinner. If so, she could discuss her plan with him then. It would give them something to talk about and would make a change from the usual fraught mealtimes where they both struggled to find something uncontroversial to talk about.

The slamming of the door signalled Niall's arrival home and Robina felt the predictable squeezing of her heart. This was the bit where he should be calling out to her, running up the stairs to take her in his arms…then they would make love, uncaring that dinner was ruined.

Wrapping herself in her dressing gown, she went to greet him. He was shaking the rain off his coat. Robina's breath caught in her throat as she took in his damp hair. He looks tired, she thought anxiously. Tired, but devastatingly handsome. As she looked at him the thought hit her like a sledgehammer. She still loved him. Completely and hope-lessly. All this talk about staying together for Ella's sake was only half-true. A life without Niall was no life at all.

'Robina! Is something wrong? Is Ella all right?'

He looked surprised to see her waiting for him. Once again her heart contracted. They had both been so stubborn. They had been in love once; surely he couldn't have lost all feeling for her?

'Ella's fine. She's sleeping. I thought we might have dinner together,' she said, feeling a blush steal over her cheeks. 'And have a chat.'

'What about?' His voice was flat. 'Is there something about the documentary you want to discuss? Because I have to tell you, I'm tired and not really in the mood.'

'No, it's not work,' Robina retorted, disappointment making her brusque. 'I was thinking of taking a couple of weeks and going to see Mum. I wondered about taking Ella with me.'

They moved into the kitchen where delicious smells were emanating from the oven. Niall cocked an eyebrow in Robina's direction, but said nothing, instead taking his place at the table.

'Why now?' he asked. 'I thought we agreed that we both needed to spend time with Ella. Or had you forgotten?'

'I miss Mum,' Robina said as she removed the lamb from the oven. She had made dauphinoise potatoes and green beans to go with the roast. Somehow the potatoes looked more like mash and the lamb was burnt at the edges, but at least the beans were fine, if a little limp and anaemic-looking.

'I just know something's bothering her, and I'd like to find out what. Apart from my brothers, who have their own families, she's all I've got.'

Neil winced then dragged his hand through his hair.

'We're your family now, Robina,' he said quietly.

'Are you? I want to believe that, but I don't know if I can.'

'I thought that's why we were going away this weekend. So we can try to be a family again. Or have you already decided that it's not going to work?' He narrowed his eyes at her. 'Are you thinking of going back to South Africa for good, Robina? Because if you are, you'd better tell me.'

'No! Of course not!' Robina replied. 'I told you and Ella I wouldn't leave, and I have no intention of doing so. Niall, why are we going round in circles like this? All I want is some time with my mother. I thought Ella would enjoy the trip. We're still going away this weekend, aren't we? And I have every intention of making it a happy couple of days.' She pushed the lamb towards Niall. 'Would you carve?' she said.

Niall attacked the roast with the sharp knife and manfully tried to cut a slice, without much success.

'Shall I get the saw from the garden shed?' Robina suggested, and suddenly they were both laughing. Niall managed to carve enough for them to share and the earlier tension drifted away as they chatted about the documentary. Watching Niall as they talked, Robina revelled in the companionship she had missed for so long. It was a start; a small step in the right direction. Her sore heart began to ease.

It was late on Friday by the time they set off. Niall had been held up at the hospital. Although he wasn't on call, one of his patients had gone into labour and Niall had stayed to do her C-section.

'I'm sorry, Robina,' he had apologised when he'd eventually made it home. 'I promised her I'd deliver her baby and I just couldn't let her down.' He sat down at the kitchen table and rubbed a tired hand across his forehead.

'What happened?' Robina asked. There had been a time when they'd spend the evenings discussing their patients, sharing the ups and downs of their medical lives, but it had been a long time since they had done that. Robina handed Niall a coffee and waited.

'She had a stillbirth at thirty-five weeks in her last pregnancy. We don't know why. God, Robina, it still beats me that we lose babies, even now when we have all this technology at our disposal, and we don't know why.'

Robina felt the familiar sharp stab of pain.

'I would have done anything to have been able to save our baby. You do know that, don't you?' Niall said gently.

Robina closed her eyes, hearing the undercurrent of sadness in his words. 'I know, Niall. There was nothing anyone could do.' She took a deep breath, summoning her courage while trying to find the words to tell him how she felt, but before she could say anything, Ella skipped in and sidled up to her father. Niall put his arm around his daughter and pulled her close.

'Every baby we lose is a blow.' He glanced up and Robina sucked in her breath at the naked pain in his eyes.

They sat in silence for a few minutes, watching Ella, who had climbed up on a chair and was rooting around in the kitchen cupboards.

'Sabrina was naturally worried the same thing would happen in this pregnancy,' Niall continued. 'So I agreed to let her have an elective section. It was supposed to be this afternoon, but then I had to take another patient to Theatre who was an emergency. I'll tell you about that later,' he said with a quick glance at Ella, who appeared to have found what she was looking for—her favourite mug. 'Anyway, the emergency took most of the afternoon, so we couldn't do Sabrina's section until after five. But, she had a healthy baby girl and is absolutely delighted. So all's well that ends well.' He grinned at her and Robina's heart did a flip-flop. The way he cared about his patients was one of the things she loved most about him.

'Maybe we should leave tomorrow morning instead?' Robina suggested. 'Ella will be ready for bed by the time we get there.'

'No,' Ella protested. 'I want to go tonight. You promised. And I'm all ready to go now I've got my cup.' She set her mouth in a mutinous line. She had been excited all day and Robina knew they couldn't let her down. Ella had even packed her own suitcase, although when Robina checked it she found it full of books and toys and not much else, and had had to pack another, more appropriate case for her.

'It's not too late, surely?' Niall said. 'I packed before I left for work this morning, so I'm ready.'

Robina gave in and soon they were following the winding roads that led them to the Highlands. She had never been to the north of Scotland before and she was looking forward to seeing more of her adopted country.

After a couple of hours they pulled up outside a cottage that seemed to be set in the middle of nowhere. Dark, gloomy mountains rose out of the darkness. There were no lights to be seen for miles. Where had Niall brought them? Where were the shops, the restaurants? What on earth were they going to do for the two days?

Predictably, Ella had fallen asleep and they left her in the car while they went to open up the cottage. As promised, keys had been left in the door.

The cottage was tiny and freezing. Again Robina wondered what Niall had been thinking. There was a stove on one side of the kitchen and an open fire on the other side, which obviously served as a small sitting room. Upstairs, Robina was aghast to find that there was only one bedroom.

'Where is the other bedroom?' she said to Niall. 'I imagined there would be at least two.'

Niall was looking baffled and dismayed. 'I'm sorry, Robina. Believe me, it's not what I expected. The website described it as luxurious with all mod cons.' He grimaced. 'I guess we can say they were a little economical with the truth.'

He looked so woebegone that Robina had to laugh. 'Never mind. We'll just have to make the best of it. We can all sleep together in the bed—it'll be a bit of a squash but, seeing as it's just for a couple of nights, I'm sure we'll manage.' All the same, a little part of her felt disappointed that she and Niall wouldn't be sleeping together alone. Even so, the thought of sharing a bed with Niall again, even with Ella beside them, was making her pulse race.

'Why don't you bring Ella in while I make us something hot to drink?' she said, keeping her voice steady. 'Then we'll see what can be done about the fire.'

Once Ella was tucked up in bed, Robina and Niall set about the fire. But the old-fashioned stove was nothing like either of them had ever seen before and soon they were forced to concede defeat.

'I'll have a look at it in the morning,' Niall said. 'There's not much point in persevering at the moment. Let's go to bed.'

There was nothing else for it. Robina was freezing and there was no way either of them could spend the night in the chair.

'I'll just use the bathroom, unless you want to go first?' she said. The room was suddenly alive with unbearable tension. Niall simply nodded.

Robina spent ages in the bathroom, first trying to get warm water out of the shower and when that didn't happen making do with lukewarm water at the sink. After washing as best she could, she slipped on the warm flannel pyjamas she had brought, refusing to think about the silky nightdress she had also packed in her suitcase. Eventually, re-alising she couldn't possibly spend any more time lurking in the bathroom, Robina abandoned the sanctuary. Niall was exhausted and would no doubt be looking forward to a good night's sleep—even if she wouldn't get a wink.

She slipped out of the bathroom, feeling ridiculously self-conscious. She hadn't felt this way since the night of their wedding—the same unsettling mixture of excitement and nerves. Niall had respected her views on sex before marriage and although it had been hard on *both* of them, the wait had made that night even more special. Not just special—sensational. Just thinking about it sent waves of heat and desire coursing through her body.

But she needn't have worried. Niall had obviously become fed up waiting for her to vacate the bathroom and had used the kitchen sink to clean his teeth before slipping into bed, with Ella curled up beside him on the far side. In the semi-darkness, Robina couldn't tell if he was asleep, but from the sound of rhythmic breathing it appeared he was.

Tentatively, trying not to disturb him, she slipped under the blankets, shivering as she felt the cool sheets on her skin. She lay there for a few seconds scared to move a muscle in case she woke Niall.

But it seemed as if she had been mistaken.

'You're cold,' Niall's deep voice said. 'Come here and let me warm you.' Robina felt his hand touch her shoulder and the shock of it was almost enough to make her leap out of bed. 'You're perfectly safe,' he said, and she could hear a hint of laughter under his words.

He rolled over and pulled her into the crook of his arm. She lay there rigidly, breathing in the familiar scent of soap from his skin. From his touch she knew he was naked—above the waist at least. Niall never wore pyjamas, and she absolutely refused to think about the lower half. She could feel the heat radiating from his body, the hard muscle of his shoulder underneath her, his fingertips just brushing her arm.

Robina was trembling but she knew it wasn't from the cold. It felt so good to be back in his arms, deliciously warm and safe, and she wondered what would have happened if Ella hadn't been sleeping right next to them. Would she have been able to stop herself from snuggling closer and running her fingertips over the hard, once-so-familiar contours of his body? Would they have made love, then talked into the night? Would Niall have told her he still loved her? But to her dismay and chagrin, she heard his breathing deepen and realised he had fallen asleep. Suddenly she was furious. How could he? How could he just fall asleep with her in his arms? As if it meant nothing and he was completely unaffected by her? Grumpily, she rolled away from him and onto her side. It was more proof, as if she needed it, that their marriage was dead in the water.

On the other side of the bed, Niall was acutely aware of every inch of his wife's body as she lay next to him. He smiled, thinking that everything was going according to plan. Well, almost. Okay, the cottage wasn't exactly the way he had thought it would be, but he had known it only had one bed and that they would have to share it. He had already suggested to Ella's grandparents that Ella stay with them tomorrow night, giving him the opportunity to get his wife on her own. He bit back a groan. If it wasn't for Ella, he wouldn't have been able to stop himself from seducing his wife and, remembering the feel of Robina's hammering heart underneath his fingertips when he had held her close, he doubted if this time she would have pushed him away. As it was, he could do with a cold shower or a freezing walk, because there was no way he was going to be able to sleep feeling the way he did. It was driving him crazy, seeing her every day and not being able to make love to her. He couldn't stop the memory of her long legs wrapped around his, her head thrown back, her long neck arched as she lost herself in their love-making. Did she have any idea what sweet torture it was having her back in his bed but not able to touch her? Sweet God, the sooner he had his wife back—heart and soul—the better.

CHAPTER NINE

WHEN Robina woke up she was alone in the bed and the delicious scent of fresh coffee was filtering through the air. She could hear the rattle of plates and Ella's excited whispers.

She eased herself out from under the covers and was pleasantly surprised to find that the house was warm.

'Good morning,' Niall said as she stretched. 'Did you sleep well?' He grinned at her and her heart flipped. Had he any idea how much of the night she had spent tossing and turning? But he, he had slept like a baby, she fumed inwardly.

'I managed to get the fire going,' Niall said, pretending not to notice that she was glaring at him. 'Once I could see what I was doing, it was quite easy.'

'And we've been to the shops,' Ella chimed in, 'to get rolls for breakfast. I'm going to help Daddy make it, then we're going for a walk, then we're going to have lunch, then I'm going to see Gran and Grandpa.' When she stopped to draw a breath, Robina laughed and ruffled her hair.

'Then I'd better get dressed, hadn't I?' She remembered about the shower. Damn, it would have to be the sink again. But she slid a glance at Niall. His hair was still a little damp at the front. Had he braved the cold water?

He flashed her another heart-stopping grin. 'Come here,' he demanded. Tentatively, Robina stepped close to him. 'See this little switch here? You have to press that if you want the shower to work.' He patted her head as if she were no older than Ella. Little did he know that Robina had started to keep score. She'd get him back—one way or another.

After her shower, Robin dressed warmly in figure-hugging jeans and her favourite cashmere sweater, before adding a pair of thick socks. She wasn't going to take any chances with the weather, especially if Niall planned to get her up a hill.

Breakfast was a mixed affair. They had managed to overcook the eggs, but the bacon was crisply grilled, just how Robina liked it. But the best thing about it was that they were sitting around the table, laughing and joking again, just as they'd done in the early days of their marriage. Suddenly Robina felt herself relax. Maybe this weekend *could* be the start of something.

Niall and Ella insisted on washing up. Shooed out of the kitchen, Robina took her coffee outside. The view took her breath away. The cottage was in a little hollow, surrounded by mountains on either side. The sun had risen and although it was still cool, the air was clear, and Robina breathed in air purer than she had thought possible. There was just the hint of a breeze, and mingling with the scent of the smoke from the fire was the salty tang of the sea, meaning it couldn't be far away. For the first time in months Robina felt her spirit soar. Out in all this beauty how could anyone feel sad? All of a sudden she was keen to set out on the walk to discover what lay beyond the hills.

After breakfast had been cleared away, Robina packed

a small rucksack with a flask of coffee, egg and cress sandwiches and an apple each. Although still cool, there was
no suggestion of rain in the air, but they packed some wa-
terproofs just in case.

Their walk took them along the side of a stream and then
gradually upwards along a rough track. Ella skipped ahead,
returning to show them various items of interest before
running ahead again.

'Tell me about the emergency yesterday,' Robina said,
curious. There was a time when every evening had been
spent discussing their patients. Their love of medicine had
been one of the things that had brought them together and
she missed their discussions, even if at times they had
been heated.

'Placenta praevia,' Niall said.

He didn't have to elaborate. Robina knew how dangerous the condition, where the placenta lay below the baby's
head preventing natural birth, could be.

'We got her to theatre in time to deliver her,' he continued, 'but then she started bleeding and we couldn't stop
it. We gave her several litres of blood as well as blood-
clotting agents, but she continued to bleed out…' He
pulled a hand through his hair. 'I thought we were going
to lose her.'

'What did you do?'

'We called in the radiologists—one of the benefits of
working in a big teaching hospital. They inserted balloons
into her major pelvic arteries, which stopped the bleeding,
and then embolised all the bleeding vessels that we couldn't
see. She's in intensive care, but doing well. I phoned the
hospital to check when we were at the shops. There's no
signal at the cottage.'

'People don't realise that childbirth can still be risky for the mother.'

'Only very occasionally, but when things do go wrong, they can go wrong pretty quickly. Losing a mother in labour—or even afterwards—is everyone's worst nightmare. No one ever wants that to happen. God, Robina, when I thought I was going to lose you…'

'But you didn't lose her. Or me.'

No, he thought to himself. Thank God, I didn't. At least not physically.

They finished climbing to the top of the hill in companionable silence. At the top they could see for miles in every direction.

'It's so beautiful,' Robina breathed. 'We could almost be the only people left on the planet.' Suddenly Edinburgh and all her heartache seemed a million miles away.

'According to the map, there's a small loch at the foot of this hill,' Niall said. 'Why don't we have our snack there? Then we can take a different route back to the cottage.'

Ella was racing off down the hill before they could stop her, her blonde hair flowing behind her.

'Does she remind you very much of her mother?' Robina asked.

Niall watched his daughter, looking thoughtful.

'Physically, yes. You've seen a photo of Mairead? Ella has the same colouring and her mother's nose. But Mairead was quiet, almost shy, and I guess we can say that Ella isn't. At least not now. After her mother died, she seemed to retreat inside herself, but since you've been in her life, she's almost back to the little girl she was. I have you to thank for that.'

'She's a child who is easy to love,' Robina said softly.

'I think so,' Niall agreed. 'But it couldn't have been easy for you, stepping into the role of stepmother.'

'She is your daughter, Niall. And now mine. I've never really felt like a stepmother.' Feeling that she was treading on dangerous ground, Robina changed the subject.

'Her grandparents will be looking forward to seeing her.'

'They haven't seen her since...' Niall broke off. 'More than a year now. She stayed with them when I was in Cape Town.'

They were both silent.

'I think I should stay behind when you take her to see them this afternoon. If I were in their shoes, I'd want to spend time with my granddaughter and son-in-law, alone, without the new wife making things seem awkward.'

'But you are my wife, and Ella's stepmother. You are part of the family and they'll love you. Especially when they see how much Ella adores you.'

Robina felt her heart melt a little at his words. Did he mean what he was saying?

'I still think you should go on your own. It's only for the afternoon. I'll find plenty to keep me occupied at the cottage.'

Niall looked at her searchingly. 'Please come, Robina,' he said softly. 'Ella's grandparents would like to meet the woman who means so much to her.'

Robina turned away so he wouldn't see the effect his words had on her. If only he had said that he wanted her to come for his sake.

In the end, Robina went with them. They followed the road across the mountain to the village of Applecross. As the road climbed up, sweeping around hairpin bends, Robina caught her breath. Every rise in the road brought new vistas of the mountains and valleys. It was wild and bleak but more beautiful than anything Robina could have imagined. No wonder tourists flocked to Scotland.

'This road's called the Bealach na Ba, Gaelic for the Pass of the Cattle, and is often impassable in winter,' Niall explained as they stopped at the summit to take in the views. 'There is another, longer way round that we could have taken, but it's not nearly as dramatic or as beautiful.'

'It is stunning,' Robina agreed. 'Almost as spectacular as the road around Chapman's Peak in the Cape.' She slid him a mischievous look. 'Remember?'

'I remember,' Niall said quietly, and Robina wondered if he too was thinking of the time they had spent together when they had first met. Then she had been showing him *her* country, seeing it afresh through his eyes.

'Why don't I drop you off at Ella's grandparents?' Robina suggested. 'Then you can have some time together on your own while I explore. I'll pick you up later.'

Niall nodded. 'And you'll come in?'

Robina nodded. 'This way they can meet me while they have some time on their own with you and Ella.' She paused. 'Do they know…?' She couldn't bring herself to finish the sentence.

Niall reached across and took her hand in his. 'About the baby? Yes, I told them. They were delighted when they thought Ella was going to have a brother or sister and very upset when they heard we had lost the baby.'

'Didn't they mind that you remarried?'

'No. They were happy for me. They knew Mairead and I had a very happy marriage and never doubted how much I loved their daughter. They saw how devastated I was when she died. As far as they're concerned, nothing can bring their daughter back and they know Mairead would want Ella and me to be happy.'

Every one of his words was like a knife cutting into her heart.

'Do you miss her?' she asked softly, not sure whether she wanted to know the answer.

Niall glanced at Robina, a strange expression in his eyes. 'I will always miss her,' he said. 'She was part of my life for almost as long as I can remember. If you are asking me whether I still love her, the answer is yes. But I'm not *in love* with her any more. She's dead, Robina, and I will always cherish her memory, but I married you. I couldn't have done that if I were still in love with my dead wife.' His words were clipped, almost cold. Robina wanted to ask him if he still loved *her*, but she knew she didn't dare— not as long as she didn't know what the answer would be.

Robina dropped them off outside Mairead's parents' nineteenth-century croft house, promising to return later that afternoon. She explored the village before finding a cosy spot in the local pub to read a book. She was nervous at the thought of meeting Mairead's parents. Would they like her? Would they approve of the woman who had taken their daughter's place? In the event, she needn't have worried. When she arrived back at the croft, Mairead's mother met her at the front door and embraced her warmly.

'We have been so looking forward to meeting you,' she said. 'Ella has talked about you non-stop.' She ushered Robina into a cosy kitchen and thrust a cup of tea into her hands. 'I'm Seonag.'

Mairead's mother was plump and curly haired, with a face that looked as if it was used to smiling.

'The others are down by the shore,' Seonag continued without stopping for breath, and Robina wondered if this cheerful woman had been as nervous about meeting her as she had been of meeting them. 'They'll be back shortly, but it'll give us a wee while to get to know one another. Now, I've just finished cooking a batch of pancakes. I hope you won't say no.' She eyed Robina as if she was already planning to fatten her up.

'I'd love one,' Robina said. 'I'm not much of a baker myself. Not really very domesticated at all, I'm afraid.'

'Niall has told us how proud he is of you and your career,' Seonag said. 'You must tell me all about it. I've never met anyone who works in TV before.'

Instantly Robina felt herself relax under this woman's obvious warmth. Had Niall really said he was proud of her? She had thought he resented her career, blaming the miscarriage on her frantic work schedule. Or had that just been her displacing her own sense of guilt onto him? She didn't know what to think any more.

'I never thought for a second that I'd end up in TV,' Robina explained.

'You are very beautiful,' Seonag said. 'I can see why they asked you. And I have seen your programmes. You come across as if you really care about the people you interview.'

'I do care,' Robina replied. 'I can only guess at how much courage it takes for people to share their personal experiences. The last thing I want to do is make them feel uncomfortable.'

Seonag smiled. 'And it comes across. No wonder Niall is so proud of you.'

'Is he?' The words were out before Robina could stop herself. 'I think he wishes I were more like Mairead.'

Seonag set down her cup and sat down next to Robina, taking her hand.

'It can't be easy being the second wife,' she said sympathetically. 'But I don't think you should compare yourself to Mairead. The two of you are as different as it is possible to be. She was always a home bird, happy to make a home for herself, Niall and Ella. It was all she ever wanted.' Tears shone in Seonag's eyes. 'She would have been so grateful to you for looking after Niall and Ella. When she learned she was going to die, her greatest fear wasn't for herself but for her daughter—and Niall.' Despite her obvious grief, she smiled at Robina. 'Mairead and Niall went to school together, played together. I can't remember a time when he wasn't in and out of our house.' Seonag looked into the distance, as if she were recollecting the images of a much younger Niall getting up to all sorts of mischief. 'Mairead was desperately worried Niall would retreat into his work as a way of dealing with his grief. He's never been one to talk about how he feels, you see, and she knew that. She loved him too much to want him to be sad. And it's obvious to me that you love him and Ella very much. Mairead would be happy.'

But he doesn't love me, Robina wanted to protest. At least, he doesn't act as if he does. He thought he'd found a replacement for Mairead and he was wrong. Seonag didn't have a clue what their marriage was really like. But when the older woman looked at her searchingly Robina guessed that there wasn't much that escaped Mairead's mother.

'We were so sorry when we heard about the baby,' Seonag continued gently.

Robina swallowed the lump in her throat. The warmth and sympathy in the older woman's eyes made Robina feel she could confide in her.

'I fell pregnant as soon as we got married,' she said. 'I was so happy, even though it was sooner than we planned.' She smiled, thinking of how excited they had both been when they had realised they were going to have a baby. 'I always thought we'd have at least four children.'

Seonag reached for Robina's hand and took it in hers.

'It's a devastating loss for a couple. I know you'll never forget the baby you lost, but in time perhaps you'll try again?'

'I don't know. Maybe,' Robina hedged. 'I don't even know if I can fall pregnant again. It's likely, even probable, that the infection after the miscarriage damaged my tubes and made me infertile.'

'Do you know that for certain?'

'No. I don't. I guess I'm too scared to find out.' Robina thought for a moment. 'But perhaps I should. At least then I'd *know* one way or another.'

The clattering of footsteps meant there was no more time to talk. Niall came into the kitchen followed a few moments later by Ella and an older man with faded blue eyes the colour of the morning sky.

'This is my husband, Calum.' Seonag introduced the older man who proceeded to pump Robina's arm enthusiastically.

'I have heard so much about you,' he said in his lilting Highland accent. 'Welcome to our home.'

Niall stood back, looking at Robina, a strange expression in his eyes.

'Mummy!' Ella flung herself into Robina's arms. 'We've had so much fun. You should have come with us. I missed you.'

The lump in Robina's throat got bigger as she caught Seonag's eye. Whatever else had gone wrong, at least

Mairead's child was happy. Even if it hurt Mairead's parents to hear Ella *call her* Mummy.

'Niall,' Seonag said slowly. 'I wonder if you and Robina would let Ella stay the night with us—if she wants to, that is. It would give us a little more time with her.' It crossed Robina's mind that Seonag had an ulterior motive for wanting Ella to stay, but she quickly dismissed the notion. Of course Ella's grandparents would want to spend as much time as possible with her. She was all they had left of their beloved daughter.

'Oh, can I, Daddy? Please say yes. Grandpa says I can stay in Mummy's old room and tomorrow morning he's going to take me out in his boat.'

'Only if the weather stays calm and she wears her life-jacket,' Calum said sternly, but there was no mistaking the twinkle in his eye.

'If you want to, pumpkin,' Niall said, ruffling his daughter's hair. 'And if that's okay with Robina?'

Robina was pleased that Niall had asked her opinion. For the first time she truly felt as if he really saw her as the mother of his child.

'Of course, if that's what you want. We can pick you up after lunch tomorrow.'

'Yippee,' Ella shouted, before turning to Robina and her father. 'You can go now.'

Niall laughed. 'I can see you want us out of the way so Gran and Grandpa can spoil you rotten. Come on, then, Robina. Let's leave our daughter to wallow in her grand-parents' undivided attention.'

There it was again. He had called Ella their daughter. As if she truly had an equal share. Maybe she had mis-judged him. Or had her own grief just clouded her judgement so she could no longer see straight? Whatever it was, she felt a surge of happiness—and hope.

After taking their leave, Niall asked Robina whether she'd prefer to stay in the village and have a bar supper, or go back to the cottage and have something to eat there. Robina felt unaccountably shy and awkward in his presence. She had so much to think about, but it was impossible to think rationally while he was so close.

'You fancy some seafood?' Niall asked. When Robina nodded he continued, 'There's a little shop on the way home where they sell freshly caught shellfish. Why don't we stop there and pick something up? I'll cook. I bought fresh bread and salad this morning. How does that sound?'

It sounded lovely, if a little nerve-racking. Robina couldn't remember the last time they had spent an evening in on their own together. She was aware of a nervous fluttering low in her abdomen. This was sounding very like a date.

'Sounds good to me,' she said through lips suddenly dry. Maybe this was the chance she had been waiting for. The opportunity to try and start over.

Back at the cottage, Niall insisted on making up the fire while Robina relaxed with a glass of wine. Soon delicious smells were wafting through the small cottage and Robina's stomach grumbled in anticipation. Her anxiety was increasing as she watched Niall move around the kitchen. She hadn't known he could cook but, then again, there were many things she didn't know about this man who was her husband.

Why, she thought, did he have to be so damn gorgeous? Why did he set her nerves on fire with one look from his blue eyes? And why was her stomach churning?

Niall smiled when he caught her looking at him—and he grinned even more when she blushed.

'You can set the table, if you like,' he said, pouring her another glass of wine. Robina rarely drank and her head was beginning to swirl, but whether it was from the wine or the way he was looking at her she didn't want to speculate.

Her hands were shaking as she set out plates and knives and forks. The atmosphere was heavy with something Robina couldn't put her finger on. She only knew she felt almost breathless and wanted to run away, yet at the same time there was nowhere she'd rather be and no one she wanted to be with more.

'Now sit, while I serve,' Niall said eventually.

Robina's heart was pounding so hard she was amazed that Niall couldn't hear it. And how she was going to swallow a morsel, feeling the way she did, was beyond her.

Somehow she managed a few mouthfuls. It was, as Niall had promised, delicious, but her appetite seemed to have deserted her. While they ate, Niall began telling her stories from his childhood. How he had grown up in the area and most of his afternoons had been spent running wild, either down by the shore or in the hills.

He made her laugh with tales of the various characters who had lived in the village and who had made it their business to send Niall home with a clip on his ear, if they thought he deserved one.

'It was like being brought up by several parents at once.' He smiled. 'There was no chance of getting up to no good with so many pairs of eyes watching you. Not that I ever did do anything very wrong, except perhaps drop a crab down the back of Mairead's T-shirt when she was eight.'

Some of the light went out of the evening at the mention

of Mairead's name. For the last couple of hours she had allowed herself to forget. But now her anxieties came flooding back. Robina pushed them away. Wasn't it time she let herself believe Niall?

As if he could read her mind, Niall laid down his fork and came to stand behind her. He rested his hands on either side of her neck. His touch was like a bolt of electricity running through her body. She longed to rest her cheek against his hand, but still she couldn't bring herself to.

He dropped his hands to her shoulders and massaged the side of her neck. Robina felt a wave of desire that stole her remaining breath. Involuntarily, she turned her head towards him.

Then, without knowing how, she was on her feet and in his arms. Her head came to just under his chin and she leaned against him, breathing in the scent of soap and outdoors and just the hint of wood smoke.

'I would do anything to remove the sadness from your eyes,' Niall said hoarsely, tilting her face, forcing her to look at him. 'Don't you know that?'

He brought his mouth down on hers and she was clinging to him as if she was drowning. He kissed her hungrily and she responded, pulling him closer, feeling herself ache from her need for him. He dropped one hand to the small of her back, the other lightly on her hip. He groaned and then pulled her closer, tight up against him, where she could feel his need for her.

He picked her up and she wound her legs around his hips. He held her, still kissing her as he carried her towards the bed. They fell in a tangled heap and then Robina was tugging at his shirt, pulling it over his head while he eased her out of her clothes. Not a moment too soon they were lying naked. Niall's eyes darkened as he looked down at her, his eyes devouring every inch of her body.

'God,' he whispered, 'I'd forgotten just how beautiful you are.' And then unable to wait any longer, Robina swung herself on top, guiding him inside her. Her body exploded with pleasure as she felt him move, and she rocked against him, unable and unwilling to control her body. She gasped, flinging her head back as his hands sought her breast, one hand staying to flick her swollen nipple, the other dropping down her belly, searching for the place between her parted legs, touching gently at first, then alternating with hard and soft strokes, finding just the right place, applying just the right amount of pleasure, remembering her body and what drove her wild. Robina cried out as wave upon wave of pleasure ricocheted through her body and then they were moving together, lost in each other.

Later, they lay in each other's arms and were gentle with one another. Re-exploring each other's bodies with hands and lips, reacquainting themselves with every inch of what had once been so familiar. The night passed without words until, finally exhausted, Robina fell asleep in his arms.

Niall propped himself on his elbow and gazed at the sleeping form of his wife. He drank in the sight of her, her long chocolate-coloured legs tangled in the sheets, her full mouth relaxed with a hint of the smile as if she was having happy dreams. God, he had missed her, and not just in his bed. He had missed everything about her; the glow in her eyes, the smile that always hovered around her lips, her touch, her laughter, her wit and intelligence. But now she was back where she had belonged and, God help him, that's where she would stay for the rest of their lives together.

Earlier, when they had been at Mairead's parents' house he had paused outside the kitchen to remove his boots and had overheard the last bit of her conversation with Seonag. Robina was thinking of having her tubes examined. That could only mean one thing. At last, it seemed, she was looking towards a future. A future with him and children.

'Good morning,' Niall whispered. She opened sleepy brown eyes and he ached to see the familiar wariness, before they cleared and the shadows in her eyes were replaced with a sleepy glow.

She raised a finger and gently touched his cheek.

'Hey, you,' she said softly.

He pulled her against him into the crook of his arm, revelling in the feel of her velvet skin against his.

'I've missed you,' he said, taking her hand and kissing each fingertip in turn.

'I've missed you too,' she said, a hitch in her voice.

'Let's never do this to one another again, Robina. Let's start over.' He felt the rise and fall of her breathing as she lay secure in his arms.

'I'd like that,' she said in a small voice.

He shifted slightly, kissing the top of her head, letting the fingers of one hand trail down her jaw, down her long neck to the hollow in her throat where he could feel her pulse against his fingertips.

'Maybe we could try for another baby,' he said tentatively. 'You could see one of the other doctors at the clinic and have a tubal patency test.'

He heard her take a sharp intake of breath and then suddenly she was out of his arms, pulling the sheet with her. She glared down at him, twin points of colour staining her cheeks.

'I should have guessed,' she said bitterly. 'I should have *known* that you wanted me back in your bed for a reason.' He reached out for her, but she backed away. 'You think if I fall pregnant again, I'll give up work and stay at home and become the kind of mother and wife that Mairead was.' Her voice was shaking with fury.

Niall was bewildered. What had he said wrong now? Then immediately he knew. He cursed himself under his breath. How could he have been so insensitive? They hadn't even talked about their lost baby, now here he was making the same mistake he had seen so many men make before him, suggesting that a new baby could replace the one they had lost, as if that was even a remote possibility. No wonder she was furious. He was acting like her doctor, not her husband. He had to make her understand she was wrong, apologise, make her see that he just wanted her to be happy.

But it was too late. Picking up her discarded clothes from the floor, Robina was already heading out of the room.

'Why don't you go and collect Ella?' She threw over her shoulder, 'while I pack up here. I think its time we returned home, don't you?'

'Wait, Robina,' he called after her retreating back, but it was too late. He was speaking to a door that had been slammed shut.

CHAPTER TEN

'I CAN'T keep it from you any longer,' Robina's mother Grace said over the phone. 'Your grandmother isn't well—isn't well at all. She didn't want me to tell you, but she's getting worse. I'm sorry, darling, but I don't think she's going to pull through.'

'You should have told me sooner,' Robina cried, distraught. 'I would have come to see her. Has she seen a doctor? What are they saying? Who is her doctor? I want to speak to him or her.'

'That is exactly why she didn't want you to know. She says the time is right for her to go, and more old people should just accept it when it is their time to die.'

Through her sorrow, Robina felt a bubble of laughter. Trust Umakhulu to say what she thought.

'The doctors say it's heart failure. They don't expect her to get better. All they can do is make her comfortable. I begged her to come and stay with me, so I can look after her, but she won't hear of it. She says she wants to stay beside her neighbours—the people she's known all her life. She says it is the Xhosa way.'

Niall, on his way to his study, stopped and listened.

'I'm coming home, whatever Umakhulu says. Give me

a couple of days to arrange things, Mum. I need to see her for myself. Please kiss her for me.'

Blinking away the tears, Robina replaced the receiver slowly. It had been a shock hearing about her grandmother. Right now, she would give anything to be back in Africa, with her mother. In her mother's arms she could let the pain out, find the comfort she so desperately needed.

'What is it, Robina?' Niall asked gently, his blue eyes soft with concern. 'Is everything okay?' He placed a hand on her shoulder, turning her to face him.

Unable to hide her tears, Robina bit her lip. 'It's my grandmother. She's not well. Heart failure, Mum says. I need to go and see her.'

Niall pulled her into his arms. Despite her grief, Robina breathed in the scent of him and revelled in the feeling of being in his arms. It had been too long since she had found shelter and comfort there. The night in the cottage had been all about sex and didn't count. Since they had come back from the weekend, a week ago, life had returned to the stilted conversations and strained atmosphere of previously. Niall hadn't even attempted to return to their bedroom, guessing rightly that she was still angry with him.

Niall tipped her chin, forcing her to look into his eyes.

'If you want to go, we should all go.'

'But what about work?' Robina sniffed.

Niall pulled away, dropping his hands to his sides. 'Can't you stop thinking about work—even at a time like this? For God's sake, Robina!'

'Not *my* work,' Robina retorted. 'We're due to take a break from filming the documentary for a month to give us time to follow up some of the patients at a later point in their treatment—you know that. And as for my books, they can be put on hold. And even if they couldn't, I would go anyway.' Robina felt crushed by his assumption, but could she really blame him? 'I was referring to *your* work,' she continued. 'Can you take time off?'

'I'm sorry,' Niall said, looking a little shamefaced. 'Of course you wouldn't let work stop you from going to see your grandmother. And me? I'll find a way to take time off. It may only be for a week, but it would mean we could all go together. No time is particularly convenient, so this would be as good a time as any. Mark and Elaine can hold the fort between them. Anyway, Lucinda's been nagging me to take time off for months now.' He paused. 'Besides, you have faced enough on your own. Regardless of what you think, Ella and I are your family now. Whatever the future brings, you have us. There's no way I'm going to let you face this on your own!'

Robina felt a flutter of something she barely recognised as hope. If he would put his work on hold, even for a short while, so he could come with her, perhaps he still cared a little?

Just then Ella skipped into the hallway. One look at Robina's face was enough to tell her something was up. She stopped dead and popped a thumb into her mouth, regarding her parents with the solemn blue eyes she had inherited from her father.

'What's wrong?' she asked. 'Why does Mummy look so sad?'

'It's all right, pumpkin,' Niall said, scooping his daughter into his arms. Ella buried her face in her father's shoulder. 'Remember how you and Mummy were talking about going on holiday? All of us together? To somewhere you hadn't been before? Well, we are going to see her mummy. In South Africa. How does that sound?'

Ella lifted her face from her father's neck. 'All of us?' she queried, as if she could hardly believe what her father was telling her. 'A proper holiday? All together? More than just a day?'

Robina saw the regret in Niall's eyes as he realised how much his daughter missed spending time with him.

'Yes,' he said firmly. 'The three of us together. All day, every day. How does that sound?'

'It sounds great!' Ella grinned from ear to ear, her small face lighting up. Still in her father's arms, she held out her hand to pull Robina into the embrace. As the three of them stood in each other's arms, Robina let hope take hold. Maybe it wasn't too late.

The next few days were frantic as Robina booked flights and tried to catch up with work. While she was away, her team would edit the footage they had already taken, ready for more filming on her return. Niall had arranged to be away for nearly two weeks, leaving his colleagues to pick up his workload. He would be back in time to carry out the egg collection on Maisie who had decided to go forward with treatment. Immediately after that, she'd be starting her treatment for the ovarian cancer, and Robina was impressed with the way Niall had arranged for her to be seen and treated so quickly. Maisie was still frightened, but seemed more relaxed now that she knew she would still have the chance to have children in the future and was loud in her praise for everyone, particularly Niall, for giving her the opportunity.

Eilidh's treatment was progressing well and Niall was quietly optimistic that the couple would have a positive outcome. Trevor and Christine Strain had had a positive pregnancy test and were anxiously awaiting the seven-week scan that would confirm the pregnancy was ongoing. Patricia and Luke were still thinking about using donor eggs, but had put their names down on the waiting list in the meantime.

All in all, between work and organising the trip there was no time to think, and that suited Robina just fine.

'I am so happy to meet my son-in-law and my granddaughter at last,' Grace said when after a very long flight they arrived at Robina's mother's home in Cape Town. It was almost midnight and Ella, tired out from the excitement of the trip, was asleep in her father's arms. Grace had never learned to drive and so they'd had to hire a car at the airport.

'We can talk properly tomorrow,' Grace said. 'After everyone has had a good night's sleep. I've put Ella in the room next to yours so you'll hear her if she wakes up during the night. I don't want her to get a fright if she wakes up and doesn't know where she is.'

Robina's heart thudded. Everything had happened so fast she hadn't had the time to think about sleeping arrangements. Of course her mother would have put them in the same room. The same bed. That was the norm for married couples. Catching Niall's eye, Robina could tell that he too was thinking of the last time they had shared a bed. She felt the heat rise in her cheeks. They had never discussed what had happened that night, both treading around the subject like wary cats, but she thought about it often. Too often.

They laid Ella down in the spare room, pulling a sheet over her, although the night air was humid. Then Grace showed them to the room that had been Robina's when she had been a child. Her little single bed had been replaced with a double, but apart from that her room was essentially the same, the books of her childhood neatly lined up in the bookcase, even her favourite teddy placed on the chair beside her bed. Robina swallowed a lump in her throat. The last time she had slept in this room had been the night of her father's funeral.

Her mother kissed her goodnight and then, after hesitating for a moment, kissed Niall too.

'It's good to have a man in the house again,' she said softly, before closing the door behind her.

Alone together for the first time, Robina looked at Niall. Suddenly he grinned and nodded towards the bed.

'It seems I am to have my wife in bed with me again,' he drawled, his eyes glinting. 'Unless you have a better idea?'

Robina, her heart racing, looked around the room. Apart from the armchair there was nowhere else to sleep except the bed. Why, oh, why hadn't she thought about this before?

'It's all right, Robina,' Niall said heavily, the veiled look returning to his eyes. 'I promise this time you'll be perfectly safe from me.'

'Too right,' Robina muttered, going to the cupboard, pulling out a pile of blankets and arranging them on the floor, while Niall looked on, baffled.

'That should do you,' she said when they had been arranged to her satisfaction. 'I don't think it'll be too uncomfortable.'

'You can't be serious!'

'Oh, but I am. There's no way I'm sharing a bed with you. Not after what happened the last time.' She looked him directly in the eye. 'Regardless of what you say, I don't trust you.' The truth was she didn't trust herself. She hadn't been able to stop herself thinking about that night—the feel of his hands on her skin, him re-exploring her body with his lips, his mouth growing ever more demanding… Stop it! she told herself as she felt a languorous heat spread through her body. She wanted him—had never stopped wanting him, but she wanted more, so much more than he seemed able to give—and she was damned if she'd accept anything less.

Thankfully, Niall seemed to realise she was serious and by the time Robina emerged from the bathroom he was grumpily punching the pillow as he attempted to make himself comfortable in his makeshift bed. He muttered to himself and Robina didn't quite catch the words, but it sounded suspiciously like 'You…belong…bed and soon'.

The next morning Robina was awake as soon as it was light. Slipping out of bed, she stepped over Niall's sleeping form and padded into the kitchen, unsurprised to find her mother already at breakfast.

'Good morning, darling,' her mother greeted her. 'Did you sleep well?'

She could hardly tell her mother that she had lain awake for most of the night as Niall had tossed and turned on the floor. So she simply nodded and helped herself to orange juice from the large fridge.

'Not having breakfast?' Her mother clicked her tongue in disapproval. 'I couldn't help noticing that you've lost weight. You're far too skinny. Men don't like skinny women, you know. At least African men don't. I can't say I'm too sure about Scottish ones. And it is not good for your health. You should know that.'

'Well, seeing as I'm married to a Scotsman, I can't see it matters what African men think.' Robina smiled.

'And you know, Mum, I've always been skinny. I take after Dad.' The two women were silent as they remembered Robina's father. Both Robina and her mother believed that he had worked himself into an early grave. But Robina wouldn't have swapped her idealistic father for the world.

'How's Umakhulu?' Robina asked. 'I'm desperate to see her for myself.'

'She's looking forward to seeing you too. She's failing, Robina; you'll need to prepare yourself for that. Why don't you and Niall go and see her this afternoon? I know Umakhulu likes the morning to herself. You can leave Ella here with me.'

'Sounds a good idea. I don't think it's a good idea for us to take Ella.'

'Good morning.' Robina swung around to find Niall standing behind her wearing jeans and a short-sleeved T-shirt. He looked surprisingly relaxed after his night's sleep, which was more than could be said for her.

Automatically Robina poured him a coffee and set it on the table. 'Ella still asleep?'

'I looked in on her and she's still dead to the world. I thought I would give her another hour.' He turned to Grace.

'You have a lovely home, Mrs Zondi.'

Grace smiled with pleasure. 'I like it. Would you like to see the garden?'

Leaving Niall to follow her mother, Robina went to get dressed.

It was hot. She'd forgotten just how hot it could get and she was unused to it. On the other hand, the warmth of the sun lifted her spirits. Here, at least, she felt as if she belonged.

Choosing a simple shift dress in bright colours that she

knew her grandmother would like, Robina dressed. It was good to be home, although the irony didn't escape her. Here they were, she and Niall, back where they had met, but things couldn't be more different. She sighed. It would soon be their first wedding anniversary. They hadn't even managed to stay happy for a single year. How had she ever believed that they'd manage a lifetime?

By the time she returned to the kitchen, her husband and mother were chatting away as if they'd known each other for ever. A few moments later, a sleepy Ella padded into the kitchen, rubbing her eyes.

'So this is Ella,' Grace said, smiling at her. '*Molo. Unjani?* That's Xhosa for hello and how are you?'

Ella tried to make the clicking noise of the Xhosa language but failed miserably and soon had everyone laughing at her frustration.

'It's not easy for people who weren't brought up speaking Xhosa like I was,' Robina soothed. 'But I'll try and teach you a few words while we are here.'

'It's hot,' Ella pronounced. 'Can we go to the beach and swim?'

Robina caught Niall's eye across the top of Ella's head. He nodded.

'That's a great idea, but after lunch Daddy and I have to go and see my grandmother while you stay with my mum. Is that okay?'

Ella nodded shyly at Grace, who was holding out a large glass of freshly squeezed orange juice.

'Then tomorrow we can all go to the top of Table Mountain, in the cable car. Would you like that?'

Ella nodded excitedly. 'But can't I come with you and Daddy to see your grandmother?' she asked.

'Not this time. Maybe in a couple of days, after we see how she is.'

Ella seemed to accept that and scurried off to get ready for the beach.

'I can take her on my own, if you want to spend time with your mother,' Niall offered.

'Oh,' Grace said, 'I thought I'd come too. Robina and I can always catch up while you two are swimming.' Grace slid a glance at her daughter and Robina sighed. She knew what that look meant. Her mother knew something was wrong and was determined to find out what.

Robina decided on the beach at Noordhoek. It had miles of empty sand and she knew it was shallow enough near the shore for Ella to paddle safely. There were also plenty of places nearby to get snacks and shelter from the sun. She would save Boulders Beach with its famous penguin colony for another day.

As soon as they had made themselves comfortable on a blanket on the sand and Ella had dragged her father off for a swim, Grace turned to Robina. 'Something's not right, is it?'

'I'm not sure what you mean,' Robina said evasively. 'We're all just a bit bushed. Work's been hectic and we had a long flight, that's all.'

But Grace knew her daughter far better than that. 'You don't have to pretend with me, darling. I know you too well. Is it the miscarriage? I was so sorry I couldn't be with you, but you were so insistent that I didn't come.'

Robina felt tears well in her eyes. She should have known that she couldn't keep much from her mother.

'It's my fault I lost the baby,' she burst out. 'I was so

busy with my new career I wouldn't slow down, even when Niall asked me to.' She laughed bitterly. 'It seems I got what I deserved.'

'Don't say that! Don't ever say that,' Grace admonished. 'You're a doctor, so you should know that these things happen, regardless of what we do or don't do. I very much doubt that the outcome would have been any different even if you had taken to your bed the moment you found out you were pregnant.'

'I know all that, in my head, but I just can't make myself believe it in my heart.'

'What does Niall say? Surely he has told you that you're feeling guilty for no reason?'

'We haven't really talked about it,' Robina admitted.

'What?' Robina didn't think Grace could have been more astonished. 'You haven't talked about the baby you made together and lost? That you are both grieving for?'

Grace's words brought Robina up short. Niall hurting? In her grief, pain and guilt she hadn't stopped to think how he'd be feeling. He'd never shown any sign that losing the baby meant anything to him. But had she given him the opportunity? Hadn't she been so wrapped up in her own pain that she hadn't really given a thought to his?

'But it's not just losing the baby. Our marriage was going wrong before then.'

'Oh?' Grace raised an eyebrow.

'I knew about Mairead before we married, of course I did. Niall never denied that he loved his late wife, but he didn't tell me he still loves her.'

'In love with a dead woman?' Grace protested mildly. 'C'mon, Robina. Listen to yourself. The woman I know would never think like that. What's happened to you?'

'She was so perfect. The perfect wife, the perfect mother, the perfect homemaker. Everything I'm not.'

'Sweetie, surely you're not jealous of her?'

'Jealous.' Robina laughed sourly. 'Of course not.' But even as she said the words she wondered if there wasn't the tiniest bit of truth in them.

'He married you,' Grace continued. 'Doesn't that count for something? He doesn't strike me as the kind of man who would marry for convenience.'

'And that's where you'd be wrong.'

Grace patted her hand and then put an arm around her and hugged her close.

'Do you still love Niall?' she asked quietly.

'Yes. I do. I can't imagine a time when I would ever stop loving him,' Robina replied. 'But I don't think he loves me.' She looked across to where Niall, his shirt removed and his jeans rolled up to just below the knee, was twirling Ella around over the waves. He was so many men, this husband of hers—the doctor, the father, the work colleague—but which part was hers? Even from a distance she could see the muscular chest and the narrow hips. She wanted him, he set her nerves alight, and he wanted her. She knew that without a shadow of a doubt. But was that the same as love? She had thought so once.

'And I think you couldn't be more wrong,' Grace said, following Robina's eyes. 'Anyone seeing the way he looks at you can see he loves you very much.'

Robina's heart kicked against her ribs. *Did* he love her? Was Grace right?

'I can't bear the thought of a life without him.'

'If you can't imagine living without him, you need to do something about it,' Grace said firmly. 'I never thought you were a woman who gave up easily. Especially not on what's important. He strikes me as a good man.'

'He is, Mum. He's good and kind and decent and sexy as hell. He's everything I ever wanted—and more. But one thing we've never really done is talk. Even after all this time, I still don't know what makes him tick—or him me.'

Niall and Ella were beginning to make their way back up the beach. Robina could hear the tinkle of Ella's laughter followed by Niall's deep rumble in the still air, although she couldn't hear what they were saying.

'You two need to talk,' Grace said quickly. 'I can't believe that two people who have to talk as part of their jobs can be so bad at communicating with each other.' She grabbed Robina by the arm. 'Talk to him. You owe that to yourself, to him and to Ella.'

There was no time for anything but a nod as Niall and Ella flopped down on the blanket. 'You should have come in with us,' Ella said. 'It was so much fun.'

'Another time.' Robina smiled. 'We have a few days yet. But it's time to get going. The sun gets very strong at this time and I don't want any of us to get sunburnt.'

'I've got loads of suncream on,' Ella protested. 'Anyway…' She reached out and touched Robina's arm. 'Can you burn? Your skin is dark already.'

Robina laughed. 'I won't burn as quickly as you, but even people with dark skin have to be careful, especially when they haven't been in the sun recently.'

'Let's get going,' Niall said. 'I don't know about everyone else, but I'm hungry again. Let's find a café and grab some lunch. What do you say?'

'I say yes. Can I have some ice cream too?'

On the way home, Robina thought about what Grace

had said. Her mother was right. She *had* been so wrapped up in her own grief she hadn't stopped to think about Niall's pain. She had pushed him away when he had tried to comfort her, freezing him out. And if their marriage had been going wrong before the miscarriage, what had she done to make things better? Realisation hit her like a sledgehammer. She couldn't just blame Niall. And her jealousy of Mairead—and, yes, she had been jealous, she admitted ruefully—had stopped her from reaching out to him. But what was she going to do about it? She shifted uncomfortably in her seat. Didn't she owe him—and their marriage—another chance? She bit down on her lip. She had been such an idiot. Was Grace right? Did he still love her? Or was it too late? No, she wouldn't let it be. There was no way she was going to give up on her marriage without a fight. Where had the fighting Robina been all these months? The woman her father had made her? One thing was for sure, though, she was back to stay.

After lunch they dropped Ella and Grace off at the house and set off towards the village where Robina's grandmother lived. Outside the air temperature had risen and Robina was glad that the car they had hired had air-conditioning.

'You didn't have to come with me. You could have stayed with Ella,' Robina said.

Niall glanced across and laid his hand briefly on top of hers. She smiled and he felt his heart thump against his ribs.

'I want to come,' he said quietly. 'She made quite an impression on me when I met her. But why hasn't she moved in with your mother so Grace can keep an eye on her?'

'Umakhulu's stubborn. She's lived in the village all her life and she told Mum that she wants to die there, surrounded by her friends and neighbours.' Her voice caught and Niall wanted to hold her. Hadn't she had enough pain in the last few months?

'What about her other children?' Niall asked.

'There was only my father. Umakhulu made sure that my father would have the best she could afford, even if that meant doing without. She sent him to school and he won a scholarship to go to high school and then on to university. In those days, it was very rare for someone from my father's background to make it to university.' She sighed. 'I think that's why he was so driven. As soon as he qualified as a lawyer, he was determined to put something back—to help those in a less fortunate position.'

'Like his daughter, then.'

Robina glanced at him. 'I don't think I could ever match him. All I can do is work hard, so that had he lived he'd be proud of me.'

Apart from the day they had met, when she had told him how much she admired her father, Robina hadn't spoken much about him. Was that why she was so driven to succeed? Was that why she had thrown herself into her job? Was the thought of failure so frightening for her? And if so, how much a failure would her miscarriage and infertility have seemed? At last, he was beginning to understand what made his wife tick.

'I also want to put something back—that's one of the reasons I donate to charity, but it never seems to be enough.' Once again her words struck home. Could it be that she felt as if she had never measured up to her father? If so, his lack of support for her career must have hurt.

'I know how blessed my life has been,' she continued,

'with the obvious exception. But who said life was fair? Who said you could have it all?'

Why shouldn't she have it all? Niall thought angrily. If anyone deserved it, it was his wife.

'I had no idea you were sending money back to Africa,' Niall said. 'Why didn't you tell me?'

'I didn't think you would mind. There was always plenty of money for us and Ella,' Robina said defensively. Why hadn't she told him? Surely she knew him well enough to know he wouldn't have stopped her.

'Of course I don't mind. I think it's a great idea. I just wish you had felt able to share it with me. You even found it easier to share your pain about the miscarriage with the public,' he replied sadly. 'I just wish it had been me.'

Robina looked out the window, knowing he was right. Why had she kept so much from Niall? He was her husband and they weren't supposed to keep secrets from each other. But he seemed so preoccupied with his own work and she with hers, there had never seemed the time to talk. And as for mentioning the miscarriage on air, in some strange way it had been easier than talking to Niall about it. She would have to find the courage to talk him about it—some time.

'Do you miss South Africa?' Niall said after a few minutes. 'You must find living in Scotland so different.' They were talking like two strangers, but at least they were talking.

'I miss Mum and Umakhulu, and the sunshine.' She smiled briefly. 'But I like where we live too. If only I could have Mum and Umakhulu, in Scotland…' She hesitated.

'Then what? Life would be perfect?'

'No.' She shook her head. 'You and I both know it's far from that.'

'It's not too late,' Niall said urgently. 'It could still be good. We could start over.'

Robina looked at him, her dark eyes glowing. 'Can people ever go back? Do you really think it's possible?'

'I think they can. If they want to badly enough,' he replied.

They drove for what seemed like miles, each occupied with their own thoughts until eventually they turned off towards the village.

Outside the little mud houses, children played and groups of men hung around talking. Women passed by with heavy buckets of water perched effortlessly on top of their heads. Washing hung in neat rows from lines strung up in back yards.

A neighbour looked up as they got out the car. Recognising Robina, she greeted her in Xhosa, her face wreathed in smiles.

Robin replied in the same language before turning to Niall and introducing him. The neighbour, Mrs Tambo, giggled and hid her face behind the brightly coloured scarf she was wearing.

'How is my grandmother?' Robina asked in Xhosa.

Mrs Tambo's smiles disappeared and she clicked her tongue regretfully. 'Not so good. But she will be better when she sees you.'

Niall had to dip his head to avoid hitting it on the low doorway. Inside, Robina's grandmother was lying in bed in a small room separated from the living area by a screen. She struggled up onto her elbows when she saw Robina.

Robina embraced her grandmother, shocked by how much weight she had lost since the last time she had seen her. Her dark skin had the unhealthy dusky hue of oxygen deprivation. Her breath sounded laboured and a quick

glance at her ankles revealed they were puffy, a sign of
oedema, which in turn was a sign of heart failure. Robina's
heart sank. Although she knew her grandmother wasn't
well, she hadn't been prepared for just how unwell she
was. She blinked rapidly. It wouldn't do to let her grandmother see how shocked and upset she was.

But her grandmother had no such reservations. She let
the tears flow and in a long stream of Xhosa told Robina
how happy she was to see her only grandchild before she
died and that she had been hanging on to see her.

'You have brought my grandson back to see me?' She
looked at Niall approvingly. '*Aiee*, but he is a man for
you.' Robina thought Niall almost blushed under the old
woman's frank appraisal.

'Hello,' Niall said softly. 'I am pleased to see you again.'

'And I you.' The words came out in short gasps as if she
didn't have enough breath left.

Robina turned to the neighbour who had remained
standing by the door.

'When was the doctor last here?' she asked in Xhosa.

She listened to the reply before translating for Niall.
'She said the doctor was here yesterday and will come
again tomorrow. He has given Umakhulu pills, they sound
like diuretics, but that her heart is getting weaker.'

'Makhulu.' She turned back to her grandmother. 'Please
let us take you to hospital.'

But the old woman shook her head firmly. 'No. I will
stay here.' She reached for Robina's hand. 'I am an old
woman who has had a long and happy life. I am ready to
die. I have seen you now. Please, do not argue with me.'

Robina turned to Niall in desperation. 'Niall, please
tell her that she'd be better in hospital. Tell her that they

can give her medicine to help her breathing and that they'll make her comfortable.'

Niall placed his hands on Robina's shoulders.

'Robina, look at me.' She forced herself to raise her head and look into his eyes. The sympathy in their diamond depths made her realise that it was hopeless, but she wasn't ready to give up yet.

'With the right medication and nursing care, she would get some more time. Tell her, Niall. Make her see.'

'She's made up her mind. This is what she wants. Do you have the right to force her to go to hospital so that you'll feel better? Because that's the only reason. You know as well as I do, as well as your grandmother does, that nothing is going to change the outcome.' Gently he pulled her into his arms, rubbing her back as if she were a child. 'I'm sorry, Robina. You have to be strong for your grandmother.'

Robina knew when she was beaten. All they could do now was help make the old lady as comfortable as possible and let nature take its course. But it was one thing knowing when a patient was ready to die, when nothing more could be done, and quite another when it was your own much-loved grandmother. Tears slipped down her cheeks and she could taste their saltiness.

'*Umntwana*, please don't be sad,' her grandmother said in Xhosa. 'Come now. Sit beside me and tell me about your life.' She patted the bed. 'I hear such wonderful things about you.'

Resigned, Robina perched on the side of the bed and, taking one of her grandmother's thin hands in hers, she spoke in Xhosa, telling her about her job, her book and the documentary she was doing at Niall's clinic.

Niall sat quietly in a chair opposite, watching. Eventually Robina's grandmother closed her eyes and fell into a deep sleep. Robina and Niall sat watching as her breathing slowed.

Suddenly there was a commotion outside and one of the neighbours came rushing in.

'Please, we need a doctor,' she said. 'Lydia's baby is in trouble, and she needs help.'

Immediately Niall and Robina were on their feet. 'Take us to her,' Robina said.

They found the labouring woman a few doors down, lying on a bed, surrounded by anxious women.

'The baby, it's not coming. She has been like this for a long time and she isn't well.'

'Why didn't she go to the hospital?' Niall asked.

'There is no money for hospitals.'

'Is this her first child? Has she had a baby before?'

'No. This is her first time.'

'Damn,' Niall muttered under his breath. 'I haven't any equipment with me.'

'There is a clinic a few blocks away. They'll have something,' Robina replied.

'I don't think we can move her.' Niall straightened up from his examination of the young mother. 'I can feel the head. Robina, go with the women and bring me whatever you can find. Gloves, endotracheal tubes, anything that you think could be useful.'

'I have latex gloves and an airway in the glove compartment of the car. I always carry that with me wherever I go, in case I come across an RTA,' Robina told him.

'I doubt we'll need the airway, not for Mum anyway, but the gloves would be handy.'

Robina fetched the gloves from the car and handed them to Niall. They'd probably be on the small side, his hands were much larger than hers, but they would have to do. Then Robina was running, followed by an excited gaggle of schoolchildren. As she ran, she prayed that she would find something at the treatment centre.

Happily there was an outpatient clinic on the go, and Robina found a nurse and explained what she needed. The nurse quickly collected some items and told Robina that she would call an ambulance and follow her as soon as she was able.

Robina, her arms laden, was off again. She was only away for ten minutes, but as soon as she arrived back she could see that the young woman's labour hadn't progressed. She handed a stethoscope to Niall.

'I know it's not as good as a Sonicaid monitor, but it was the best I could do.'

Niall leant forward and listened for the baby's heart beat.

'Too slow,' he said quietly. 'If we manage to deliver this baby, it could need resuscitating. Did you manage to find a paediatric endotracheal tube?'

'Yes, I don't know if it's the right size. But one of the nurses is calling for an ambulance. Hopefully they'll be better equipped.'

'Could you explain to Lydia what's going on? I tried while you were away, but I don't think she understood me. Tell her that she needs to push as hard as she can with the next contraction.'

Niall's steady voice gave Robina comfort. Her heart was pounding against her ribs. It had been so long since she had done any obstetrics. There hadn't been a call for it when she had worked as a GP, most of the deliveries taking place in well-equipped hospitals. Lydia looked so young, so alone and vulnerable. She couldn't bear it if anything happened to this baby. She had lost hers and was damned if she was going to let Lydia lose hers. No other woman was going to experience the loss she had, not if she could help it.

She slid a glance at Niall. How could he be so calm? Although he had delivered hundreds of babies, it had always been with experienced staff around and the latest equipment, plus a fully equipped theatre. This was a completely different scenario, but he didn't seemed fazed in the slightest. Didn't he care? But when he looked up at her she could see the muscle twitching in his jaw and the concern in his deep blue eyes. Of course he cared. How could she ever have doubted it? Hadn't she seen him with enough patients to know that?

'The baby's not progressing down the birth canal. Normally I would do a forceps delivery, but I don't have the equipment. You are going to have to help me, Robina.'

They worked together as if they had done so for years, each knowing instinctively what the other needed. Without the right equipment, Niall had to improvise, using his hands to guide the baby down through the birth canal.

Finally, the baby slipped out and into Niall's arms. Quickly Robina took the clean towel the women had fetched and wrapped the newborn infant tightly. But she could see that the baby was floppy and hadn't taken a breath and her heart thumped painfully against her ribs. They couldn't lose the baby now. Not after everything they had been through.

She caught Niall's eyes. 'Where is that bloody ambulance?' she muttered under her breath.

'We don't have time to wait for it. We need to get this baby breathing, right now.' He took the tiny infant from Robina and laid it gently on the table the women had prepared.

'Could you pass me the endotracheal tube, Robina?' His voice was calm, giving no indication that intubating a neonate wasn't something he would have had to do as an obstetrician. At the hospital, there were always highly experienced paediatricians around to take over the care of the baby once it had been born. 'You'll need to deliver the placenta. Can you do that?'

Robina nodded as she passed across the tube that Niall would attempt to slip into the baby's airway. She had the easy job.

Please let it be all right, Robina prayed silently, before turning to the mother who was lying exhausted on the bed.

'My baby,' she said. 'Why isn't it crying?'

'You have a little girl, a daughter. But she needs help to breathe. The doctor is doing everything he can to help her. You have to stay as calm as you can. We still need to deliver the placenta.'

Robina knew that Lydia would be straining even more than she was to hear the sound of a cry, but as the seconds passed slowly, it was deathly quiet. She glanced across the room, but could see nothing except Niall's broad back. Then suddenly she heard him give a grunt of satisfaction.

'The tube's in and we have an airway, and baby seems to be pinking up with a good pulse. Tell Lydia that although the baby isn't out of danger yet, it has a good chance.'

The lump in her throat made it difficult for Robina to speak. 'Your daughter is breathing,' she whispered to Lydia in Xhosa. 'It will be a couple of days before we can be sure, but the doctor thinks she'll be all right.'

The wailing sound of the ambulance was like music to Robina's ears. The baby needed to be in Special Care, and the sooner the better. She and Niall, especially Niall, had done everything they could.

Niall carried the baby, still wrapped in a towel, across to Lydia. Despite the tube, the baby was making small movements with its little fingers. Lydia stroked her baby's cheek with a tender finger.

As Robina looked down at the baby her throat closed. If only things had been different and she too had been able to accept a baby into her arms. He or she would have been loved much. It was as if all the suppressed love she'd had inside her had built up like a dam. She realised that she had been too frightened of letting that dam burst, unsure if she'd ever recover from her grief. That was why she had pushed Niall away, instead of seeking the comfort he had offered her.

Looking into his eyes, she saw them darken and knew he too was thinking of the baby they had lost.

'I should go with them in the ambulance,' Niall said, once Lydia had been wheeled into the ambulance and her baby placed in the portable incubator.

'Of course.' Robina nodded tiredly. Now that the drama was over and she felt the adrenaline seep away, she felt wrung out and on the verge of tears. Today hadn't turned out the way she had imagined.

'I don't want to leave you,' Niall said urgently. 'Not when your grandmother…' He didn't have to finish the sentence. Not when her grandmother might die at any time. 'But the baby might relapse. Although the paramedics will look after Lydia, I still need to be there just in case.'

'I know.' She gave him a small push in the direction of the ambulance. 'Go. I'll be all right.'

But still Niall hesitated.

'Go!' Robina said more firmly. 'Right now that baby needs you.'

'I'll be back as soon as I can.' With a last long look at Robina, Niall jumped into the ambulance then, with the siren blaring, he was gone.

Robina returned to her grandmother's side. The old lady was still sleeping, but her breathing had become more laboured in the hour that Robina had been away and she knew it wouldn't be long before her grandmother passed away. She used her mobile to phone Grace, to warn her that her mother-in-law was slipping away.

Distraught, but unsurprised, her mother said she would take a taxi and bring Ella with her, and would be there as soon as she could. Robina didn't tell her that Niall had gone to the hospital and that she was alone. She knew her mother would be even more anxious if she knew, and there was no point in increasing her worry when there was nothing she could do.

She held her grandmother's hand and let the tears fall. And as she guessed, the old lady died without opening her eyes again.

CHAPTER ELEVEN

THROUGHOUT the journey to the hospital, Niall was torn in two. He knew Robina's grandmother only had hours left— if that—and he hated the thought of Robina facing it alone. Once again, he was unable to help his wife when she needed him most. Once again, he had let her down. But he had no choice. He couldn't stop his baby from dying, but he wasn't going to let anything happen to this one.

'I am going to call her Lucky,' whispered Lydia, who hadn't taken her eyes off her baby.

'It's a good name,' Niall agreed. The baby was doing well and he was pretty confident that it wouldn't need to stay in Special Care for very long. As soon as he had seen mother and baby safely into the hospital, he would go back to Robina. He prayed he wouldn't be too late.

And sure enough, by the time he had passed Lydia and Lucky across to the hospital staff and filled out the paper-work detailing his treatment, a couple of hours had passed and he still had no way of getting back to Robina.

'Where can I hire a car or find a taxi?' he asked the driver of the ambulance that had taken them to the hospital.

'Sorry, man, but there is no car-hire place open near here. You'll have to go to the airport to find one open.'

'What about a taxi?' Niall asked.

'There is a taxi rank over there.' The ambulance man pointed to a large group of people queuing across the road. 'But it takes a long time. It must first go to the other villages along the way. If you want a taxi that takes you there directly, you will have to phone, or go to the airport.'

Seething with frustration, Niall looked at his watch. All that would take time he didn't have. The thought of Robina alone was eating him up inside. He called Grace, hoping she would have a better idea, but there was no reply. Robina had probably called her to let her know about her mother-in-law and she'd be on her way to the village.

Niall swore under his breath. There *had* to be a way to get back to Robina.

'You're in a hurry?' the ambulance man asked him.

'A very big hurry,' Niall replied.

'In that case, I will take you myself. My shift has finished for the day.'

'But it's miles,' Niall protested, feeling the first stirring of hope. 'Well out of your way.'

The ambulance man shrugged. 'You helped someone you didn't know. Now I must help you back—it is the custom.' He held out his hand. 'My name is Tambo.'

Soon they were careering up the road in Tambo's rickety car at well over the speed limit. But Niall couldn't bring himself to tell him to slow down. All he cared about was getting back to Robina.

It seemed an interminable time before they pulled up outside Robina's grandmother's house. Niall thanked his rescuer effusively, offering to pay for the petrol. But Tambo only looked offended as he waved away the money. 'I told you, it is my duty. One day, maybe somebody will do some-

thing for me and the favour I did you is returned.' And with
another wave of his hand he drove away in a cloud of dust.

As soon as Niall entered the room, he knew he was too
late. The room was filled with keening women and Robina
was sitting by the bed looking stunned.

'Is she gone?' he asked gently. When Robina nodded he
strode across the room and wrapped her in his arms. 'Oh,
my love,' he said. 'I'm so sorry.'

He felt her relax into his arms for a moment, but then
she straightened and pulled away.

'Mum is on her way with Ella. She and I will need to
stay, it is the custom, but you must take Ella home. It will
only distress her to be here.'

'Ella knows about loss,' Niall reminded her gently. 'Let
us stay. We're your family too, and everyone needs their
family at times like this.'

Robina smiled wanly. 'I'll have my mother. Honestly,
it's better if you go. I'll be all right. As Umakhulu said, she
had a long and happy life. She didn't mind dying, she was
ready to go.'

'Don't push me away again, Robina,' he said.

'I'm not. I…' She hesitated and Niall could tell she was
only just holding it together. 'I'll need you later.' Her voice
caught and, despite feeling wretched for his wife, Niall felt
a surge of hope. She'd admitted she needed him. It was a
start. He owed it to her to let her do things her own way.
But this time he would make her talk to him. This time he
wouldn't let her push him away. She had to know he loved
her and wanted only her. They had to start talking—find a
way back to each other somehow.

'I'll go when your mother comes. But I'll be waiting
for you. Whenever you need me, I'll be there. I'm not

going to let you go through this alone. Do you understand?'

She gazed up at him, her large brown eyes luminous.

'I understand.' She brought a hand to his face and gently touched his cheek. 'How's Lydia's baby?'

'She is going to be fine. We can go and see them in a day or two if you like.'

'I'd like that. One life into the world and another out. I understand that now. It's time for us to talk about our baby. Not here, but later.'

Reluctantly Niall released his wife and watched her being swallowed up by the crowd of women. Hearing the sound of a car, he went outside to find his mother-in-law and daughter emerging from a taxi.

'Could you hold on a minute?' he asked the driver.

Grace looked at him, the sound of keening drifting across the still night air.

'I'm too late,' she said softly. It wasn't a question.

'I'm so sorry. I think she was just holding on long enough to see Robina,' he said. 'I have seen it before in the dying.'

'How's my daughter?' Grace asked.

'She's okay. I think she's going to be all right. I think it's *all* going to be all right.' He could see from Grace's expression that she understood the true meaning of his words. 'She wants me to take Ella back to the house. I'd rather stay, but it's what she wants.'

'You should go. I'll be here with her,' Grace said. 'But later, when it all hits home—that's when she'll really need you.'

He watched as Grace enfolded her daughter in her arms, regretting that once again he hadn't been there when she needed him most. He swore that as long as it was in his power, his wife would never again face anything alone.

Niall woke to hear the sound of Robina tiptoeing around the room. Although she was quiet, too many years on call had made him alert to the slightest sound.

'You're back,' he said, stating the obvious.

'Only to shower and change,' Robina said. 'Then I'm going back again. I brought Mum home so she could have a rest.'

Niall propped himself on his elbow. In the dawning light trickling through the curtains, he could see the lines of fatigue and grief etched on Robina's face. He longed to reach out and pull her into his arms, but a sixth sense stopped him. He had rushed her before, and he wouldn't make the same mistake again—the stakes were too high.

Instead he eased himself out of bed and touched her lightly on the shoulder. 'I'll make you something to eat, shall I? Or would you prefer to sleep for a couple of hours?'

Robina lay down, still fully clothed, on the bed he had just vacated. 'A couple of hours' sleep, I think, then some breakfast would be lovely.'

Niall hesitated, before lying down beside her and pulling her towards him so that her head was resting on his chest. At first he felt her stiffen and then she relaxed into his arms. Although it took every ounce of his willpower not to pull her closer, he lay there simply holding her, until her breathing relaxed and she fell asleep.

He breathed in the faint smell of her perfume and revelled in the velvet feel of her skin under his fingertips.

One loss had pushed them away from each other. This time he was determined that another would pull them together.

When Robina opened her eyes the sun was high in the sky, and the space next to her empty. Niall was up. She felt a pang of loss as sharp as any physical pain. Umakhulu was dead and she would miss the old lady terribly, but for the first time in many months she didn't feel alone any more. There had been something healing in the way Niall had held her, undemanding and yet—there.

Niall shoved the bedroom door open with his shoulder. He was carrying a tray with a pot of coffee and some toast and cereal. Suddenly, Robina's stomach revolted and she fled to the bathroom, only just making it in time. That was all she needed now, with so much to do—a tummy bug. But after she had been sick she felt better. When she emerged from the bathroom, Niall was waiting for her, looking anxious.

'Are you okay?' He frowned. 'Perhaps you should go back to bed for another couple of hours?'

'Please don't fuss, Niall. It's just a bug—I'll be fine. Anyway, there's so much to do.'

'Tell me what and I'll help.'

'There's not much you can do, Niall. Just keep Ella company.'

He didn't see much of Robina in the days leading up to the funeral. He and Ella spent most of the time exploring, either down on the beach or going for a drive. When Robina did return to get some rest, she was usually asleep within minutes. Then as soon as she was awake, she would be off again. He hardly saw her eat and he worried about her, but every time he tried to tempt her with something she pushed her plate away. Grace also looked tired and drawn but she was more concerned about Robina.

'I'm worried about her, Niall. She's so thin and unhappy,' Grace said.

'I'm going to take her away for a couple of days after the funeral. Would you look after Ella for us?' Over the week he had been finalising the plan he had put into action weeks ago. He hoped it would be enough to convince Robina. 'If you think Robina will agree.'

'I think that's rather up to you, don't you? Look, Niall, I don't know what went wrong between you and my daughter, but I hate to see her so unhappy. If you don't love her, let her go so she can move on with her life.'

'Is that what you think? That I don't love her?' He leaned across in his need to convince her. 'You couldn't be more wrong. I love Robina more than I have loved anyone before, or imagine I will love anyone again.' He hated discussing his personal life, it really wasn't his style, but he knew for once he needed to put his pride to one side.

'More than Mairead?' Grace raised an eyebrow at him and Niall realised where his wife had inherited the razor-sharp look that could turn men into babbling children.

'I loved Mairead. I won't pretend I didn't. But she's gone and it's Robina who matters now.'

'Then I think you'd better use the time to make her believe that,' Grace said gently. 'Because, Niall, I have to warn you, if you don't you could lose her for ever.'

All of a sudden Niall was nervous. What if he had left it too late? What if she left him after all? But that wasn't going to happen. He wouldn't let it.

'Over my dead body. In that case, she's coming away with me even if I have to throw her over my shoulder. I'm warning you, there's no way I'm going to lose her now, so you'd better get used to having me around.'

CHAPTER TWELVE

NOTHING and no one was going to keep him away from the funeral, Niall decided grimly, and then afterwards, once they were alone, were going to talk. He planned to set off for the cottage as soon as the funeral was over. While she had been busy with the funeral arrangements he had put the finishing touches to his plans. He'd had no idea what to pack for his wife, so he'd more or less chucked everything she had brought into the suitcase. Ella was going to one of Grace's neighbour's to play while the funeral was taking place. Then she would stay with Grace until he and Robina returned from their trip.

The funeral surprised him. Instead of the sad and sombre affair he had expected, there was singing and dancing. It was more a celebration of life than a mourning of death. He forced himself to join the men as they clapped and danced—even though he felt ridiculous. This was his wife's country and her customs and he was determined to be a part of it. Robina laughed when she saw his ungainly attempts, but he was glad he had made the effort when he saw how touched she was. She looks at peace with her grandmother's death, Niall thought. Perhaps if they had marked the loss of their child, they too could have mourned properly and taken comfort in each other. He had learned more about himself and his wife in the last few weeks than he had in all the months since they had met. It was make-or-break time, and he was damned if he was going to lose his wife without a fight.

'This isn't the way back to Mum's,' Robina said as Niall turned left instead of right. 'You need to turn around, Niall.'

'We aren't going back to your mum's house. I've arranged for us to spend a couple of nights away. Alone.' His voice was determined, his face set, and Robina sensed immediately it would be useless to argue.

'We don't have to keep up appearances for Mum's sake,' she said tiredly. 'She knows things aren't good between us.'

'Nevertheless, we're going. You've been through a lot in the last few days and you need time to recharge your batteries. We'll be returning to Scotland in a few days' time, and it will be back to work for both of us. For once,' he continued sternly, 'you are going to do as you are told, and let me look after you.'

Robina knew that it could easily be the last couple of days that she and Niall would ever spend together and her chest tightened with the pain of it. She would make the most of every last hour, so that later she could store up the memories.

'Where are we going?'

'Wait and see,' Niall said.

It was one of those perfect summer days, Robina thought as they followed the coast road. Just enough breeze to keep the temperature at a bearable level and to stir up the sea enough to keep sailors and surfers happy.

As she cracked her window open a couple of inches, the smell of fynbos mixed with the salt of the sea in a tantalising mix and memories of childhood holidays came rushing back. She had hoped to be bringing their child to the same places one day. Robina swallowed hard. She had promised herself that she wasn't going to think sad thoughts. For these couple of days, she was going to only think of happy things.

'Any news from the clinic?' she asked, wanting to keep the conversation on neutral ground. She knew Niall kept in touch.

'A few more pregnancies.' He reeled off a few names that Robina recognised. 'I never quite relax, though, until they're safely delivered.'

As he continued to follow the coast road, Robina began to suspect where they were going. And sure enough a short time later they drew up in front of the cottage that had belonged to Robina's grandparents—the place she had brought him to when they had first met.

'Let's stop here for a while,' Niall suggested.

Baffled, Robina slipped out of the car and joined him outside. The 'For Sale' sign had been removed and the cottage had recently been painted. Obviously someone had bought it. Although she knew it was inevitable that the cottage would be sold, she felt a pang of loss. It was another connection with her past life that had gone.

'I didn't realise it had been sold,' she said sadly. 'Mum never said. But I guess she's had other things on her mind.' She looked down to the beach, remembering how she had played there as a child, and the even more vivid memory of the first time she and Niall had kissed. How long ago it all seemed. 'Why did you bring me here?'

A smile spread across Niall's face and Robina once more felt a pang. That goofy smile of his always undid her.

'What's so amusing?' she asked.

'The image of you running along a beach, all long legs and flowery bikini.'

'Oh, no,' Robina groaned. 'Mum's been showing you the baby album, hasn't she?'

'So what if she has? You were a beautiful baby and an even more stunning teenager. I loved seeing those photos of you,' he continued softly. 'Part of me is jealous I missed all those years.'

Robina's heart missed a beat. Suddenly she felt inexplicably shy in his company. Deep inside she felt a blossoming happiness she hardly dared let herself trust.

Niall dug around in the pocket of his trousers. 'This is where we are spending the next couple of nights.' He looked like an excited schoolboy, Robina thought. So pleased with himself.

He opened the door and Robina gasped with surprise. The house had been painted from top to bottom, the wooden shutters repaired and the pine floors re-sanded and polished. Scattered across the floorboards were rose petals, leading towards the spare room.

Robina raised an eyebrow at Niall, who was looking a little bit like a boy who had been caught stealing apples.

'I'm not very good at this sort of thing,' he said. 'Do you like it?'

She wandered through the rooms, noting that the beds had been made up with fresh new linen.

'You rented it from the new owners?' she asked,

moving towards the large picture windows that over-looked the sea. Niall came to stand behind her, resting his hands on her shoulders.

'Not exactly.' Niall shuffled his feet. 'Look, can we sit down?'

The sun was beginning to set, turning the sky a flamboyant mixture of red and gold. All at once the tension of the last few days seeped away and as it did, Robina felt her head spin. She grabbed a nearby chair as the room swam in and out of focus.

Immediately Niall was by her side. 'What is it, Robina?' Taking her arm, he steered her into the chair. 'Put your head between your legs for a moment.'

'I'm all right.' Robina waved him away. 'I think the last few days have just caught up with me.' She shivered. 'It's a bit cool now that the sun's going down.'

Before she knew what was happening, Niall picked her up in his arms. For a moment she was tempted to struggle, but she couldn't help herself from laying her head on his shoulder. It felt so good to be in his arms—to find the comfort and shelter she so desperately needed. Niall laid her on the sofa and covered her with a rug he found over the arm of the chair.

'Don't you move a muscle.' He glowered at her. 'I'll get some heat into this place and sort us out some supper.'

It was strange to have Niall looking after her. Strange, but nice.

She watched him rattling around with the fire, his mouth set in a determined line as he tried to coax a flame from the pot-bellied stove. 'Should have stayed in the Scouts a little longer than I did,' he muttered, but eventually, after several goes, the fire was lit. 'At least it's slightly easier than that last place in Scotland.' They smiled at each other, remembering. Robina was the first to look away.

The light continued to fade, the room lit only by the flickering fire. Neither made a move to switch on the lights. The sound of the sea crashing against the rocks echoed the tumult of emotions that were zinging around Robina's body. Niall pulled her into the crook of his arm and they sat in silence, listening to the sea.

'You still haven't said why you brought me here.' Robina broke the silence.

Niall sucked in a breath. 'It's my wedding present to you. A little bit of Africa that will always be yours.'

Robina felt her blood chill. What was he saying? Was this where he told her it was all over, and the house was somewhere for her to live while they dissolved their marriage?

'I can't believe it's only a year since we met,' Niall started hesitantly. 'When Mairead died, I thought I would never know happiness again. But I had to try and make everything all right, for Ella's sake.'

The ice around Robina's heart solidified. This was the part where he reminded her how important his daughter's happiness was and that nothing mattered except providing her with a secure, happy home.

'Then I met you. And from that day meaning came back into my life. I didn't expect ever to meet someone like you. I didn't expect to be happy again. Not really. But the moment I met you, I knew that life would never be the same again. At first it felt like a betrayal, but I couldn't help myself from loving you. Every minute away from you was torture. I knew those kinds of feelings couldn't be wrong. I was lucky. To be able to find love again.'

Slowly the icy tendrils around Robina's heart began to melt.

'When you agreed to marry me, I thought life couldn't get any better. But when you told me you were pregnant with our child, it did. I knew perfect happiness.'

'But…' Robina interrupted.

Niall placed a finger gently on her lips. 'Please let me finish. I haven't been very good up until now at letting you know how I feel. You know I'm hopeless when it comes to talking about emotions, but I have to make you understand.'

His eyes were like the sea; stormy, impenetrable.

'I don't really know when things started to go wrong,' Niall admitted. 'I guess I had found more than I ever thought I'd ever have again, so I didn't pay attention to how you were feeling. I left you alone too much, I see that now. Just as I see I should never have asked you to live in the home Mairead and I shared.'

'You had your reasons,' Robina said softly. 'And remember, I agreed.' She smiled wistfully. 'But I did find it difficult to live up to Mairead.' This time it was she who stopped his words with a finger. 'She seemed so damn perfect. Beautiful home, great mother—everything I wasn't.'

A flash of pain crossed Niall's face and he pulled her closer. 'Why didn't you tell me you felt that way?' he said softly. 'I had no idea. You always seemed so confident, so secure in yourself. You have your work and not just any career either. How many women would sell their souls to have what you have?'

And she would have given it all up in a heartbeat to have Niall loving her and her baby back. 'Remember that dinner party we had, soon after we married? The one Lucinda and the others from the clinic came to?' she said.

'Vaguely.'

'Well, I don't think I'll ever forget it. You didn't know then that I don't do cooking, not least because I'm hopeless at it, but I thought I should make an effort. I wanted everyone to think I could at least match up to Mairead.'

Niall frowned. 'I remember it now. But why would you think that whether you could cook or not would matter in the slightest?'

'It seems silly now,' Robina admitted. 'But back then, I don't know, it seemed to matter. I spent hours in that damn kitchen trying to produce something edible, but one look at Lucinda's face when she tasted the first course told me all I needed to know.'

'You did go a bit overboard with the spices. It's the first time I've seen Lucinda's face go as red as a beetroot.' Niall grinned.

'Poor, brave thing tried to swallow, but the others couldn't manage it. You had to go out and get us take-aways. It was awful. I felt so embarrassed. Mairead, I'm sure, would have produced something that wouldn't have been out of place in a restaurant.'

Niall laughed then his face grew serious again. 'I'm sorry, I shouldn't laugh. But nobody minded. And, yes, Mairead was a terrific cook. But that's what she liked to do. She often talked about opening a restaurant when Ella was older.'

'*I* minded. I already felt so inadequate next to Mairead. I know it sounds silly now, but at the time all I wanted to do was hide until everyone had left.'

Niall pulled her closer. 'I had no idea you felt that way. To me—and I'm sure to everyone else—you were this confident, successful woman who had just produced a best-selling book and had appeared on TV. Mairead would have admired *you*. Did you think anyone cared at all that you couldn't cook? I certainly didn't. It was never a reason why I married you.'

'Why did you marry me, Niall?' Robina forced the words past the lump in her throat.

A silence, interrupted only by the crash of waves, stretched between them before Niall spoke.

'As I said, after Mairead died, I thought I would never fall in love again. I didn't want to. Ella was enough for me. And then, when I met you, here in South Africa, I tried to pretend that it was just an incredible physical attraction. That was all. But nevertheless I still felt so guilty. It seemed like a betrayal of my love for Mairead.' He paused, his expression dimming as he turned to her. 'I don't expect you to understand.'

'I think I do. Go on,' Robina prompted.

'Then when I went back to Scotland, I couldn't get you out of my mind. From the moment I woke up until I fell asleep, your face was there. The thought of you, your smile, everything. I couldn't settle or concentrate. Even at work. I tried to put you out of my head, but I couldn't. I knew we had to be together. It was as if I had met the other part of my soul. The missing piece of my heart. I knew I loved you and that we had to be together.'

'And I came to you.'

'Yes. You gave up everything for me. Your life here in South Africa, your family, your job, everything. I know now I should never have asked that of you.'

'I did it willingly. A life without you was no life at all.'

'And we were happy at first, weren't we?'

'But everything started to go wrong so quickly, I didn't

even notice until it was too late. Until I lost the baby.' Her voice caught. 'You blamed me for the miscarriage, I could see it in your eyes, but I blamed myself even more. If I'd slowed down, if I'd listened to you, I could be holding our child right now.' This time Robina couldn't prevent tears from coursing down her cheeks.

Holding her face in the palms of his hands, Niall wiped her tears with his thumbs.

'Shh, Robina, I didn't blame you. God, how could you ever think that? As a doctor you know nothing anyone could have done would have made a blind bit of difference.' He swallowed. 'Losing the baby was like a kick in the chest, but coming so close to losing you was unimaginable hell…'

She frowned. 'Everything's a blur after the miscarriage. The last thing I remember was going into labour and then you looking down at me, almost as if you hated me.'

'Oh, my darling love.' He brushed his eyes with the back of his hand. 'But you are right to a degree. If we are going to be honest with each other then I have to tell you this, even if I feel like a total bastard. When you got the infection and collapsed, I was terrified. When I saw you lying in ITU looking so pale, not knowing if you would live, all I could think about was Mairead. I was angry with you. Angry with God, with everyone. I thought I was about to lose the most important person in my life again and I cursed myself for falling in love with you.'

'I saw it in your eyes. It was the first thing I saw when I came round. I thought you were angry with me for losing the baby. Then I thought you had only married me because you wanted a mother for Ella. I knew then I had lost you. I turned away from you, because I couldn't bear to see the reproach in your eyes.'

'You wouldn't let me comfort you. You looked at me as if you couldn't bear the sight of me.'

'Only because every time I looked at you I was reminded of what I had lost. Not just the baby, but any future children. The infection on top of everything was the last straw. We both know that it's probably put paid to any chances of me having more children. Anyway, even if it hasn't, I don't think I could bear the thought of going through another pregnancy that might end in miscarriage. And you want more children, don't you? You made that perfectly clear that night in the cottage.'

Niall groaned. 'You wouldn't think that a man who is used to dealing with women every day could be so inept. How can I speak to them so easily, yet get it so wrong when it comes to my own wife? I thought if we had another baby it would bring us back together. It was stupid, crass and insensitive of me. I was a fool.'

'Yes, you were.' Robina hid a smile. A warm glow was spreading throughout her body. But she still wasn't convinced Niall loved her for what she was, faults and all.

'And you don't know that you can't have more children. We would need to look at your tubes before we can be sure, and even if they're damaged there is IVF, which admittedly wouldn't mean you couldn't miscarry again. But, Robina, I don't care about having more children—not unless you want to. Can't you see what I'm trying in my uniquely clumsy way to say? I want only you. You are enough for me. Just you. I wanted our baby because he was part of you. A symbol of our love for one another.'

Robina's heart was starting to sing. Did he mean what he was saying? Did he really still love her?

'But I wanted that baby,' she cried. 'Only *that* baby. I

know you don't care as much as I do but, God, Niall, it hurts. It feels as if a little bit of my heart has been ripped out and is gone for good. I don't want to ever forget about my baby.'

'And neither do I,' Niall said sadly. 'And we won't. We'll find a way of remembering and acknowledging our first child. But I can only thank God that you lived. Had I lost you too…' His voice cracked and Robina could only guess how much it was taking it out of him to share his feelings with her.

'I am not a demonstrative man,' he said after a moment. 'I wish I was. But it's not the way I was brought up. We Scots are used to keeping our emotions in check. But you have to know that I love you. I can't imagine a life without you. All I want is to spend the rest of my life with you, making you happy, growing old together. I know it's maybe too much to ask after everything, but do you think you could love me again? As I know you once did?'

Robina looked up at him. His intense blue eyes were alight, but there was an uncertainty she had never seen before in the tension in his jaw. He turned to her and gripped her by the shoulders, his fingers almost digging into her flesh. 'If you can't…' His voice was hoarse. 'I'll let you go. It will kill me, but I won't keep you, not even for Ella's sake.'

'Do you promise me that you'll love me for ever?' Robina teased, suppressing a smile. 'Do you promise we will spend the rest of our lives reminding each other? Even if it goes against everything your Scottish heart rebels against?'

Niall looked her directly in the eyes. Whatever he saw there must have convinced him. Slowly his lips stretched in the wide loopy smile that made her heart somersault.

'But you have to tell me too,' he demanded. He pulled her close and dropped kisses that took Robina's breath away up and down her neck. She could feel the answering heat low in her abdomen as her heart began to sing.

'Of course I love you, you idiot. I could no more stop loving you than I could cease to breathe.' She wrapped her arms around his neck and, turning his head towards her, found his mouth. 'Now, don't you think we've wasted enough time?'

As soon as Niall and Robina retuned to Scotland they started redecorating their home. Despite feeling cosseted and loved by Niall, Robina felt tired and drained from the trip. She suspected that she was still recovering from the loss of her grandmother, and knew that eventually time would continue to heal the wounds left by the loss of her baby as well as her beloved Umakhulu.

Too soon it was time to return to work and wrap up the documentary. She was thrilled to discover that so many of the patients they had followed had fallen pregnant, and although her heart would always ache for the loss of her child, she couldn't help but share in the joy.

On the last day of shooting, after John the cameraman had left, Niall turned to her. There was a new softness in his eyes and a tenderness in his touch.

'Remember we discussed you having your tubes scanned?' he said. 'Why don't we ask Elaine to do it now?'

Robina felt a flicker of anxiety. Was she ready to face the truth? But she and Niall in one of the long talks they'd had since reconciling had decided to consider IVF as an option. But before they headed down that road, they both agreed it made sense for Robina to know for certain how badly her Fallopian tubes had been affected by the infection following the miscarriage.

She took a deep breath. 'Well, I suppose we have to know some time, so why not?'

Niall gripped her hand. 'I'll be right here with you. But whatever the outcome, remember I love you. You and Ella are all I'll ever need. I couldn't be happier than I am now.'

Robina lay on the table, her lower half covered with a towel as she waited nervously for Elaine to start.

'First, I'm going to do a scan of your pelvic region to see if your ovaries are working normally. Then we'll do the tubal patency test. Okay?'

She smiled reassuringly at Robina.

'Why is it that all the stuff we tell our patients means nothing when we're on the receiving end? Perhaps every doctor should be forced to have regular medical examinations to keep them real?' Robina asked them both.

Niall squeezed her hand in sympathy, his eyes glued to the monitor. Suddenly Robina saw him frown and edge closer to the screen. Her heart plummeted. Whatever he was seeing there, it didn't look like good news. Cold tendrils of dread curled around her spine. She wouldn't cry. She had shed enough tears to last a lifetime. Whatever the future held, at least she and Niall had each other for comfort and strength. She could face anything, knowing that he loved her.

'Do you see what I am seeing?' Niall asked.

His voice sounds strange, Robina thought. Please let me be strong, she whispered to herself. At least knowing what they were dealing with, they could decide on the future. If children weren't on the cards, well, they would face that too.

But, incredibly, Niall was smiling, as was Elaine. It was obvious that they weren't the patient, Robina thought grumpily. She'd like to see how they would feel in her shoes.

And had she really thought that Niall had turned over a new leaf? Where was his supposed sensitivity in that smile?

Now he was grinning. He picked her up in a bear hug that almost had her on the floor and crushed her to his chest.

'Oh, my love. My sweet darling girl. You know how you have being feeling lethargic and nauseous over the last few weeks?'

Robina barely had room to nod, she was being held so tightly.

'Well, that's because you are pregnant. About six weeks, by the look of it.'

Robina wriggled out of his arms. 'I'm pregnant?' she whispered, hardly able to believe what he was saying.

'Yes. Most definitely pregnant. It must have happened that night in the cottage.' Niall was still grinning from ear to ear.

Robina felt a wave of excitement wash over her. But almost immediately it was followed by an even stronger wave of fear.

'I could miscarry again,' she said softly. 'Maybe we shouldn't get too excited.'

'It's possible,' Niall agreed slowly. 'But somehow I've got the feeling that this time everything is going to work out fine.' And as Elaine left them alone, secure in each other's arms, Robina knew for certain that, whatever the future brought, she would have Niall there, right beside her.

EPILOGUE

ROBINA looked around the house, checking everything was in order. The guests would be arriving any minute to view the preview of the documentary and she wanted to take a moment to reflect. All the staff were coming, as well as Annette and Mike with their little girl and Eilidh and Jim and Trevor and Christine with their baby boys. Maisie, who had been given the all-clear, was bringing her new boyfriend, and Patricia and Luke, who were just beginning treatment with donor eggs, were planning to pop in as well.

As she looked out of the window, watching as the first snow of the winter covered the garden, Robina sighed with contentment. The house, apart from Ella's room, had been redecorated, and while she had kept much of Mairead's colour scheme in the walls and carpets, Robina had added splashes of vibrant reds and oranges in the soft furnishings. Now it truly felt like it was her home.

The last few months of her life had been the happiest she could remember. Although in the early stages of her pregnancy she had been anxious, Niall had been there to constantly reassure her, and the day Johnny had been born she could have sworn he had tears in his eyes. Now they talked about everything, both determined that they would never again leave anything unsaid. Weekends were spent as a family, but they always made time for just the two of them. They planned to holiday in their cottage in Cape Town at least once a year, so their children would come to understand and love their mother's country as much as they both did.

Robina picked up the photograph from the side table and studied the familiar features of her father. At last she understood he'd be proud of her whatever she did. Robina had decided not to return to her show until Johnny was a little older, but had started on her third book. She had more than enough to keep her busy. Niall too had cut back on work and most evenings managed to be home in time for them all to have supper together. He still had to work some weekends, but Robina knew he wouldn't be the man she loved if he didn't care about his work as much as he did.

She felt a movement behind her, and strong arms slipped around her waist, pulling her close.

'I've checked up on Johnny,' Niall whispered in her ear. 'I think he'll be asleep for a couple of hours yet and Ella's still at her friends'.'

Robina turned around to face him, smiling up into his beloved face. 'Are you suggesting what I think you are?'

Niall traced the curve of her cheek with a long finger. 'Have I told you recently that I love you?' he said, moving his finger to her chin and tilting her head, forcing her to look at him.

Robina made a show of checking her watch. 'Not for ages.' She laughed. 'Not since this morning, at any rate.' She blushed, remembering their dawn love-making, the familiar heat in her abdomen spreading through her limbs yet again. 'But feel free to tell me again.'

Niall picked her up in his arms and looked down at her, his eyes darkening. 'I love you, my love, my heart. And when I get you upstairs, I'm going to show you just how much.'

Robina wrapped her arms around his neck and looked him directly in the eye. 'That's good, *sthandwa sama*, my darling love, because have I told *you* lately how happy I am with you and my second chance family?'

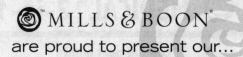

MEDICAL™ 2-in-1

Coming next month

THE NURSE'S BROODING BOSS
by Laura Iding

Dr Brock Madison can't believe Elana Shultz works in his new A&E department! Even though she's a daily reminder of his troubled past, Brock simply wants to spend the rest of his life with this nurse in a million – if only Elana will let him in…

EMERGENCY DOCTOR AND CINDERELLA
by Melanie Milburne

When charismatic Eamon Chapman discovers the vulnerable beauty his co-worker Erin Taylor hides behind a prim and proper persona, he finds himself wanting to give this innocent doctor the fairytale happy-ever-after she truly deserves!

CITY SURGEON, SMALL TOWN MIRACLE
by Marion Lennox

Dr Maggie Croft's decision to have her late husband's baby has left her juggling pregnancy with the care of a small town community! Maggie can't afford any distractions, until the arrival of irresistibly gorgeous Max Ashton changes her mind…

BACHELOR DAD, GIRL NEXT DOOR
by Sharon Archer

When single dad Luke Daniels returns to Port Cavill, Dr Terri Mitchell remembers him all too well! Soon Terri has fallen for Luke and his young daughter, but can she convince this doctor to let her heal his troubled heart?

On sale 2nd April 2010

MEDICAL™

Single titles coming next month

A BABY FOR THE FLYING DOCTOR
by Lucy Clark

Doctor Phemie Grainger prides herself on her cool resolve –
until a chance encounter with her professional idol,
Gil Fitzwilliam, throws her into turmoil! As she starts to fall
for the English doctor's charm, Phemie can't help
wondering if, with Gil at her side, her dreams of holding
her very own baby might one day come true…

NURSE, NANNY…BRIDE!
by Alison Roberts

Nurse Alice Palmer's world is turned upside down
when the new A&E consultant is none other than her
teenage crush, Andrew Barrett! The attraction she feels
to him is hard to deny, so when Alice becomes part-time
nanny to his beautiful little girl, it's as if fate has dealt
her the most remarkable hand of all…

On sale 2nd April 2010

millsandboon.co.uk Community

Join Us!

The Community is the perfect place to meet and chat to kindred spirits who love books and reading as much as you do, but it's also the place to:

- **Get the inside scoop from authors about their latest books**
- **Learn how to write a romance book with advice from our editors**
- **Help us to continue publishing the best in women's fiction**
- **Share your thoughts on the books we publish**
- **Befriend other users**

Forums: Interact with each other as well as authors, editors and a whole host of other users worldwide.

Blogs: Every registered community member has their own blog to tell the world what they're up to and what's on their mind.

Book Challenge: We're aiming to read 5,000 books and have joined forces with The Reading Agency in our inaugural Book Challenge.

Profile Page: Showcase yourself and keep a record of your recent community activity.

Social Networking: We've added buttons at the end of every post to share via digg, Facebook, Google, Yahoo, technorati and de.licio.us.

www.millsandboon.co.uk

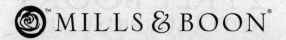

2 FREE BOOKS
AND A SURPRISE GIFT

We would like to take this opportunity to thank you for reading this Mills & Boon® book by offering you the chance to take TWO more specially selected books from the Medical™ series absolutely FREE! We're also making this offer to introduce you to the benefits of the Mills & Boon® Book Club™—

- **FREE home delivery**
- **FREE gifts and competitions**
- **FREE monthly Newsletter**
- **Exclusive Mills & Boon Book Club offers**
- **Books available before they're in the shops**

Accepting these FREE books and gift places you under no obligation to buy, you may cancel at any time, even after receiving your free books. Simply complete your details below and return the entire page to the address below. You don't even need a stamp!

YES Please send me 2 free Medical books and a surprise gift. I understand that unless you hear from me, I will receive 5 superb new stories every month including two 2-in-1 books priced at £4.99 each and a single book priced at £3.19, postage and packing free. I am under no obligation to purchase any books and may cancel my subscription at any time. The free books and gift will be mine to keep in any case.

Ms/Mrs/Miss/Mr _____ Initials _____

Surname _____

Address _____

_____

_____ Postcode _____

Send this whole page to: Mills & Boon Book Club, Free Book Offer, FREEPOST NAT 10298, Richmond, TW9 1BR